THE CASE OF DR. SACHS

THE CASE OF THE SACCUS

The Case of Dr. Sachs

MARTIN WINCKLER

Translated from the French by Linda Asher

SEVEN STORIES PRESS
New York / London / Sydney / Toronto

Seven Stories Press
140 Watts Street
New York, NY 10013
http://www.sevenstories.com

In Canada:
Hushion House, 36 Northline Road, Toronto, Ontario M4B 3E2

In the U.K.:
Turnaround Publisher Services Ltd., Unit 3, Olympia Trading Estate, Coburg Road, Wood Green, London N22 6TZ

In Australia: Tower Books, 9/19 Rodborough Road, Frenchs Forest NSW 2086

Library of Congress Cataloging-in-Publication Data

Winckler, Martin.
    [Maladie de Sachs. English]
    The case of Dr. Sachs / Martin Winckler.
    p.   cm.
    ISBN 1-58322-056-9/1-58322-261-8 (pbk)
    I. Title.
PQ2683.I456 M3513 2000
843'.914—dc21   00-030787

9 8 7 6 5 4 3 2 1

College professors may order examination copies of Seven Stories Press titles for a free six-month trial period. To order, visit www.sevenstories.com/textbook, or fax on school letterhead to (212) 226-1411.

Book design by Cindy LaBreacht

Printed in Canada.

To Pierre Bernachon,
Christian Koenig,
Olivier Monceaux,
and Ange Zaffran,

who were as expert at telling stories as at giving care.

NOTICE

As their names indicate, all the characters in this book are fictional.

If the events described in these pages seem truer than nature, that is because they are: in reality, all things are less simple.

This said, even if they are not intentional, any resemblances to real persons or events are, probably, inevitable.

M.W.

PREFACE

There are several extant versions of the Hippocratic Oath. The one reproduced at the start of this book appears on page 3 of a medical treatise printed in Algeria in 1939. It is markedly different from the original Greek text. Despite its omissions and awkward turns, this is the version to which Bruno Sachs tries to remain faithful.

❀

Certain passages of this novel were read in public in the course of the seminars "Literature and Medicine" and "Testimony and Fiction" held in two different locations in France: in Cérisy-La-Salle in 1994 and in Villa Gillet, Lyon, in 1995. The quality of the attention and the reactions of the persons present have been very important to me.

ACKNOWLEDGMENTS

I must express my gratitude to the inhabitants of "Play" and of the "Lavallée District." They wrote these stories with me.

I would also like to express my affection for the persons and characters who, near and far, have accompanied and supported me over the past ten years:

Adam A.; Alain A.; Alain C.; Alethia N. & Josiah N.; Alice K.; Ally McB. and Bobby D.; Andrew H.; Ann and Howard S.; Anne and Jean-Louis S.; Anne-Marie G.; Anneke and Bernard T.; Anthony E.; Ariane K.; Arko O.; Armande N.; Aube, Laurence, Philippe and Yves M.; Betty and Dick H.; Bill E.; Brent S.; Bud P.; Burt L.; Carine T.; Caroline B.-D.; Cary G.; Cherie S.; Chris N.; Christiane O.; Christophe P.; Claire L.; Claude P.- R. and Daniel Z.; Dan S.; Danièle, Juliette and Eric P.; Danielle B.; David K.; David M.; "Data" C.; Dean S.; Debbie W.; Denise C.; Dennis F.; Dharma & Greg M.; Dick W.; Dominique and Alain F.; Dominique M.; Dominique N.; Donald B.; Dougal J.; Ella F.; Emmanuelle P. & André G.; Eugene H.; Flavia L.; Franz K.; Frank P. & Tim B.; Fred A.; Frédéric M.; Frédérique et Christophe M.; Gary C.; Gates MacF.; Gayle L.; Gene K.; Gene T.; Hector E.; Nathalie and Gérard D.; "Gertrude" T.; Harry M.; Hélène and Pierre-Jean O.; Janet and Isaac A.; Jacky C.; Jacques B. & Jean-Jacques C.; Jacques C.; James Y.; Janet and Isaac A.; Jean Claude B.; Jean-Paul H.; Jean-Paul S.; Jerry L.; Jerry O.; Jill H.; Jim L.; Jimmy S.; Joëlle and Lelia M.; José L.; Judith and Martin T.; Julianna M.; John S.; Jonathan B.; Jonathan F.; Juno N.; Ken W.; "Kiko"; Kyle MacL.; Lance G.; Léo F.; LeVar B.; Lily M. and Rick S.; Linda A.; Lois and Clark K.; Louis A.; Luc J.-D.; Mady and Raoul M.; Mandy P.; Marie-Laure C.; Marie-Noëlle C. & Serge T.; Marike G.; Marina S.; Maryse H.; Mark F.; Martin L.; Michael C.; Michael D.; Michael M.; Michel H.; Michel M. & Joël D.; Michèle and Alain G.; Michèle and Jean-Pierre D.; Naomi R.; Neal Y.; Nicole D.; Noah W.; "Noisette" H.; Olivier S. & Pascal G.; Patrick S.; Paul O.-L.; Peggy and Chuck S.; Philippe B.; Philippe L.; Philippe M.; Randee Dawn C.; Raphaël M.; Richard B.; Richard P.; Robert J. T.; Rod S.; Ruth W.; Sam W.; Scott B.; Sean C.; Sharon L.; Sherilyn F.; Sophie and Félix B.; Stephen B.; Steven H.; Sylvie and Pierre A.; Sylvie C. and Jean-Pierre B.; Thierry F.; Tom F.; Valérie-Angélique and Christophe D.; Vibeke M.; Victor B.; Vincent D.; Violaine H.; Whoopi G.; Wil W.; Winnie H.; Yasmina M.; Yves L.;

my sister Anne R., writer and teacher in Aix-en-Provence (France);
my brother John C., and my colleagues Aaron S., Jeffrey G. and Phillip W., doctors in Chicago (IL);

Pierre, Mélanie, Jean-Baptiste, Thomas, Paul, Olivier, Léo and Martin;

and M.P.J., my beloved.

CONTENTS

PROLOGUE

It's an old two-story building, set in the middle of an asphalt courtyard.

On the outside wall, beside the rusty gate, a brushed-steel plaque announces

BRUNO SACHS, M.D.
General Medicine

The street door, with its flaking dark-green paint, stands ajar. At the end of the entry hall, the words "Waiting Room" are stencilled on a pinewood door, above a card listing the office hours in neat red, blue, green, and black handwriting. To the left rises a dingy stairway.

As a small metal sign suggests, I ring and enter.

❋

The waiting room is a big tiled space, cool, bright, and high-ceilinged. The walls are covered in a light blue paper with darker blue stripes.

Across from the door, toward the garden, a few chairs ring a low table full of magazines. I murmur a greeting to the people there, and take a seat.

On the side toward the courtyard a big wooden desk, bulky and undistinguished, holds a potted plant. To my right, a man in a polo shirt, shorts, and sneakers is reading a daily paper. To my left, a middle-aged woman is talking in a low voice to a teen-age girl whose eyes are riveted to the floor. Farther along, beside the connecting door with its closer mechanism, a young, very pregnant woman slumped on a chair keeps a tired eye on two children three or four years old. The little girl, who seems to be the elder one, is playing teacher to a row of stuffed animals set up on a small red wooden bench. Her baby brother, sitting on the big square of carpet covering that corner of the room, is piling up blocks with a frown of concentration.

The man sighs and turns his newspaper over. The teenager glances at me sidelong. The middle-aged woman pays me no attention and goes on talking to the girl. The children play. Their mother digs through her purse. I glance at my watch. I turn around. Behind me on the wall, between the two big windows, a dish-faced clock says it's after ten.

It rained earlier. The windows are misty, but now the sun is coming through the clouds and warming the children's corner. The doorbell rings. An elderly woman, short and obese, comes panting in, followed by a very thin and very stooped old man. She collapses onto a bench, raises her eyes to heaven with a moan, grips her purse to her chest, sighs noisily. The old man circles the table and sits down too. I cross my legs and open my book.

PRESENTATION

(Wednesday, September 12)

THE OATH

Before Professors of this Institution, before my dear fellow students and according to the Hippocratic tradition, I promise and swear to be faithful to the laws of honor and honesty in the practice of Medicine. I will care for the poor without payment, and will never demand more payment than my labors justify. When I am admitted into households, my eyes will not see what occurs there, my tongue will keep the secrets confided to me, and my position will serve neither to corrupt morals nor to promote crime.

In respect and gratitude to my Professors, I shall pass on to their children the instruction I have received from their fathers.

May men grant me their esteem if I keep faith with my promises.

May I be steeped in opprobrium and disdained by my colleagues if I should fail to do so.

1

IN THE WAITING ROOM

Tires hiss on the wet asphalt of the courtyard. I raise my head. A beam of light crosses the ceiling. An engine turns off. A car-door slams. The street door shakes, keys jingle. I slide a finger between two pages and close the book on my crossed knees.

The waiting-room door opens and, black bag in hand, you enter, shaking your keyring.

"Good morning, everyone…"

Murmurs greet you. You walk past us, open the connecting door and hold it with an elbow. With the other hand you separate out one key from the bunch, you unlock the second door, you open it. You pull the key from the lock, you slip the bunch into your pocket, you enter. Silently, the connecting door falls shut behind you, pulled to by the airspring.

A few instants later, you reappear. You have taken off your parka, your pullover or your jacket, and put on a white coat whose sleeves you're rolling back. You give us a questioning look. On my left, the man folds his newspaper and stands up. You offer your hand, you step aside and motion him in. The connecting door closes behind you both.

I return to my reading.

2

HOW IT BEGINS

I step in, my newspaper or magazine under my arm. As the connecting door closes in silence, you shut the inner door, pushing hard with both hands.

The room is bright, the walls are covered in pale blue paper with a slightly deeper blue stripe. To my left, sheer curtains hang at the window. In the corner are tall pinewood shelves holding grey boxes stuffed with files. To my right, more shelves, a tall case set perpendicular to the wall, divide the room in two. Standing against the rear wall, your desk is a plain wood slab painted white, supported by two sawhorses of dark-blue metal tubing. In front of the desk is a rolling swivel-chair covered in beige fabric; right of the desk are two seats upholstered in black; you wave me over to them.

"Sit down."

You move to the desk, you sit in the rolling chair. You close the big red book before you, you shift a prescription pad. You swivel toward me, you set your left elbow on the painted-wood table top, you raise your eyes. You smile.

"Do sit down, please."

As I take a seat, you ask in a kindly tone, "What can I do for you?"

I consider what to say.

3

A CONSULTATION

"Well, I don't know where to begin…"

You nod, "Mmmhh." You swivel toward the shelves, you reach into one of the grey boxes. You pull out a brown envelope. As I explain the reason for my visit, you take a grid-lined form the shape of a postcard from the envelope and lay it on the tabletop; you pull a black fountain pen from the chest pocket of your white coat, you unscrew the cap, you press it onto the shaft of the pen, you draw a line on the filecard, you write the date at the left margin.

"Now then…"

Leaning over the gridded filecard, you write.

❀

As you write, you sit bent over the painted wood tabletop. Behind you, brilliant light pours through the yellowing voile curtains and the sheets of translucent plastic on the panes of a big window. Without setting down your pen, you turn your head toward me. The lenses of your glasses are faintly tinted; I can't tell if you're looking at my mouth or my eyes.

From time to time you lower your own eyes to the file card and write some words. You occasionally interrupt my account to ask a question:

"When did this start? Was that the first time? Every day? During meals or between? Are there some days when you don't feel it? What about at night? Or today, for instance? Have you taken anything for the pain?"

You comment on my answers with a "Mmmhh" or an "I see." You write on the file card, you nod, "Yes, that must be very uncomfortable…"

Eventually, you lay down the pen.

You turn your back to the painted wood tabletop and you point to the low cot standing two yards from us, against the wall between the medical office and the waiting room.

"Well, let's have a look. I'm going to ask you to undress and lie down here, if you would."

＊

As I take off my shoes, you cross the room.

At the far side of the room, past the tall crowded bookshelf that functions as a screen, I glimpse a small washbasin with an electric water heater above it, a rolling table with all sorts of instruments, and the end of an examining table on chrome-tubing legs. Against the wall facing the door, a baby scale reigns atop a varnished pine shelf-unit.

You turn on the water, you pour liquid soap into your cupped hands, you lather them.

"Is your appetite good?"

"Uhh… average."

I put my clothes (my polo shirt or my blouse, my trunks or my skirt) on the chair in front of the window, between the cot and the shelf-unit. You rinse your hands and you wipe them with paper towels that you discard in a small metal trash can with a pedal opener. I am still standing, in my underwear. You walk back toward me. You point to the cot. "Lie down there, please."

I take a couple of steps, I stretch out on the white sheet—a bit cold, a bit rough to the touch. My head presses into the slightly oversoft pillow. Stretched out along the wall, I can hear voices sounding from the waiting room. You lift my clothes off the backrest of the chair, you lay them on the bench where I was sitting a few minutes ago, and you bring the chair over to the cot.

You sit down beside me.

＊

From a small chest at the head of the cot you pick up the blood-pressure gauge, I give you my right arm, you wrap the grey armband around it. You pick up the stethoscope, you fit the tips into your ears, you lay the cup against the crook of my elbow, you grasp the rubber bulb of the blood-pressure gauge, you tighten the valve, and you start to inflate it. It tightens. With your fingertips you gently loosen the valve. It hisses.

"One-thirty over eighty—good."

You unwrap the armband and lay it on the little bureau. Brandishing the cup of the stethoscope, you lean toward me and apply it beneath my left nipple. It's cold. With your other hand, delicately, you take my pulse.

You listen.

"You've got a nice regular heartbeat. Breathe deep."

Between breaths you move the instrument around my chest, from top to bottom, then more to the left.

"Good. Now sit up." I rise. "Lean forward."

I bend. You shift the stethoscope cup into your left hand, you lay your right delicately on my shoulder. "Breathe hard. Mouth open."

You move the stethoscope systematically down the length of my spine, on the left and then the right, from top to bottom.

You pull the plugs from your ears and the two metal prongs clack together. You lay the instrument on the little bureau. You half-rise from the chair and sit behind me on the cot. You set your left hand flat on my back and tap on it with your right index finger bent. That produces a deep, hollow sound. You slip your left hand a bit lower and you tap again, regularly, from top to bottom, on one side and then on the other. Then you put both hands flat along my ribcage.

"Say 'ninety-nine!'"

"Ninety-nine."

"Louder."

"NINETY-NINE!"

"Good. Lie down again."

You sit down on the chair and I stretch out on the now faintly warmer sheet. You lean toward me, you lay your right hand on my belly. With your fingertips you palpate, starting on the left side. Your hand moves around my belly, counterclockwise.

"Am I hurting you?"

"Uh—it's just unpleasant, that's all..."

"Your digestion all right?"

"Uh—it's okay..."

Then you slip your left hand between my back and the sheet ("No, don't move") right and then left, and you press my flanks between your two hands, one side and then the other. As you do it, you ask casually, depending on the patient, "Do you have any trouble urinating?" or "When did you last have a gynecological exam?"

From the other side of the wall I hear the doorbell shrill. The door to the waiting room opens and closes again. Heels click on the floor tiles. A chair scrapes.

You sit back down. You put your left hand flat on my belly, and you knock on it with the knuckle of your bent right index finger. You move your hand and knock again, from left to right, from top to bottom. It sounds hollow.

Then you palpate my groins, my thighs ("Bend your knees") and you put your fingertips on the tops of my feet, or behind my ankles.

"Sit on the edge of the bed."

I sit up, I put my bare feet on the mat. You feel for something in the pockets of your coat, you don't find it, you get up, you reach your hand over to the desk and pick up a little black metal flashlight, you turn it on, you sit down again, you adjust the beam, you delicately lift my chin.

"Stick out your tongue, say 'Ahhh!'"

"Ehhh…"

From a cardboard box on the little chest, you take a tongue depressor, you raise it in a slightly threatening way but smiling apologetically. "Could you open your mouth a little wider? 'AAAhhh'?"

"EEEhhh…"

"Again—'AAAAA'," you urge, aiming the little flashlight. Desperately I stick my tongue out.

"EEAAAhhh…?"

"Very good."

Gently you slip the wooden stick between my cheek and my teeth, on one side and then the other, then finally onto my tongue. I start to cough, I gag, you pull out the tongue depressor.

"I'm sorry," I say with tears in my eyes and close to retching.

"Don't apologize… When did you last have your teeth looked at?"

I swallow my spit with some difficulty.

"Uhh… a long time ago…"

You toss the tongue depressor behind you, into the blue plastic sack of the big straw wastebasket.

"Look at my nose." (You shine the little flashlight at an angle into one eye, then the other. With the tip of your thumb you pull my lower lid down.) "Look at the ceiling."

The ceiling is not completely white. Someone must have laid on a couple of coats of paint a good while back. It sags in the middle. Cracks show near the walls, and faint greenish stains indicate a creeping mildew.

"Good…"

You get up, you stick the flashlight into the pocket of your white coat. You point to the standing scale by the window. "Come let me weigh you."

You lean in. "Is that your usual weight?"

"Uh… yes."

You go back to your chair.

You uncap the black pen, you bend over the lined card. You raise your head and, seeing me still standing, motionless, on the scale, you say, "Get dressed, please."

❊

You don't watch me dress.

I sit back down on the black cloth chair. You turn to the left, you lean down to the lower shelves, you pull out a prescription pad and some Social Security forms, you lay them out in front of you on the desk.

You open up the big red book lying to one side, you scan the salmon-pink pages at the front and then the white center pages.

"So, what did we say… mmmhhty-seven kilos, right?"

"Uhh… yes."

The telephone rings.

※

There are two telephones on the painted wood slab you use as a desk. One is grey, on a portable base; the other is black, buried in the corner near the shelves under magazines and the big red book.

The grey telephone rings.

"Excuse me…"

You pick up. "Hello?"

From where I sit, I sometimes hear a shrill voice cry "Hello, Edmond? Is that you, Edmond?" and you say "No madame you must have dialed wrong," and you hang up. But more often, I hear nothing of the phone voice, and you answer "This is he… Yes, hello Monsieur Kelley…" You reach for your appointment book, you open it. You flip the pages. "Mmmhh… When did you want to come? This morning I'm full until noon, half-past… Yes, the afternoon would be easier… I'm booked again from five on. Shall we say four-forty-five?" You pick up the black pen, "I've marked you in. Not at all. Goodbye, then, sir." You hang up and look at me. "Excuse me…"

You close the appointment book, you look again into the big red volume, and finally you push it away from you. You open the prescription pad, you write. On top, the date: September 12. Then my name, at the same level as yours, and you underline it twice. Lower down on the slip, your hand writes out, in capital letters, the instructions as you recite them for me aloud: "All right then, you'll take such-and-such a medication, two pills three times a day for six days," or: "Such-and-such a syrup two tablespoons every night at bedtime for three weeks…" You lift your head. "Mmmhh… what do you take when you get a fever or a headache? … You still have some of that? … Do you want me to put down for some more? Two packs—will that be enough? … Do you need anything else?"

You add—or you don't, depending on the answer—the name of some third item.

With a brisk turn of the wrist, without lifting the pen, you sign, bottom right on the prescription slip.

The telephone rings. You pick up.

"Hello… Ah, no, ma'am, this is not the Provincial Credit Bank…" You hang up.

You detach my prescription slip, you pull over a pad of Social Security forms and in an easy rhythm your hand fills out the space for PATIENT'S LAST NAME FIRST

NAME (TO BE COMPLETED BY PHYSICIAN ACCORDING TO PATIENT'S INFORMATION), then the boxes headed SERVICES PROVIDED: 1: DATE OF SERVICES; 2: DESCRIPTION OF SERVICES BY NOMENCLATURE/CODE; 3. PRESCRIPTION ISSUED; 4: ORDERS: A) CONFINED TO BED, or B) UNCONFINED, before signing at number 5: SIGNATURE OF PHYSICIAN CERTIFYING SERVICES PROVIDED. Under CHARGES you write in column 6: AMOUNT (IN FRANCS) OF FEES COLLECTED, then with a single long line you cross out columns 7: SURCHARGE FOR SPECIAL REQUIREMENTS, 8, 9, and 10: TRAVEL COSTS, before pausing briefly over Space 11: TOTAL DUE, and signing your name again at 12: SIGNATURE CERTIFYING PAYMENT.

"Thank you, Doctor. What do I owe you?"

You fold the medical form in two and slide the prescription slip into it. You hand them to me and tell me your charges.

I open my wallet or I borrow your pen. You fold the bills or the check and slide it into the chest pocket of your shirt or your white coat. "Thank you."

In the big appointment book you mark "C" for "Consultation" beside my name. You stand up, I stand up, you cross in front of me, you open the inside door of the examining room, I slip the papers into my purse or my trouser pocket, you push open the connecting door and walk into the waiting room, I collect my magazine or my newspaper from the painted-wood tabletop, I leave the consulting room. With your back holding the door, you shake my hand, "Goodbye."

Someone has already stood up. I hear you say "Come in."

I leave the waiting room.

4

THE PERMIT

I lay my health booklet on the desk. "I'm here for my permit." I open the booklet, pull out a card with my photograph. I hand it to you.

"Ah, I see. Well, strip to your underwear so I can examine you…"

❈

From the little chest at the head of the cot, you pick up the stethoscope, the blood-pressure cuff. You take my arm, you wrap it in the gray band, you apply the stethoscope cup to the crook of my arm, you slip the tips into your ears, you pump. It tightens. You deflate. It hisses.

"One-thirty over eighty—good."

You undo the armband and set it back on the little chest. You lay the stethoscope cup against my chest and you listen.

"Breathe deep… You have a nice regular heartbeat. V'you been playing soccer long?"

❈

Sometimes it's: I just took it up again. After a long time. I used to play a lot. But when you're working it's not easy. And also I thought I ought to get into shape a little, first. What with everything you see happening.

Sometimes it's: Five or six years now, I did a little basketball and handball, but I wasn't enjoying it anymore—not too nice an atmosphere. So I changed clubs, now I play soccer over in the next town and it's fine.

Sometimes it's: I'm just starting, and I'm not here by myself, I came with a buddy, or the coach—he's my buddy's dad—brought us in, all the kids from the club—in two shifts, two Wednesdays in a row after the the game, the waiting room's barely big enough for us all to sit down, and when you come in, at three o'clock, three-thirty, we look at you half-nervous, half-cracking up, we watch you struggle with your keys and your two bags, talk to your secretary who's waiting for you there kind of impatient and she tells you the schedule's already full-up, all the appointments are taken. You frown, you go into your office, you slam the door behind you, and then a long time after, you come back out and you say, "Okay, let's go two at a time—Madame Leblanc, if anybody asks for me, say I'll call back later… Who do I start with? Come on, kids, get moving, I'm not going to bite you!"

I'm cool, I grab my permit (and my health booklet, if my mother remembered to give it to me) and I go in with my brother or my cousin or a buddy, you close the door behind us, you take the booklets out of our hands, you go sit at your desk and you say, "Strip to your underwear."

While I'm taking off my trunks and my jersey, you look at our permits (and our health booklets if our mothers remembered to give them to us). Then, when we're both in our underpants, you turn to us and wave us over. You ask How old are you? You put that cold doohickey against my chest, you look at my throat, my teeth, my ears, you stick that little flashlight in my eyes, you feel my neck and under my arms. Next, you have me stand on one foot and then the other, on tiptoe, on my heels, then you tell me to lie on the cot, you feel my belly, you make me sit up and cross my knees and you take a little hammer with a round head wrapped in dark rubber and you tap on my knees and my feet jump. Next you make me get on the scale, and then finally you tell me to get dressed and you put the other guy through the same routine, or else him first. When it's over, while the second guy is getting dressed, you open the health booklets again, you look up at one of us and you say, "You're going to need a booster on your DT/polio one of these days," or "If you've never had mumps, it would be good to get a vaccination, I'll put down a note to your mom." And only after that, when you're just about to send us out and call in two other guys, do you pick up the permits from the table and Bang! you give them a whack with the stamp, you sign it, and you ask "V'you been playing soccer long?"

✳

"Say ninety-nine."
"Ninety-nine."
"Louder."
"NINETY-NINE!"
"Good. Lie down."
You put your hand on my belly. You feel around a bit everywhere, even behind. You push your chair back a bit. "Turn this way."
I sit up on the edge of the cot. You pull down my eyelid with the tip of your thumb. "Look at the ceiling."

27

You lift up my hair. You look at my forehead. "You have a lot of acne…"

"Yeah, actually, I was wondering if you could…"

"Sure. I'll give you something." You pull your chair back a little more. "Good. Get up now."

From the little chest at the head of the cot, you reach into a cardboard dispenser and pull out two limp translucent rubber gloves.

"Lower your underpants."

Leaning forward on your chair, you examine me. With your gloved hands you touch, you press, you weigh right and left. And then you toss the gloves into the blue plastic bag in the big straw wastebasket and I pull up my underpants.

"Turn around."

You get up, I feel your fingers run down the length of my spinal column.

"Lean forward. Do you ever have pain in your back?"

"Uh, no…"

"Turn your head to the right, that's it. To the left. Lean it to one side. To the other. That doesn't hurt? Good."

You stretch an arm toward the wall beneath the window.

"Come over here so I can weigh you."

I get onto the scale.

"That's fine, you can get dressed."

You go back to your seat.

While I was getting dressed, you took the permit from the desk, you stamped it, you signed it, then turned it over to look again at the photo attached to the front. Now you open the health booklet.

"You're… sixteen… Mmmhh… yes, that's what I would have said. Time for a booster vaccine this year. It's not urgent, but keep it in mind. I'll write you a prescription for it. Is there anything else you want to ask me?"

"Uh, for the acne…"

"That's right, I was forgetting."

You turn on your heel, you lean down to the lower shelves to get a prescription pad, insurance forms, you set them down on the desk in front of you. You look up at me. I'm still standing.

"Sit down, please!"

5

THE RENEWAL

"I'm here for my Pill."

You swivel around to the shelves to get my file, a brown envelope from which you take some grid-lined file cards and some folded sheets held together by a paperclip. "How've you been since… Hey, it's six months! Didn't I write you a prescription for a year's worth?"

"Uh, no…"

"That's odd. Oh, I see. I wanted to take a vaginal smear."

"Yes, maybe…"

You ask me a few questions, always the same ones—whether I'm tolerating the Pill all right, whether I've gained any weight, have any breast pain, if sometimes I forget to take it, if I smoke, if I get headaches… You note down my answers on your filecard. Finally you say, "Okay then, let's examine you…"

"Uhh… well, I—my period started yesterday."

You raise your head, look at me briefly, smile. "Well, it's not crucial—I won't bother you this time, we can do it next time you come."

On your gridded filecard, in red and in block letters, you print it so big that I can read it from where I am "GYN. EXAM + SMEAR NEXT VISIT."

You push back your rolling chair, you point to the cot. "Lie down there, I'll take your blood pressure."

6

AMÉLIE

The door opens, you come out and you step aside to let a young woman pass. You shake her hand.

"Thank you, doctor, goodbye."

"Goodbye, madame."

You lean toward the child looking at you wide-eyed, still grasping the stuffed bear she found lying on the little red bench when she arrived.

"Well now, honey, something wrong today?"

"Oh," I say, "don't even ask, six months now it's going on, I'm getting sick of it, you coming Amélie? Come, sweetie, we're going in to see the doctor."

Amélie wrinkles her brow and rushes over to me. I take her in my arms. You smile. You bring us in. I put her little satchel on one of the benches covered in black cloth. Amélie won't let me go, so I open the satchel with one hand, I take out her health booklet, I put it onto your tabletop.

"I've already been to the doctor—I mean the doctor in Deuxmonts—two weeks ago, it was a Thursday, you weren't in or else it was some other afternoon when you don't have office hours, I think?"

"Sure I do…"

"Okay, anyhow I didn't want to wait, I'd just picked her up at the sitter, she told me the baby was cranky and I saw right off something was wrong, she wanted to be held all the time and she kept whining. I just went back to work three months ago, so I thought she was making a scene. Actually, she's been giving me a hard time, naturally when she was born I took a year's leave, so now I watch out because she can throw a fit. My husband worries the minute she gets the slightest little thing, he's crazy about his little girl, but me I don't want to be pushed around so I says we'll just see. Only, when I undressed her for her bath, she started crying and that's not like her, she adores her bath, so then I think, Something's wrong, I took her temperature she had a hundred and two and it kept going up. The doctor said she had a cold and sore throat with complications…"

"Complications?"

"Yeah, a touch of earache… Anyhow, he put her on antibiotics, but the next morning she started to vomit so I called him back and he ordered something else, but she finished that the day before yesterday and it's starting up again."

"It's starting again?"

"Yeah, she's been cranky since this morning, she was over at my in-laws, we were gone for a week my husband and I we haven't had a vacation in a long time, and when we got back my mother-in-law told me she was getting sick yesterday, she's got a runny nose, she's coughing, at night she snores and keeps waking up, so I says it better not be starting up again this is the fifth time since November it just keeps going we gotta find some solution…"

"Mmmhh. Let's take a look. Undress her…" You open up the little health booklet.

I look around for the changing table, but it was that doctor in Deuxmonts the other day who had one. You examine children on the cot against the wall. I lay Amélie down on the sheet to undress her and you ask, "The doctor didn't write anything in the record when he saw her?" But Amélie starts howling and I can't get her jumpsuit off.

❄

Sometimes it's just hell, she keeps yelling and squirming, I can't do a thing with her, and I hear you roll back your chair.

"May I?"

You point to the cot. "Sit down beside her."

You pull over a chair from under the window, you sit down and you look at Amélie still lying there.

Amélie looks back at you. You say, "You still have your same big blue eyes, pumpkin… Okay now, I'm going to undress you and see if we can figure out why you have a fever."

Amelie keeps the suspicious sulk on. You put out your two hands. She gives you hers, and you sit her up.

You say, "I'm Doctor Sachs, you met me before, but a long time ago, you may not remember. Today your mommy didn't bring you for a shot, she brought you so I could help you feel better. I know you don't like people to make you lie down—little children and babies don't like that, and at your age you don't trust strangers…" You slide down the zipper tab of her jumpsuit. "Zoom!" You take hold of one sleeve. "Now, first one arm!" Amélie pulls her arm out of the sleeve. "Other arm… one foot… two foot…" And she lets you pull off her suit without a peep, never takes her eyes off you, and all the rest of her clothes the same way. When it's finished, you hold her little hands, you tug gently. "Upsy-daisy!" And there she stands, straight up on the cot. "Come sit on mommy's lap."

You lift her up, sit her on my lap, and she shoves her thumb into her mouth.

✸

But sometimes she's manageable, and while I pull off her jumpsuit, her cardigan, her pullover, her wool skirt, her tights, her blouse, her turtleneck and her body-suit, you circle the bench where I left the little satchel, you pick up something from the baby-scale on top of the varnished pine shelves, and just as I'm taking off her undershirt—"Can I leave on her diaper?"—you hand her a big transparent rattle with colored balls tumbling around inside it. Amélie pulls her thumb out of her mouth, takes the rattle, and shakes it.

"Daaaada?"

"Sit down and put her on your lap."

I sit on the cot. You pull over the chair from near the window, you settle onto it. You take the stethoscope from the little chest. You slip the tips into your ears, you look at Amélie, you say "This is cold," you set the cup of the stethoscope against her chest.

Amélie looks doubtful, but she doesn't cry. She sticks her free thumb into her mouth. After a few seconds, as you're moving the stethoscope around on her chest, she takes her thumb out of her mouth, moves the rattle from one hand to the other, and reaches the free hand toward the black rubber tubing.

"Don't touch!" I say.

You shake your head slightly. "That's okay..."

While she takes the tube in her fist and pulls on it, you move the cup over her chest, then over her back. She starts coughing, that hoarse cough she gets a lot during a nap or at night that makes her gag and scares us so much, especially my mother-in-law, because me, I know that as much as she coughs, it doesn't stop her from all kinds of dumb tricks but still, she's had it for a really long time and my mother-in-law keeps on telling me I should take her to a pediatrician.

"She often cough that way?"

"Constantly. Sometimes she coughs all night, and the minute I go into her room she starts crying, can't get her back to sleep. My husband says to take her into bed with us, for him it's easy, he falls right back to sleep, but me no way. So of course I have trouble getting up in the morning..."

You put the stethoscope on Amelie's back as she tugs harder on the black rubber tubing. Your head follows the pull and pretty soon you're nose to nose with her.

"Yahhhnanaaa...," she sighs.

You take the stethoscope out of your ears, and the metal tips clack together. Amélie hasn't let go of the tubing. The rattle drops to the floor. I pick it up. You take a little plastic cone out of a cardboard box on the chest and attach it to a kind of pocket flashlight.

"We're gonna look in your ears, pumpkin."

"She doesn't like that…"

You lean toward Amélie, you slide along her cheek, you slip the cone into her right ear. Amélie holds very still, but not a peep.

"Onnnne ear… good."

You straighten up, you change sides.

"And the otherrrrr… earrr. Good."

"Naaanana?"

"That's all, pumpkin."

"What's she got?"

"Just a cold and sore throat, nothing else."

"Nothing in her ears?"

"No. Did she have much fever this afternoon?"

"I don't know, I didn't take her temperature, I came right over but—" I lay my hand on Amélie's forehead—"I don't think so, no—just I was scared it was going to start up again, you don't think we should do something? Take out her adenoids, or give her globulin shots? My sister did that with her son… a shot three times a week for eight weeks, they say it does them good…"

You look doubtful, you shake your head, you offer Amélie your pinky finger, and her little hand closes around it. "Mmmhh—that's not necessary. It's autumn already, and until they're about two years old they get lots of colds. Later on things get better…"

You turn around, you take the health booklet from your desktop, you leaf through it.

"My colleague didn't write anything down here, last time?"

"Oh, he never writes down anything, by now I don't even bother to bring along the booklet—you know, doctors don't write things too often…"

"That's too bad… All right then, you can get her dressed…"

You get up. You push the chair back beneath the window. You sit down on the desk chair. You lay out the health booklet, you take your pen, you write.

Amélie starts sneezing—once, twice, three times.

"Ahchoo, ahchoo, ahchoo!" you say without turning around.

Now naturally she's got a noseful and a mouthful, she wipes with her sleeve and splashes everywhere, and I don't have a handkerchief on me.

Still holding your pen you get up. You cross the room. You take some paper towels out of a wall dispenser, you hand them to me.

When Amélie is dressed, I come back and sit on one of the black cloth chairs. She trots along behind me. She goes over to the table where you're writing out the prescription, she's still clutching the red and green rattle, she looks up and hands it to you.

"Tah!"

"Thank you, little bug. All right," you say as you fold the prescription slip and the insurance form, "no antibiotics this time—that'll get better by itself, you just give her something to lower the fever for a day or two, I'll order a little cough syrup unless you've already got something at home…"

"You're not even prescribing nosedrops?'

Before you can answer, the phone rings.

ANGÈLE PUJADE

Two rings, and you pick up.

"This is Doctor Sachs…"

"Hello, Bruno! This is Angèle."

"Hello, Madame Pujade. How are you?"

"Very well. I'm not disturbing you?

"Never."

I laugh. That's always your answer. "Tell me, can I put another woman onto your schedule tomorrow?"

"Mmmhmm… The schedule's crowded?"

"Yes, rather. You already have three procedures and three—no, four consultations. But this is a woman who'd like to go with you in particular—Jean-Louis is sending her to you."

"Jean-Louis Renaud?"

"Yes, it's one of his patients… But I could ask her to come in next week."

"No, we don't want to make her wait around for a week, it's hard enough as it is. Mmmhh… I'll come in a little earlier. At half-past twelve. Will that do it?

"Very good, thanks, Bruno. See you tomorrow, then!"

"See you tomorrow, Madame Pujade."

I hang up and turn to the dark-haired young woman with somber eyes. "It's on for tomorrow!"

Her glance wanders about. She smiles, forcing it a little, and nods. "Thank you…"

"You'll see," I say, "it'll be just fine. Bruno—Doctor Sachs—is very… very gentle."

I don't know what made me say that. Maybe to lessen the sadness and the anger churning inside her.

8

_____

MARIE-LOUISE RENARD

"Hallo, doctor honey!"

"Hello, Madame Renard. Sit down."

The telephone rings. You give a sigh.

"Oh, excuse me…"

"You go right ahead, I'm not in a rush!"

While you're answering the phone, I put my purse on the corner of the desk, I take off my shawl, I hang it over the back of the chair, I take off my jacket, I lay that on top, I open the zipper of my smock, I take off my smock, I lay it over the jacket, I unbutton my cardigan, I take off my cardigan, I lay it on top of the smock, I unbutton my dress, pull it off, lay it on top of the cardigan, I take off my slip, I put that on the seat of the chair because otherwise everything's going to fall, and now that you hung up, I look around at you. "Sh'd I take off the girdle?"

You smile. "You're fine like that… What brings you here today?"

"Well, like always, I'm here for my medicines. And then for the blood pressure, too, it's not so good lately, everything spins around in the morning when I get up and at noon when I just finish eating, and at night when I take off my stockings, I straighten up and everything's spinning, it's like swirling around, I feel like it's gonna throw me down… And I hurt, ohnomygod can a person hurt so bad, such pain such pain such pain…"

I close my eyes, I shake my head, I sigh, I nod, I sigh again and then finally with my hand on my breast, "I always have pain here… in my heart."

I look at you. You're very tall. You look less like a boy, more like a doctor, than when you first got here, but you're still just as tall. I'm not.

You point over to the cot.

I sit down, ohnomygod it's so low. I stretch out, ohnomygod it's so cold. You pull over the chair from under the window and you sit.

You put the earpieces on. You take my blood pressure. It squeezes, but I know it's for my own good. It hisses.

"How much do I got this time?"

The telephone rings.

"Oh, nuts!" you say.

"Not your lucky day, huh? They don't leave you in peace a minute to work!"

"Excuse me, please…"

The armband goes flat. You take a couple of steps over to the desk, you pick up.

"This is Dr. Sachs, can I help you?… Hello, monsieur… Yes… No, it hasn't come in yet. I think it should be in tomorrow's mail… Yes, I'll call you… Not at all, monsieur—goodbye."

You hang up.

"People are always bothering you, when you're a doctor!"

"Mmmhh…"

You pump it up again, it squeezes. You watch the needle. You wrinkle your eyebrows. You pump again. It squeezes more this time—what a person's gotta go through to take care of hisself! You look at the needle. The thing hisses very soft. I feel like a twitch in my arm. You nod.

"That's fine."

"What is it this time?"

"One-fifty over eighty."

"Really? But last time it was a hunnertanforty. That's awright, you think?"

"Yes, you know, it can vary a little from one time to the next."

"But I don't understand, I never have the same two times in a row when I come in. And I do take my medicine, though. And if I ever forget—mind you, that's not often—then I get up in the middle of the night to take it, so how come it's not always the same each time I come in?"

"Because it does vary. Between one-fifty and one-forty there's no big difference…"

"You're not gonna change my medicine?"

"No, it's just fine as it is…"

"Oh, good, I'm glad, I had so much trouble getting used to it! Still, a hunnert-anfifty, that's a lot, right? We don't want it to go up again like last year, you weren't around, I hadda call some other doctor…" Through the wall I hear the doorbell ringing.

"Really? Was I away on vacation?"

"No, but it was a Sunday and your machine said you woun't be in until Monday morning…"

"Yes, once in a great while there's a Sunday I don't work…"

"Ah, that's always how it is! When you need a doctor he's never there when he's sposed to be. No, I mean, I'm not talking about you. I'm glad to have you here. Before, I used to have to go all the way over to Lavinié, my son coun't always take me so I'd ask the neighbor and I'd give him money for the gas, but it was a whole business. And then I'd have to wait an hour there, even two hours—I gotta say, that Lavinié doctor always had a real big crowd! But you, here, when you started you didn't have too many patients, of course, so when I heard you were going to be seeing folks in the old school building, I was glad, it's not so far, and besides I see you go by on your way in in the morning, and when I go to the grocery I look to see if you're still there, and I can come in before it gets crowded—"

Somebody knocks at the door.

"I don't believe this!" You get up, annoyed, you open both doors.

I hear a voice, singsong, a little whiny. "Hello there mister?... Would you be wantin to buy a basket maybe Doctor?"

"No, thank you. I have everything I need."

"Yer lady she's here maybe?"

"No, this isn't where I live. Excuse me, I have a patient with me…"

"Awright, it don matter, bye…"

You close the door and come back to the cot. You're even taller when I'm lying down.

"She's not from around here, she don't know you got no Lady…"

"Mmmhh."

I tease you a little. "Good looking fella like yourself, you'll find somebody soon enough, be a pity you din't…"

"All right, then, Madame Renard, you can sit up now."

"Yes… but I need help—Aagh! Ohnomygod, it's so low, your cot, doctor honey!"

You help me sit up.

"They're a pain, them gypsies, I don't see why the mayor lets'm camp over there on the land by the stadium, I told him, Lucien, I said, you shoun't let them set up there, next thing ya know there's breakins and they leave all kinds of filth around, their kids don't even wear shoes, they're dirty you woun't believe.."

"Breathe deep…"

I breathe.

"Ohnomygod listen to that whistle. But you know, my bronchitis, it did go away with the syrup you give me last time…"

"Mmmhh. So I see…"

"Yeah that's good but I got my heart bothering me… And there's my legs. Ohnomygod! Them capsules you give me the other time, that helped for a day, maybe two, and then it started up again. Acourse, I had it fifty years already, it's not gonna go away overnight…"

You lean toward my legs. "Where does it hurt?"

"A little lower down…" You press on my shins. "Aiiyee! Yeah, ohnomygod that hurts, yeah, right there…"

"That's the muscle… When a person's a little heavy, like you, the muscles in the legs have to work a lot harder…"

"Ohnomygod! Gotta say I worked plenty hard in my life! I tell my husband, 'Marcel,' I says, 'It's just godamighty not right to be this tired.' It's not my circulation?"

You shake your head. "Uh-uh."

"Well, that's good. But I got my heart, too, ohnomygod is that awful! Just the other night, such awful pain I had! My husband was scolding me because I kept him up, he laid hands on me before I went to bed but it didn't help a bit, I still hurt…"

"Laid hands?"

"Well, yeah, you know that—Marcel has the *gift*. He used to do healing, he could *stop fire*. Acourse now he don't do it so much nowadays, only to me, and I don't think it works for me these days…"

"You still have that same pain under the breast?"

"Yes, there at the heart… Shoun't I take off my girdle?"

"No no—lean forward…"

I lean over. You leave your chair, you put a knee on the bed next to me and you press your two thumbs right between my shoulder blades. "Oowwwwiiie!"

"Mmmyes, I see what it is—the same as before. It starts between your two vertebrae—here, feel?"

"Owww!—yeah, that hurts…"

"And then it comes around to the front…"

"Oowwiie!…"

"That's not your heart, it's between the ribs… a pinched nerve."

"Ah… So it's not worth it you should do a cardiogram, huh?"

"Tch—uh-uh. Come get on the scale, Madame Renard."

You give me your hands, you help me stand up.

"Ohnomygod, I sure ain't lost any weight!"

I go over to the window. You crouch down and slide the scale in front of me.

I climb on real careful. You hold me by the hand. You let go. You look at the numbers I can't see from up here. "How much, today?"

You go back to your desk. You look at my record. "Same as last time."

I get down off the scale. "I get dressed now?"

"Mmmhh… yes, of course, please!"

I pick up my slip from the floor where it fell, I put it on, then the dress, I button that, I pull on the smock and slide the zipper up, I put on the jacket, I throw the shawl over my shoulders, I go over to the black-covered seat by the desk, I sit down, I put one hand on my breast ohnomygod such pain, and the other on the desk on top of my change purse.

You're busy writing very tiny on the sheet you took out of my big thick file.

You get to the end and turn it over. The other side is already full. You shake your head. You open a little file cabinet under the window, you pull out a fresh sheet. In the corner, top left, you write my name, RENARD Marie-Louise, and you underline it three times. Up in the right corner you put a number, 18 I think, and you circle it. Then you start writing again but too small for me to see, my eyes aren't what they used to be.

"What kind of medicine you giving me? Because the last thing helped, but not for long…"

You raise your head, you look at me over your spectacles.

"Which one gave you the most relief?"

"Ah, I don't remember… Nothing much helps me now, except them fat green capsules you prescribed last time, I had to get them made up by the pharmacist lady. They're really fat but now and then they do me good except when I can't get them down my throat. So then I open them up and mix the powder into my soup, but they don't work so well then…"

"It's true, it's better if you don't open them… Do you still have some left?"

"Ohnomygod yes! You gave me enough for three months but I wasn't having trouble so I stopped and when it started up again the other night, I says to myself better not take just anything, I'm gonna go back to my little doctor, for once in my eighty-somethin years I got a doctor right here on my own corner, I might as well take advantage! In the first place, I already paid in on the tax for it, and then besides you're so nice…"

"Mmmmhmm… Well, so then I'll just order you your blood-pressure pills…"

"And something for sleeping too…"

"Mmmhh…"

"And some of that cream so Dad can give me a rub when I hurt. Could you come by the house for him tomorrow morning? This afternoon he couldn't come in because he had to go look in on the mayor, but he wanted to see you and he's so impatient, he don't like to sit and wait…"

You open up the big appointment book. "Not tomorrow—it's Thursday, the office is closed… Is it urgent?"

"Ohnomygod no! You know how Dad is, he likes you a lot because you take good care of him, not that he's so easy to take care of, I can tell him 'Don't eat that, it's bad for you' or 'Take your pills it's for your own good,' you should hear him, he gives me an argument, he gets nasty, but with you he's all sweet…"

"So then it can wait till Friday?"

"Friday, okay, but the neighbor's taking us to the pharmacy in the afternoon, so could you come by in the morning not too late?"

"Fine, then Friday morning."

You push back the appointment book, you add a few words to the sheet, then you file it with all the papers in the big brown envelope held together with Scotch tape, and you set it on a pile of other envelopes just like it on a shelf, between two grey boxes. You write the prescription, you fill out the Social Security form, and you give me them both.

I already opened my purse and put out the bill I folded in four before I come in. I get up, you get up, from inside my smock I pull out the plastic case where I keep my blood test results and my insurance card, and I put the prescription slip inside.

"Ohnomygod I got so many papers, and I don't understand a thing about them. Lucky I give all that stuff to Madame Grivel the pharmacist or to Madame Lacourbe her technician there and they figure it out, they're so nice, they even bring us the medicine to the house sometimes, otherwise we have to ask the neighbor and it's a whole big business, acourse we do pay him for the gas… Well! I hope this works."

"I'm sure it will. And be sure to take a green capsule before every meal, you'll have a lot less pain."

"Oh, I hope so, doctor honey! Because when I got pain like that, Ohnomygod it's rilly awful…"

You walk ahead of me, you open the two doors, I see Marcel. I turn around, but you already closed the door behind me. Marcel stands up.

"Well?"

"Well, he says I gotta take care of myself because it's serious and I can't just act like it's nothing."

"Oh, okay. Did you tell him I wanted to see him too?"

"Yes, but he can't today or tomorrow, he's busy, so he'll come around and see you Friday, we can't be botherin him all the time."

"Oh, okay. Because I got almost no medicine left and my stomach's starting to bother me again…"

"It don't matter. He tole me you not taking it tomorrow won't make it no worse. All right, so, let's go!"

"Oh, okay."

I open the waiting-room door, Marcel walks past me, he goes out into the courtyard and then I hear somebody calling me.

"Madame Renard!"

I turn around. You come out of your office. "Your cardigan. It fell on the floor."

"Oh, are you nice! Thank you, doctor honey!"

9

MADAME LEBLANC

The telephone rings. Once, twice. I pick up. "Hello!"

"Hello, Edmond? Is that you, Edmond?"

"Ah, no, ma'am, you've reached the doctor's office in Play. You must have dialed—"

She hangs up. It's always that way. I set down the receiver, and it starts to ring again. "Hello?"

"Hello, Madame Leblanc."

"Oh, hello, Doctor!"

"I'm switching the line over to you, I'm on my way home."

"Wait, I'll get my book... Let's see, I made one appointment for five o'clock and another at five-twenty..."

"And I made one for five-forty—Monsieur Roché."

"Monsieur Roché. Okay, I have it down."

"I'm going to lunch. If anyone needs me for house calls, I'll do them after three-thirty. Unless it's an emergency, of course..."

"Fine, Doctor. You'll be at your house?"

"Yes, sure... Enjoy your lunch."

"Thanks, Doctor, you too. See you th—Doctor, Doctor!"

"Yes?"

"I forgot to tell you, a friend of yours, Madame umm... Markson, tried to reach you this morning but you were already out on a call. She'd like you to phone her."

"Ah. All right... mmmhh. Well, see you later."

"Goodbye."

I hang up and close the appointment book.

CATHERINE MARKSON

The telephone makes me jump.

"That must be Bruno," Ray says.

I pick up. "Hello?"

"Kate? This is Bruno…"

"Yes, we were expecting your call…"

"How is he?"

"Not bad, but—I don't know what to think. I'd better put him on."

"And what about you," he says in that voice that makes me shiver. "How are you doing?"

"It's hard…"

"Yes."

"Here's Ray."

I turn to Ray. He takes the telephone with one hand, holds onto me with the other, makes me sit down on the edge of the armchair beside him. He starts out in English:

"*Hi, buddy!*… Yeah, not too terrible. My white count's started climbing… You know how whites are—always invading!" He laughs and starts coughing.

"Yes, I've got some fever and I've begun to have that uncomfortable thing in the—how do you say 'chest' in doctor-language? The thorax… No, no, I'm not in pain, *honest.* Yes, I've got some and I take them when I need to but *not at this point in time.* Yes. You're nice to call me back, fella, but I just wanted to ask you—your colleague out here—you know, Thérame—he wants to put me in the university hospital, Professor Zimmermann's unit… Yeah, that's it. You know him?"

I squeeze Ray's hand.

"What do you think? Is he a genius or a nut?… Hey, makes you laugh when I talk like you, huh?… So you do know him?"

He turns toward me and nods reassuringly.

"Good, but tell me—they won't drive me too crazy? And Kate will be able to come in whenever she wants?... Well then, if I don't feel any better in a couple of days, I may go. *It's a real pain in the ass, but when you gotta go*—(one of his English tag lines). Yeah... yeah, he said I shouldn't put it off, but you know I don't like hospitals... Yah, boy. Don't worry—you'll come over when you can. (In English again:) *Seeyalater, Alligator! Bye...* Wait, I think Kate wants to talk to you. Watch out what you say to her, she tells me everything. *Bye, buddy!*"

Ray hands me back the phone and signs a thumbs-up to reassure me.

"Bruno?"

"Kate, I know Zimmermann, he's a good guy, he'll do what's needed to keep him going without putting him through too much. But he shouldn't wait. And it will be hard..."

"Yes. I know. Thérame told us what's involved."

"When he's decided to go into the hospital, let me know, okay?"

"Okay..."

"Give him a hug for me."

"Yes, thanks, Bruno..."

"I—I send you one too."

"Yes..."

I hang up. Ray starts to cough again. He is pale, and when he coughs his face tightens and turns livid with pain. He sits up in his easy chair. He takes my hand in his two.

"*See*, you should've married him, instead of taking on an old man like me who could drop dead in front of you any minute..."

I look at him through my tears. He takes me in his arms.

"*I'm sorry, honey*, I'm talking stupid."

"You're not rich enough to make me a merry widow. And I certainly wouldn't have married Bruno."

"Why not?"

"He's way too independent. Or uptight. Or impotent."

"*Wow!* You've got sharp teeth, as you folks say around here. *Explain...*"

"D'you know many guys who live alone at thirty-six or -seven?"

THE BUTCHER

The door opens, I hear the bell. I wipe my hands and push open the swinging door from the back room into the shop. You're standing there looking over the sausages.

"Ah! The doctor! How're things with monsieur?"

"Things are fine, thank you…"

"What can we give monsieur?"

"Well, I don't know… maybe some lamb chops…"

"How many?"

"Um—three?"

"Three chops, coming up!"

You don't say a thing while I cut the meat and then crack the bones by a couple of big smacks with the cleaver.

"Lots of folks sick these days?"

"Enough…"

"Myself, I don't have a minute to look around! Can't wait for vacation!"

"Coming soon?"

"Oh well, not till next month, that's the slow season. Still, with the kids, it's not so easy going away anywhere…"

I lay the meat on the scale.

"They're well?"

"Perfect! But it's a lot of work. Good thing my wife took her year's leave, otherwise I don't know how she could've managed!"

"Well, sure, triplets…"

"That comes to nineteen francs fifty!"

As I'm folding the wrapper, the door to the back room opens and my wife comes in. "Hello, Doctor!"

"Hello, Madame Didier…"

"I was actually meaning to call you, the babies are due for another shot… It was supposed to be done in August—it's not too late?"

"No, we're still within a couple of weeks. I'll give you the slip for the pharmacist—when you've got the vaccine, call me, I'll come by some evening on my way home."

"You wouldn't mind doing them Saturday noon? That way if they run a fever, Sunday's a little quieter, and Monday the shop is closed…"

"As you like. I'll go get the slips from my car."

You lay out the exact amount on the counter, you pick up the meat, and you step outside.

"Go finish up in back," my wife tells me. "I'll wait for the doctor."

THE NEXT-DOOR NEIGHBOR

I'm setting the table. A car door slams. I glance through the living-room window. Your car is stopped in front of the cottage gate. Without turning off the motor, you step out of the car, I go back to the kitchen, you open the letterbox sitting on top of its post twined in brambles, you pull out a pile of papers and leaflets, I rinse the salad I had soaking. You climb back into the car. You slam the door. You get right out again. I work the salad-spinner. You open the gate, you get back in the car, you pull in and park under the linden tree. My pressure-cooker starts hissing. I lower the flame, it goes out, I light it again. Your car door slams. Your briefcase in hand, the mail under your arm, you cross the yard. With the other hand, you shake out your keys. You unlock, you go inside, I put the salad in the salad bowl, you close the door behind you. I hear paper rustling, the cat's scratching around in the waste basket. I give him a smack.

Later on, I see smoke coming out of your kitchen window. A smell of grilled meat floats across to me. You grill meat a lot. I've never said a word to you since you moved in. I run into you once in a while in the butcher shop, or the superette, and you always greet me, but I've never had any business with you. You live alone. You have company in from time to time, in the evening, but you're not noisy people. A woman from the village—she's the sister-in-law of some brother-in-law by marriage of my husband's cousin—comes in on Tuesdays and Fridays to do your housework and ironing. When I told her you looked nice, she said you were very nice and not snobby, but she wouldn't tell me any more than that.

13

MADAME DESTOUCHES

The telephone rings. Once. Twice. Someone picks up.

"This is Doctor Sachs."

"Doctor? This is Madame Destouches. Could you come to my house this afternoon?"

"Of course. What's troubling you?"

"Oh, well, I still have some medicine left, but my leg-ulcerations need checking, and also I'd like you to take a look at Georges—his stump is hurting him lately. I can see it, I give him one of my pills for the pain, but he doesn't always want to take any and he gets worked up. And you know how he is when he's worked up, there's no controlling him…"

"I understand. I'll come between four and five, before my office hours."

"Thank you, Doctor, I'll expect you."

I hang up. Standing behind me, a cigarette butt in the corner of his mouth, Georges doesn't say a thing. He shuffles out of the kitchen.

MADAME LEBLANC

It's three forty-five. I pull out the plug, roll up the wire, and put the vacuum away in the closet. On the desk, I line up the prescription pads and Social Security forms on the left, and in the middle I put the mail I found on my desk when I got in. You were already gone when the postman came. The telephone rings.

"Madame Leblanc?"

I can almost always tell if you're irritated, tired, or cheerful. Today, at noon, when you transferred the line to me, your voice was calm and steady. It still is—maybe a bit foggy, the way it is when I wake you up on mornings when you've been on call all night.

"Yes, Doctor?"

"What's the schedule?"

"Well, there's little Romain Bologne—his mama didn't take him to the outdoor play center this morning because he wasn't feeling well. For the moment he's over at his nanny's, Madame Duhamel at La Marinière."

"La Marinière—where's that again?"

"You went there once—it's on the Tourmens road, a mile or so outside Play, there's some woods and then a road off to the left?"

"Mmmhh…"

"Do you know where I mean?"

"No. Well, I'll find it."

I turn toward the big military map tacked to the partition behind my desk. "I see it on the map—it's just after Les Bordes, old Madame Rosten's house, you know?"

"Mmm… vaguely. Was it urgent?"

"No—well, the nanny didn't say. I think he has a fever and certainly a bad cold."

"All right. First I have to go see Madame Destouches and her son."

"Do you want me to get the records ready?"

"No, I'll fill them out when I get back. What time is it?"

"Almost three-fifty."

"I'll be leaving the house in ten, fifteen minutes. I'll be back at the office around a quarter of five. See you then."

"See you then, Doctor." I put down the receiver.

I don't put a lot of faith in your estimates. You're often late. Sometimes I think you don't quite grasp how fast time flies. But I'm used to it. And I always know how to reach you if I need to.

CONSULTATION: IMPOSSIBLE
(First Episode)

I cross the office courtyard. A black bicycle, with a big wicker basket attached in front, is parked in the shade next to the entrance. I wipe my feet, I ring, I push open the door to the waiting room, I stick my head in. Pen and appointment-book in hand, Madame Leblanc comes out of the examining room.

"Hello, Madame Leblanc. Is the doctor with someone just now?"

"Oh, no—he's out on house calls at this hour."

"I didn't know, I've never come in for myself…"

"I'll give you a copy of his schedule." She hands me a half-sheet of paper with typing on it. "Wednesdays, the doctor sees people by appointment from five o'clock on. This afternoon, unfortunately, he already has a lot on the book. Is this urgent?"

"Uhh—no. That is… I've needed to come in for a long time and I keep putting it off…"

Madame Leblanc consults the notebook open on her desk. Her finger slides along a dozen names. She sighs.

"Yes… This afternoon he has an awful lot of work. Unless—if it's urgent, he might be able to squeeze you in between two other—I could ask him…"

"Uhh—no, it doesn't matter, I don't want to make a problem for him. I'll come back some other time. Can I keep this sheet?"

"Of course, that's what it's for! Would you like to make an appointment for Friday?"

"No—no thanks, I'll come again," I say, and I leave the waiting room.

For once I decide to go to the doctor's—it's just my luck.

16

THE NEWSDEALER

The door opens, the bell jingles. I leave my order sheet, I lift aside the curtain that separates us from the shop. You're standing at the newspaper rack.

"Ah, it's the doctor! How you doing?" I put out my hand.

"Hello, Monsieur Roubaud. Doing fine, thanks…"

"Lots of folks sick these days?"

"Mmmhh… Depends on the day. You wouldn't have *Le journal des lettres*, by any chance?"

"Ah, no—I don't get that. Is it a weekly?"

"Monthly."

"I can order it for you, if you like."

"No, don't bother, thanks."

I don't insist. Several times now you've asked me for magazines I don't know, or a daily I never carry; I've tried to order them for you but I never manage to get hold of them. When the outlet is too small, the distributors act like it doesn't exist.

The door opens again. It's Monsieur Amila come to pick up the local paper. As he enters, he steps aside to let in a short woman I don't know; she must live in one of the new housing developments. I go back behind my counter. While I chat with Monsieur Amila, you linger a good while at the periodicals stand, you leaf through movie and computer magazines, sometimes the comics. When there's nothing you like, you take some weekly or a television magazine. It also happens that you leave without taking anything, and as you go out you always say "Have a good day, Monsieur Roubaud," even if it's already six in the evening.

After a few minutes, you turn around and discover the video section. Not all the shelves are up yet, and lots of the cassettes are piled on the floor. You examine all of them before you pick one. You come up to the counter. While I'm giving Monsieur Amila his change, you bend over the stationery display. You look at the fountain pens, the ball-points, the felt-tips, the rollers with metal tips or plastic tips, the fluorescent underliners and the indelible markers, the specialty pencils, the erasers, the pencil-sharpeners. You take the cap off a felt-tip and I see you looking around for something to write on. I hand you a little pad.

"Thanks."

You sign your name on the pad several times. You always do that to try out a pen.

"That one's not very fine—you like a fine point, don't you?"

"No, medium… the fine point's a little fragile."

"I can see that! Doctors do a lot of writing—prescriptions, certificates…"

You nod, less to agree than to show your lack of enthusiasm for the way that felt-tip writes. You put it back in the display case and you set down the periodical and the video cassette in front of me.

"Ah, so you have a VCR, Doctor? I just bought three hundred cassettes, all good interesting movies you'd probably like…"

"Yes…"

I look at the cover of the one you've chosen. I don't know the title. "I haven't seen that one yet. I haven't had a chance to look at them all, naturally, but the salesman told me it was good."

"Would you mind if I made a little suggestion?"

"Of course, Doctor!"

You point to the twelve X-rated movies sitting smack in the middle of the display rack. "It might be better to put those where children can't see them, don't you think?"

"Ah?… Oh yes, of course, you're right. I did it all so fast last night, I didn't think about it, and besides I haven't got much space. But I'll take care of it—thanks for the advice!"

While I make out one of my very first membership cards for you, I see you cock an eye at the box of disposable pens I opened a little while ago. You uncap one, you try it on the pad of grid-lined paper, you nod your head approvingly, and you take six of them. Three blues and three blacks.

"They seem good. I hope they won't break down too soon."

"Ah, when a person writes a lot like you do, naturally you need the thing to hold up… Those, I've heard nothing but good things about them. I think I'll order more, they've got them on special."

"I'll recommend them to my patients. They often borrow my pen to make out their checks."

"Oh, that would be nice of you—give us a little advertising!"

Behind you, old Madame Malet just came in, she trots over to the TV magazines. I hand you your brand-new Video-Club membership card, I slip your seven disposable pens (three blues, three blacks, and at the last moment you picked up a red one too) into a paper bag, and I take the bill you've pulled out of your wallet. As I give you your change, I ask, "Shall I make you a receipt?"

"Thanks, don't bother."

"You're sure? I do it all the time, after all."

"No, no thanks, you're very kind. Have a good day, Monsieur Roubaud..."

"Yes, you too... oh, Doctor!"

You turn back to me and I jingle the key-ring you left on the counter.

As your car pulls out, Madame Malet asks if you're the one who's standing in for our doctor while he's off on vacation, and I explain that no, you're the doctor from over in Play. That's too bad, she says, it's a little far to make him come, and anyhow we're used to our regular doctor. "Mind you," I tell her, "he would certainly make the trip, he does come over this way to buy his newspapers and his stationery, he uses quite a bit, especially pens and packs of paper, of course—doctors do a lot of writing."

17

MADAME DESTOUCHES

A car door slams. I see a figure pass quickly by the kitchen window. There is a knock at the door.

"Come in!"

You come in. You duck so as not to hit your head. You close the door behind you.

"Oh, leave it open Doctor, it's nice out. It'll give us a little air..."

"Hello, Madame Destouches. Hello, Georges."

"Say hello to the doctor, Georges."

"Lodoctor."

Georges takes the cigarette stub out of his mouth and gives you his hand without looking at you.

As usual, you put your bag on the kitchen table. You pull out the stool and sit down.

You look at me over your round glasses. Since you're always stooped, you often look at me over them. Your hair is a little too long. Your face is grey with beard even when you've just shaved. You often have a little half-smile, but not today. You're wearing a worn leather jacket, your pockets always look full enough to burst. You're always nice with me, as if we've known each other for a long time. And I do owe you my life.

"Ah, I don't know where I'd be if you hadn't saved me..."

"Yes, well, it's really the surgeon who saved you."

"Yes, Doctor Lance too, I owe him a lot, but after all, you're the one who sent me to his unit."

"Mmmhh... It was the only thing to do, and any doctor would have done it. You had an obstruction, I couldn't leave you like that."

"But still, I didn't want to go to the hospital, you remember? I was so scared of dying there, at my age. And you sent me anyhow!"

"Yes. But you're still here, and I'm really glad of it."

"And what about me?" Georges exclaims, behind me.

"How are your legs, Madame?"

"Oh, still the same. The ulceration on the left leg doesn't change, the nurse says it's clean, but the one on the right is getting deeper and deeper. I should have put on that stuff you ordered for me a few months ago—that closed it up nicely— but they don't reimburse for it and it's too expensive for me. And then look how long I've had these ulcers—imagine! Even the graft they did on them didn't hold, my arteries are too bad, I knew it wouldn't hold. Well, at least I've been comfortable for a while…"

"Six months?"

"Oh, at least! Georges, could you go get me my box from the wardrobe, so the doctor can see how many dressings I have left?"

Georges tosses his stub into the sink and circles the table. You stand up to let him get by into the bedroom. When he's through the door, I lean over to you and say very low:

"He's drinking a lot these days. Madame Barbey keeps finding empty bottles in the shed when she puts out the garbage in the mornings. When his stump hurts, it gets to him (I touch my finger to my forehead), it affects his system, and he drinks even more."

You listen to me, you turn your head toward the depths of the bedroom. Without lowering your voice, you say, "And what does he take for the pain?"

"I give him one of my Dolévits when he's very worked up, but sometimes I'm afraid it'll make a bad reaction with…"(I mimic the drinking movement.)

Georges comes in with a plastic basket in his hand. He sets it down on the table without a word. I count the packages of compresses, the rolls of adhesive, the rolls of gauze and the tubes of Vaseline. You take a prescription pad out of your black bag. Georges hasn't gone back to stand at the window, he's still leaning at the main door, just to your left. You look up at him. I'm ashamed at the sight of him—he's dirty, he's not shaved, when he's in pain like that he sleeps in his clothes because he hasn't got the strength to change them, and today it's been a week.

"So, Georges, how are you feeling?"

"Me, doctor? Okay, okay."

"Your mom tells me your arm's been hurting you lately?"

Georges looks at me, with that dazed baby look he's always had. "Uhh, yeah, that's for sure, it's hurting more. Must be the weather."

"Come in here, let me take a look at you."

You push open the bedroom door. Georges grumbles a little but he obeys and shuffles into the room ahead of you. Without a glance at me, you follow him and close the door behind you.

ROMAIN AT HIS NANNY'S HOUSE

Somebody rings the doorbell. Nanny Colette comes out of her kitchen and opens. It's you, with your black doctor's bag in your hand, you slip your bunch of keys into a pocket of your leather jacket, you spot me, you smile, you look at Nanny, you tell her "I'm Doctor Sachs," she brings you inside. Curled up on the living room couch, I watch you come closer, put your bag on the floor, and sit down on one of the two seats right across from me.

"Hello, Romain... So, what's going on with you, little guy?"

"Well, early this afternoon at the outdoor center he complained of pain in his stomach, so his mama went by to pick him up, and she left him off with me because she had to go back to work."

"Did he have any fever?"

"I don't know, I didn't check it." Nanny Colette takes me in her arms, lays her hand on my forehead. "I don't think so."

"Well, let's just see..."

Nanny Colette tries to lay me on the couch but I don't want to let go of her. She hugs me, tells me you're not going to hurt me, but I don't know you very well, I saw you once a long time ago and I remember Mommy was very upset that day.

"Do you want me to undress him?"

"Just take off the bathrobe..."

You stay in your seat. You tell Nanny Colette to sit down and hold me on her lap. You open your doctor bag, you pull out that long black thing that you stick in your ears, and you put the other end on my tummy. I squeeze up tight against Nanny Colette. You lower your head. I can't see your eyes any more. You take the round thing at the end of the black tube and move it around on my tummy, then on my back. "Good!" you say, and there's a clack when you pull the instrument out of your ears. You raise your hands to my chin, you touch my neck, my head, it doesn't hurt but I'm a little afraid.

"Let's look at your eardrums..."

You pull a black box out of your bag, you take an ear-light out of it, and before I can say a thing, Nanny Colette turns my head against her chest.

"We're going to look into your ears, bunny," you say.

I feel you stick something into my ear, like when Mama cleans them, but this doesn't hurt.

"Can we look at the other side?"

I turn my head. That doesn't hurt either. I let go of Nanny Colette's shirt.

"Now can I look in your mouth?"

I shake my head.

"Do you want a spoon?" Nanny Colette asks you.

"No, thanks. I never use a spoon." You lean toward me. "You open your mouth for me to look inside, but I won't put anything in there. Okay?"

I stick my tongue way out. You smile. "Ah, I can see your tongue, but I can't see your teeth…"

I open my mouth so my teeth show. You dip your head down, you turn the flashlight to the right, to the left, then you straighten up and turn out the light. You slip it into your pocket and you feel around my neck very gently.

"I'm going to check your tummy now. Would you stretch out on the couch?"

Nanny Colette gets up, I lie down, I pull up my pajama top.

"Show me where you were hurting, before."

I point to my belly-button. Your fingers are warm, they tickle a little.

"Do you hurt right now?"

I shake my head no.

"Are you hungry?"

I nod my head yes.

"He didn't have a snack?" you ask Nanny Colette.

"No, and he didn't eat at lunchtime, either."

"All right—I think you can give him a little something. A chocolate cookie?"

"A banana," I say.

"A banana!" exclaims Nanny Colette. "That's awfully heavy!"

"He hasn't thrown up, and I think he's already better. So we can give him whatever he feels like having."

"But what do you think was the matter?"

"Mmmhh… I don't know. (You tap around my tummy again.) But it's not appendicitis."

"Good, that's what his mother was afraid of… I've got to say, she does worry easily, but in my opinion this is a pretty healthy child. My second one, at his age, he was always having one earache after another, but with Romain it's very rare he comes down with something. Tell me, though, Doctor—"

"Mmmyah?"

"What if he complains about his stomach again?"

"I'm going to order you a sedative syrup. But I'd be surprised if he needs it."

I get up, I pull at Nanny Colette's shirt, she bends over, I tell her something in her ear, she says, "Yes, go get it, darling." When I come back, with my banana, you've put your instruments back into your bag and you're flipping through my health booklet. I peel my banana. I come over to the table. You're busy writing in my booklet. I eat my banana standing up next to you while you write. Every now and then you give me a quick sideways look over the top of your round glasses, and you smile.

19

MADAME LEBLANC

The telephone rings. I wipe my hands and walk toward the desk. I pick up.

"Medical Office, Play—hello?"

"Hello, is this the Provincial Credit Bank?"

"No, no, sir—you must have dialed wrong. This is Doctor Sachs's office."

"Oh, I see!" He hangs up.

✴

The door opens. You come in, your bundle of keys in one hand, your leather briefcase in the other. You walk rapidly past the three people already waiting, murmur "Hello everyone," and you plunge through the open door into the consulting room. I copy a test result onto a record card, I put the card into the folder and the folder into the filebox marked *Per-Tes*, I gather up the boxes holding the *Per-Tes* and *Tet-Wim* records which I've just reorganized, and I follow after you into the consulting room. You've set your briefcase against one of the dark-blue tubular sawhorses, and the keys on the big red book. You take off your windbreaker and your sweater and you shove up your shirt-sleeves. I put the *Per-Tes* and *Tet-Wim* boxes back on the shelf. Standing at the sink, you soap your hands. I take the filebox *Win-Zaf* and carry it out into the waiting room to copy in the test results.

You come out of your room slipping into your white coat, you lean to look over the appointment book lying open in front of me. You examine the names I've written there. You make a face. You murmur:

"Mmmhh… Better not to book me two people for the same time slot."

"I know, Doctor, but for this woman"—(I point to a name in the margin with the end of my pen)—"it was an emergency… I put down her number for you if you want to ring her back."

"Fine. You did the right thing."

"And then, this gentleman"—(I point to another name)—"has already called twice for his results. The mail came late, I put it on your desk."

"Mmmhh… He's worried…"

"And also, could you write a prescription for Madame Renard, she took some green capsules and she actually thinks they helped her, but she doesn't have many left."

You look at me with astonishment. "She said they helped? You're sure?"

I nod yes, yes.

"Well, then—with a little luck maybe we can get her down to under two visits a week!"

I think to myself that you're an optimist. Madame Renard calls, visits, or stops by "just in case" three or four times a week since the first month you opened your practice. You straighten up, you look at the big round clock hanging between the two windows, then you say to the three persons sitting in the waiting room,

"I'll ask you to bear with me for another moment—I have to make a phone call."

I look at my watch. If you have calls to make, that's going to take some time. I smile at the three people seated around the low table. One of them, someone I don't know, returns the smile and plunges back into a book. You step into your office, with a quick move you push shut the inside door and it slams behind you; meanwhile, by means of the spring mechanism, the connecting door pulls to noiselessly and finishes with a click.

20

IN THE WAITING ROOM

The connecting door closes with a click. I lay my book on my lap, I stretch, I turn my neck from left to right and from right to left, the telephone rings.

The secretary picks up: "Doctor's Office, Play... Ah, good evening, madame..." The young mom has taken the two children onto her lap, she's reading them a *Babar* from the rickety children's-book shelf. I see the secretary purse her lips, she's sorry: "All the appointments are filled this evening... No, I can't put you through, he's on the other line just now," she begs pardon, she's extremely regretful, "Yes, tomorrow would be better, goodbye Madame Renard..."

A man comes in, about sixty years old, maybe a little less—country people always look a little older than they are. He takes off his cap and reveals a balding pate. He greets the secretary, exchanges a few words with her, sits down on the edge of a chair. From his jacket pocket he pulls out a small booklet, a Social Security form, and a carefully folded prescription slip; he sets the whole collection on the low table before him.

Next to me, the teenager is more and more sullen; her mother has left off talking to her. The old gentleman draws his wallet from his pocket, and from the wallet a bill that he folds in four and slips into the booklet lying on his cap.

I uncross my legs, stretch them out to relax them, fold and cross them again, re-open the book.

SOLO DIALOGUES

I

PRESENTING COMPLAINTS

What can I do for you?

It's about my daughter. She didn't want to come but I made her.

It's about my little boy. He doesn't eat a thing. He still wets his bed. He won't sleep. He throws temper tantrums. He screams when I turn off the TV. He wakes up at night and comes into our bed, I have to take him in with me so he'll sleep, and my husband has to get to work at five in the morning so he goes and sleeps in the boy's bed. (Or else) He's not toilet-trained. He's not talking right. Can't get him to eat meat. At school he's a demon, the teachers complain. (Or else) He's had a cold for three weeks and he had antibiotics twice and and he's not getting better, you've got to do something. (Or else) He only likes yogurt and bread-and-butter, after-school snack is his best meal. He looks skinny to me, he should be getting some vitamins.

It's for my second-month visit, I know it's not required and I'm not sick, but since they pay for it…

It's just to get his stitches taken out, but he's scared.

It's for a refill on my Pill, or my vein medicine, or my tranquillizer, or my heart medicine, or the ointment for my hemorrhoids.

It's to renew my hundred-percent coverage document, or my insulin prescription, or the nurse visits to dress my leg ulcers every day morning and evening Sundays and holidays included for a month.

It's for my blood test they do every month on the prothrombin levels this month it was thirty-five instead of twenty-five last month but I ate leeks and especially be sure to write down *home visit* on the order last time I couldn't get them to pay me back, thank you.

It's for a form I got from the Social Security from the hospital/from the insurance/from the mayor's office and I can't understand it at all they told me I have to get you to fill it out.

What brings you here?

Nothing new, same old stuff.

Tell you one thing, I'm not good.

Listen, I'd be very glad not to be here.

I'm bringing my mother in to see you, she was going to a doctor in Tourmens but she can't stand him any more, she's mad at him because he wanted her to have an operation and she didn't want it...

It's not for me, it's for my husband. He won't come in, so I decided I would talk to you about him, because I should tell you that for the past six months he's been coughing and drinking and flying into a rage with me the kids everybody, and his boss said if it stays like this he can't keep him on.

I just came to tell you that my grandmother died the day before yesterday and the funeral is tomorrow.

I came to show you my test results.

I came to ask you if by any chance you could help me out. Here's the thing: I'm an addict and I'm getting clean and I need some morphine pills because that's the protocol, you get clean by taking morphine in smaller and smaller doses, it's a doctor in Tourmens who prescribed that—you probably know him, Doctor Bober, at the hospital—the thing is, right now I'm having a rough time so if you could give me a prescription for morphine pills, just a few, to get me home, no I'm not from here, no I have no family in the area just some buddies and I'm passing through but I just need a couple of pills...

I came in because people told me about you, they say you're good at treating asthma/sinus infection/warts/headaches/depression/rheumatism/boils/old people and that you're very gentle with children. My neighbor has an aunt you take care of, she told her sister who lives near my mother-in-law. So I thought I'd come see you, doesn't cost anything to have a look, huh? We pay enough in for it. But I warn you, I'm a real case!

How's it going since the last visit?

Not so good, or I wouldn't be here!

Me, I'm okay, my wife's not so good.

Better. Not perfect yet, but better.

The same. Those medicines of yours didn't do a thing for me.

It's no worse, but I still have trouble sleeping.

Well, it doesn't hurt me anymore, but now it's itching.

I keep going.

You're going to bawl me out, I didn't take the medicine like you told me to, when you saw my blood pressure was higher you told me I had to take one in the morning and one at night but after three days I felt okay so I started taking it just the one in the morning. So naturally the package lasted longer, so I didn't come back after three months like you told me to, for sure you're going to bawl me out...

Doing fine, but I'm running short of medicine so I came in to get it renewed.

Not bad, but you asked me to come by to see if everything was back in order.

What's wrong with you?

I didn't go in to work this morning, there was really something wrong I couldn't stand up, I was shaking I was cold I was hot my head was spinning I felt like throwing up but it wouldn't come, I decided it was my blood pressure dropping—even normally it's not very high—and when my husband saw me in that state he got mad, he told me I'd better call the doctor, but I didn't want to bother you since I know you have so much to do, I told my boss I wouldn't be coming in to work this morning and then I called here, and your secretary told me that you were having office hours so I asked my neighbor to bring me over, since I can't drive, this way we can stop at the pharmacy on the way home, I've had this for a long time and my boss said You need a rest.

I have a cold. I'm coughing, I'm spitting up phlegm, I have a sore throat, I have a stuffed nose, eyes, head, my ears hurt, I can't swallow, I can't hear a thing I can't see a thing I vomited all night, I had a hundred-and-four fever last night I just managed to get myself over here today somebody told me you don't do housecalls, if I'd known you do I'd have stayed in bed, my eyes are all stuck closed I can't stand up my head is spinning this never happened to me before I really think I've never been this sick in my life, you've gotta help me I've gotta go back to work tonight and there's no way I could take off.

I'm pregnant. My husband's been hoping for this for years, and me too, and it never happened. So we stopped believing it would. We got used to the idea of adopting. And then two months ago I skipped my period, I think That's it, it's all over, maybe I'm only thirty-seven years old but still this must be early menopause. And then two weeks ago I start throwing up like a sick person, my breasts swell up, I'm going to the toilet all the time, finally I decide This isn't natural, last week I went to the pharmacy to get a test and it came out positive. My husband went crazy he was so happy, see this is a second marriage, he was never able to have a child with his first wife, and as for me, my first husband beat me, so every time I got pregnant I arranged to get rid of it without telling him, and then finally my doctor put in an IUD and he cut the thread very short so my ex wouldn't feel it and since I kept getting infections in the tubes because my ex didn't wash every day and also because daytimes he'd go get it someplace else but still that didn't stop him at night—you know how men are—so I thought I was sterile. And actually the gynecologist told me I was. So when this second husband found out I was pregnant, naturally he was crazy happy, me a little less so because after all I'm thirty-seven that's not real young to be having babies, the bottles the diapers and all that, but him you can imagine he was in heaven—a man can be thirty or forty, makes no difference to him he's not the one who carries it. Only, then—yesterday I went to the gynecologist he did a sonogram and right away I saw there's just no way, that's why I came to see you today, I know you won't tell my husband. I'll say I had a miscarriage, he'll be real disappointed but it won't be the first time and he knows what I went through before my divorce. You understand, I'm already thirty-seven and sure he's been waiting for this a long time and he was starting to lose hope and about adopting I told him yes because I saw how much he wanted it whereas me, after all I went through with my husband—the first one I mean—-it really didn't appeal to me a bit, in fact not intercourse either I'm not crazy about that but still I have to admit my husband—the second one—he's very sweet and he's a hard worker, he does a lot of things around the house so of course I thought it'll really make him happy even if it does come a little late, we could adopt some kid who's already bigger, that wouldn't be so hard, but getting pregnant like this when I didn't expect it it really gave me a shock. So when the gynecologist told me what was up, I thought I would die, I kept thinking about it all night long and whatever way I looked at it, I don't see any other solution. You understand, I'm already thirty-seven, my husband's forty, and really, twins, I don't think I can do it.

Not feeling too well, from the looks of you.

I don't know what's the matter with me, but my back's been hurting for over a week now, I thought it would go away but it's still there, it starts here behind the shoulder and goes down in front, under the breast, it clutches when I breathe and at work it's no fun, working sitting in front of a screen you get into bad positions, I mean it was already giving me headaches even before, all those colors, and on top of that we work two people on the same machine, my partner keeps switching things around, she likes a blue screen and that's a strain for me, only the black's good

(or else) The other day I went to the bathroom, I sat there I was knocked out, I work standing up, see, and my foreman came in looking for me he found me there he says to me if it was too much for me I should just change jobs

(or else) It hit me the other day when I tried to push my fridge out to mop behind it, I felt this pain that went through my buttock and down to my heel I couldn't move my husband says What happened to you and I had to lie down and ever since then it doesn't go away even at night, I don't sleep I even had to take my husband's sleeping pills, you know he works nights and he takes a pill on his day off or else he doesn't get any sleep, and now I've been taking them for the last three nights but I don't want to get used to them

(or else) You understand, it's exhausting to keep holding your arms up to tighten the bolts under the engines, the assembly line never stops so you can catch your breath, and besides you're standing right in a draft and I've always been sensitive to the cold but no I didn't take any aspirin I thought it'll go away and I wouldn't have come in if my wife hadn't made the appointment for me, in fact I nearly cancelled but she would've had a fit

(or else) You know, I'm no sissy but the minute I start to make some movement my neck jerks me right back into line I have to say I'm sick of it by now it's months, your colleague the rheumatologist decided to do this—what do you call it?—"manipulation" and right afterwards it felt a little better, but the physical therapy sessions didn't help at all. In fact, I wonder if I did the right thing going to him, all he did was stick me under the heat lamp and then he'd leave the room I'd hear him talking next door and fifteen minutes later he'd come back do three moves on me and whup! right to the cash register. I thought he might be working on a whole bunch of patients at once, whatever, I still hurt and I've got to find some solution.

What's wrong?
    My stomach hurts.
    I'm losing my hair.
    I have a wart.
    I only see out of one eye.
    I feel lightheaded, would that be blood pressure?
    My back hurts.
    I'm always thirsty.
    My foot hurts.
    It makes me uncomfortable telling you this but I've got a pain in an embarrassing place.
    I can't move any more.
    I'm bleeding.
    I can't manage.
    I've got a thing there, in my mouth. It scares me.

Why have you come to see me this afternoon?
    Because I don't know what to do anymore.
    Because this has been going on too long.
    Because this can't go on any longer.
    Because I didn't have much choice—if it was up to me, you know, doctors—the less I see of them the better I feel.
    Because my mother/my father/my boss/my husband/my wife/my son/my daughter/my grandchildren/my neighbors/everybody told me to come in, but frankly, *I* know I don't need any doctor, just because I'm tired doesn't mean I need a doctor and besides, you gotta die of something.
    Because I'm due for a booster shot. Is it going to hurt?

SOLO DIALOGUES I

Because I still need some massage sessions, that helped me and the physical therapist told me I could ask you to prescribe some more, I really do have less pain, even my husband thinks I'm more relaxed.

Because I didn't go back to the barracks last night, I called in sick but really I'm okay and I need a medical excuse slip.

Because I'm afraid my husband has something bad and doesn't want to tell me, so I decided to ask you directly and of course I won't tell him I came in to see you, you can trust me!

Because I've gotten fat.

Because I've gotten thin.

Because I can't sleep.

Because I keep sleeping.

Because I can't stand my children any more.

Because my father hit me.

Because I cry all the time.

Because I have bad thoughts.

Because I have no more ether in the house.

Because I'm not getting along with my wife/my husband/my daughter/my son/my mother/my father/my brothers and sisters, especially now with my grandmother's estate.

Because I'm sick and tired of breaking my butt for nothing.

Because I'm only thirty and already I hurt all over.

Because I'm already forty and I'm starting to get worried.

Because I'm over fifty and it's about time.

Because I'm nearly sixty and I'd like to keep going.

Because I'm seventy-plus and my son worries about me.

Because pretty soon I'll be eighty and I want to die in my own house.

Because I'm ninety and, you know, I'm tired of living.

What's the trouble?

Well, I don't know, you tell me! I'm not a doctor.

THE CASE OF DR. SACHS

HISTORY

(Tuesday, October 7)

So, you going fishing?
No, I'm going fishing.
Oh, I thought you were going fishing.

Moron Story

0

1

2

3

4

5

6

7

8

9

10

11

12

13

14

15

16

17

18

19

20

21

21

MADAME BORGES

The door opens with a creak.

Hair shaggy and face drawn, you appear at the door of your room, wearing a slightly too-short pair of sweat pants, a T-shirt, and a shapeless lounging jacket that you button up clumsily at the sight of me. You yawn like a lost soul. You don't have your glasses on. You're shuffling around in worn old moccasins.

"Good morning, Monsieur Sachs," I say as I go on ironing.

"Good morning, Madame Borges... Excuse the way I look, by this time I should've been up a while already."

"Were you on call again?"

"No, but I forgot to switch to my answering machine last night, and I got a call at three in the morning..."

"Oof—it must be hard getting up!"

"Mmmhh, but not as hard as it was for the patient: he was having a terrible asthma attack."

You don't say who it was. If it's someone in the village, I'll certainly hear about it at the grocery this noontime.

"Lots of people are asthmatic, it seems to me..."

"Mmmhh..." You head for the kitchenette.

You stop in front of the stove, you pick up the pot, you scratch the back of your neck. You glance at the clock on top of the refrigerator, you turn on the radio on the kitchen table, you turn it off again almost immediately.

You fill the pot. You turn on the gas. From the cupboard above the sink you take a stoneware mug, you pick up the plastic cone from the drainer, you set it on top of the mug, you arrange a paper filter inside it. You take a half-full packet of coffee out of the fridge, you pour three spoonfuls of ground coffee into the filter, you close the packet, you have second thoughts, you open it up again, you take a

22

23

24

25

26

27

73

quick look inside, you add another spoonful of coffee to the filter, you lift the filter-cone off the mug and you set it on a white porcelain pot that's not much bigger.

You shuffle across the room. In the bedroom, you open the window and push back the shutters. You tug the bedcovers into some order on your rumpled bed. I fold the shirt and lay it on the pile. You take a journal, a book, and a notepad from the night-table. I pick up a pair of brown corduroy trousers, slightly worn in the seat, I set it on the ironing board, I lift the iron.

You circle the room, you scratch the back of your neck, you mutter. "Say, Madame Borges, you wouldn't have seen my glasses anywhere?"

"Nooo... Before, when you came out, you weren't wearing them..."

You put the books on the kitchen table, you lift up the newspapers, the maga-zines piled in a corner. You circle the room again, looking under the things on the coffee table, under the cushions on the mattress-and-boxspring draped in a big multicolored throw that you use as a couch. You slide your hands into the cracks of the old sagging armchair. Finally, you rub your eyes, you scratch your cheek, you massage your head, you set your fists on your hips and you sigh.

"Mmmhh..."

I fold the trousers over the back of a chair and start on the blue jeans.

You go back into the bedroom.

The water boils up in the pot. I set down my iron and go pour water over the coffee. You reappear, you make a vague attempt at straightening out your glasses, but when you put them on they're still lopsided. You watch me pour the coffee, you smile, you reach a hand out.

"Thanks, Madame Borges, leave it, I'll take care of it..."

"It's no trouble, you know."

"I know, you're kind, but still. It's like the other day—you shouldn't have done the dishes, you have plenty to do as it is with the cleaning and the ironing. I do the dishes when I come in at night, mornings I don't always have time."

"I know, that's why I do it. You know, in my house I don't like to see the kitchen messy, well it's the same here, I can't help it, I tidy up. And anyhow, three knives two plates—it's no big deal."

"Yes, but I..."

"Yes, Monsieur Sachs?"

"No, it doesn't matter, it's very nice. May I?"

You take over the coffee pot. I return to your jeans. I glance at the time display on the VCR beneath the tiny television set standing between the window and the unused fireplace in the living room: ten of ten. The telephone rings.

"Ah, damn!" You slam down the saucepan and pick up the phone. "HELLO!... Yes, good morning, Madame Leblanc, excuse me, I'm not complete-ly awake. Yes, two housecalls last night. No, no, it's okay, thank you... Oohh, Madame Renard? (You roll your eyes to heaven.) What's bothering her? Can it

74

wait a little, till I have my breakfast? And you have other housecalls scheduled? What time is it now?... Yes, I'll be there in—mmmhh, say three-quarters of an hour. Yes, fine. Thanks. See you later."

❀

"A little coffee, Madame Borges?"

"I wouldn't say no!"

"Oops, I put in two sugars—but I didn't stir."

"Thank you, Monsieur Sachs."

I set down the iron, I turn the spoon.

"It's good and hot, I'll wait a minute for it to cool. Tell me, Monsieur Sachs—uhh, Doctor—can I ask you a question?"

"Of course."

"One of my sisters-in-law—well, she's not really a sister-in-law, she's the sister of my husband's brother-in-law, you know, the one who's married to a man who works at the Provincial Credit Bank—they just had a little girl, and they had to keep her in an incubator because she was born premature—not by much, three weeks. So anyway, she's all right, but what's bothering them is that her mother can't breast-feed her. She was told that would be best, but no matter how hard she tries to bring up her milk, it isn't coming, and that's got her in a state, of course they'd waited a long time, her pregnancy tired her out, at the age of forty-two that's pretty much what you'd expect. So they're giving the baby milk from the breast-milk bank but my sister-in-law says it's not as good as her own milk, she gets these ideas, naturally, with the things you hear about—is the milk good, who does it come from... I tell her that it *is* sterilized, though, and she shouldn't worry—isn't that so?"

"Mmmhh? Of course, you're quite right... Go on."

"Well, she was asking whether there's something she could take to bring up her milk but they told her there isn't anything for that. So she's upset, she wonders whether her baby will develop allergies or eczema, she's in a state. I think she's worrying a little too much. Don't you think?"

"Yes... a first child at forty-two, people do get very anxious."

"That's what I told her. I told her, 'You'll see, they do just as well on the bottle.' It's true—my second, she wouldn't take the breast at all. With the bottle, though, at ten months she was drinking it all by herself, sometimes she'd even have two in a row. And you've seen the size of her now!"

You smile as you lift your cup.

"It's like my neighbors with their son, they're upset because at fourteen months he's still not walking. They say he's lazy, I keep telling them it'll come—he gallops around on all fours, or he stands up and pushes chairs around on the tile floor, but he doesn't want to let go, so that worries them, but it'll come!"

"Mmmhh… I walked at sixteen months."

I stop ironing and look at you. "Really?… It's true, we didn't use to rush kids off to the pediatrician every minute. Still, sixteen months—that's unusual."

"Isn't it? And you see where it got me."

⚙

I've almost finished ironing. You gulped two big mugs of coffee and three slices of bread slathered with cream cheese.

"I'm leaving the dishes in the sink, but promise you won't touch them, okay?"

"Whatever you say."

While I put away the linens in the cupboard in the living room, I hear the bathroom pipes rumble. I'm folding up the ironing board as you come out of your room. You're wearing a yellow pullover, a blue shirt, jeans, beige socks and black shoes. As usual, you've cut yourself shaving, and you've stuck on a little bit of adhesive—today it's under your chin.

"Madame Borges, you wouldn't have seen my watch anywhere, by chance?"

"Um—it's not on the kitchen table?"

"Is it? Yes, thanks."

"While I think of it, when you go to the superette, could you pick up a little distilled water for the iron?"

"Uhh—of course, would you write it down so I don't forget?"

You put on your watch, you pick up your scarf from a chair, you pull on your windbreaker, you take the book and the journal from the living-room table, you slip them into your briefcase, you circle the room lifting up cushions and newspapers.

"Madame Borges, you haven't seen my keys anywhere, by chance?"

You finally remember that they're still in the raincoat you were wearing yesterday, you go out, you pull the door to behind you, you think again, you stick your head back through the gap:

"Have a good day, Madame Borges, see you Friday!"

"Goodbye, Monsieur Sachs—Friday."

Outside, I hear you slam the car door, start up, gun the engine, and leave. I go into the kitchen, I open the pantry closet, I take out the broom and the dustrag. In the hall, I lift the lid of the bench under the window and take out the vacuum cleaner.

In a while, after I've washed your two spoons and your plate, I'll go in to do the bathroom. I don't clean the bedroom each time, you say it's not worth bothering. From time to time, though, you ask me if I'd mind vacuuming or—this is rare—

changing the bed. Making it, rather: those days, there's only a rubber cover on the mattress and you've washed the sheets and hung them out to dry. I never touch the papers, notebooks, magazines and books, pens, pill boxes, tissue packets, envelopes and other things piled up along the edge of the desk, which is crowded with an enormous electric typewriter. It's a small, small room, and it's very hard to vacuum in there without knocking into the furniture, but I should do it more often. When I think it begins to need doing, even if you haven't asked me to I give a little swipe with the dustcloth to the mounds of books piled up on your night table. Because books, I'm sorry, they really do collect dust and at night it's just not healthy.

22

YVES ZIMMERMANN

I remember the first time I saw you. I mean, really saw. And listened to you, not just heard you. You were standing beside a patient's bed and I asked who was handling her case. You answered, "I am, Monsieur." You were twenty or twenty-two, you were one of the interns on the unit that year; there was nothing particular about you—you were tall, dark, taciturn, a little stooped. You always used to roll up the sleeves of your labcoat and your forearms were naked. I looked at you over my glasses and I said, "Tell me about it." You stood beside the patient and you said, "Madame Malinconi came in three days ago with thus-and-such presenting symptoms," you summarized the situation very quickly, very tersely, and then you stopped. I had nothing to ask you. You had summed up the problem in six sentences, and were done. That exasperated me—the intern knowing better than the chief what the patient's problem was, that looked bad. I said, "Is that all?" You answered, "That's all." "Is that really all? You're sure?" And the patient began to cry. I said, "Why are you crying, Madame?" I looked at you, I asked, "Why is she crying?" You gave me a stubborn look, you crossed your arms and tipped your chin toward the other staff. I turned to the head nurse, the two residents, the senior resident, the six interns, the student nurses, and the nursing aide just coming into the room, carrying a tray (if I recall, there was another patient in the next bed.) I asked again, "Why is she crying?" No one answered. I got up, I told you, "Fine, answer me when you know the case," and I left the room intending to slam the door behind me. But you darted behind everyone, you followed me into the hallway, and you're the one who closed the door on them all. I turned around, I looked at you over my glasses, and though I'm six-foot-two you looked almost as tall as I am.

"All right, then: what's wrong with her?"

And you told me, tersely, in a few sentences, the history of that woman who'd tried to go home two days after she was admitted even though her doctor had referred her for an acute pulmonary edema that nearly killed her, her blood pressure was 220 on admission, she weighed a hundred-and-ninety on a height of five-feet-three—I didn't see how we could get that under control without a standard workup, minimum; back then, getting the meds to therapeutic levels would take at least a week, not to mention the dietician and initiating treatment—but that her problems with job husband mother-in-law moving house and I don't know what-all else, anyhow her whole freaking daily life, seemed to matter more to her than her freaking symptoms.

"Okay, okay! But why wouldn't you say anything back in the room?"

"There were fifteen people in there, monsieur."

So then I looked at you through my glasses and I saw you for the first time. You were twenty or twenty-two years old and you were already angry.

23

MADAME LEBLANC

The telephone rings. I pick up.

"Medical office…"

"Hello, Edmond? Edmond, is that you?"

"No, Madame, you must have dialed a wrong number—"

She hangs up. I hang up, and it rings again.

"Doctor's office, Play—hello?"

"Hello—when does the doctor come out to see people in their own house?"

"Well, today the doctor is doing housecalls in the morning. Did you want him to come by?"

"Yes, it's for our father, he's not in awful good shape…"

"You're Madame—?"

"It's not for me, it's for our father, Monsieur Mirbeau, over in Les Genêts, the doctor was here before once…"

"Very well, I'm putting it down."

"But I gotta talk to him before he comes over because our father won't look after himself and he doesn't take his medicine so we wanna tell the doctor to push him a little…"

"I see. Do you want Doctor Sachs to call you back?"

"Well—"

I hear tires squeal on the asphalt. I look up. The white car pulls up right in front of the waiting-room window. "Wait a moment, madam—the doctor's just back. If you'll hold on a few minutes I'll put you through to him…"

You get out of the car, you look at me through the panes, I signal to you and point to the phone. You take your briefcase out of the back seat, you lock the doors. I go on patiently holding the receiver on my shoulder. The waiting-room door opens and, with your briefcase in one hand and your bundle of keys in the other, you come in.

"It's Monsieur Mirbeau's daughter calling…"

"Monsieur Mirbeau?" You frown, puzzled.

"Yes, over in Les Genêts—she says you've been there before."

"Mmmhh…"

You go into the office. I see you set down the briefcase against the shelves, you pick up the phone, you sit down on the rolling chair, I hang up and go over to close the inner door, pulling on it hard.

From the waiting room I hear a murmur of your conversation. After a few minutes, the telephone on my desk rings faintly, which indicates that you've hung up. I wait another few minutes, but you don't come out. I pick up the appointment book, I knock at your door.

"Yes?"

I go in. You're seated at your desk, writing. You look up.

"Will you be going to see Monsieur Mirbeau this morning?"

"Mmmhh?… Yes, at about eleven-thirty…"

"You already have three other calls to make…"

"Ah… all right."

"And Madame Reverzy asked if you could get there before eleven o'clock, because she has to leave for work."

You sigh. You lay your hands flat on the painted wood slab that functions as your desk, you close your eyes and you nod your head. "I'm waiting for the postman and then I'll leave…"

❀

I have a clear memory of our first meeting. It had already been a year since I was laid off at the factory. The grocer said you were setting up practice in the old schoolhouse, and that you'd probably need someone to answer the phone, to clean house or iron—maybe at home too, since you lived alone. I thought, "What can I lose?" I phoned you up, you answered right away because you were spending all day long down there, hanging wallpaper, painting windows, building shelves. I said, "Hello, Doctor, I'm Madame Leblanc, I wondered if you might need someone to answer the phone and clean up at the medical office, but maybe the job is already filled?" There was a long silence and you answered, "That's funny, someone mentioned you to me this morning and I was going to call you."

You came over to my house. You were smiling, friendly. You seemed very young, but I'd heard you had been standing in for several doctors—at Deuxmonts, at Lavinié, and even farther away at the other end of the district, at Forçay. You needed someone half-time, to answer the phone, to greet people when you were out, and to keep the place in order. But not to do housework in your home. ("Better not to mix the two, you know.") I offered to find you someone for that if you wanted; you said yes, sure, that would be a help. And then we walked over to the office together. It was exactly what I was looking for, a job right nearby, even if it was part-time, just to be out of the house.

The striped pale-blue wallpaper—I thought it was pretty, and unusual for a medical office. It brightened things up. The little low cot I thought was nice too, it's true a person's never really at ease on a table that's too high, and children and old people have trouble getting onto it. You said, "I expect to be starting at the beginning of May—when could you begin?" and I said, "Right away. I'm sick of being shut up inside my four walls, my husband says it's not good for me at all and the children don't like it either."

I told you you'd have to give me some instructions for when a person called in an emergency, what should I say if there was an injury, or a poisoning? And I'd have to take first-aid training, they run classes twice a year at the town hall, the firemen from Lavalleé give the course. You said, "I'm glad to have met you so quickly. I'm very lucky not to have to go looking for someone," and "I'm sure we'll get along very well," and I answered, "Sure, no reason why not!"

That was seven years ago. We were supposed to start May 2, but you were away that whole first week, because your father died. The morning of Monday the 2nd, for the first time, I opened the office at 8:30. At 9:30 I'd already had three calls. I tidied, polished, answered lots of phone calls and saw lots of people who stopped in for information. You called me three or four times, to ask if everything was going all right. Well, gosh, I was managing pretty well, I said, and if people were going to come in or call that much the next week, you'd be overloaded with work very soon and you might need me full-time! You laughed, "I sure hope so!" Still, in those early days, we really didn't see many people. With the little electric typewriter you brought me, I typed up the office hours, recommendations for women on the Pill or the IUD, advice for young mothers breast-feeding or giving bottles, advice on children who don't sleep and on which medications shouldn't be mixed with alcohol, what to do for wasp stings or snakebites (I don't think we have any dangerous snakes around here, but you never know, when people go on vacation), in case of car accidents or drownings, or when someone's swallowed pills. You'd written everything out by hand on a lined pad and, typed up, each page came to exactly half a sheet. Then I put the slips on my desk in the waiting room for people to take. I also made up a sign showing the times for open office hours (in black), for appointments (in blue), your day off (Thursday, in green) and the telephone number for reaching you (in big print and in red). And as you asked me to do, I added *FOR HOUSECALLS PLEASE PHONE, IF POSSIBLE, BEFORE 10 A.M.*

After three months I found that I really liked it: managing a medical office, greeting people, taking calls. That's how I became your secretary.

The waiting-room door opens. "Good morning, Madame Leblanc! I have a registered package for the doctor…"

I look back into your consulting-room. You're bent over something, one of the three little wheels of your chair is tipped up from the floor, the two others are doing their best to stay put.

"Doctor, it's the postman!"

The wheel hits the ground, you swivel around, you get up and come through the two doors.

"Good morning, Monsieur Merle. I'll sign that for you…"

You scrawl a neat round signature on a form. "There you are… So, you getting around all right? Not too much water?"

"No, it's okay," says the postman, touching his cap. "It's only the little roads where the ditches are overflowing, but you just have to watch out. The rain better not keep up too long like this… All right then! Good day now, folks!"

You go back into your office.

Besides the package, the postman has left the regular mail, bundled into two elastic bands. I sort it.

There are magazines—lots of magazines, magazines every day. Big envelopes with official acronyms: Regional Medication Agency, Health Ministry, Regional Council, Tourmens Media Library. Catalogs of furniture, of medical equipment, of women's lingerie, toys, business gifts and other gadgets. And of course there are the pamphlets everyone gets in their mailbox: SuperStuff, MegaFrozenFoods, HugeHiFi, HyperMerchandise. There are offerings for real estate investments, invitations to car dealers, sales on amazing wines or truffled foie gras with Christmas delivery guaranteed on orders received before December 10. Then finally there's the real mail: white or brown envelopes with letterheads of doctors or hospital departments, and sometimes a letter or two with the address written in an awkward hand and, to judge by the feel, probably containing a stamped self-addressed envelope. Before I put the mail on your desk, I always make sure there's nothing addressed to one of your colleagues in the area. It happens sometimes that the post-office people mistake one doctor for another, early mornings when they're sorting.

I set aside the free medical magazines, four-color on slick paper, proclaiming the virtues of drugs with spectacular effects on varicose veins, brain circulation, rheumatisms, hypertension, cholesterol, excess weight, but you told me once they served no purpose except to make their makers rich. I tie the prospectuses and the ads into big bundles that pile up under the shed behind the office. Once a year, the district highway overseer collects them for recycling. When he leaves, his panel truck is three-quarters full.

Among the publications you subscribe to, two are medical weeklies, and one of those is in English. The others are monthlies: "*Le journal des lettres*," "*Cinéma/*

Cinémas," and "*Entertainment for Men,*" a thick magazine that comes carefully wrapped and which, unlike the two others, you never put out on the reading table in the waiting room, probably because it's in English.

There are also medication samples that drug companies send us without charge, and whose packaging is sometimes torn and then taped back together, which indicates that they've been opened before getting here—and, in fact, they're short two of the four pill boxes or three of the six tubes of cortisone listed on the invoice. When I tell you that, you look up smiling and you murmur, "Someone must have needed it." Myself, I just think it's not right for post-office workers to help themselves to things along the way.

✸

You open your mail without haste, without rushing, starting with the magazines (the ones you would sometimes spend some time over, sitting at your desk with the door open, back when I used to wait desperately for the telephone to ring, because sure, that first week it never stopped, people kept calling out of curiosity, to see, but then afterwards when they were supposed to come in, it was another story. "He seems nice but we're used to our doctor," or "These young folks don't always know as much as the old guys," or "It's strange he's not married, isn't it?" and I worried, I knew that I was costing you a lot, if you didn't get more patients than that, you wouldn't be able to keep a secretary, even part-time) and ending with the letters from the hospital or with the letterhead of some testing laboratory. Often there's one that you're waiting for particularly—the patient has already phoned me several times in the past few days to ask if it's come, and when it finally does, I pull out the file and put it on your desk beside the mail. Or the telephone rings and as soon as I recognize the voice of the person calling, I answer, "Oh yes hello, Madame (or Monsieur) Sand. Yes, the doctor just received it this morning, I'll put you through to him."

I knock on the study door. "Doctor, it's Madame Sand! About her mother's blood test."

As you pick up, I go in and lay the file and the expected letter in front of you.

JÉROME BOULLE

The telephone rings. Finally! I pick up: "Doctor Boulle here."

"Hi, Jérôme, it's Bruno."

"Ah, it's you—how you doing?"

"Fine. I won't take your time, I just wanted to know if you could cover my emergency calls between twelve-thirty and three. I have to be over at the hospital."

I look at my watch, it's ten-thirty. "No problem, I haven't had a thing to do all morning. Same with you?"

"Mmmhh…"

"It's really quiet, huh? Five years ago, Tuesday was a heavy day, but with all these new doctors coming in and these specialists setting up on Boulevard Gustave-Flaubert…"

"Yeah, it's not easy…"

"What about you? You have a lot of work?"

"Mmmhh…"

"Yeah, same here. What a jackass job, people think we're their servant-boy, one day they call up crying and you're the only one who can save them, the next day they switch sidewalks when they see you coming out of the bakery. And if only there was some way to do a juicy diagnostic workup now and then, but forget about it! That's for the fancy specialists… Actually, yeah, I have to tell you a story. Last week I saw a gorgeous case of—"

"Wait, just a second—yes?" (muffled sounds at your end, you must have put your hand over the mouthpiece) "Excuse me, Jérôme, I have to get off. We'll talk later. Thanks for this noontime! So long!"

"So long."

You've already hung up. Can't talk to you anymore. You're too hard to pin down. You've always been a funny character. A few years ago, before you set up here, you brought me a baby to look at, some little nephew or godson, I think. You were finishing your residency at Tourmens. I wanted to take a couple of weeks' vacation, I had a lot of work at the time, I asked if you wanted to cover for me. You hesitated, then you made a point of letting me know that you planned to set up practice in the area. I wondered if you were on the level, I'd never heard a young colleague lay his cards on the table like that. But you were serious, you really did have scruples about invading my territory. I told you it didn't matter, and that was true—I had so much work I could barely manage. So you stood in for me a little—two weeks here, three weeks there. My patients liked you fine. They said you were talkative, but nice. And you didn't do too many dumb things, it's true. I invited you for coffee once or twice, you did the same once or twice. But you never came to dinner, even when you were substituting; you preferred to go home. I thought you had a girlfriend, I suggested bringing her along, but you gave me an odd look and said you lived alone. I didn't insist—anyhow, my wife doesn't care much for you. She doesn't care much for doctors.

A few months later, you came to see me saying you couldn't decide between two locations, Play and Marquay, and that you'd go where I'd mind the least. I had practically no patients in Play, but lots in Marquay. That's how it is with villages—two of them can be equally far from a doctor, they've just got different habits. The people from Marquay have been coming to this office for fifty years; they come not to see me, Doctor Boulle, any more than they used to come for Doctor Sturgeon, whose practice I took over; they just use "the Deuxmonts doctor." Lots of my Marquay patients were already looking forward to your setting up practice there; the mayor was making you offers; it could have cost me some business. So of course I said go to Play, and you said all right. But I thought that in the end you'd find some excuse to go back on your word. And then, no. You actually did set up at Play. The town board rented you the old school. For a long time I thought you were a little nuts. In that backwater they take their medical care from all over the place: they call me in, they call the doctors from Lavinié, from Lavalleé—sometimes even the ones from Saint-Jacques or from Saint-Bernard-de-l'Orée, and they're almost ten miles away—but it's always been like that, none of us and none of our predecessors ever really managed to get a foothold in Play, not among the oldtimers nor in the new subdivisions either. Maybe because lots of the young people work in Tourmens and go to doctors on the boulevards there before heading home, or they bring their kids into town to see the pediatrician. *My pediatrician*— that sounds like a bigger deal than *My G.P.*, even if he doesn't have to do anything more than weigh their lousy brat, vaccinate it and order nose drops for its drippy nose. I thought, he won't pull it off in Play; a few months, a year or two, and he'll close up shop, it can't work, he's picked the worst place, it's a little suicidal, I've seen guys like you borrow to set up a practice, have a rough time, and after eighteen months pull down their shingle and go somewhere else, or turn into bureaucrats— medical inspectors for a Social Security office or an insurance company—and spend their days counting how many prescriptions their former colleagues are writing ("those two bottles of tranquillizer on the mother's prescription slip—now, they wouldn't by any chance be going to the sister-in-law who's been taking a stupefying amount of them?"), or checking that the husband's sick leave is really for lumbago or a twisted ankle and not for acute lazyitis, getting their kicks out of dropping in by surprise at eleven in the morning thinking, "If I catch that faker hoeing his garden, I'll fix him good." Frustrated, bitter, but not doctors anymore.

During those periods when you covered for me, my patients adopted you. They'd say you were very attentive, that you would come by to check on them even if they hadn't asked you to, and refuse to take payment—kind of "This is just a friendly call." Annoying. But what annoyed me even more was you'd leave me these long comments on my files, and then on top of that, when I came back, you'd give me detailed accounts—everything: lab test results, phone discussions with specialists, stories the family told, previous medical histories that I'd never managed to extract from them, the list of medications they were taking secretly, your opinion on their surgery, your feelings—everything! You reminded me of these characters you don't see anymore, I knew a couple of them and they wound up badly, like mining-company doctors in the Niger or G.P.s in some godforsaken hole in the Massif Central, housecalls fifty miles away in every direction, no hospital closer than a hundred, snow in winter and those impassable roads you have to slog through on foot to do a home birth. Just your type: single-minded, hypermoral, kind of jerky. Very jerky. Very highly esteemed. Well, not by everyone, actually. I was talking about you once with Genevoix, the pharmacist in the next district—or rather *he* was, at the lunch Arbogast & Gruesome gave for the doctors who took part in that study on *The Treatment of Depression in Pubescent Girls in an Open Setting*. In the middle of the meal, he asks me if I know you, out of curiosity I say A little, then he tells me you give him a big pain: when a patient walks into his shop, he can always tell if they're coming from you, there are less than three items on the slip and he can make it out from way back behind the counter. But on top of that, when he starts to tell them they should take the meds this way or that way, the patients stop him—they've already got the whole backside of a prescription slip covered with detailed instructions, and you even give people free samples, aspirin or antibiotics or cough syrup, that you cart around in the trunk of your car nights and Sundays, or that you take out of a drawer in the office after 8 p.m., to spare them having to run to the pharmacy. If he keeps that up, Genevoix was saying, he might just as well take over our job, nobody'd complain! Anyhow, he was really pissed off, and I didn't tell him it sometimes happened that I give them away, too, those samples—it's the only way, when a little old lady is alone in the middle of nowhere you can certainly give her the penicillin you've got in the trunk, let's not kid ourselves.

Once you opened your office, a lot of my patients changed doctors! Coming from some of them, that hurt me. Fine, the nuts—the phantom stomach-aches,

HISTORY (TUESDAY, OCTOBER 7)

the minor and major pains, the constantly constipated, the manipulative nympho-maniacs, the surgery-obsessives, the chronic alcoholics, the couples who beat each other up only when there's an audience—those I was just as happy to be rid of. They must have landed on you the way they did on me when I started out, it's inevitable. Anyhow, there's one you got for sure—that's old lady Renard, the biggest pill-popper in the whole county, according to Genevoix.

Finally things settled down. Some people came back, and it even happens sometimes that patients of yours leave you for me. People I'd never seen, who're disappointed in you: not firm enough, not Doctor enough, a little too hot-grog-and-aspirin. Especially the oldsters. They've paid into the health insurance for forty years, they see open-heart surgery on television, every day they get bom-barded with bulletins on a new treatment for Parkinson's or for Alzheimer's, so they want medication, surgery, x-rays for their sore foot, sonograms for their liver ailments, color scans for their headaches. And it's not only the oldsters. There's the teachers too. Ah, the teachers! Anxious, demanding, nitpicking know-it-alls. We talked about it once, way back—you called me up, embarrassed: one of my patients wanted to change doctors but she didn't have the guts to ask me for her record, she wanted you to get it, and it was too thick for you to manage without it. That really got to me (It made me feel sick—a patient I'd been following for seven or eight years, the first years I'd see her three or four times a month, twice a week when one of her kids had a sore throat, and she'd grab the chance to talk about her problems, I'd tell her to come in the next day during office hours without an appointment, hoping that when she saw the full waiting room she'd drop it, but nothing doing!) but I grinned like a good sport and came over to put her file right into your own hands. You brought me into your flaming-new study, it still smelled of wet paint and wallpaper paste, it wasn't very big, you'd put in a divan (that went very nicely with the part-shrink part-father-confessor image that people had of you, and that was starting to annoy them), and I told you that this Dominique Dumas had used up all the doctors in the area one after another—too hysterical to be satisfied, too anxious ever to calm down, too much the teacher to believe what you said, and whatever you did, she'd always find some way to put you in the wrong—and that, all in all, I was glad you'd be the one stuck with her now. After-wards, though, I did wonder how things turned out with her. When I'd meet her in the street, she was much more cheerful than before, I was dying to ask you what happened to her, but of course I never did (because, you bastard, you never answer any of my questions. I remember once I called you and said, "Hey, I saw one of your patients last week!"

"Yes?"

"Yes, Madame Mouillaud—you'll never guess what she's got!"

"No, and I'd rather you didn't tell me."

"Why not?"

"If she went to see you, she didn't intend you to go passing it on to me."

"Uh, no, of course not... but certainly colleagues can discuss a case..."

You said No, curtly and finally, and I understood that you were vexed, but also that you didn't want to have to tell me when some patient of mine came to you. Comes on all virtuous but actually he's protecting his own little turf!). Later on, though, I did hear the news from a neighbor, a grandmother who couldn't get over it, she was so shocked: "Really, now I've seen everything!" she tells me that all of a sudden Madame Dumas left her husband and her two kids to set up house with a girl who was a student of hers! My jaw just dropped! After all the soap opera she put me through—"You think I'm still a woman, Doctor? Since my pregnancies, I've gotten fat, my breasts sag, my husband doesn't want me any more, I think he's got lovers, anyhow I feel no desire for him either, my friends tell me I should leave him but I can't deprive my kids of their father after all, and besides how would I manage, all alone?" and the rest. Anyhow, I'd have to sit and listen to her for an hour sometimes, until one day she's going out the door—it was late, there was nobody coming in after her—I hear her say with her eyes glittering, "Some nights I'd be willing to give myself to the first comer!" That's all I'd need! My life's not complicated enough without screwing patients after visiting hours! Anyhow, when I heard she threw everything over, I called you on some pretext or other. "So listen, have you heard? Madame Dumas threw out her husband and she's shacking up with a high-school girl. Would you have guessed she was a dyke?"

You answered me, "No." Then, after a minute, "But it's the first thing she told me."

⚘

Despite that, you always phone the day after you've covered for me to talk about patients of mine you've seen. That seems a little neurotic of you, but I'm not about to reproach you for it. And also, we do each other favors. You don't go out much, so evenings I give the service operator your number and I take off, I go to... oh, to training seminars, or to drug-company dinners, or I take Dolores to a movie— that keeps me out of the dumps and her from sulking. In exchange, I cover your calls on Tuesdays when you go to the hospital, and on an evening now and then. But you're not away much.

From time to time, when I pass you on the road, you blink your headlights, we both pull over, we swap mail that's come by error (one of the labs always mixes up our addresses, but every time I phoned to straighten them out, they thought I was you, so I've stopped bothering), you ask me for news of patients you've seen for me. That reminds me of when I was starting out—I used to get really upset over people I just saw one time who didn't come in again. These days, I have other troubles.

I don't think you have a huge practice. It's six or seven years since you started, but from what I hear, you're struggling. In fact, there's one sure sign: you haven't changed cars since you began, even though after four years you can't deduct for amortization on a professional vehicle any more. The only explanation is that you haven't got the wherewithal to buy another one. I keep hearing you'll be leaving Play. I know, that's only a rumor too, but rumors always have some basis in fact.

25

MADAME LEBLANC

The telephone jingles on my desk. You were on the line and you just hung up.

Mornings like this one, when you don't have a lot of housecalls, you come in a little late. You stop for a moment to look over the empty pages of the appointment book, you go into the consulting room, you drop your briefcase and your medical bag beneath the desk and, without sitting down, you open the mail. Sometimes you pick up the phone and dial a number, and I close the connecting door. Or you've just gotten in and the telephone rings and a man asks to talk to you, or else a woman comes into the waiting room and hands me an envelope: "I have some tests to show the doctor." You always take the call, you almost always receive the people who turn up (and it sometimes happens that you keep them with you twenty minutes when they were "just stopping in with a quick question," and that then, after they leave, you plunge into some magazine or write for a long time in one of your notebooks. When I say timidly that I'd like to dust in there, you look at your watch and you exclaim "Good heavens! Eleven o'clock already!" and, gathering up your keys, your briefcase, your bag, your jacket or your raincoat, you rush out to make a few housecalls that aren't awfully urgent but the people did phone between eight-thirty and quarter of nine, if not the night before. One day, just after you left, as I was filing the form for one of those unexpected office visits, I couldn't help reading your last sentence. In capital letters you'd written "SHE DRIVES ME NUTS!"), but sometimes you're in a hurry to leave, you fall all over yourself with apologies and you ask them to call back or to come in again that afternoon.

In the early days, you would arrive at the office a half-hour after me and, since there weren't many calls, you would spend a long time on the telephone. One day, I told you that—if you didn't mind—you could stay home mornings, since I'd be in anyhow; I could phone you if there were any housecalls. Startled, you answered that you'd rather be on hand in case someone came in. I then suggested that maybe, if it wasn't too expensive, we could get another line put in. So that patients could reach us when you were talking on the phone. You blushed and then, with no comment, you rang the phone company.

That second line, with an unlisted number (you asked me not to give it out), rings rarely during my work hours. Now that I think of it, it's a long time since I've heard the rather slow, rather sad female voice that often used to call for you when you weren't in, and sigh deeply before hanging up.

✳

I come out of your study. I lay the appointment book near the telephone. Mornings you're not often in a good mood, even less so on mornings after a night on duty. It's as if you didn't feel like working. When you've had a heavy day, I understand that. Seeing sick people all day long, that must be tiring, but sometimes, when the phone calls get less frequent, I worry, I think patients may not want to come anymore, people are so changeable. The two first years, you'd spend hours in the examining room without seeing more than one or two people the whole day, and the townsfolk would ask me with a worried look if you were earning enough to live, if you weren't going to leave. I was concerned that if you didn't have enough patients, you couldn't go on paying an employee, even half-time. But you'd often say you were glad to have me and I'd answer that I was glad to be here, because I like keeping up the office, putting the instruments in order, copying out the test results, answering the phone, greeting the people who come to see you, writing down appointments. I couldn't find better work than this, three minutes from the school and five from the house, what with all the unemployment there is. Since you came, you've gathered some loyal patients, whole families, young folks, old people. You've built yourself a practice. Not one as big as other doctors in the district have, but people appreciate you a lot, they say you listen well to them. Not everyone thinks that, of course not, it takes all kinds. There are people who came a lot in the beginning and then don't anymore; I realize that as I put away medical records, I recognize names that I haven't written in the appointment book for a long while, so then I look at their card and the last date you noted down goes back two or three years and I ask myself why all of a sudden some lady or some man you used to see two or three times a week, a person you'd sometimes spend an hour over, has stopped coming, as if there was a falling-out. Even when a health problem gets better, people always need a doctor from time to time—for the children, or for a certificate or some little thing; but this, it was like from one day to the next they're finished with you, and it's not because they've moved, I still see them at the bakery or the superette or on the road from Play to Lavallée. They're taking their child to school or they're going home from work, so they do still live around here. But actually, you have more and more patients anyhow, even if there are still quiet periods, like the summers, for instance. Almost everyone here goes on vacation in August, but you stay put.

For a while now, I've sensed that you're not as patient as you used to be; you're often silent, irritable, and sometimes you're curt with me on the phone. Some late afternoons, you switch your calls to my line after office hours, you leave for Tourmens, and when you get back you seem unhappy at having several appointments; but you have work because people are pleased with you, in fact they say so, and that's why they come. I hear them, in the bakery or at the grocer's, they say, "Doctor Sachs, at least you can talk to him, and he explains things." Of course you did get a good part of Dr. Cronin's practice at Langes, because the town's growing old and so is its doctor. The young people come and build in Play because it's closer to Tourmens, and there's a gym, the commune is more dynamic thanks to this mayor—he actually helped you set up practice. And besides, Dr. Cronin is old-school—a very good doctor, granted, but he never says anything, and he prescribes so much medication. When I see that you have a lot of appointments I'm happy, your practice is growing, I've even seen people come all the way from Tourmens and farther to see you. A lot of people come because someone's told them about you, people know you're reassuring, you're an upbeat kind of doctor. For a few months now, I've been coming in to open up the waiting room Saturday mornings, because you're not back from your housecalls yet, and I always find eight or ten people waiting for you outside in the courtyard. And I don't understand, now that your practice is growing, why you're not pleased, why you're so often sad and edgy.

The study door opens. You bend over the appointment book, you write down the sequence you'll be doing your calls in, so that I can reach you in an emergency. You look up at the wall clock the soccer club gave you last year in thanks for the free medical exams you did for the junior team, and you leave the waiting room. "So long, Madame Leblanc…"

"So long, doctor. Will I see you before noon?"

"No, I think I won't have finished in time. I'll go directly to the hospital. If you have an emergency call between noon and three, tell Dr. Boulle, as usual. He's staying in. Enjoy your lunch, Madame Leblanc."

"You too, Doctor."

I go back to sorting the mail. I slip the test results behind the patient's initial in the thumb-tabbed file. On the corner of the desk there's a handbook on free medical services. I put it into a big envelope containing all kinds of documents to bill the health administration for everything patients don't pay for directly out of pocket: consultations for work-related accidents, medical aid, day-care attendants' health certificates, requisitions from the police for night-time blood-tests on intoxicated persons, assault-and-battery reports, burial permits. The envelope is jammed full, because you never send off the papers. Sometimes I'll hear your car door slam, the waiting-room door open, and you go into your office. Without a word, looking distracted, you pick up your pen, or your keys, or your wallet hidden

HISTORY (TUESDAY, OCTOBER 7)

under a prescription pad, and you go back out again. You almost always forget something as you leave.

Once I have the prescriptions clipped to the right insurance forms, the thick red book closed up, the pens put back in the jug that houses them, I gather up the three magazines still in their plastic wrap next to the wastepaper basket and pile them into the broom closet, then I go back to clean the instruments soaking in the sink at the bottom of a pink plastic basin filled with antiseptic liquid.

Finally, I hear the engine turn over, the car leave the courtyard. Just then, the telephone rings. I turn off the faucet, I head for the desk, I pick up with the fingertips of my rubber gloves.

"Doctor's office, Play—hello?"

"Hello, Madame Leblanc, it's Madame Sachs. You're well?"

"Hello, Madame! Yes, very well… and you?"

"Oh Lord, just all right. You know, I'm getting old. Is Bruno there?"

"I'm so sorry, he just left. But I know where to get hold of him, if you want."

"No, no, it's nothing urgent, just tell him to call me back when he's got a moment…. He has office hours this afternoon?"

"Yes, after three or three-thirty, when he gets back from the hospital… and then appointments from six o'clock on…"

"I'll call him, then. Good day, Madame Leblanc."

"Goodbye, Madame!"

When I've hung up, I take off my right glove and, in the margin of the appointment book, right beside the line for three o'clock, I write, "Call your mother back."

❋

A truck brakes in the street. A man in a gray uniform climbs out, holding a canvas sack at arm's length. He comes in and greets me, hands me the sack and an envelope with the monthly bill in it. I give him back a sack full of white coats for laundering. He says goodbye and leaves.

I pull the clean coats out of the sack, I hang them in the metal closet in the waiting room, among paper towels and rolls of examining-table sheets, boxes of tongue depressors, cleaning products, toilet paper, prescriptions, insurance forms and sick-leave certificates still sealed in their carton, packets of cotton, blood-draw vials and the pre-stamped tubes for sending them off to the lab.

You didn't used to wear a white coat. For the first two or three years, you'd do consultations in a sweater, or even in a shirt, and you'd roll back your sleeves. And then one day, after you'd stitched up an injured man (he'd been in the back seat without a seatbelt, the driver braked, he was thrown forward, his head hit the dome light—it was an old car—and he was almost totally scalped) you called me at home, full of apologies, it was half-past noon or one o'clock. You had to go home and change clothes to make a house call, would it be too much trouble for me to come in a little early to clean up?

There was blood everywhere. On the cream-colored leatherette and the chrome frames, on the fabric stretched over the back of the shelf unit that screens off the alcove, on the rolling table, on the little fridge where I keep the vaccines, on the floor linoleum and even on the wallpaper, because the treatment alcove isn't very big. There was blood in the sink, piles of bloody compresses in the garbage, and in the metal basins, blood and needles, blood on the suture thread and the instruments you'd used.

The next day, you came back from Tourmens carrying white coats made of washable paper. At first glance, like that, they looked like the real thing. You'd put one on now and then, for doing stitches or for treatments that were a little delicate. After two or three trips through the washer they were like papier mâché. Not very neat-looking. One of your patients, Mr. Bester, works at the linen-rentals company; he didn't dare say anything, he didn't know how you'd take it, so I talked to you. And I suggested he leave you a brochure.

Since then, you wear a real coat, almost all the time. When you get into the office, you put down your things and slip on a clean one, even if it's not time yet for consultations. At the beginning, I wondered what the patients would say: since you'd started practicing, you'd examine people in shirtsleeves, like all your colleagues. Children, of course, don't much like men in white coats, especially if they have bad memories of a hospital stay; when they don't know you, they wince a little at the sight of you. But the adults didn't say a thing. Actually, yes, one of your earliest patients, and one of the oldest—Madame Absire. One morning, she was going by in the street, she saw your car in the courtyard, she came in. You received her before office hours. When she left, her hand on the doorknob, she smiled and said, "It's nice you wear a white coat. You look like a real doctor."

26

INAPPROPRIATE THOUGHTS

Knock, and it shall be opened unto you.

As you enter, she—it's almost always a woman—greets you, apologizes (I don't usually call on you) for troubling you, explains (But today I just can't go on it's not possible anymore) what made her call you in. Often, but not always, it's for a child or an old person.

It's my father and he won't listen to reason.

or:

It's my youngest child and I didn't go to work.

or:

He has fever, or diarrhea, he's vomiting all over the place and it worries me, he's not usually like that,

or:

He doesn't get up anymore he's not eating I wanted you to take his blood pressure and do something to get him moving.

And while you're listening with one ear to what the woman—half-frantic half-guilty—is saying, you look wearily at the half-filled health booklet or the results of blood tests ordered every two weeks by their regular doctor ("He's away right now and I don't much like the doctors who cover for him" [and/or] "Our regular doctor's very nice but he's awful busy so since you were on duty this morning") and you decipher the mother's meticulous notes [at age one month: 6 bottles 120 cl each + one teaspoon orange juice; at 2 months: 5 bottles 140 cl with cereal in the bedtime one (just a half-teaspoon so he'll sleep a little longer, till five or six in the morning but no later, because otherwise he doesn't wake up before nine and that throws him off completely, and besides can't let him get obese)] or the illegible orders of three successive doctors—an ENT: nasal inhaler + syrup (If you'd heard him coughing at night!), an ophthalmologist (They changed his glasses six months ago to bifocals and he won't wear them because he says they make him dizzy but it's crazy because after all they did cost him twenty-five hundred francs out of his own pocket), and a covering doctor seen one night for a sudden unexplained fever: antibiotics + anti-inflammatories by suppository + drops for memory and tonic (to make him eat because he/she's lost weight over the past three months and is it normal for a ten-year-old child/for an old lady of seventy-five to get thin like that and not swallow a thing anymore?)—or again, in a report on a hospitalization two or three years back, the laconic comments of a pediatrics resident: "Hospitalized 12/24/89 to 12/26/89 for unexplained fever (I thought he caught cold at the outdoor center)/diarrhea without dehydration (My neighbor's son had that and now he's paralyzed)/constant crying (My mother-in-law kept saying he'd get over it but I could tell he had something wrong). Clinical exam satisfactory, additional tests (Blood count electrolytes chest x-ray urine spinal tap) negative, released after three days with symptomatic treatment" or from a geriatrics-staff doctor: "Admitted 1/6/90 for anorexia and confusion, longstanding hypertension well-controlled, no diabetes or neurologic signs, general exam negative (I don't understand how they couldn't find anything wrong with him), up to day 3 of hospitalization walking the halls (And into the female patients' rooms to talk, that annoyed everyone especially at night), demanding to go home, moderate stay expected (But my sister never wanted him in at all, still she's not the one who has to go to his place when he falls out of bed and the lady next door phones us because she can't pick him up—she's ninety-four herself—but when once in a while we want to leave town for three days to see our children who live two hundred kilometers away, it's hard, we don't feel secure about him, so from our side, we'd rather they kept him in, at least for a few weeks, but naturally he wouldn't hear of it: his dogs his chickens his rabbits, who'd take care of them? You know how old people are! So they let him go home), release after two weeks with customary treatment plan."

Women are funny, they're all the same with their children, with their parents —always the same battling, the same concern, the same worry that they weren't told the whole story, they can tell things aren't quite right, they feel it in their bones, and maybe they've got only their intuition to go on but Any way I look at it I bet they find something serious in the end, What do you think, Doctor?

Headache and fever could it be meningitis? Fever and stomach pain could it be appendicitis? Stomach pain and vomiting could it be intestinal blockage? Vomiting and headache could it be a brain tumor? Chest pain could it be a heart attack?

And those are just the admitted fears, the expressed fears, the imaginable fears.

But there are the others, the forgotten, ancestral fears, passed on wordlessly from grandmother to daughter-in-law over the bed where the little one (or the old man) is writhing with his 102 fever, his cough, his pallor, his torpor, his scorched tongue, his jaundice, his moans, his groans. The fear of sicknesses that used to be fatal—measles, whooping cough, diphtheria, typhoid, tuberculosis— that people think have disappeared because nobody talks about them, and now today there's AIDS besides (I insisted he should get tested, you understand, he's always given blood, they didn't use to require an examination, but with what's going on these days), cancer, myopathy, that lung disease—you know, what do they call it? (My neighbor, Madame Baudou, she and her husband couldn't have children so they adopted two little boys from Madagascar who they already had a lot of trouble with—she's really very brave!—and then all of a sudden she gets pregnant at thirty-nine well of course they wanted to have it, imagine, their first little daughter! So then the poor little thing was sick from the minute she was born, I mean not very but the mama could see her baby wasn't well, and the doctors couldn't figure out what it was, to tell the truth they didn't believe her, but what with seeing her back on the unit time and again, they realized that it wasn't just in her head, and finally they diagnosed it—cysts... something with fibers... cystic fibrosis, that's it—and now the little girl goes to the hospital every four days to have an intravenous treatment, antibiotics inhalations respiratory massages, sometimes it's weeks before she comes out and even then she's not always in good shape, she coughs she coughs she can't stop, sometimes you think they shouldn't let her go home like that seeing how the Baudou place is out in the fields and it's actually pretty damp in the house. But the doctors say that if they keep her too long in the hospital there's a risk she'll pick up even worse germs than if she stayed home) and the exotic sicknesses that you can't see, that nobody talks about, but they're spread by toothbrushes (There's good reason to worry about sending your children to school) so by comparison, the sicknesses that carried off our grandparents, the sicknesses we had ourselves when we were kids (I certainly remember when I had measles! I got to stay home from school!), they look harmless, old-fashioned, even if we do remember that they used to just kill off an adult in his prime, that sometimes they'd leave a child an idiot or a cripple (in my class there was a boy who had a paralyzed arm from polio, and when he ran he'd shove the hand into his pocket so it wouldn't bounce around).

And then there are the irrational fears, the everyday fears, the fears that nothing can quell because that's life, you live you suffer you cry, you see children cry, you see children suffer, you see your parents get old fall down not get up again because they just don't want to anymore, you tell yourself that one of these days (no you don't tell yourself, you're too scared to think about it, even though you do think about it anyway without letting on too much) it'll be your turn and they won't be around anymore then to help you—your children, in the first place, you can't expect anything from them, they go off they have their own life and besides you know how it is, Doctor, children only think about themselves, it doesn't help to warn them they'll feel bad about it later, we were the same way at their age.

And then in the hallway, just before going into the bedroom, or afterwards, in the kitchen, the women sum up or give a rundown of the symptoms, they voice their worries, their complaints, their expectations, their requests:

She hasn't eaten for two weeks, I get mad I spank her but still all she'll swallow is pasta or bread-and-butter and nothing else, steak won't go down, she won't listen, she has a fit, I thnk it's just wrong she's going to grow weak get anemic on me, it's just not normal that she doesn't eat a thing, no nothing at all nothing absolutely nothing you can believe me. My husband said I had to bring her in to see you because the boys, he didn't pay all that much attention, but his little girl, well that's another story!—the minute she gets sick he goes out of his head! So I called you (It's true, though, she often kicks up a fuss. I don't go along with it too much but my husband, well, his little darling is always right), because frankly she really needs something she's white as a sheet, she must have some vitamin deficiency and naturally from not sleeping she's exhausted, it's weeks already, it can't go on like this.

or else:

She's really suffering but she won't admit it, she's always been afraid of bothering people but she can't stand up, in fact my brother agrees but he couldn't come in today, she wouldn't let us call the doctor she absolutely put her foot down, but of course we could see that it was bad, so we had you come here because she's afraid to go to the hospital, of course it wouldn't be pleasant but suppose she has to? What do you think Doctor? Wouldn't it be better if she went in for treatment, got her strength back? Hospitals aren't the end of the world, right? You'll see, Mama, you'll be fine there, listen to the doctor, he's going to examine you carefully and he'll tell us what he thinks, but we can't just leave you like this you know, this can't go on, isn't that right Doctor she can't go on for long like this?

or else:

He's been coughing for a week now and I give him the syrup but it doesn't stop, daytimes it's okay but the minute I put him to bed he coughs and he coughs all night long. Oh no, it doesn't wake him up, but for myself, I can't get back to sleep, my husband doesn't like it because I keep getting up to give him a drink or to quiet him down if he starts crying, and sometimes he manages to climb out of his crib and he comes into our room so we'll take him in with us and myself I always give in to get a little peace but my husband has to be up at five to go to work so he goes and sleeps on the couch and of course the next day you can't get near him. If he hears the boy coughing when he comes home he gets on my back right away so naturally I'm at the end of my rope, the three big kids are already a handful, and then here's the little one so darling, so sweet, so cute, when I hear him cough that gets me all upset, because if it was just the cough, I know that'll eventually get better even if it is already two weeks, but on top of that he doesn't sleep. And that's how it's been ever since he was a tiny baby. Nothing helps. I used to give him baths, they say that calms them down, but nossir as soon as I'd put him in bed he'd yell, I couldn't understand why. Naturally I'd pick him up especially since his father couldn't stand him yelling, he'd finally tell me to go get him. And me—I was fed up, I'd say, No! we've got to let him cry, he's not gonna die from it, if I go back in there we'll never see the end of it, and he'd insist, Maybe there's something wrong with him, maybe he's sick? I could tell him a million times, No, he's faking, the minute you pick him up he'll be fine, but he'd never listen to me he'd wind up going in to get him and of course as soon as we held him the baby'd start chattering away and laughing and my husband would say See, he just wanted to be with us that's all, and we'd keep him till midnight, sometimes until two o'clock, he never got sleepy and we were falling apart. That act went on for months, you can get mad but really you can't go spanking him every minute and you can't really just let him keep yelling either. He's been better for a while lately we were starting to get a little sleep but now here's this cough, so you can see why I'm at the end of my rope, it's just lasting way too long now!

or else:

He doesn't leave his bed, he won't get up, he won't get dressed, he won't do anything, and this was a man who was always busy puttering with some project, it's as if he has no taste for anything anymore, he throws me out whenever I say something but we can't leave him like that, since he's been living alone he's let himself go, he's slowly dying away, he doesn't even feed his dog, he forgets everything—forgets to take his medicine, to turn off the stove when he cooks, evenings he falls asleep in his clothes with the door open, and when he gets up at night to go do his business he thinks it's daytime and he leaves the house, that's how come one night they found him in some little back road, he'd slipped into the ditch alongside and couldn't get out, luckily it hadn't rained for three weeks or he would have spent the night in the water, but the most amazing thing is he didn't even realize it. Sometimes, even, he doesn't recognize me, he has no idea what he's doing anymore and I don't know what to do and we tried calling the doctor and taking him to a specialist, but nobody can tell me if there's some way to treat it or how long it will last…

The women don't know what to think, so they talk. They've lost their bearings, they're confused, they're desperate. They're sure they're the only ones to feel and see what's happening, but it's so hard to get it across—the doctors don't always take the time to listen and neither does he/neither does she, when a person's sick he's not about to listen. And I can't handle it anymore, Doctor, you understand?

Yes, you do understand. You understand that she's in deep shit, and that she's asking you to get your hands in there.

Because, when you push open the door to the bedroom, you see that the cough, the exhaustion, the loss of appetite, the tears, the fever she's telling you about—all of that is just an excuse, a pretext, and doesn't come close to telling you the real story.

You ask yourself, But what does she want? And it's the child or the old guy himself who gives you the interpretation.

By a gesture, a look, a word just faintly louder than required, he sketches the picture:

the ineradicable anguish of the daughter who cannot accept her father's oldness, his approaching death, his weariness, that bellyful that keeps a person lying in bed and banishes all desires, the sad smile of a person who wants no more of it, who's fed up with the goddamn wonderful full life, had more than enough, had it up to here, let's just drop it at that, leave me the hell alone, can't you give me a little shot that'll finish with it, I'm not asking a lot; I know some people want to keep on going but really as for me I've had it;

the vampire-like anguish of the mother who can't understand how her former baby could be not quite that any longer, how he could grow up and say no and pelt her with his bowls of soup full of its little vegetables so nicely peeled so nicely simmered so nicely strained—and along with the vegetables, all the frustrations she'd like to force him or her to sop up—her little boy racing around, her little girl already talking (It's wild how fast they grow up), whose trousers are too short, whose blouses are too tight, and who just can't stand being their mothers' sponges any longer.

And it's clear from their faces—from their silent, noncommittal gaze—that they're waiting to see whether you're some new agent for the enemy (a mercenary practitioner, an erudite killer-for-hire); whether you're going to join in the chorus of alarm bells, the concert of sirens, the way the ones before you went along with it (a little blood-sample here, a little X-ray there, and a diet and pills and shots; and when that really couldn't continue, then: We'll get an expert opinion and hospitalize her for a few days not long just to see what's going on—Oh, I didn't dare ask you Doctor with all the trouble you've gone to but since you mention it if you think it's really necessary) and who eventually wearied of it but who'd rampaged long enough by then to give support to the frantic love of the devoted daughter, the suffocating love of the tearful mother, to sustain her in her certainty (I know what I'm talking about I'm his daughter after all) that something is wrong and that it needs solving (I'm not a doctor but I am his mother after all), or whether— by what miracle?—you just might be the type who'll put up some resistance—

"What did you say?"

"I said it won't be necessary to hospitalize him."

And the face of the old man, the face of the child or of the adolescent, turns up, brightens: Could it be that—?

"Anyhow, not right now."

"But you're not going to do anything?"

"Of course I am! And you're going to help me, aren't you?" you add, looking at her with determination written all over your face.

"Uuhhh… well yes, of course, but…"

"But?"

"But you're certain you don't need to at least do some blood tests?"

"I'm certain; the last one was only Thursday." And thereupon, you take her hand and you sit her down, and you say, "You're feeling very anxious…"

"Well, I sure am! And if it was just my son/daughter/father, it would be easy, but—"

"… But this is the straw that…"

"Right! after the load I got last year it just keeps—"

And she starts recounting her whole life, her freaking woman's life, and while she's recounting it, the other one—the person you were supposedly called in for—senses that he's no longer the point, that she's not on the front line here, and he reaches a hand toward the bed table to pick up his urinal flask, she sits up in bed to play with her dolls; and after a moment, when he feels that things are getting out of hand, when she decides that it's taking forever, she says, "Mama, I'm hungry," he calls, "Did you bring me back the newspaper?" because it's all very well whatcher doin there, fella, yer very nice to pay her a little attention, gives me a breather, but don't forget that what she's here for is to take care of *me*.

✳

Of course, it's not always so simple, it depends on their age, it depends on the season, it depends on the people, it depends on whether school's still in session or it's just before vacation break, it depends on whether it's been dragging along for a week or for years, it depends on whether the mother and the father are sworn to suffer together through the rest of their lives or are just waiting for the first crisis to split up, it depends on whether the brothers and sisters are talking to each other or are already squabbling over the inheritance of the not-yet-dead relative.

It depends on your own condition, too. On your patience. On what you did in the course of the day, or the week. On what you still have to do before you go home. On the evening ahead—if you're on standby call or going to a movie. On the outlook for tomorrow: a day off, or a day on. On the state of your back, on the state of your feet, on—in short, it depends.

And then in any case, whatever you say, whatever you do, however much you hold their hand or listen, however much you find them touching or strangleable, you still think: women are funny. They don't see why a person wouldn't want to eat what they've cooked, when they've cooked it specially for the person. Because if he doesn't eat, it can't be that the person doesn't like the dish—they only cook dishes the person likes—but that the person doesn't like *them* anymore. The proof is that he eats just fine at the café-restaurant, at the neighbor's, or at the senior-citizens' banquet; he devours everything in sight at the school cafeteria or at the baby-sitter's or even at the grandmother's (The *paternal* grandmother's. The one who was so good at making treats in the old days for the little boy whom the girls married so they could cook their own treats for him, but who keeps asking for the ones Mom used to make—Mom, who couldn't believe her ears when the daughter-in-law phoned her to ask for the recipe: "But I always thought he hated that!" and the younger woman—the Man-eater, poised to become a Mother herself, to triumph in her turn, says: "Well, *now* he loves it!", and goes on, between gritted teeth: "… as long as I make it the way *you* do…" and he (the father of the kid writhing with disgust on his chair) half-smoothly, half-astounded, half-jerk, murmuring "Who, me? Hate creamed spinach? It was just that I had to eat it at the cafeteria every day. But when *you* made it, Mom, I *adored* it!") and meanwhile back at the house he's pitching the plate at her from the other side of the room, so you have to wonder who he takes after!

And you, you're sniffing out that it's a done deal, that the situation is never going to change. The babies may spit out the mashed vegetables, they may pick at their potato casserole, push away the pot-au-feu, but still when they grow up the girls are going to cook the way their mothers did (or the opposite, which amounts to the same thing) for the sons of other women—for guys who will spend their time bemoaning the matchless taste, forever lost, of mythic maternal dishes whose fragrance, savor, existence can—just barely—be rescued from oblivion only by their sons' act of remembrance.

Oh, they believe you, the mothers, when you tell them that the kids won't let themselves die of hunger, but they have trouble understanding why their kiddies won't eat what the mothers have killed themselves cooking for them with such love and care. They don't understand that the kids want to—and can—eat and live their lives without the mothers to help.

Oh, they believe you, the daughters, when you say that an old man can't eat like a forty-year-old laborer, that his eyesight's not what it was, that he moves less quickly, that he does everything sparingly, that he's tired… (But up until his stroke, six months ago, he was so healthy!)… that the thing is to respect his rhythms, support him, go along with him, but not expect more of him than he'll be able to give as time goes on. But the daughters refuse to see that he's grown-up enough to die without the daughters to help.

Women are funny. They don't want to do like their mothers. They don't want to undergo what their mothers did. Or what they made the fathers undergo. They want to prove that they're good daughters; they're terrified of being just another housewife. They're afraid, finally, that their menfolk—big or little, young or old—could do without them. Women are funny, loving men who love them so poorly, and turning out other little boys who'll grow up to love other women still less well than they love their mothers, even though they don't love their mothers the way the mothers want to be loved. And as for the daughters…

"What do you think, Doctor?" asks the woman (the mother, the daughter) seeing you musing over the health booklet which is practically empty and yet so eloquent, over the pile of test results at once perfectly normal and yet so indicative.

"Mmmhh. Well, madame, we'll make it simple…"

HISTORY (TUESDAY, OCTOBER 7)

27

ANGÈLE PUJADE

The door opens and closes without slamming, footsteps sound in the hallway. Presently you appear at the office door. I look at my watch: one-twenty-five. As usual, you're late.

"Hello, ladies."

"Hello Bruno!" "Hello, monsieur…"

"You're all well?"

"Fine," I say. "How about you? Want coffee?"

"No. Thanks. Later."

The secretary appears behind you. "Hello, Bruno."

"Hello. What's on the schedule?"

"There are three women today, and two consultations. Can you come by and sign some prescription forms before you leave? I have none left."

"All right."

You slip into the closet we use for dressing. I hear you open a metal locker, close it again. Soon you return, in a white coat. On the chest pocket, the word DOCTOR is prominently marked. You bend over some files lying on the desk. You flick the first page. You say nothing.

"Would you like me to go get the first woman?"

"Mmmhh… No, thanks, I'll go. Where is she?"

"In Two."

You take the file and step firmly toward the second room. This isn't your usual way. I go into the treatment room to prepare the instruments.

28

PAULINE KASSER

The door opened.

"Madame Kasser?"

I turned around. He was standing there, in a white coat.

I said, "Yes. Shall we get started?"

He looked taken aback. He smiled, stammered: "Well, uhh, yes... sure, let's get started."

I picked up my bag and my raincoat. I left the room ahead of him. He said, "First door on the left..."

I walked into a room like the one we had just left. The blind was lowered, light rose from a sconce on the wall. In the center of the room stood a GYN examining table. I saw a rolling instrument stand, a machine with large glass jars along the top, a stool.

"You didn't bring a nightgown?"

"Yes, but I didn't know I was supposed to put it on."

The nurse-assistant showed me into a little bathroom. "If you'd please undress..."

I put on the long black T-shirt I'd brought, I came back into the room, I stretched out on the examining table, I positioned my thighs in the supports set up for the purpose.

❀

I don't remember everything that happened next, only flashes. His hand lying on my abdomen as he leaned over me to say, "Excuse me for not introducing myself—I'm Doctor Sachs, I'll be doing the procedure. Has someone already explained to you how it works? Anyhow I'll let you know what I'll be doing, as I go," his voice again as he prepared the instruments, trying a little awkwardly to put me at ease—as if it were possible to put a woman at ease in such a situation—asking me what I did and, in response to my sigh ("I'm an editor...") his voice saying, "Editor. That's a fine profession."

I raised my head to scrutinize his face. He seemed to be sincere. I said, "It's just an administrative classification. It's not as glorious as it sounds."

"Still, it's fine: *editor*…"

❋

I don't know any more, I don't want to know any more, about what happened next. Much later, he came back to see me in the room. He asked if I felt any pain; I said yes, a little still. He sat on a chair against the wall, he laid my file on his lap, he asked me again how I felt, if I had questions for him, any concerns to raise. And because, with my head turned toward the door, I kept silent, holding back my shame and anger, it took no more than his "*It's hard…*" to set off my tears.

❋

Still later—they'd brought me a dinner tray—he stopped by the room again with Jean-Louis Renaud, who'd come to see how I was doing. The two of them stood at the foot of the bed. When I'd gone to consult him the week before, Jean-Louis had given me the names of three doctors. I remembered only one of them when I called in to the Family Planning clinic. Watching the two of them talk now, sensing the complicity, the warmth between them, seeing the way he laid his hand on Jean-Louis' arm, I understood why that was.

"If you like, I can insert a IUD in a month, when you come in for your follow-up visit, and then you'll go back to Doctor Renaud for your regular care."

Jean-Louis let out a little laugh. "It's usually the specialist who sends the patient back to the GP! But if Pauline agrees, I have no objection."

He looked at me. I said "Yes, sure, it's fine with me."

❋

He came back to see me one last time. He had taken off his white coat, put on a distressed-leather jacket. A pen was hitched to the neck of his sweater. He was carrying a briefcase. He pointed to my tray, frowned, rubbed a hand over his chin. "Have you eaten anything?"

I shook my head no.

"It's important to eat, you know, you mustn't leave without eating a little something. At least a fruit cup. All right?"

I didn't answer, I looked at him. His hair was a little too long and in need of a shampoo, he'd sliced himself up shaving that morning: there were tiny smears of dried blood on his neck. His shirt collar was pretty worn out, and when he smiled saying goodbye, I noticed for the first time that one of his upper front teeth had a little chip in it.

29

YVES ZIMMERMANN

The telephone rings. I set down my cup, I pick up. "Zimmermann here—hello?"

"Hello, Professor."

"Hey, Sachs! You're well?"

"Moderately."

"You here at the hospital?"

"Yes, in the abortion clinic. But I didn't know if you had a patient with you."

"No, I'm struggling over some crappy file here, can't make head nor tail of it. Do you have time to come by for coffee?"

"No, I've got to get back to Play. Tell me, I had a friend sent over to you—he's been bad for weeks, but it was a big struggle to get him to go to the hospital. You may not have seen him yet—"

"Ray Markson, is that the one? Yeah, I saw him an hour ago. Very nice guy. He's American?"

"Australian, but he's lived in Tourmens for over fifteen years. I met him when I was spending my year in Kangarooland. A few years later he spent a sabbatical here, and he stayed on."

"Uh-huh. So, you're worried—"

"There's reason to be, no?"

I think a minute, I hesitate. When a person asks you a question, always consider whether he wants to hear the answer. "Well... wait till we have the whole new workup completed, so we know exactly what's up with him. Has this been going on for long?"

"Months. One day Thérame, his doctor, did a count and it was clear that things weren't good, but Ray didn't want to hear about it. He didn't want to worry his wife, he wanted people to leave him alone, he had books to finish. He's a historian... He just asked Thérame to keep me informed; he wouldn't even talk to me about it privately. I don't dare look his wife in the eye—she thinks I only found out he was sick the same time she did. Now that it's gotten worse, I've been thinking I should have sent him over to you long ago."

"That wouldn't have made much difference, you know. This bitch of a thing stays asymptomatic for months, years sometimes, it's better not to touch it. In a way it's good he held off. If he'd come in last year, Bloch hadn't retired yet, I couldn't have kept him from grabbing the case, your friend would have been put through the whole damn business—leucocyte tracers, monoclonal antibodies, experimental chemo, the kitchen sink… But now—"

"Yes?"

"We'll do as little of all that as possible…"

"Oh. It's that bad?"

"Well, you know, intractable anemia that could turn into acute leukemia any minute—that can't be good, and there're a bunch of complicating factors. But as your good old teacher Lance always says, "Let's not bury him too quick, he might not lie still."

"Yeah…"

"Doing as little as possible doesn't mean doing nothing. We'll give him a transfusion, he'll feel better from that alone. If his whites stay stable and if his pneumonia isn't from some freak source, we'll send him home quick, I'll see him twice a month in the office, or in the day hospital if he should need a transfusion now and then. But we won't go pestering him more than that."

Bruno doesn't answer. I can tell it's hard for him. This Ray Markson seems awfully nice. And his wife is splendid. After a minute, Bruno says,

"I'll be coming into town tomorrow—will you be around?"

"At your service. Incidentally, what can I tell Markson if he asks me any questions?"

"Everything. The truth, if he asks for it. But not in front of his wife."

"Fine. Gorgeous, that wife. You know her well?"

"Huh? Oh, yeah, sure, we were at university together."

"So you must have laid her! How is she?"

He explodes. "Shit, Zim—you're a real jerk. I'm in no mood for joking around!"

"Excuse me. I'm sorry. Anyhow, it's a pity for him. And for her. They look like they love each other a lot."

"They adore each other…"

I sigh—it hurts me for his sake, this whole story. I've often thought the boy is too sensitive for this business. He should only be seeing healthy people, they've got enough problems to keep a good doctor busy.

"Listen," I say, "we've got an interdisciplinary staff meeting scheduled for Saturday morning, we'll certainly be discussing this case with our exchange docs from the University of Rochester—they're here for the month. You want to come?"

"I don't know. I'm supposed to work until noon…"

"No problem, we never finish before two. If you're coming, I'll hold his file for last."

"Thanks, Zim, I'll owe you. Okay, then—see you tomorrow."

"Tomorrow, pal."

I hang up. I'm annoyed with myself for teasing him. I don't know if he laid that pretty little Madame Markson, but to judge by the way she talked about him this morning, he's not done with her yet.

30

CONSULTATION: IMPOSSIBLE
(Second Episode)

Two bicycles and two mopeds are standing along the waiting-room wall, and three cars are parked in the courtyard, but not yours. The windows are fogged over, the street door is ajar. I wipe my feet. In the corridor, two umbrellas hang dripping from the old coathooks. To the schedules posted on the door, someone has taped a card saying

TODAY, TUESDAY
ONLY
OFFICE VISITS WILL BEGIN AT 3:30 P.M.

By my watch it's a quarter past four. A dozen people in soaking-wet coats look up. Two of them greet me. Here I thought I could walk right in. Madame Leblanc told me it usually wasn't too busy on Tuesday afternoons. I sigh, I look again at my watch, and I go back out. The kids will be getting out of school. Maybe I should have made an appointment. For once I take the time to go to the doctor—just my luck.

31

A PRESCRIPTION

Sitting on the edge of your rolling chair, you're writing on a card.

I come back and sit down on the black upholstered chair. You turn to the right, you bend down to the lower shelf, you pick up a prescription pad and insurance forms, you lay them out on the desk in front of you. On a prescription slip you write the date and my name and you pause for a few seconds, ballpoint hanging over the paper, pen tilted, then you shake your head and set the pen down.

You open the big red book lying to the side, you turn to the salmon-colored pages at the front, then to the white pages in the middle, you read attentively, you look back at the salmon-colored pages, your fingertip moves down a list, you sigh, you glance at me over your glasses, you ask: "And what about the medication I prescribed for you last time?"

"Oh, that didn't do a thing for me, absolutely nothing! Look, me and constipation, we go back thirty years, you can imagine I've tried just about everything, it works for two-three days and that's it, just never can go normal. After a while it affects my whole system, my husband gets furious. Not that there's not plenty of specialists, but I've seen them all, and no one's ever been able to help me. With all the things they can do these days, I don't understand how come they haven't figured something out. Now, it does run in my family, my mother was like that and I actually think my daughter—oh, she doesn't say so, but I know her..."

You pick up the ballpoint again. Slowly you close the big red book, and as you write you say, "Okay, you can try this..."

I stretch my neck to read it. "What are you giving me?"

You say, "A laxogenic with tribismuth," or "Paraffin oil and prune," or "Dr. Scheckley's Purgative."

"That's what I thought! Don't bother, I've had that! It does even less for me than the other ones. The only thing that makes me go is SoftStool. I've been taking it for years now. I know they say it gives you cancer, but if I don't go every day I don't feel right and it's just no way to live."

I see you stop writing, sit up straight, look at me in silence for a long time, and I expect to hear you sigh. But no, you tear up the slip, you drop it into the wastebasket, I expect that you'll pick up the pad again and in a rage write down what I'm asking you for, and that you'll say (as all of you say, sooner or later, when you realize you won't manage to treat me with your thisses and thats—but *I* know exactly what I need, *I'm* the one who's constipated, after all!) as you hand me the prescription slip, "Here! The fee is such-and-such!" in a tone of contempt (though we contribute plenty and I pay you besides) or even screaming at me like the doctor I used to go to before you set up practice (he was a young one, too, I thought he seemed nice, actually, and he used to listen to me, but one day he flew off the handle and screamed at me that—that I gave him a—that I made him—So I just picked up my things and he never saw me again. I was so shocked that I didn't remember to pay him, and that never happened to me in my life, but in this case it's understandable. I asked my son to send him a check because I didn't want to owe him even if that's no way to treat people. And right after, quick as a wink, I came to see you, you'd already been in Play for a few years by that time but I'd never had occasion to come by since I was satisfied with my doctor up till then) or like your colleague over in Deuxmonts, who said (not to me but to my sister who has the same problem except that she's depressive for the past ten years besides, and when they give her antidepressants of course that throws her system off, but if she stops taking them, she goes into a tailspin, so there's no way out): "Madame there's nothing more I can do for you" (really, I'm not joking!) but instead you pick up the file card, you note something down, since it's very small I can't read it (and for a moment I thought you were going to open up the big red book again to look for something else, or else suggest sending me for some more X-rays or to see a specialist (and of course I would say All right, if I have to, but you know I've already seen everything had everything, so what good will that do?) and as far as I'm concerned, I can't see why someone would refuse to give me SoftStool when I ask for it, since that's the only thing that makes me go! If it was that bad, you wouldn't be able to buy it! And besides, cancer no cancer, a person has to die of something, it only happens once, at least afterwards you don't suffer any more, whereas being constipated all year long from the first of January to the thirty-first of December is really no way to live); then, very relaxed, you take another slip, you write my name and the date, and right below that: "SoftStool: three times a day for six months," you sign, you fill out the form, you fold it in half and slide it quietly over to me on the desk. You cap your pen, you slip it into your breast pocket, you swivel your chair around and lean toward me, one arm resting on the desk with the hand dangling and the other hand on your thigh, and looking at me over the top of your glasses you say, "And apart from that—how are things?"

32

MADAME SACHS

The telephone rings. I look for the remote to lower the sound on the television, I reach out to the wireless telephone beside me, I press the button. The clock on the VCR says ten to five.

"Hello?"

"Hello, Mother."

"Hello, son! It's good to hear you."

"Mmmhh. Madame Leblanc said you called this morning. How are you?"

"All right—you know, all right. Still the same... I'm tired."

"Since when?"

(You don't call me every day. Once a week, rarely twice. When I feel it's been a while, I call Madame Leblanc. I know she'll tell you to phone me back when you get in from your housecalls. Or at night, if you haven't had time. Sometimes, if you forget, I'm the one who calls you back.)

"Bruno?"

"Oh, hi, Mother..."

"You didn't call back, is there anything wrong?"

"Not at all, but I was busy."

"Oh, you had a lot of house calls?"

"Yes."

(You always answer yes, but it wasn't always true. In the early days of your practice, you used to tell me you were seeing a good many patients, but Madame Leblanc confided sometimes that she was worried, that the patients were taking a while to come in, she wondered if you'd be keeping her on, she was afraid she was costing you too much. You said she was a pearl, and I agree. It's clear she loves her work, I hear it in the way she answers the telephone when you're out on calls or when you want to have lunch at home without being interrupted. She's not much older than you, so you'll be able to keep her a long time.)

"Hello, son!"

"Ah, hello, Mother!... I was going to call you."

"I phoned your house around one o'clock and there was no answer. Didn't you have lunch?"

"No, I had an emergency, a heart attack. You didn't try me at the office? Madame Leblanc would have told you that."

"I didn't want to bother her at lunchtime. Was it serious?"

"Was what serious?"

"The emergency."

"Mmmhh... not anymore. He was dead when I got there."

"Oh my lord, how horrible! Was it a young man?"

"No, no! Sixty-five..."

"Sixty-five is young! You know how old I am?"

(You know exactly how old I am. You always call me on my birthday. You've never missed it. Not even during your year away in Australia. That year you used to write us twice a week. Your father couldn't get over it. When you were at medical school you didn't call home much. You'd talk a lot with your father about what you were doing at the hospital, what you were hearing in your classes, that gave him pleasure, that was some consolation for the fact that you didn't want to go into his specialty, where he could have helped you. Now that he's dead you don't call me every day. Once a week at most, sometimes twice, but that's rare. When you were a student you had no phone, you had to go hither and yon to call home, whereas now of course you do have one, in fact the other day when I said to Madame Leblanc "I don't have much luck, often when I try to reach Bruno the line's busy," she told me you'd had a second line installed back in the first year. So a person could always get hold of you ("What, Madame, you didn't know that?" "Well, no! See, I might be his mother but he doesn't tell me everything!" "Oh, madame, it probably didn't occur to him, he has so much on his mind, shall I give you the other number?" "Oh no, no, you're kind, I don't want to intrude... oh, if you insist... But please don't tell him. I just, you know, for my peace of mind... I have no one else but him, I'll only call it if there's an absolute need, you're sure he won't be angry with you if I use it?") in an emergency.)

"Bruno!"

"Mother? What's up?"

"Nothing, son, nothing, don't worry, I'm fine! Just that I heard someone interesting on the radio before, and I thought, well, Bruno'd be interested in that, so I taped it and I'll give you the cassette. You know that program where they talk about books, in the morning on Tourmens Radio?"

"'Speaking Up'…"

"That's it. Well, today, the guest was a woman doctor who just published her work-diary—I thought I'd buy it for you, I'll tell Elsa to pick it up at Diego's shop, she seemed very nice, the doctor, she had a good voice and I'm sure you'll like it, from listening to her I thought she must practice the same kind of medicine you do."

"Really? What's that—my kind of medicine?"

(Actually, I wish I knew. You never talk about it. At least, not since your father died. And when he was alive, you were still a student, I didn't pay much attention, I thought, He's still got time to change his mind…)

"Madame Leblanc told me you were out of the office at noon today."

"Yes, I was over at the hospital."

"You go there often?"

"Yes, Mother, every Tuesday at noon."

"Really? You work down there?"

"Sure I do, Mother, ever since I started practicing here I have one session a week there. Sometimes more, when I cover for colleagues who are away."

"What unit is that again? The other day a friend of mine asked me where you worked and I couldn't tell her, I sounded real smart."

"In the abor—in Family Planning. That's where women come for contraception or when they want to… interrupt their pregnancy."

"Ohhh—that can't be much fun. Excuse me, I'm changing the subject, but tell me, your article—you know, the one you were working on last week when I called you—when is that going to be published?"

"Mmmmhh… It takes a while, you know. They'll discuss it at an editorial board meeting, and they'll certainly ask me for some revisions before they publish it. Maybe in two or three months."

"You remember to send me a copy!"

"Of course, Mother, I always do."

(You often send me issues of the medical magazine you work on. The first few times, you were a little reticent ("You know, Mother, it's very technical stuff." "Well, son, I *was* married to a doctor! Of course I'm not trained, still I did type your father's articles, I'm not a complete ignoramus!") but you eventually did send me one and then another one and yes, at first I didn't understand everything about it, but gradually I came to understand a little more and I decided that I actually wasn't so stupid. I saw that what you were writing was less and less like medical articles and more and more like…

Still, I suspect you don't show me everything you write. You send me your magazine, but you could easily be publishing articles somewhere else as well without my knowing it. And the more you do that, the less you discuss it, even less than you discuss your patients or your friends.

But I know you spend long hours with pen in hand or sitting in front of a typewriter. That doesn't really surprise me. I always wrote a good deal myself. When the family scattered to the four corners of the country and sometimes even farther away, I would type my letters and, of course, I used to type the drafts of your father's articles. When he fell ill, he very soon developed trouble writing, so I would type to his dictation… So actually, the fact that you enjoy writing you get from both of us, but that you learned to type comes mostly from me…

What surprised me most, reading your magazine, is that you were writing stories your father used to tell. He'd be amazed to know how much time you spend writing, almost as much as you do practicing medicine. I say that because you never go out, except to have dinner with Diego and the Marksons. When I call you at home in the evening, you always answer instantly, as if your hand were waiting on the receiver.)

"Yes?"

"Good evening, son! Your voice is odd—is something worrying you?"

"Evening, Mother… No, but almost every night, the phone rings at this hour and whoever it is hangs up without saying anything."

"Oh, that must be infuriating!… I'm calling because it's a long time since I've heard from you and I was missing you."

(Of course you don't call me every day—not even every week—and if I didn't insist that you come to dinner Friday nights in memory of your father, I wouldn't see you very often, either, although you live not even ten miles from Tourmens and come in here to the hospital every Tuesday. I keep asking if you couldn't stop by for just a minute, or have lunch on your way to the hospital, but you always answer that you do a great many house calls that day and that you're always running late. And when I say, Still you could give your mother a little phone call between patients, you answer that you haven't got much time with your patients and I say, I don't dare call in to you I don't like to bother you, and almost just as quick you answer, You never bother me, Mother… and that makes me happy, almost as much as having you phone me when I'm not expecting it.)

"Hello Mama, it's Bruno…"

"Ah, son—what a nice surprise! You know, I was just thinking about you!"

"Really?"

"Yes, see, I turned on the TV and I came across a medical program, I thought you'd certainly be interested, so I'm taping it. They're talking about contraception and wanting babies, we can watch it together Friday night because you know, I don't quite get everything but you can explain it to me."

"Mmmhh… I never watch medical programs."

"Really? But still, on that topic! You didn't know that was on? Actually, though, why are you calling me at this hour? This isn't your usual time—I hope you're not on duty?"

"No, not at all, I was working."

(The first time you said that, I didn't say anything, the second time either, but the third time, I laughed, "What kind of work can you be doing at ten o'clock at night, son, you're not on call every night, are you? I hope you're not seeing your lady patients at the house!" "No, but now that I'm on the editorial board of this magazine, I read manuscripts, I edit copy, I proofread, I rewrite…" and that reminded me of what Monsieur Juliet, your junior-high teacher, told your father one day: "Your son's not a scientist, he's literary!" Your father, of course, was not pleased to hear that, you can imagine! His son, *literary?* Whenever I reminded him of that story, he would shrug his shoulders and grumble, "That knucklehead doesn't know a thing about it," but the fact is that you always did read a lot, even when you were twelve, thirteen years old you would spend hours reading and, when you didn't come straight home from school, I'd have to go look for you, you'd be reading between the stacks in the Mall Bookstore, or sitting under the murder-mystery shelf at the library, I don't know when you found time to do your homework. Sometimes I'd go into your room and I'd see you slipping something into the bureau drawer and later, when I went to see what you were hiding (I thought I'd find comic books or a detective story, or the *Mystery Magazine* I bought every week and tried not to leave around because it had rather risqué pictures in it) I would find only notebooks full of stories, lists of titles, characters' names, lines copied from books, songs, and I'd think, Monsieur Juliet wasn't so far wrong, but of course I'd never say a thing to your father so as not to rile him. Besides, you always said you were going to be a doctor like him, and you are.)

"You don't regret it?"

"What?"

"Going into practice."

"No, not at all, why?"

"Because I see you enjoy writing for that magazine, maybe you'd rather have done that than medicine…"

"No. I was offered the job of editor-in-chief and I turned it down."

"Really—why? yes, of course, stupid of me—you'd have to be there full-time, it wouldn't leave you the time for the office."

"Uhhh… yes, but mainly because I don't want to spend my time getting other people to write, and I have other things I want to do."

"You're writing a book!"

You're silent.

"I guessed it!" (I was pleased!) "Look, I'm your mother after all, I know you pretty well!"

(That day, you hadn't wanted to say any more about it. Later on, you told me it was a novel, of course I'd suspected that and I was both uneasy and annoyed at the idea; it stuck in my mind.)

"A novel? You're not going to be like those men and women who go on about their miserable childhoods and say bad things about their mothers, I hope!"

You burst into laughter.

"No, Mother, it's nothing like that. It's a book about my experiences as a doctor."

"Oh, good. That's better. Yes, you must see an awful lot, with all those sicknesses... The other day on the television—you know, the show I taped for you last week but we forgot to watch, that's all right, we'll see it some other time—well, just before it, on the news there was a young man, he must have been your age, who was there to talk about some very rare disease he'd caught somehow. He'd had a really terrible time, the poor fellow, and he'd written a book about it with his doctor, they were both on and it seemed interesting, I thought you might have heard about it. I sent Elsa to buy it for me, if it interests you I can lend it to you when I've read it."

"Mmmhh... If you like."

"All right, son, I'll get off now, it was nice of you to call me, but the telephone's expensive and besides you have patients waiting."

(And you answer: Yes, or you answer: Not too many, but I do have some articles to write, and I say: I know you're never short of things to do. I suspect you read and write even when you're at your medical office, because you've always been like that, you'd spend your time reading and listening to music, and even nowadays you never go out, except to go to the movies from time to time, and you're often on call. Apart from the Marksons and Diego, you don't see anyone, except for that doctor group that has discussion meetings—Balint, I think you called it?—once or twice a month. Right now you don't even have a girlfriend. For a long time you haven't had anyone at all. There was a time when I even wondered whether you... didn't prefer men. Of course the idea was absurd, but it plagued me. I really got quite upset about it. I didn't dare raise it with your father, he would have blown up at me—a son of his, *preferring men?* But still, it tormented me. And then one day on the radio I heard a woman talking about her son, she was saying that he and the male friends of his she knew were generally very, very close to their mothers, they told them everything, they were very affectionate, they had very good relations with them. And I found that comforting and painful at the same time, because you—it's not that you're not affectionate, but you are secretive, remote. And in fact what she said may not be true of everyone, because Serge, my cousin Yvette's son, really is *that way*, and he's never gotten along with his mother, not at all! And with his father, we won't even talk about it. The day they learned he was like that, you can imagine, it gave them a real shock. And then, with time, things settled down and now they get along much better. True,

Yvette's husband died, the poor woman—that did bring her closer to her son. He even introduced her to the boy he lives with—well, it's a man who could practically be his father, but apparently they love each other very much. Yvette even says she's pleased to see Serge so happy, so peaceful. His... friend is a very fine man, very cultivated, you would never think he was... And she always used to worry that Serge would end up with some girl she couldn't get along with! Here, obviously, there's no such problem. I can sympathize with her. When you've got a son, you always worry a little; you think, I just hope he doesn't fall into somebody's clutches, young folks get infatuated so easily and then suddenly they look up and find they're stuck. Anyhow, the point is it was reassuring to hear the woman saying that on the radio.

In the end I said to myself, It's not that he doesn't like women, it's more that he's the sort who doesn't like many people in general. I remember when you were fifteen you had no friends at the lycée except for Diego—and he's not married yet either—and you'd spend hours together reading and listening to records, it's a little like that now too, if you're still immersed that way in your articles or your books it can't leave you much time for meeting someone.

When you were at medical school I did often ask you, lightly, "Son, don't you ever invite your classmates to go out for dinner or a movie?" I thought there must be lots of girls in your classes, girls love going to the movies, when I was young myself I loved that—but each time you gave me a funny look and answered, "No I haven't got time for that." I could see that it irritated you for me to ask and that you were answering that way to avoid upsetting me. Nowadays, when I ask questions, you can say you don't feel like answering. Look, you could have loads of girlfriends and I wouldn't know it, right? Well, a mother can't be blamed for feeling some concern for her child—what's more natural than to want your child to be happy?—that's why it troubles me knowing you live alone, at your age. I'd have been very pleased to see you marry Catherine Markson, but she fell in love with Ray and who could blame her, such a brilliant man!

Still, a couple of years ago, for several months you were seeing a young woman your age, a teacher. You even brought her over here several times. She wasn't pretty, she dressed very badly, she looked older than you, but she was polite and very cultivated—naturally, being a teacher. At the table, though, she wolfed down her food. It was surprising how much she could put away, I mean it was a pleasure to see such a good appetite but if I didn't know she earned a living, I would have thought she couldn't afford to eat every day. And then, too, although she seemed to like my cooking, she never asked me for the least little recipe. That's what tipped me off. I said to myself that things weren't likely to get very far between the two of you, or she would have wanted to make you the dishes you like, but that didn't seem to interest her. Every now and then I'd ask you for news of her: "Speaking of which, how is—?" I kept forgetting her name, it's awful, I remember it was the same name as some theater actress, it's on the tip of my tongue, but this memory of mine—it's dreadful. And one day you answered "We're not seeing each other any more." I don't know why it didn't work out. It's true that aside from liking my cooking she wasn't very demonstrative. Well, that's how it is. These days, young people meet and then, if it doesn't work in a couple of months, they'd just as soon drop it. Actually, it's better that way. In my day, if you had a yen for some fellow, you had to be very careful or you'd find yourself with a bun in the oven and have to get married, it was awful, but unless you had the means to do something about it...

Even so, I hope you won't spend your whole life alone. One day I was teasing you, I asked if there wasn't some patient you'd like to see outside of work. You shot me a look as if I'd said something heinous and you very curtly declared: *People who do that are filthy bastards.* That knocked the breath out of me; I said you were being excessive. You and I both know stories of doctors who take advantage of a situation, of course, but it's certainly not the majority! And besides, the women it happens to—you wonder whether they didn't bring it on themselves to some degree. Some of them even do very nicely from it, I've seen men desert their wives and children and get a divorce for the sake of some patient... But it really irked me to hear you react that way; after all, I did marry your father (Yes, I know, we were both single and I wasn't his patient, but I could have been. When we met at my cousin Roland's wedding (at one of the most elegant hotels in Algiers—we were still all living there—and come to think of it, that's funny, I was with Yvette) your father—of course I didn't know then that's what he would become—he was pacing around restlessly and he'd jump every time the phone rang. It made us all laugh. Yvette liked the look of him—she always had an eye for the men—whereas I thought he was too thin, and since he kept pacing like that, she went over to where he was on the pretext of getting a little sandwich and she just asked him right out, laughing, why he was acting so edgy. He answered, "I'm on call, I'm sure someone's going to phone me to deliver a baby." Just then the telephone did ring and it was for him! Roland's parents insisted he should come back afterward, they were very close friends with his parents. When he came in two hours later, Yvette was dancing. (You don't think she'd be waiting for him! She was dancing with Bernard, a boyfriend of hers at the time, a darling boy, he was killed in a terrorist attack, the poor fellow. He was on his way to the beach, he walks past a café, he sees two friends sitting at a table, he stops to say hello and just then a car goes by and the men inside it spray the terrace with a machine gun because the café owner refused to join the O.A.S.* —Bernard was killed instantly and four other people were wounded, when I think of his mother, the poor woman, it breaks my heart... But I do think we were right to get out.) Anyhow, your father did come back, all

---

*French colonialist militia fighting the Algerian independence movement.

wrung out from the delivery, and when I saw that, I told him to sit down, I'd make up a plate for him, and we started talking. Well, you know that man—when he wasn't under stress he adored telling a story. I was only listening with one ear, I was looking at him thinking that he was really awfully thin, that bothered me terribly you can't imagine, I couldn't see myself with such a thin fellow, and then in the end luckily that didn't stop me! After all, he was a doctor, actually his professor had just made him his senior resident, and I was pretty impressed, which was a good thing, because otherwise you wouldn't be here!) So I thought that among your patients there might be some young women who'd be very happy to marry my son, doctor or not!

"Uhh, excuse me, Mother, I have to get off the phone, I have patients waiting and I was at the hospital all morning, so I was late starting here…"

"Yes, of course, son, I don't want to hold you up. And the telephone's expensive, you can call me back later. Otherwise, it doesn't matter—if we don't talk before then, I'll see you Friday night as usual."

"Umm… Yes. If I'm not there by eight, don't worry; and don't go to any trouble, when I finish late like that I'm not very hungry."

"I don't worry, son, I don't worry, take however long you need to, I'm in no hurry, you have work to do, but me… I'll tell Elsa to make something simple that I can reheat. From my end, you know, I'm so tired I just stay put, I wait for you, I read or watch a movie, that's all I've got to do."

33

IN THE WAITING ROOM

My eyes reach the bottom of the page and I suddenly realize that they've scanned the lines without retaining any of the meaning. My thoughts were straying back to our short conversation yesterday.

❋

The telephone rang once and you picked up. Waiting for your voice, I couldn't help smiling.

"Doctor Sachs here, hello."

"Hello, Monsieur, I'd like to come in to see you…"

"I see. This evening it's a little tight. Is this something urgent?"

I smiled more and more, I couldn't stop. "No, not really. What are your office hours tomorrow?"

"Well, in the morning by walk-in from ten to noon, or else the afternoon by appointment."

"Then I'll come in tomorrow morning around ten."

"As you like. Have you got a record here?"

"No, this is a first visit."

"Do you know where the office is?"

"Uh, no, I don't know the town of Play at all, I live in Tourmens."

"Oh really—you're coming a long way. Well fine, it's not hard to find."

"Just a minute, I'll get a pencil." Among the papers piled on the table, I finally managed to find a pencil stub and a torn envelope. "I'm ready."

"All right: coming from Tourmens, you get off the highway and come into Play, cross right through town, and just before the exit sign at the end of the square, you take the little dead-end street to the right. The office is at number seven, but I suggest you park in front of the church."

"I've got it. Till tomorrow, then. Good evening, Monsieur."

I hung up. I picked up the book again and looked for the passage I was reading just before dialing your number.

❇

A knock at the door; it opens halfway.

A woman enters, she is pretty and elegant, her face is sad. She greets the secretary; apparently they know one another. She sits down beside me, smiles at me faintly, and her gaze wanders off.

The teenager and her mother are increasingly agitated. At several points, the woman laid her hand on her daughter's arm, and the girl jerked it away with an extremely violent look. The mother has a cowlike gaze, the manner of a self-sacrificing martyr, the sort that says "Oh-why-are-you-so-mean-to-me-when-I-do-everything-I-can-to-make-you-happy-my-little-daughter…"

I shiver. I return to my reading.

34

MONSIEUR GUENOT

The door opens. "I'll see you now."

I get up, my cap in my hand. From the table I pick up my case with the health booklet and prothrombin record, the Social Security form, and the prescription slip I brought along. You put out your hand.

"Hello, Monsieur Guenot."

"Hello, Monsieur—uh, Doctor."

You step aside to let me pass. The connecting door pulls to by the air-spring mechanism as you shut the inner door with a shove. "How're you doing?"

"Well, I'm here about my prothrombin, like every month…"

"Mmmyes."

You settle in at your desk, you lean over to the file cases. You straighten up with a brown envelope in hand.

I pull the latest blood test results from my booklet, I lay that on the table and my cap on the chair. "It went down since last time."

"Did it? Let's see… Thirty-one percent. Last time, you had thirty-four—that's about the same. If your prothrombin rate is anywhere between twenty-five and thirty-five percent, it's perfect."

While you were reading my record, I took off my jacket and my vest and undid my belt. "Okay well, you could maybe have a look at me. Should I get undressed?"

"Yes, please…"

I take off my pants, I lay them on the chair. I take off my sweater too. "Socks off too?"

"If you want."

"Lie down?"

"Yes, please."

You swivel around on your rolling chair. You get up, you take the straight chair from near the window and you bring it over to the cot. "Well now, what's new since last time?"

"Oh, not much, I had a little cold, but with that syrup you give me it went away. Not much left, better write me down for some more, if you don't mind. I gotta come in pretty soon for the flu shot?"

"Yes, this month. But you still have time."

The armband tightens. You deflate slowly. It hisses.

"One-forty over eighty—that's good."

"What? Last time I had one-thirty!"

"Same thing. It varies a little from one time to the next, but it's the same."

You ask about the sleeping, the appetite, the digestion, the wife.

"Holding up…"

You ask me if I'm tolerating my medicine all right and I tell you yes, on that, I'm tolerating it all right, lucky thing the wife called you that time four years back when I took sick, cause they told me at the hospital if it wasn't for you getting me treated right away I'd a stayed in that state but now I come out of it fine. And the specialist said if I keep on watching myself and taking my medicine, that shouldn't happen again, so now I'm real careful. Heck, you gotta take care of yourself.

You listen to my chest. You sit me down. You pick up the rubber mallet from the little shelves and you say, "Sit on the edge of the cot."

You knock on my knees, my ankles. "Perfect."

"So everything's okay? The old horse not about to drop dead?"

You smile. "Far from it! In fact, you seem to be in tiptop shape…"

"Shouldn't complain—seventy's not like twenty! But I'm holding up… Heck, I take care of myself."

You get up. "Come over here and let me weigh you."

I climb onto the scales. Without my glasses on I can't see the numbers. "Did I lose?"

"No, no change since last time."

I get off the scales. "Should I get dressed?"

"Mmhhh…"

You go back to your desk. I sit in the black-covered chair, I put back on my shirt, my socks, my pants, my shoes. You pick up your pen. I take out my case and I watch you write the date on the prescription slip, then my name up by yours, and down underneath in capital letters the name of the medicines you been giving me since the first time, that time I come to see you when I was leaving the hospital where you sent me because I went off my mind. Course I don't exactly remember that, I woke up one day in a bed that wasn't mine and some ladies in blue smocks told me "Hello Monsieur Guenot how are you today?" And I said hello back but that's all. I didn't know how to say anything else but hello hello hello hello, they'd ask me if I was hungry and I'd say hello, they'd tell me the wife was coming in and I'd say hello, I was going nuts because I couldn't talk normal and I didn't know what was going on. That lasted three days easy until the doctor in charge—a little

HISTORY (TUESDAY, OCTOBER 7)

bald man, he must be a good doctor since he's the boss, but he's not too nice, sort of stuck-up, and he scares people—he tells me he'll be giving me some new medicine for my treatment but that he can't guarantee how it's gonna work out.

I was crying a lot.

I was crying because I didn't know what was happening to me, the wife would come see me afternoons and I couldn't talk to her I kept saying the same thing over and over hello hello hello hello and nothing else would come out. And her too that made her so sad naturally because she likes having our chats, now that the kids are gone the daughter telephones "Hello Mama" and "We'll be over on Sunday to see you" and then "Goodbye," but that's all, so naturally her and me we gab together a lot, keeps us busy.

And then there was that young lady, the speech trainer—I'd go see her at her office three times a week. At first she used to ask me questions I was supposed to answer yes or no by nodding my head and I was answering right so she made me do some simple things, orders like, that she'd write down on a paper, like Close your eyes, Give me your hand, and little by little probably because the medicine was working I started talking again and now I have almost no problem, only every now and then I hunt a little for some word but they say that's normal anyway at my age, especially after what I had.

When I got outta the hospital, the doctor in charge asked me to come in once a month to see how things are going and to give me more of that medicine, since they don't have it even at the Ramparts Pharmacy, and that's the biggest one in Tourmens, only at the hospital. Every time I come back to see him, I was talking better. After six months I was almost the way I was before. Sure, seventy's not like twenty, but heck! when you take care of yourself, you hold up okay. He seemed really surprised, he would check me out from top to toe, he'd always ask me the same questions—What day is this, What are the colors in the flag, Who's the president of France—and I couldn't figure out why he seemed like he was annoyed that I gave the right answers—after all it wasn't magic, I was reading the newspaper again and acourse I knew the elections weren't gonna be for another two years—but he didn't seem to like that very much, even though he'd say it was good. One day, he told me they couldn't keep on giving me that medicine, cause it cost a lot and I didn't seem like I needed it anymore, but that he didn't know what would happen when they stopped it. Well, I was feeling all right, so I says it's not worth it for me to keep on taking it. One day, I seen that poster about flu shots in the pharmacy window and I says to myself I got weak lungs I should go get that, specially since after age seventy they reimburse for it and Heck! gotta take care of yourself. So I come in to you, and when you saw me in the waiting room you smiled. When I walked into your office, you shook my hand and said, "I'm glad to see you so well." I'd took along my vaccine and my prescription and my last blood test, it was forty-four that time and I had a little cold so I was worried, but you told me, "It's not very serious, just keep taking the same dose and we'll do another blood test in a few days. And I'll order you a little syrup for that cough." I asked you, "Should I keep up my treatment?" and you said "Mmmhh."

That meant yes.

And I says, "It was a lucky thing the wife called you last year when I got sick, because they told me at the hospital that if you hadn't of put me in I'd still be like that, but this way I come out fine and that if I keep getting checkups and keep taking my medicine it shouldn't happen again, so now I watch out. Heck, ya gotta take care of yourself. Okay, so the doctor in charge wanted to see me regular every six months, but he's not giving me that special medicine anymore anyway so I been thinking maybe there's no point going back to him, if you'd let me be your patient?"

You looked up, you put down the pen and you smiled. "I'd be very glad to, of course, but didn't you have a regular doctor before I sent you over to Neurology?"

"Yes—Doctor Jardin, at Lavinié, but he's not so young, and when we called you it was a Sunday and he don't want to be on duty Sundays. His wife just sends you right to the hospital without him lifting a finger. You, though—you came to the house, you gave me a real examination, and you saw right off that I needed to go in. So if it's all right with you to keep taking care of me…"

"Well now, I'm very touched. But right now you look in fine shape. You shouldn't have to come in very often. Every three months—that should be enough."

I was doing fine, it's true, but every three months with a monthly blood test— that didn't seem like enough to me, specially since the test never comes out the same twice in a row, thirty-four one time, twenty-eight the next, it's like it depends on what I eat (now that we're retired, the wife and me we like to take trips with the senior club, we go on the bus for a day at Mont Saint Michel or for a week to Italy, and we don't eat regular like at home, so I always come in to see you right before, just to check that my prothrombin isn't too bad and to renew my medicines so I don't run out. The thing is, on the blood-pressure medicine they give you only twenty-eight pills in a pack, where the package for the prothrombin medicine comes with a lot more. And on that one I don't take a whole pill, I take three-quarters the first day and then a half on each of the next two days, except when the prothrombin goes up, then I take three-quarters of a pill for two days and a half on the third, or, if it's too low (that mostly happens when I eat asparagus or when I haven't urinated enough) I don't take it on the night I get the analysis back, I call and the lady who answers the phone tells me when your office hours are and either I take a half a pill for three days until I see you again if you don't have time before, or else I come in the next day) and then, with the chronic bronchitis, I cough now and then and when that goes on too long, the wife gets worried, I don't like to take the syrups she has in the cabinet, you never know how long they been open. So I'd rather come in every (myself, I feel safer that way. You know me better than if I'm seeing you three times a year, and even if somebody doesn't like it, I don't care. People talk, they say we shouldn't spend so much, that Social Security is running out of money, but myself I don't see things that way, your health is important or else it's not worth working all your life and then not take care of yourself. Besides, you never make remarks. Not one way or the other—you never say things like "I wondered what ever became of you I thought you didn't want to see me anymore," the way some doctors do, to hear them talk you'd think they owned a person. You, no, that's not your way. So much that sometimes I hear stupid talk, naturally people always gab, like "He must not have very many patients, he doesn't turn anybody away, you never have to wait long at his office and when you call him he always comes over the same day, so I wouldn't be surprised if suddenly we hear he's leaving." I been hearing that for a long time already, that you're gonna leave, but acourse all that is just stories, would you of gone and set up practice here just to take off all of a sudden? Besides, they can talk, all I know is you been taking care of me five years already, a visit every) month, and you said, "All right, whatever you like," and you wrote out my prescriptions in capital letters, for my medicines and a blood test once a month by the nurse. And putting "At home" on the order, else I don't get my money back.

You hand me the prescription slip, it's easy to read can't make any mistake and I open my wallet to get the little notebook where I have you write down the number on the prothrombin count. There's almost no space left, I been coming so long, but heck, ya gotta take care of yourself.

35

THE SPECIALIST

You come out of your office. You usher out the man with the cap, I stand up, you shake his hand.

"Goodbye now, Monsieur Guenot."

I straighten my skirt and turn to your door but you stop me with a gesture. "I'll have to ask you to wait a moment—I've got to make a telephone call." The connecting door closes again. I sit back down.

❋

I hear the knob turn on the inner door. The connecting door opens. You come out, you glance at me with some surprise, I stand up, I walk in ahead of you. You point to two black-upholstered chairs and invite me to have a seat.

I sit down, I cross my legs. You sit down as well.

"Yes?"

"I phoned you this morning—I'm Doctor Geneviève Nourissier, I'll be practicing in Tourmens as an associate of Doctor Bazin's in his vascular clinic."

"Really? He has too much work?"

"Well, yes, there's plenty to do, his practice has increased enormously in the past eighteen months. I'd covered for him several times and he proposed a partnership."

I watch you. With your elbow resting on the edge of the painted surface you use as a desk, you listen to me, stoop-shouldered, almost hunched, and looking faintly irritated.

"Yes?"

"Well… Soon we'll have a very advanced scanner for vascular imaging with real-time 3D color Doppler ultrasound."

You smile. "Oh really?"

You tilt your head to one side. You rub your chin, then your eyes, then you take off your glasses, you lean back in your chair and you ask, "And what did you want to talk to me about?"

"Uh… well—mainly I wanted to introduce myself, and then to learn what your needs might be as to vascular imaging…"

"My needs?"

You raise your eyebrows. You lay your glasses on the painted desk. You lean down toward the floor, you lift your trouser leg, you finger your calf, you straighten up, you shrug your shoulders and purse your lips doubtfully.

"Ha-ha!" I go, to show I get the joke. "I mean your *patients'* vascular needs."

"My patients? Well, you know—their needs tend to be in a very different vein… In fact, that's the main pulse behind their seeking care."

I sit there flabbergasted. You lace your fingers together. You gaze at me in silence.

I consider whether you're not just razzing the hell out of me.

36

MONSIEUR GUILLOUX

I step in, gasping for air. You offer me a seat, and then you hear the whistling coming from my mouth as I catch my breath. Your head jerks up in alarm: *"How long have you been in this condition?*

"For… (I take another breath) three months."

A fit of coughing takes me, I hurt, tears come to my eyes, I'm nearly suffocating. You lay your hand on my shoulder. You press me to sit down, but I raise my hand and shake my head. I pull a handkerchief from my pocket, I wipe away the foam that comes to my lips. I take off my jacket, I unbutton my shirt, I don't lie down on the cot because it's worse when I lie down. I settle into a chair instead.

You listen to my chest, you look into my throat with a little lamp, you examine my neck, you feel in my armpits, the hollow behind my clavicles. Finally, you lay me down partway, wedging a big pillow behind my back. You feel my abdomen. You spend a long time examining my abdomen, especially around the liver.

I breathe very slowly, to avoid setting off my cough again.

You ask if I've lost weight.

I tell you Yes, I don't eat much, I have too much trouble swallowing. You nod without speaking.

You reach into the drawer of the little chest at the head of the cot and take out two glass vials. You prepare an injection, you tell me it will make me feel better, that for the moment you're going to prescribe very little, just some pills I'm supposed to dissolve in a little water, but above all an exam by a specialist.

"A fibroscopy. It involves threading a slim tube through the nose, to get down and explore the bronchi. To see what's going on there. We've got to find out why you're having such trouble."

You stand up. Before letting me dress, you ask me to step onto the scales over by the window. I've lost fifteen pounds. My wife did say my trousers are very loose on me.

You return to your swivel chair, you pull out a white medical form. I sit down on one of the two chairs covered in black cloth and you ask me my name, my age, my address, my telephone number.

You open the prescription pad, you slip the cover beneath the first few pages, you write. First the date: October 7. Below that, my name on the same level as your own, and you underline it twice. Your hand slides a few inches down the page and writes some words I can't read.

"I'm giving you a letter for the specialist."

You're writing in a rush. You stop once, you crumple the sheet, you start afresh. In the middle of the page, you stop again. You pick up the telephone, you clench it against your shoulder while you dial a number. Waiting for someone to answer, you tap the sheet with the tip of your ballpoint, not looking at me.

"Hello? Hello, this is Doctor Sachs. I'd like an appointment for one of my patients. Yes, it's urgent. No, it can't wait till next week. Fine, put me through to him. Thank you."

You look up at me, you nod your head and close your eyes, as if to say I won't have much more of a wait. You set to writing again.

"Hello, Philippe, this is Bruno. Excuse me for interrupting you in a consultation, but I'd like to send you a patient I'm seeing for the first time this afternoon. He's wheezing very badly, he's lost weight, and he absolutely requires investigation. That's right. Tomorrow morning? Ah, that's excellent. Eleven forty-five? Wait, I'll ask him."

You turn to me, I nod my head to say I'll do it.

"That will be fine. It's a Mister Guilloux, Gaston (and you give him my date of birth, my address, my telephone number). Fine. Again, thanks, that'll be a great favor. Yes, whenever you like. Thanks enormously."

You hang up. "I'll give you his address."

You finish the letter. You write more slowly, carefully this time. You read it over. You nod. You sign it.

You fold the letter and slip it into an envelope whose flap you fold down without sealing it. On the envelope, you write the specialist's name, his address, his telephone number, and the time of the appointment. You hand it to me.

You ask me if I feel any better, I say Yes, the injection is beginning to work on me. You tell me more about the examination. You explain how the procedure will go, but I don't hear your explanations. I ask you if I'll have to have an operation. You say that will depend. On what they find.

You don't name any illness, and I don't ask you to.

The next day, my wife goes with me to your specialist colleague.

He's a very gentle man. The examination is long but it goes easily. Afterwards, he has me sit down in his office and he tells me I have cancer of the larynx.

SOLO DIALOGUES

II

SKETCHES FROM MEMORY

At the time, I was a resident in medicine, it was summer, we were even more understaffed than usual, he was filling in as a nurse. He was a third-year student, if I recall. The boss took him on because his father had phoned him, they'd been senior residents together. This guy didn't know how to do a thing, he always seemed like he was born yesterday, and he was underfoot all the time. He was constantly on my tail, asking questions about everything, and worst of all, having opinions on everything.

One day, they brought in a fifty-year-old man with acute pancreatitis. The guy was rolling on the floor with pain, and howling.

Sachs says, "Don't you think he's overdoing it a little?"

I didn't answer. I sent him out to get me something, anything, in some other unit, so I wouldn't have to look at him. Afterwards, when I'd managed to sedate the patient—I had to give him I don't know how much morphine before he could stop screaming—I cornered the idiot in the office and really gave him hell, I told him the next time he said something like that I'd break his face. And that if he didn't understand what I was talking about, he could just go find himself another job. The next day, he comes into the office and says, "I want to apologize to you."

He babbled on, some great thoughts about Pain and the Doctor's Role, and then he said he was heading off to apologize to the patient.

I told him he was a little late. The guy had died during the night.

❋

One day, my mother-in-law came to spend a few days with us. When my husband saw how many different medicines she was taking, he said she was going to get sick from all that—I should mention she's very tiny, she's a featherweight with the appetite of a bird. He felt that once she'd swallowed her pills, her capsules, her powders, her drops, and her cough syrup along with her soup, there couldn't be room for anything else. And in fact, she ate almost nothing. So he brought her in to see you and they came back delighted because you'd told my mother-in-law that her medications would be more effective if she took them at the end of the meal, and you told my husband he'd done a good thing bringing her in to make sure the treatment was right for her. So then I brought you my mother too, from Tourmens. Since her hip fracture, she'd had a bedsore that just wasn't getting better. The first time, you said that at her age it would take a long time. She answered that she didn't care, as long as it did heal eventually. I brought her in over several months. You would examine her bedsore very carefully, you'd measure it to see if it was getting any smaller, you were very gentle, and you prescribed very little for her—Vaseline, bandages, a tiny bit of ointment, told her to rest her leg on a cushion, to massage around the wound, to sleep on her side, to walk a lot, to eat well— and in the end it did heal. The last time I brought her in to your office, you said the thing had closed up by itself, that all you'd wanted to do was keep it from getting worse, and I know you weren't saying that out of modesty, but she would never go along with that. She said, "It took time, but if you hadn't treated it the way you did, it would never have healed." Usually, doctors don't take the time to wait for sick people to get well, they don't help sick people to deal patiently with their sickness. Doctors aren't very patient. You are.

✳

I come by every year for a check-up. You look me over from head to foot, you give me an electrocardiogram and you order a complete blood workup (you always tell me putting "complete" doesn't make much difference, but I insist). You're a very good guy and you're very clear, but I do think you ask some questions that are a little too personal. My private life, after all, has nothing to do with my health.

✳

One morning I passed out in a café. The owner got scared, he called the firemen. I wanted to go home, I told them it was just my period, but they forced me to go to the hospital. What with all the shit I was going through at the time, I hadn't eaten anything since the night before. And on top of it they had to give me a lot of grief on the pretext I'd fainted before I could even eat a croissant.

I was freezing there on an examining table when a guy in a white coat came into the cubicle. He looked at me funny. I thought: Great, one more asshole who's gonna have a little fun feeling me up.

He gave me a gown. He sat down on a chair, he took off his glasses, he said, "I'm the resident. Excuse me if I start yawning, I haven't slept since yesterday morning. What's going on with you?"

At the time, I was ashamed of what was going on with me, of what I was doing, I wished I could disappear down a hole, but I didn't have the strength anymore to lie, so I told him everything. After a minute he stood up, he went out, he came back with a hot chocolate and a sandwich and left me alone. After a quarter of an hour, he came back in again, he took my blood pressure, then he picked up the telephone and called the ER director to say he didn't see any need to keep me, what with all the admissions they'd had during the night. Then he tore up the sheet they'd put my name on when I came in, and he told me to go home. And when he saw I wasn't moving, he reached out his hand, he got me up, he gave me my dress, he smiled.

"Go home, gorgeous."

He blushed, and then he went away.

With my daughter, it wasn't the obstetrician who delivered me, it was a young doctor. The midwife showed him what to do and the obstetrician stood by. The young doctor was very gentle. It was my fourth delivery, I knew it would go well anyhow, but for him, it was his first. When the baby was born, he put it on my stomach, he stood beside me for several long minutes looking at it, touching it. He was more emotional than my husband was.

I'll never go to him. I don't trust him. There's something about him that's not right—one day I saw him looking over the porn movies in the same video store I go to.

Didn't I tell you I dislocated my jaw? I was scared to death when it happened! I'd heard of it, it used to make me laugh, but boyoboy, there's nothing funny about it. You look like a fool—you can't talk, you can't close your mouth, and if you try to force it it hurts like hell. I went to his office. He looked totally alarmed, he didn't know what he was supposed to do. He tried closing my mouth gently but I'd already tried, that didn't work. He tried pulling forward, pushing back—nothing, and I was starting to get antsy, I could see myself already at the emergency room, general anesthesia, the whole bit, waking up with my jaw all laced up with metal wires, having to eat through a straw, I wanted to cry. And on top of it, I still felt like I had to yawn. He was sitting there next to me, I was stretched out like a jerk on his cot wondering how much longer we were going to stay like that before he'd decide to send me to a specialist, and all of a sudden he gets up without a word, he pulls a little book off the shelf and I hear him talking to himself, he's saying something like, "Okay, the jawbone fits into the skull this way, so, logically…"

He puts down the little book, he makes me get up off the cot and sit in one of those black padded chairs he has, and he puts on some gloves. I'm not feeling too confident, but he tells me, "Don't be scared," he sets his thumbs on my back molars, he presses gently downward, and clack! I feel it go back in place. Just like that. He looked totally amazed. As for me, I was pretty relieved. And happy.

It happened to me three or four more times before I decided to let the jaw specialist operate on my ligaments. Naturally, each time it happened I called Sachs, and I was in luck, he was always there, even on a Sunday the last time it got me. Each time, of course, it only took him a couple of seconds. He offered to teach my wife how to do it, but you know how it is, I'd rather have him. Either you've got the knack or you don't.

✻

I see you whenever I get a slight intestinal upset. It doesn't happen to me often and I'm well otherwise. I bike wherever I go, I garden, I go to the senior-center lunches, so it's fair to say things are pretty good. Even my son always says I look fine. Still, now and then I have some pain here, on the side, and I think maybe it's cancer and I go in to see you. One day the woman next door—who's younger than I am (she's only eighty-one), she'd never been to a doctor in her life—one day she started bleeding. You told her she'd have to have an examination. And then you sent her for an operation. And she came home, she told me, "It was an early cancer, he saw it right away, they took it out and that's that." So now, when I have a pain, I say to myself that if *I* had one you'd spot mine right away too. You check me over, you press exactly where it hurts and you tell me that it's not the colon, it's a big muscle that goes right behind it, it attaches in the back and goes through to the abdominal. I actually do often have trouble with my back, since I have to bend to garden and hoe—I never did enjoy doing it but it has to be done, otherwise nothing would grow. Every time, I ask you if you're absolutely certain it's nothing serious, that I'm not getting cancer, and you answer, "For next year I don't promise a thing, but right this minute I am certain that that's not cancer." That always makes me laugh. And you've never been wrong, because here I am still. Sometimes, when it hurts me too much, you give me medicine for two or three weeks. I take some for a few days and when I don't feel bad anymore I stop. You did tell me that I could start up again whenever it comes back, but I'd rather come in to see you, just in case a cancer does hit me—from one year to the next you can never tell.

When I went to put in my request at the abortion clinic, they told me a doctor would have to examine me. You're the one who saw me. You asked me the same questions as the nurse—the date of my last period, whether I took any medicines, whether I'd ever had the operation before. I was sick of it, I was answering in monosyllables. You put down your pencil and crossed your arms. You said, "It's a hard decision to make. Do you want to talk about it?" I didn't want to talk about it. I couldn't talk about it. I remember that that day my heart was icy, it hurt the way it does when you put bare fingers into snow, I felt detached and torn up at the same time.

You looked at the sheet, you saw that I had one child, and you asked if I had a boy or a girl. I said, "I have a girl—she's mixed-blood."

You tilted your head and said, "All children are mixed-blood."

That made me smile, I said, "Yes, genetically speaking, you're right…" and then you asked what work I did.

"I don't know if I should tell you. You'll laugh at me."

"Why?"

"I'm a night nurse. Pretty ridiculous, huh?"

"To be a night nurse?"

"No, to get caught like this. Nurses are supposed to know how to manage these things…"

You took off your watch, you brought it up to your ear to see if it was working, and after a minute you said, "Being a caregiver doesn't make a person immune."

❀

I never went to him. His office is a hundred yards from me and all my neighbors go to him, but I have my doubts, with everything that goes on these days. I've heard some things that aren't very Christian. Apparently at night, in his private office, he does abortions because he doesn't make enough of a living.

❀

Once when I was in training rotation at the Family Planning Clinic, I went along on a housecall. He asked a woman if she was having pain. She answered, "Yes, but it's bearable."

He went on: "On a scale from zero to ten, how much pain would you say?"

"Uuh… six or seven."

He went and got her a pill.

On the way back to the clinic he told me that all the women say, "It's bearable," and that many of them would refuse to take anything for the pain, claiming it wasn't that bad. So he had made it a practice to ask "how much." Over five, they never refused his pill.

❀

I had gotten into the habit of coming by at noon on Wednesdays to show you the kids—there was always some shot they needed, a checkup for school sports, a cold or a bump of some kind—and once in a while I'd take the occasion to discuss my painful periods or the knee that still hurts ever since my accident. Wednesdays by noon there's often nobody left in the waiting room. I found it more convenient. Sometimes we'd arrive just as you were getting ready to leave. I'd say, "I can come back this afternoon," but you'd say, "No, no, come on in, as long as I'm here."

One day coming through the courtyard I saw you standing in the waiting room, looking in my direction. I came in with the children. You smiled, you told them hello, you ushered us in. At the end of the visit, at the door, you said, "Are you aware that you almost always come to see me at exactly noon?"

I didn't like that. I never went to you again.

❀

When I went to him, I'd had stomach pain for months. They'd done every possible test without finding a thing. He hadn't been in practice very long. I said to myself, a young doctor probably knows a little more than the old fellows. The pains would hit me without warning, afternoon or morning, even while my husband and I were having intercourse. He told me it could possibly be psychological. I was ready to believe him, seeing how things weren't going so well with my husband. I went to see him twice a week for three or four months. He'd keep me an hour, sometimes two. My husband wasn't awfully pleased when I got home but obviously he couldn't say much. The doctor offered to see him too and he did go once or twice, but my stomach-aches weren't getting any better. He'd keep saying, "It's been going on a long time, it can't get better overnight." Myself, I thought it was getting to be pointless. One day I had enough of going in and reciting my life, and I cancelled the appointment. A few days later, when I went to the toilet, I found the explanation. I phoned him. When I told him what I'd found, there was a long silence, I thought the line had gone dead. He couldn't have been awfully proud of himself. Finally he said, "I'll come by and leave a prescription in your mailbox." Two pills fifteen days apart, and that was it! He didn't charge me for that—it's a good thing too, after all the useless sessions! Since then, I've never had stomach pain, but we don't go to him anymore, we have someone in Lavallée. That doctor's not young but he doesn't go looking for fancy problems. This one, when we meet in the street or at the bakery, he still waves hello, but I act as if I don't see him. I mean, it's his fault I suffered for so long. Psychological, my eye! It's really not very hard to treat somebody for tapeworm.

❋

I called the night my wife had her stroke. She was lying in bed with her breath rattling, she wasn't responding. I really thought she was about to die in my arms. You came right over. And it's far to here from Play. On the telephone, I had trouble explaining things to you, it was three in the morning and I was completely frantic. When you got here you saw that my wife was in a very bad way, her left arm and leg were all limp, her rale was getting louder. You said she had to be hospitalized and that's what I was afraid of. But there was nothing else to be done. You called the ambulance because I couldn't manage to dial the number, and you called the hospital to alert them we were coming. You stayed till the ambulance came, they must have taken almost an hour to get there. While we waited, you wrote a long letter. From time to time you went back to check her, you took her blood pressure, you listened to her heart, you spoke to her to see if she was responding. When the ambulance workers came you helped them take her down—the stairway is very steep. This used to be a barn, our son put in the upstairs room for us.

At the hospital they took good care of her. They put a drip in her, they gave her something to make her comfortable, but she'd had a brain hemorrhage and the life-support doctor told me it was very critical. She died the next day.

After the funeral, I went in to pay you for the housecall. I'd tried to do it that night as the ambulance pulled up, but you'd said "Let's do that later."

And then I asked if you'd take care of me from then on—not that I'm sick, but I have a little osteoarthritis and also my wife used to say I should have my blood pressure checked now and then but I didn't really want to bother a doctor just for that. You asked me if I had a regular doctor before, I said yes, the same one as my wife, but when I called him they'd given me your number because it was nighttime. So you asked me if I wouldn't rather keep on with him, but I said, "No, you know—you're the one who took care of my wife when she had her stroke, so it's only right it should be you."

❋

I won't have any more to do with him: the last time I went, he refused to prescribe my anti-cholesterol medication. He says it doesn't help and it's dangerous. But really, if medications did more harm than good the doctors wouldn't be prescribing them! He says cholesterol is less serious than my asthma and cigarettes. But

I'm not asking him to stop my smoking, I'm asking him to treat my cholesterol. The other day he said, "I don't treat cholesterol, I treat people, at your age you've got plenty of time to die of other things than cholesterol." I said, "Well, if that's the best you can offer me," and I left. Puh-lease! Who does he think he is? I know better than he does what I need, after all. Who's the patient here?

❋

Seven years ago, I came to see you because I was late and I was staining. You examined me, you found I had a little infection. You prescribed some antibiotics and a pregnancy test. I didn't see the sense, I didn't want to see the sense, but I did it anyway and it came out positive.

My husband was against having it. He'd always wanted a girl, and he was afraid it would be a third boy. I cried, not letting him see—I didn't want to saddle him with a child I was carrying by mistake, unless he wanted it. With my heart aching, I went back to get you to send me to the clinic. You were very young then. My story shook you. You didn't seem very much in favor of my having an abortion. You said that after all the odds were one in two that it would be a girl. You even said you'd be willing to meet with my husband and talk it over with him, but I told you I didn't want you to, that it wouldn't solve the problem, that it was complicated.

Finally, because I couldn't decide what to do, you eventually said Look, the pregnancy was just beginning, I had time to think about it before coming to a decision, I shouldn't act impulsively.

You were right. I did think about it and come to a decision. I told my husband that with the infection, it would be dangerous for me to abort. I knew he wouldn't go in to ask you any questions. He said all right, since that's how it is. And then he added, "And who knows, maybe it'll be a girl."

Manon will be seven next spring. My husband adores her and she adores him. Naturally, you're the one who vaccinates her and takes care of her since she was born. She's almost never sick but she loves you—she has the slightest little cold or scratch, my husband gets frantic, and she soothes him by saying, "We'll just go see Dr. Sachs."

One day last year, her father picked her up after school; she fell down and cut her elbow open. He got completely frantic. I was at work, so he couldn't reach me. Manon told him, "Don't be scared, Daddy, we'll go see Dr. Sachs and he'll fix it." He brought her over to you, he was very uncomfortable, of course—he wondered what you'd say—but he didn't have much choice. You didn't ask any questions. You took care of Manon, she wasn't a bit scared and she told me afterwards that she hadn't felt a thing. Later, her father told me how, when you saw him turning green at the sight of you preparing your instruments, you suggested he come hold Manon's hand. That made him feel much better.

Now, when Manon is sick, it sometimes happens that it's her father who brings her in to you. You still don't ask any questions, and I know you'll never say a thing to anyone. Even so, some day my husband will learn the truth. It might be Manon who tells him. She's young still, but she doesn't like lying. Since my husband adores her and he's a good man, it's probably better that it come from her. Yesterday when she and I were alone in the car, she said, "It's so nice, having two daddies!" Someday, it's sure to slip out of her.

❄

I remember that last year a friend came to see us with a distant cousin of his, a doctor. My husband was furious with doctors at the time. He began talking about his recent hospital stay, saying he'd lost forty-five pounds but with all their tests they hadn't been able to find anything wrong with him. The young doctor began snickering and declaring in this cocky tone that nobody just loses forty-five pounds, that my husband must certainly have something wrong, that the people at that hospital were just incompetent, and he offered to call back later with the address of someone good, someone we could go see using his name, who would doubtless figure out what he had. I wished he would choke.

As he was leaving, he came to tell me goodbye while my husband was talking with our friend. I murmured, "He has an inoperable tumor and he doesn't know it." He went white. He never called back.

CLINICAL EXAMINATION

(Monday, November 18)

By way of poetic justice,
the doctor dropped
onto his chair sighing,
"My patients are killing me."

Sacha Guitry

37

A NIGHT CALL

I hang up, I rub my eyes. I shouldn't have eaten that pizza, I still feel it sitting in my stomach. Well, at least I'm not the one who has to go out, and this call doesn't sound like much fun, either.

I dial your number. I wait.

It rings. Once. Twice. Someone picks up.

"Hello?..."

"Yes, doctor, I'm awfully sorry to wake you—this is the service, Operator 24. I have a call for you."

I hear you bumbling around at the other end. You sigh, you're probably rubbing your eyes. "Mmmhh... Okay, go ahead."

"It's a baby who's running a fever and keeps crying..."

"Really? His mother didn't drown him—I mean immerse him in a cool bath?"

"Uhh—I don't know. Maybe she has no bathtub. Shall I give you the address?"

"Yeah. Wait, I need a pencil... Is he very bad?"

"He didn't sound as bad as his mother, he was babbling in the background while she was on the phone with me. He had 100 all day, but it was 104 tonight when she got up to cover him."

"Cover him? With a fever?"

"I'm just telling you what she said... I asked her if you could ring her back, but she insists on a housecall. Unfortunately, it's at Sainte-Sophie-sur-Tourmente."

"I see. I was wondering if I could get out of it... Go ahead, I'm taking it down."

I give you the address, some little place with a flowery name miles from your house. I was conscientious about taking down the directions the woman gave me, but I looked on the military map you had me buy the first day you signed up with our service. Sainte-Sophie is one of the most out-of-the-way villages in the district, in the opposite direction from your usual area. The house is hidden in a network of little streets not always clearly marked. I describe the most practical way for you to get there—a compromise between what I see on the map and what I was told by the person who lives there.

"Fine, well, I'll go on over. If you get anything else between now and then, catch me—don't let me go back to bed."

"No, of course not. So long, Doctor."

You hang up. I'm glad I'm not in your shoes.

❋

I'm not sleepy anymore, that call completely woke me up. I look at the battery of phones and answering machines that cover the counter. I have only two lines plugged in tonight, yours and one for a colleague of yours a few miles away in the next district. He's got a wife, but he routes his calls through us when he's on duty, so that she can go off for the weekend with their children. I suspect he's very happy to be rid of her: he's much more relaxed when she's away.

I enjoy working with you. You often have very funny stories. And you don't treat me like shit, the way most of your colleagues do. You're fairly talkative. You comment on things, you explain. That calms me down—I don't always have the appropriate reflexes for answering the phones. I must say, people do call for any old thing, especially at night. They think I'm your wife or your secretary, they tell me their life stories, and I have to struggle to drag out the reason they're calling, the exact address and the telephone number (sometimes you phone them back, you advise them to take this or that remedy they've got in their medicine chest, you reassure them and avoid going out. Other times, you're still half asleep and you take down my directions wrong, you go right instead of left, you lose your way, you wind up miles from your destination and you call me again to read back what I've got written down. At worst, you call up the patient and ask them to direct you, but they still greet you with, "You had an easy time finding us?" Luckily, it doesn't always go like that story you told me a while back, one Sunday when neither of us had much to do. I was asking you if it was awfully hard looking for houses off by themselves in the dark, and you told me how one winter night you were covering in an area you didn't know at all, and someone wakes you up, it was a stroke or a heart attack or a hemorrhage, anyhow something serious way out in the middle of nowhere, they give you some vague directions in a huge panic, you get them down as best you can, you jump into your car, you take off and of course, since it's pitch dark out, you lose your way in a bunch of little roads. You go around in circles, you're swearing, you're furious, and there's not a sign anywhere to help you out. Finally, you see a light, a stable, a woman coming out with a bucket in her hand, she and her husband are milking the cows, it's five in the morning. You ask the woman for Monsieur Bailly's house, in a place called "La Bulle."

The woman looks at you puzzled. "Oh, that's not in these parts! No, it's not around here."

She calls her husband, she asks him, he rubs his chin and shaking his head very perturbed, he says, "Oh, no, not around here. And to get there from here…!"

They have no phone, so you figure you'll have to set off again blindly, but the man points the way.

"You turn around, go back. After a mile, you'll see a crossing. You stay straight on. Another mile and a half along there's a fork, you take the left, then again the first left and go another half mile maximum. There you make a hairpin turn and just as you leave it you'll see a little track going off to the right, be sure not to take that, you keep on till you get to the stone cross. Just after the cross, you turn left on a road that runs down a hill and at the bottom you take the right. After two hundred yards you'll see a little lane. La Bulle's down there, there's a sign but it faces the other way, you don't see it till you've gone past it. The house is way at the end there." And it actually was!) and when it's something I know about and they're willing to listen to me, I give them bits of advice, like "Have him suck some ice cubes, that helps with vomiting…" or "If you have aspirin give some to your husband while you're waiting for the doctor…" and if I really hear panic sweating out of the receiver, I tell them that I'll let you know and you'll be right along.

You often told me that at night it's almost always the same thing, the same anxieties, the same refrain over and over—women worried because a child has a fever or diarrhea or is vomiting or crying, men having trouble breathing all of a sudden for no obvious reason—and I get the feeling it makes you angry when I report that kind of call, that you're controlling yourself, because your groggy voice spits out acid: "Did you tell him that in the time it takes me to get there she'll be dead already?" or "Fine, so her husband's crying. What does she want me to do— spank him and put him to bed?"

The strangest thing is that when you get home (you often call in when you're back, to see if any other calls have come in meanwhile) you seem odd, as if your anger had dropped away in the course of the trip, in the course of seeing that the kid who was coughing or shitting or shivering is a lot better, but that the mother— the mother's got loads to tell and that she's getting even with her husband for the great old time he had with his pals the night before, leaving her stuck at home with the kid (You'll see, you bastard, you'll pay for that, you can shove your big nights, cause if you think come Sunday night you're gonna get laid you got anoth- er think coming you can bet on that), or that the guy who can't breathe is no asth- matic or emphysematic (those people know they are, they know their sickness like the back of their hand and they'll tell you what's up right away), he's just a pathetic little twerp hitched to a ball-breaker old lady who's been hollering at him all after- noon for some clumsy move he put on a sister-in-law of a cousin-by-marriage at the wedding banquet they got home from late that morning (You'll see, you bitch, you wanna ruin my Sunday night movie with your stupid screaming—just watch, you'll pay for that. You know my palpitations? that I used to get when I was smoking two packs a day, my heart would beat like crazy and you were scared I'd die in the night, remember? Well, they're back!) anyhow, to make it short, nights you see a lot of getting even.

You—when I wake you up, you say They'll pay for this! and you swear you're going to charge them extra for Nonessential Trip at Patient's Insistence. But then when you get home you're heartbroken, nearly destroyed, miserable at having witnessed so much emotional misery, so many stifled hatreds, so many accumulated misunderstandings.

Sometimes, too often for my taste—and for yours, I imagine—it's the real thing, blood and drama and horror,

the car crash with five people in the little red GT (people say that when he's got a girl in the passenger seat, a young guy with a brand-new license tends to lift his glass a little less and his accelerator foot a little more, but that's not always true) and of the five you find four badly bashed-up and one dead, the driver's girlfriend hit the pylon when they missed the turn,

the hemorrhage from the uterus with an inoperable cancer, here she was thinking she could die peacefully at home but now she's got to go back in,

the sudden infant death.

And then there are the nuts the rejects the not-all-there, the crazy ladies with chronic constipation who call at midnight for someone to come write a prescription for laxative "at home" and if possible to come in the back door so as not to wake up the husband, the violent cases from the "barracks" (a kind of bunker-apartment house in Saint-Jacques, the dormitory development for the spare-parts factory, every weekend you get three or four calls from down there) who beat up their wives and wave a gun at the neighbor who's come over to try to calm things down, whose own wife calls the constables who get you over there because sure, they may be the state police power, the arm of the law, the sword of justice, but they've got wives and kids and when there's a disturbed individual they'd just as soon ask a doctor to stick a shot of Valium into his butt before they go packing him into the van... When I asked you if it wasn't a little scary you said yes but that practically every time, the gun wasn't loaded because the guy was so drunk he couldn't find the cartridges.

And then there are the anxiety cases terrified of spending another night alone with themselves I've got no parents anymore no friends anymore my children have left home my neighbors are away on vacation I have to talk to someone or I'll go off my rocker

the hysterics having their weekly crisis

the teenagers flipping out

the inconsiderate ones who coolly phone in for an extension on their sick leave, Yes I know it's eleven o'clock at night but tomorrow's Monday and Monday mornings you can never get in to see a doctor, they're just too busy.

And now and then, there are people who you have the feeling (you tell me when that happens, calling in afterwards, you're tired but a little excited, almost joyful: I'm not sorry I went out there, that's someone who I really have the feeling) you've helped, a little old man who fell out of his bed and you managed to calm everyone down so they don't pack him off to the hospital, a youngster who smashed his face on his bike in the middle of the night and who you sewed back together, a pregnant woman sick with bronchitis who was worried about losing the pregnancy from coughing, a traveling salesman who was supposed to hit the road at five a.m. and got hit with a terrible toothache, a prodigal son who starts up his old asthma attacks again whenever he comes to visit his parents—it's very damp around here—and who mindlessly forgot his vaporizer back at his own house where the weather is warm and dry and this never happens to him, a woman who didn't want them to bother you but her neighbor insisted because she thought the woman was really in poor shape, whom you found sitting up in her bed with a cup of herb tea in hand, and who said apologetically, "I'm so sorry to have bothered you," beside whom you sat down to talk a little and, when you left, you only took her blood pressure but, there at the other end of the line, as you mention her without saying what she confided, I hear you on the verge of sobs.

And then there are the others, the ones nobody can do anything more for—those who just died, suddenly or after a long illness, in their courtyard or on their beds; the old folks, the youngsters, the middleaged ones, the widowers, the popular beloved ones, the down-and-out, the suicides…

I shiver, I yawn, I warm up some coffee. I open all the drawers looking for a book or a magazine the daytime operators here might have left behind. I find a paperback, I read a few pages but very soon I'm drowsing, I slump down, and feeling my head droop, I stretch out, you know it's not worth ringing me, if I get other calls I'll phone you, if it's at seven-thirty in the morning for a housecall sometime before noon, the way it often happens around here, I'll note it down and let you sleep as long as possible besides now it's Monday morning three a.m., in theory things should be fairly qui—*shit shit shit the telephone's ringing!*

CLINICAL EXAMINATION (MONDAY, NOVEMBER 18)

38

MONSIEUR AND MADAME DESHOULIÈRES

The telephone rings. I go out into the hallway.

"Doctor, it's for you—your office…"

You look up, you sigh. "Thank you."

You stand up to answer. Meanwhile, I glance into the bedroom. The ring hasn't wakened my wife.

On the kitchen table are the prescription slip you were writing out, your blood-pressure apparatus, the flashlight and the reflex mallet, the teaspoon I set out for you but you haven't used, the containers of the medicines my wife's been taking till now. I hear you answering in monosyllables, then hanging up. I finish pouring water over the coffee filter. You come into the kitchen, you sit back down.

"Do you have another housecall to make now?"

"No, they were calling with a bloodtest result…"

"Can I give you a cup of coffee?"

You stop writing, you rub your eyes, you lift off your glasses. "Mmmhh. That's awfully kind. I must have slept three hours since Saturday. I'll need coffee if I want to work properly today."

"I'm so sorry to have made you come…"

"I'd said you could phone me at home."

"But if I'd known you were on call as well…"

"If you'd known that, your wife would have told you that she could wait even longer."

"That's true—and that wouldn't have been good for her. Now, at least, she'll be able to sleep."

I put a cup in front of you, I pour the coffee into it, you take two sugars from the box, you stir with the spoon, you lay it back down, you write.

You're leaning over your prescription pad. You hair is a bit too long, a bit dirty. Your shirt collar is very worn, your leather jacket looks as old as I am and I'm not so young anymore, your cheeks are grey with whiskers—the least one could say is that you don't look very tidy. But it's been a hard night.

My wife likes you a lot. Many times, she's said she would have liked a son like you. But when we got married that was no longer possible. I already had children myself, but for us together it was too late. I thought we would have a good life anyhow; when you reach retirement you think you'll turn it to good use, indulge yourself a little, travel, fix up the house the way you always meant to but never had the time for—and then boom, sickness hits her without the slightest warning. Here I am, ten years older than she is, I thought I'd be going first, they always say men live less long than women, that women have more resistance, and then no.

I pour myself a cup of coffee and sit down with you.

"Before my wife got sick, I didn't know this sort of disease even existed."

You nod. "There are more kinds of disease than all the doctors put together will ever know."

"Is that true? But with so much scientific progress…"

"Sure, there *is* progress, but not always in the areas where it's needed."

"And about her sickness—what do they know?"

You stop writing, you stir the spoon in your cup. You look at me over the tops of your glasses. "They know how it evolves. They know pretty much how to relieve the symptoms. But they don't know how to cure it."

"No, of course, I wasn't expecting to see it cured, neither was she. Doctor Jardin… In fact, that's why we came to see you in the first place. With him, after a few months—it's true we'd called him in quite often, but she was suffering so much and she was having such trouble doing the least thing, I came to the point where I didn't know what to do. I'm not a doctor and besides I'm seventy-two years old, after all—anyhow, one day we didn't ask him to come out here, my wife wanted me to take her in to see him, even though it was torture just to walk her from the car into his office. We waited an hour and a quarter in the waiting room because, you know, Doctor Jardin always books two or three appointments for the same slot, so it's always crowded. When he called us in, she sat down and she started to cry, I'd never seen her cry like that, and she said, "Doctor, I can't stand it anymore, it's too painful, I've had enough, my husband is exhausted, do something!" And Doctor Jardin looked at her, he looked at me, he raised his arms to heaven and he said, "Madame Deshoulières, there's nothing more I can do for you!" And he went and sat down behind his desk. And that—that said it all!"

You look at me uncomprehending.

"You've never been to his office?" I ask.

"No…"

"It's not like yours—it's minuscule, people are always standing around the waiting room because there are only four chairs, and not even a couple of blocks for the children to play with, whereas at yours I saw there was a whole corner just for them—I mentioned that to my granddaughter when I told her she could bring her children to you; when there's nothing for kids to do you can't keep them in line—and then inside Doctor Jardin's consulting room it's tiny too. There's an examining table, but it's far too high for older people like us, so he only does a partial examination, with us sitting on the chair. We take off just our tops, if that. Sometimes he doesn't even have us roll up our sleeves when he takes our blood pressure. My wife, for instance—he never took the trouble to examine her the way you do each time, and besides even if he'd wanted to, she couldn't have climbed up on the table, I can just about manage it myself, a patient's not properly set up at all because the table's jammed into a corner between the door and the window. And you're always sitting there doubled over, because the end of the table is always folded up, otherwise he couldn't open the door! But the worst part is his desk. In fact it's not even a desk, just a narrow wooden countertop, tall, like the ones they used to have in old-time pharmacies, you know what I mean? they're not made for sitting at, they're for standing behind, the pharmacist would set the medications on the upper ledge and file his papers or his money on the shelves behind it."

"I see…"

"It's a handsome piece, of course, and since the space isn't large, he chose to use that instead of a desk because otherwise, with the examining table, the file cabinet, and the two chairs for the patients, there'd be no room to move. But do you think he'd ever set his pulpit back against the wall, in the corner? That would take up less space, and then besides, you'd be able to see him! But no! He set his counter facing the chairs, and when he'd get down behind it to write a prescription or to answer the phone, you couldn't see him at all, it was as if he weren't in the room! Sometimes when he stayed on the phone a long time, I'd feel like knocking on the counter and shouting, 'Halloo! Anyone in?'"

You start laughing. "You should have done it!"

"What good would it do? I say that not because he's a doctor and I was a butcher; I'm still twenty years older than he is, and to me he was a whippersnapper… But my wife wouldn't have liked it. Well, the last time we went there, he was down behind his desk like that, you couldn't see him at all, we were wondering what he was up to back there. Then my wife made a terrific effort, she pulled herself up and, as I was getting to my feet to help her, she said, 'Pay the doctor. We're leaving.' She wouldn't let him make out a Social Security form for her because she felt it would be cheating people who've sweated blood and paid into the system for forty years; she said 'Goodbye, Doctor,' and we left. And then, as we got to the car, she told me a friend had spoken well of you and as long as we were out anyhow she'd rather go to see you than go straight home."

"So the first time you came to see me she'd been sitting for an hour and a half at Doctor Jardin's office, and then another hour in my waiting room?"

"Yes. But you know, we had no sense of that hour going by. My wife was—I don't know how to say it—she was *better*, it was as though she felt relieved. In the waiting room she said, 'We should have changed doctors a long time ago, he had no interest in my case, it was too much work for almost no pay. But nobody has the right to treat people that way,' and I said, 'Still, how do you know this one is any good?' and she said, 'It doesn't matter, he can't be worse!' And what's more, when we got there your waiting room was full but everybody had a seat, and two young people got up to give us theirs. At Doctor Jardin's, that would never have happened—that day two elderly people I knew slightly had given us their seats. They would have been ashamed to leave us standing, my wife and me, but since they were tired—as tired as we were—they left. If I'd known, I wouldn't have let them give up their turns like that... In your waiting room, there were children playing quietly in the corner with stuffed animals, it was pleasant, there was sun, the windows were open, the cherry tree was blooming—is that yours?"

"No, unfortunately."

"...And then, when you came out of your consulting room, the way you said goodbye to the person who was leaving, and then hello to the one who got up, and the way you greeted us, when we'd never been there before..."

You shrug your shoulders, as if to say that's pretty small potatoes.

"It's not big, Doctor, but it's a lot, because not all doctors are like you. The other day on the avenue when you went by in your car, you waved to me. It was the first time in my life a doctor had waved to me. It's a small thing, but it says everything... Mainly, though, I wanted to tell you—I don't know how things are going to turn out, I can see very well that my wife is worse, that she's suffering more and more. It's sad, because there are people who'd like to come see her and talk with her, but now that's not possible any longer; I stuff her with painkillers and she sleeps all the time, so I offer them a cup of coffee and they talk with me instead, but it's not the same thing. I'm not stupid, I've seen people die, I certainly expect she hasn't much time left, but I wanted to tell you—The day we went to see you for the first time, when we came in to your consulting room and you helped her sit down, you remember? My wife said, 'I've come to you because Doctor Jardin said there was nothing more he could do for me.' And we both saw that you were shocked. You answered—I'll remember it the rest of my life—'*Whatever the trouble is, there's always* something *we can do*,' and when we left, you'd kept us for a long time and yet she felt better. She walked to the car without my help, and for two weeks—I'd never seen her like that since the beginning of her sickness— she took heart. She would get up in the morning, she was in less pain, she even cooked several times, and I believed it, you know? and so did she. Now I know it was mainly that you had lifted our spirits without telling us lies, without promising she'd get better...

"I know she's going to die, she says so too and she isn't even angry, she's the one comforting me—she says we just have to blame it on bad luck, she tells me

CLINICAL EXAMINATION (MONDAY, NOVEMBER 18)

I'm still healthy and I'll be able to marry again. Of course, I couldn't. Not after living through all this with her. But even though I know she's going to pass on… not that I want that, but it's unbearable watching her suffer so… I wanted to tell you that those two weeks—two weeks isn't a lot when you've suffered every minute for three years—but she's always been grateful to you for those two weeks. And so have I."

And then it catches me by surprise, and I'm annoyed with myself because I never do this—but I start crying like a little boy, and I can't any longer see a thing, or hear a thing, or feel a thing except the tears on my cheeks, the sobs that rack me, and your hand on my arm.

39

MADAME LEBLANC

The telephone rings. I drop the sheet onto the cot and reach for the telephone. I pick up:

"Doctor's office..."

"Hello—Edmond? Is that you, Edmond?"

"Oh no, Madame, you must have made a mistake, you've reached the doctor's office in Play..."

She hangs up. She does this regularly. I think it must be an old woman who doesn't see too well anymore, she doesn't manage to punch the right buttons, or maybe she still has an old dial phone that's gotten arthritic with age. I've tried to talk to her and set her straight, but she always hangs right up. She always phones around ten-thirty, eleven o'clock—must be for her son, or a brother, with that old-fashioned name. It's not even certain that they live in the area. To judge by her accent, she's not from this district... Old people don't like the telephone, they feel that every call costs a lot so they talk very fast with no pauses, they have trouble understanding what you tell them and trouble holding a conversation, as if they needed to have the other speaker right in front of them to be sure that what they're saying is actually understood and that what they've understood is actually what was said to them. They have trouble responding to questions, they have trouble giving road directions, they have trouble speaking into a void. For them, the telephone is a test. And the answering machine you switch on from Saturday noon till Monday morning—it's a torture. The darn thing talks and talks, it just keeps talking. It goes too fast, and whatever it says is useless (The doctor's office is closed until Monday morning at 8) or incomprehensible (In case of emergency Saturday or Sunday, please call Doctor Pasini in Saint-Bernard-d'Orée, at 2-4-5...) because even when you speak slowly and enunciate, it's too fast: the doctor's name, the name of the town, the telephone number—it's so long, it's impossible to remember, even if you repeat it—especially since they never think to have paper and pencil in hand because they were expecting to talk to you directly. For some of them it's even more complicated, like Madame Bellisario, over in Marquay. She's nearly deaf. Her husband was very frail, and whenever he had a bad spell she had to phone for a housecall. Since she couldn't tell what she was hearing—it might be a live person or the answering machine—as soon as she heard the sound of a voice she would give her name and her telephone number, she'd repeat it twice very slowly and she'd ask to be called back. If within five minutes no one had rung her, she'd do it again. And if she still didn't get a callback, she'd phone some other doctor and start her routine… Her husband died in the space of a few days, he had a blocked artery in his thigh, they have a daughter-in-law who works in the bank in Saint-Jacques who told me. At the hospital, they wanted to amputate because gangrene was setting in, but you were opposed. At the time, his daughter-in-law was mad at you for saying no, she even called you to complain, but you explained to her that he was going to die anyhow, that the operation would just make him suffer for nothing, whereas he could be made comfortable without cutting off his leg. I wouldn't have wanted to be in your shoes, having to decide like that what should be done, and against the doctors at the hospital besides. It's true that generally doctors do decide things, without explaining why, without considering what the patient or the family is feeling… Like with me when I lost my job. Whenever I went into the agency to look for work, I'd get the hiccups. Terrible hiccups. Once it started it wouldn't stop. Over the months, it got worse. It hit me whenever I went into town, in the stores, in the street, in the parking lot. The slightest incident—some irritation, some upset, it must have affected my nerves—it would start up again. The doctor I saw at the time—and he was a big specialist, too—told me that the only solution would be to operate, to cut the nerve in the diaphragm or something like that, and to me that seemed pretty drastic. There must be something they can do for hiccups without needing to cut! Eventually I was getting hiccups every time I was a little upset or on edge—at home, at my in-laws, and even at the school when I'd go in to see my son's teacher. They're terrible, hiccups—they start without warning and just don't let go, like the torture I saw once in a movie, where a prisoner was tied up under a faucet and a drop of water would fall on his head regularly every four or five seconds, and that incessant tapping on the top of his skull wound up driving him insane. The hiccups are just like that, they jolt your whole body, they disturb your breathing, you feel icy and you're so afraid they'll come back that you're always waiting, you hold yourself ready for the next jolt, like for an earthquake, except that this is inside you. And you can't do anything anymore—what can you do when you've got the hiccups with no letup?

It got so I couldn't cook, couldn't iron, couldn't sew in peace. If it came over me while I was reading a story to my children, I'd have to call my husband to come finish the book. If it happened on the telephone, I would have to hang up. I was in tears about it, I just couldn't stand it.

When I started working here in the office, like a miracle it eased up. I would still get hiccups from time to time, but much less often. That made me think that it might have something to do with being laid off, and the fact that I hadn't found another job. After a few months, I was worried that you might have to close for lack of patients, things weren't going well, and I started having hiccups again. One day, my husband said, "Listen, you work for a doctor, and you've never talked to him about your problem!" I didn't want to bother you, of course. But finally, one morning, I had an attack as I was getting out of bed, so right then I decided, and I went off to open the office. It was a Saturday, I don't work that day but I do open the waiting room on my way home from picking up bread, that way the patients can go inside even if you're late, and you don't have to drive into Play just to open up if you're heading out from home on a call, say, to Sainte-Sophie. Things were quiet and there was no one there yet, so I sat down in the waiting room. And then I started to think what I was going to tell you, it seemed ridiculous being a doctor's secretary and never raising the question (of course it sometimes happened that you'd send me home with medicine when I had bronchitis or a cold; still, everyone catches those, but my hiccups I wouldn't wish on anyone) and I thought you'd tease me, in a nice way (You certainly know how to tease when you want to, for example when I mention medical programs I've seen on television. My husband and I always watch those, but you say they exaggerate, that life isn't like that), but when you came in and saw me sitting in the waiting room along with three other people, you didn't say anything, you saw something was really wrong. You acted as if I was just a patient like anyone else, you greeted us all and went on in to your study. When you came back out, I stood up because I'd been the first one there. Madame Renard came in just after me—it made me smile to go before her. Usually, when she doesn't get there first, she manages to start a conversation with her neighbor ("Ohnomygod, I'm in such pain! Have you ever seen anybody in such pain?") and convince the person to let her have his turn—somehow he's always the first one in line, I don't know how she manages to spot who that is, but she always does! Anyhow, that time she didn't dare, for once.

You had me take a seat inside. You sat across from me, you looked concerned, and you said, "What's wrong, Madame Leblanc?"

"Oh, it's nothing serious, Doc—(sorry!)—tor!"

I put my hand beneath my neck, to catch my breath, I tried to swallow my saliva. When you saw me like that, on the verge of tears, you laid your hand on my arm and you said, "Take your time... "

"Yes but (sorry!)—there are people waiting..."

"Today you're my patient, so it's not your concern."

"You (sorry!—oh, my!) you know, I've had this a long time and I've never (sorry!) had a chance to discuss it with you but you see, ever since I lost my job, I mean (sorry!) mean my job before this, at the factory, I've been getting (sorry!) the

CLINICAL EXAMINATION (MONDAY, NOVEMBER 18)

hiccups, you see, exactly like this, in the beginning it was only when I would go (sorry!) to the agency to find work, but later it began to come on me all the time and I tried everything, I saw every doctor in the (sorry!) district and I even went to a neurologist at the hospital, Doctor D'Or—(sorry!)—"

"D'Ormesson?"

"Yes. But nothing helped, and I was really desperate because it was happening at night too. I tried (sorry!) to go sleep on the couch but my husband didn't want that, he wanted me to stay (sorry!) with him, but he'd go whole nights without sleeping. And of course, you can un—(sorry!)—derstand it's not easy to have intimate relations when you've got (sorry!) hiccups like this..."

"Yes..."

"When you hired me (sorry!), I felt better (sorry!) right away, I stopped getting hiccups so often, I was able to go out again, I could go into town, see my parents, have friends over, because you can imagine, I was ashamed not to be able to do things... without being jolted that way at any moment. You know, it's torture when you try to put on makeup and it comes and jolts you without warning, you stick mascara in your eye and I won't even talk about lipstick... Yes, it makes you laugh (You'd started laughing, and I was laughing too) but when it happens every day twenty-four hours a day for weeks at a time..."

I suddenly realized that my hiccupping had stopped. When it stops short, it's almost painful.

"It's quieted down," you said.

"Yes... It's mostly when I'm upset that it comes on. You know me—it's nearly ten months now I've been working with you—I'm a bit of a maniac around the edges, when things don't go the way I want them to I'm not happy. These days, I don't know why, it's started up again, so my husband said I should come in and talk to you about it. And I thought, it's true—I've been to every doctor in the area and several at the hospital, and I never discussed it with Doctor Sachs. But waiting here for you and seeing people come in after me—that upset me. I didn't realize you had so many patients on Saturdays..."

"It's not like this every Saturday."

"Yes, but still, next time I'll make an appointment."

"Certainly not! The next time you need to see me, I'll come into the office earlier, and that'll do it. Besides, I'm glad you came. I've been wanting for a while now to ask you if you were happy working here."

Of course I was happy, I was very happy.

We talked for a few minutes about the office and then you asked me about my hiccups. In the end you said you agreed with me: I wasn't sick, it had to do with my anxiety, actually it was a way of reacting. You prescribed something for me, but not to stop the hiccups—to prevent them.

On the prescription slip, I read:

As preventive, take with a large glass of water one capsule containing:
   Galactose 4mg
   Sucrose 3mg
   Fructose 2mg
   Lactose 1mg
   40 capsules 10mg each

The pharmacist made it up for me in green capsules. Little by little, my hiccups stopped bothering me. For a few weeks, I took a capsule before going into town, and that went well. And then gradually I'd forget to take them, but the hiccups didn't come back, and when they did, they didn't last for hours, as they had. After three or four months, they'd completely disappeared.

I kept the prescription, I've even kept the leftover capsules, just in case. But since I've been working at the office, listening to people talk about their little problems and the way you treat them, I've come to understand that the capsules aren't the most important thing. It's the thought of taking them that calmed me down. It's not what they had in them that did me good, but what they represented. In any case, it worked. If the problem started up again, I'm sure they'd would work again too. Of course, it doesn't happen that way for everyone. With Madame Renard, for instance, I think it wouldn't work as well. But her condition is worse than mine.

❀

The round wall-clock shows 10:05. The phone hasn't stopped ringing since I came in. I put the examining room in order, changed the sheets, cleaned the instruments, and put the containers into the autoclave for sterilizing, tossed two white coats into the laundry basket, vacuumed the consulting room and the waiting room and, after ironing the two sheets I washed on Sunday, I tidy up the medication bag you dropped off on your way home to lunch, shower, and shave.

You had practically no sleep all last night. When I saw how the telephone kept ringing this morning, I thought you wouldn't have any peace all day, but the calls were mainly to arrange appointments. So far, the only housecall you're supposed to make is to Madame Destouches, to renew her medications and make out her vouchers, and probably look in on her son. Two women were talking in front of the bakery and I heard them say that Georges Destouches had been hospitalized overnight.

I was never much of a chatterbox, but since I work here I talk even less. At the beginning, I thought people would ask me lots of questions, but actually, they don't much. They do ask me—especially at the grocery or the bakery, because that's where I run into them—whether you're in, whether you can come by sometime in the day, whether you're very busy. Generally I answer, "Of course," to the

CLINICAL EXAMINATION (MONDAY, NOVEMBER 18)

first question, "Certainly, but you should call the office later, I don't have the appointment book with me," to the second, and "Yes, but he still makes time to see new patients," to the third. I don't want people to think you're as overloaded as your colleagues. Those doctors, when you ask for a housecall, they never come before the next day.

In the black medication bag I check to see that the plastic cases have enough disposable syringes, needles, suture thread, scalpel blades. I replace medication packages that are empty or partly-used with full ones, so you never run out. The bag also contains gauze compresses, rolls of adhesive, scissors, different-size latex tubes for bandaging fingers, sterile gloves, disinfectant materials, a sealed tin for disposing of used needles, and a kind of transparent plastic bottle with holes at each end for giving asthmatics their inhalants.

You see a lot of asthma patients. It *is* awfully damp in these parts, because of the Tourmente. People rent little gardens along the river and then they build sheds, which over the years they turn into cabins and then regular little houses, and after ten or fifteen years they're coming to spend every August there with their children and grandchildren. Sometimes they lend or rent them to young couples hoping to find a permanent house, but the winter's not very healthy, and nights you get calls for (and I hear you grumbling in the morning about mindless people who bed down their) babies coughing in badly heated rooms with mold on the walls.

I check the box of morphine. There are only two vials left. On your appointment book I put a reminder to get more at the pharmacy.

You use a lot of morphine. And also aspirin, analgesics, tranquilizers. People are in often in pain at night. Or they're frightened. During the day, it's different. When I started working for you, I made myself a memorandum of advice to give in emergencies. I didn't want to make any stupid mistakes. But one day you told me:

"Emergencies are one of two things. Either the person is dead already when the doctor gets there, or else he's not on the verge of dying, and there's plenty of time to give him first aid and send him to Tourmens by ambulance—eight miles isn't so far."

I was surprised, actually. I said urgent calls did sometimes come in at night—people who'd fallen down, somebody needing stitches. Asthma attacks.

"Yes, but they're no more urgent than the same things during the day. What makes them 'emergency' is the anxiety, the pain, the fear of dying or of seeing someone die. At night, all of that is worse. Real emergencies, where saving lives does call for speed because time is crucial—those're mostly accidents."

That reminds me of the call I got once at noon at my house, one summer—a farmer was pinned under his tractor...

The telephone rings.

※

"Doctor's office, Play—can I help you?"

"Hello, Madame, this is the supervisor at the Family Planning unit. May I speak to Doctor Sachs?"

"I'm sorry, the doctor is at home—he was on call last night. Do you want his personal number?"

"Thank you, I have it, but I won't trouble him. Could you just remind him that he made an appointment for one o'clock today?"

"Oh really? He's supposed to go to the hospital?"

"Yes, to see a woman who couldn't come at any other time. Since it's not his usual schedule, he asked me to remind him. Shall I give you her name?"

"Yes… All right, I've got that. Goodbye, Madame."

Hanging up, I think how you're not going to be too pleased. Monday afternoons, your office hours are always jammed, and if on top of that you've got to go over to the hospital between one and two—!

On the appointment book I write, "1 p.m. appt. Hosp. (Madame Kasser)."

40

MADAME DESTOUCHES

Through the window, I see your car parking on the square. You step out, you close the door, you open the trunk and take out your black bag. You close the trunk. You move a few steps in our direction, you stop abruptly. You look at what you're holding—it's not your black bag, but a leather briefcase. You shake your head left to right, you retrace your steps, open the trunk, put the briefcase inside and pull out your doctor's bag.

"Madame Barbey, the doctor's here!"

My home aide's voice sounds from the bedroom. "Ah, just in time, Georges is waking up. He won't let me undress him!"

"Leave it then, the doctor will take care of it."

"Yes, because I mean, it must be three weeks since he changed his socks, so you can imagine what the rest is like."

You knock and come in. "Hello Madame Destouches."

"Hello, Doctor. We were expecting you…"

I pull back my walker so you can get into the kitchen. You wait while I go, with difficulty, to sit down in my armchair, then you pull up the stool, you set down your bag, and you take a seat.

"So, how did the night go?"

I sigh and shake my head. "Well, not too bad at first, but he started to get restless around six-thirty, he was shouting in his sleep. I'd only gotten to sleep at dawn myself, and he woke me up. I'm sick of this, you know. And on top of it we gave you trouble last night…"

"That's what I was there for, on call. He had a gash on his forehead; they were right to bring him in so I could stitch it up."

"I just had a feeling something had happened to him, so I called my daughter to go look for him. Her husband wasn't too pleased, of course, but after all it *is* his brother-in-law. Georges never goes out at night usually and then all of a sudden he decides to go visit some… some fellow who lives on the Entre road. The man's a little simpleminded, so he gets along well with Georges. But Friday, Georges collected his disability benefit, and I know that when he left the post office he stopped at the store to get some wine. I won't have that here—before, he used to hide his bottles in my husband's old workshed, but Madame Barbey makes the rounds and brings me anything she finds, so he's got to go hide it somewhere else. And since his… pal—you know, the fellow I mentioned—lives along the way…"

"… he dropped in on him last night…"

"Yes, that's it. But he knows I worry when he doesn't come home, because he'll just set out, no matter what condition he's in, no matter what the weather's like, he just starts walking along the highway, it's a good two, three miles after all, and his arm hurts him. And then in the condition he was in, he didn't manage to get very far…"

"Your daughter told me they found him in the ditch."

"Luckily it hasn't rained for a while, he could have drowned or died of cold— I kept thinking that after they brought him back from your office and put him to bed. Please excuse us now—he's so heavy that they couldn't get him undressed, he wouldn't let them… Oh, I've had enough, Doctor, you know? really more than enough, it only gets worse, if this keeps on he's going to end up like my husband, who died of cirrhosis—one night, even, he had so much to drink that he fell under his car, the door opened and he slipped out under the wheels…"

"Under the wheels?"

"Yes, I know that sounds hard to believe, but that's what the gendarmes said— he fell out the door and the car rolled right over him! So I'm very glad Georges can't drive! My husband had to get a new license five different times, and that cost a lot of money in those days… But Georges falling into ditches—that's no better…"

You nod your head, you open your bag, you pull out a prescription pad, a sheaf of Social Security forms, you lay them on the table beside the plastic basin. "What do you need?"

"Oh, everything, doctor. The nurse said to tell you we have no compresses left, or liquid soap, or detergent wash for the ulcer, or Vaseline… I'll need two or three elastic bandages—they wear out fast—and some rolls of adhesive. And then my heart medication, of course, and the sleeping pills…"

"And how are your legs doing? Did the nurse already come by this morning?"

"No, not yet. If you like, Madame Barbey will undo my dressing, so you can see."

"Let's do it together."

You lay your pen on the table, you pick up the plastic basin, you set it on the floor and you lift up my right leg. I lean back in my chair, because the leg is stiff. You set my heel on a little footrest you pulled from beneath the table. Once my foot is secure, you unroll the dressing. As usual, when you've unwrapped two or three layers, we see that there's staining over the ulcers. As you go, the stain grows

CLINICAL EXAMINATION (MONDAY, NOVEMBER 18)

larger; by the end the bandage is green with pus. Underneath that, the gauze pads are stuck to the wound. You drop the bandage strip into the plastic basin.

"I'll need some liquid soap."

"Madame Barbey!"

"Yes, Madame Destouches!"

"Could you bring me the dressing basket from my closet?"

You take the bottle of liquid soap, you pour a generous amount onto the gauze pads. From your bag you take a pair of gloves in a transparent packet. You slip them on, you pry the pads gently from my leg, and you drop them into the plastic basin.

You look at the ulcer, with your gloved fingers you palpate the puffy skin all around the wound.

"Mmmhh. It's not too bad, at this point…"

"Oh, it's been a lot worse than this, doctor. Now, at least, I don't hurt, and the leg isn't too swollen."

"Mmmhh. Ask the nurse to put a Vaseline dressing on this one again. Let's look at the other."

On the right leg, the ulcer is on the inner side of the ankle. On the left leg, it's on the outer side. It has to do with the way the legs rest on the mattress at night, you told me. Because of my back, I always have to sleep on the same side, that's why.

You take off your gloves, you drop them into the plastic basin, and you turn back to the prescription pad.

"I'll need you to certify the visiting nurse for another month, and also the certificate for the home aide—I really wish I could get her for six hours a week, but I'd be surprised if they gave me that."

You write, leaning on the kitchen table. When you've finished making out the prescriptions and the certifications, you take out your blood-pressure apparatus.

"Oh, it must be very high, after the night I had!"

"One-fifty over a hundred—you're right."

"Do I have to increase the medicine?"

"No, let's wait a couple of days. I'll come by and check it again."

Madame Barbey comes out of the bedroom and puts her head through the kitchen door. "Doctor, I don't like to mix in, but you should come look at Georges, he's not good."

When you come back, a few minutes later, you don't say anything. When it comes to Georges, you never tell me what you think, what you've found. You only say you've prescribed something for him, or that it's not worth doing, that the thing will heal by itself (Georges always heals—if it weren't for the drinking and the stump, you'd say nothing can do him in, even when he gets the flu he's up in a couple of hours. Madame Barbey says nastily that alcohol is a preservative, but it's because he's always been sturdy, even when he was little. He walked late, he talked even later, he still talks rather badly and he was never very smart, but he is very strong. He lost his arm in a machinery accident, and since then he's on disability, but he doesn't know what sick is. Look, he can't have absolutely everything against him!), but you don't tell me anything else. Once I asked you what you thought, but you said you couldn't discuss it, even if it was my own son.

You put away your instruments and your papers. You gave me my change. Before she left, you took Madame Barbey's blood pressure, since she has no time to stop by your office these days. After going in to say goodbye to Georges, you come back into the kitchen one last time.

"Doctor, I have to tell you…"

"Yes?"

"My daughter and my son-in-law… They want to put Georges away."

"What do you mean?"

"They want to have him put in a sanitarium, I don't know where."

"When did they say that?"

"Last night, after they got him to bed. They were furious, they said they'd had enough of him, that they were going to ask you to certify him for hospitalization somewhere…"

"And what do you think about that?"

"I don't want to, Doctor. I know Georges is impossible and that it's wearing me out, but he's my son, he's always lived with us since his accident, and when my husband died I had no other man in the house. You know, my husband—he wasn't his father. Georges doesn't know that of course, I never told anyone, not even my daughter. Just my husband, and now you. I know it won't go any farther…" I look at you.

"Of course not."

"His sister doesn't love him, she's ashamed of having a handicapped brother who drinks, so she'd really like it if he weren't around. Since he's older than she is and he's strong, she's afraid of him, and so is my son-in-law, because next to Georges he's tiny… But Georges isn't mean, I've never seen him hit anyone. The only harm he does is to himself, really. I don't want him put away. I wanted to ask you—I'm ashamed to ask you this, it's not right—I wanted to ask you… if it's possible, when I die, don't put him away, Doctor… I know you can't promise me that, but there you are—I did have to say it, and now I have."

I turn away to the window. "Goodbye, Doctor."

"Goodbye, Madame Destouches."

41

CONSULTATION: IMPOSSIBLE
(Third Episode)

On my way back from the school at a quarter to twelve, I see your car in the blacktop courtyard. Someone is walking into your office. I hurry to take the children to the house, I drop them with my neighbor (Mélodie is impossible when I take her along to the doctor, and I can't leave her alone with her brother) and I go back to see you.

I hurry through the courtyard. Your car is still there. I push open the door to the waiting room. It's empty. The connecting door is closed—you must have someone in with you. I sit down. I wait. Ten minutes go by. I don't hear anything from the other side of the partition.

I look at the magazines on the table, nicely arranged in piles; I don't touch them.

Ten after twelve. I'm going to have to go back and feed them.

The connecting door opens.

Madame Leblanc appears, a package under her arm. "Hello, Madame, what can I do for you?"

"Well, I was waiting to see the doctor…"

"Oh, he's gone, he had an appointment at the hospital."

"But I saw his car in the courtyard…"

Surprised, Madame Leblanc looks out the window. "Ohh, I'm sorry—that car belongs to Monsieur Troyat, the man who lives right next door. He parks it in here sometimes. If you can come back later, the doctor has office hours after two-thirty… Was it urgent?"

"Umm… no, just that I've been meaning to see him for a long time now. Oh well, for once I decide to come in—it's just my luck!"

42

ANGÈLE PUJADE

Your step sounds at the far end of the hall. Ever since the clinic moved to this new space, we can hear you coming from way off. Halfway along, I see you smile.

"Hello, Madame Pujade."

"Hello, Bruno! I was waiting for you. Your secretary told you I called?"

"Yes, but I hadn't forgotten the appointment, I'd put it down in my book."

"I wasn't worried!"

You laugh softly.

"Hello," says a voice behind us.

Three seconds earlier, she'd been sitting at the other end of the hall. You turn around, your face brightens. "Ah! But—you're early!"

She barely suppresses a smile. "Uh… no, I don't think so."

❋

Bruno looks at his watch. He seems completely flustered.

"Oh, yes, you're right, it's me—I'm twenty minutes slow. I'll be with you in a second."

And he disappears, blushing, into the closet we use as a dressing room. We hear him struggling with the metal lockers, dropping his keys, smothering a curse. She and I look at each other without speaking. She hasn't lost her smile, but I think she too is blushing. At last he emerges; he hasn't buttoned up his white coat, his collar is twisted, his hair tousled, he's shoving up his sleeves.

I hand him the file.

"Thank you. Come in, please!"

The consultation goes on for a long time. Three-quarters of an hour. For a follow-up visit with insertion of an IUD, that's a bit long, but then, Bruno always takes his time.

When the door opens again, I turn around, I see her move past him, very slowly. She's looking at him, she keeps looking at him as she comes out. He's looking at her too, there's something strange about him, with his hand on the doorknob. They say nothing.

Finally, their looks break off; she walks to my desk, I smile at her. She says nothing.

He stays behind her, he sighs, he says in an almost inaudible voice, "Are there any papers to fill out for… Madame Kasser?"

"No, we took care of everything beforehand. Shall I book another appointment now?"

She hesitates. She looks at me, Bruno steps forward.

"No," she says. "No, I'll make one later."

"Fine. Goodbye, then, Madame!" I offer my hand, she grips it warmly.

"Goodbye, Madame Pujade, thanks for everything." She turns to Bruno. "Goodbye."

"Goodbye…"

She looks at him one last time, very briefly, and she leaves.

❀

You lay the file on the desk, you look dejected. You don't say a word. You stand there, silent, motionless. Then you disappear into the cloakroom, to pull off your coat, slip on your sweater and your worn leather jacket—I've already suggested gently that you should buy yourself a new one, you told me that the pockets on this one had molded by now to your pens and your keys, and I don't think you were joking.

You shamble slowly off. You look as if you're lugging the whole weight of the world there in the pockets of your old jacket.

43

IN THE WAITING ROOM

I look up. A flash of light hits the ceiling. An engine slows, then falls silent. A car door slams. The street door rattles, keys jingle. I slip a finger between two pages and I close the book on my crossed knees.

The waiting-room door opens and, with your briefcase in one hand, your key-chain in the other, you enter the waiting room.

Murmurs greet you. You respond by a half-smile and a nod. You open the connecting door and hold it back with an elbow. With one hand you separate one key from the bunch, you unlock the inner office door and you open it. You pull the key from the lock, you slip the bunch into your pocket, you enter. Silently, the connecting door pulls shut behind you.

I reopen the book.

Someone rings twice from outside. The waiting-room door opens. A tall heavy man enters, stoop-shouldered, ill-shaven, unkempt. He looks around him, greets us all with his eyes down, "Lady-gemmen." He crosses the room in three strides, stops at the secretary's desk and stands there.

He's sucking on a rather disgusting cigarette stub.

He's got only one arm.

A few moments later, you reappear. You've taken off your jacket, your sweater or cardigan, and rolled up your shirtsleeves. Without letting go the connecting door, you step forward holding out a prescription slip. The man raises his good arm to take it.

"Thank you, Doctor."

"Not at all, Monsieur Destouches."

With a clumsy move of his only hand, the man folds the slip, slips it into his pants pocket, and leaves the waiting room.

Someone stands up. You hesitate, then stop him with a gesture.

"Can I ask you to wait just a moment? I have a telephone call to make."

The patient sits back down. You vanish, we hear you close the inner door, while the connecting door slowly pulls shut by the air-spring mechanism.

I take up my reading again.

44

DIEGO ZORN

The little doorbell rings. I look up from my book.

A pretty brunette has just come in, she nods to me. I've never seen her before, it's a pleasure to see new faces, goodlooking ones. Overeducated heads are often ugly.

She greets me, hesitates, slowly circles the table of new books, slows at the translations, sighs, comes over to me.

"Do you carry children's books?"

"Yes, certainly—upstairs. I'll take you there."

I stand up to accompany her but the telephone rings.

"Excuse me... Mall Bookstore—can I help you?

"Diego? This is Bruno..."

"Hey there, Nox! Long time! When do we meet?"

The brunette signals that she'll manage without me. I settle back into my rolling chair. I watch her slowly climb the spiral stairs. She has very pretty legs— a bit aspirin-white, but very pretty.

"Mmmhh... Dunno. Don't feel much like moving right now."

"Where you calling from? You're not working today?"

"Yeah, yeah. I mean, in theory I am. I've got a roomful of people waiting, but I don't feel like working. Feel more like putting a bullet through my head."

I straighten up sharply. "Hey—something wrong? What's going on with you?" Bruno doesn't answer.

"It's—it's Ray's sickness, right? Is that it?" I offer.

"Ohmyohmy, that had slipped my mind, thanks so much for reminding me..."

"I had dinner with Kate last night, she acts like nothing's happening, but she's completely lost. She even asked if she could spend the night at my house..."

"Really... So she's taking it pretty hard."

"Yeah. Listen, it bums me to ask you this question, I know you don't stand for it, and you know my own feelings, but when"—(I inhale deeply, tears spring to my eyes) —"I mean... when should we expect to be scraping Kate up off the pavement?"

You say nothing, you sigh. Then, "How do you expect me to know that? When he got to the hospital, six weeks ago, Zimmermann wasn't very optimistic, but then he goes into spontaneous remission, and all he needs these days is a transfusion now and then. So I don't know. He could live very nicely for several months, or several years. Or a sudden pneumonia could carry him off in three days... or his white cells could start climbing, and then..."

"Yeah... Here's another indiscreet question." I look up to be sure the brunette hasn't moved back into earshot. "Has she—has Kate asked you for... help, since Ray got sick?"

"Help? She hasn't asked me to hold her hand, if that's what you mean."

"Because hearing her say 'Diego, Ray's in the hospital for the night, would you let me spend the night with you?'—it's just a little surprising."

He explodes. "So what? You're a big boy, aren't you? You know how to say no when you don't want something!"

"You're an ass—that's not it. But you know her. The truth is, it's not my big-brother shoulder she wanted. What she wants is..."

"Is what? Quit your bullshit!"

There's more than fury in your voice, there's an anguish I can always spot ever since I know you. I shut up. You don't say another thing. "Okay, I'll let you get back to work—"

"Oh, lay off, I'm the one who called you!"

"Yes, but I'm the one who brought up Kate. Sorry. I have a feeling that's not what you called me about—am I wrong?"

"Yes. No. I dunno. I forget." He pauses a minute, then: "Diego..."

"Yes, pal, tell me..."

"You know what's the worst trap, in this business?"

I restrain myself from teasing him; I don't answer.

"It's... —ession."

I don't hear him because the stairway's shaking again, and for good reason: the brunette's coming back down!

"It's what? I missed that!"

"Nothing, drop it..."

"Wait, Nox, I have a customer here—You getting off?"

"Yes, yes I am, I've got to do some work. We'll talk."

"Okay. Later."

I hang up with a sigh. The brunette hands me two books. I give her a dumb smile. "*Algerian Cookery*, and Henry Miller, *Sexus*—well, not exactly children's books!"

She flushes and looks daggers at me. "No, but they were on sale... in the bin, right alongside."

She eyes me hard, and I surrender. "Forgive me."

"It doesn't matter. I'd like to find something for my godson. His birthday's coming soon—he'll be twelve on December 20. I have no idea what to give him."

"Okay, now I'll make you a decent proposal: come back two weeks from Saturday; the holiday specials will be in, all unpacked and on display, and my nephew will be here. He's about the same age, you'll describe the kid to him and he'll tell you exactly what you need."

She glances around the room, she nods, smiles finally. "Okay, fine. Saturday two weeks from today, right?"

"Right. The seventh. We'll have plenty of time to order if I don't have what you want in stock."

Watching her leave, I think how, if I had it to do over… Oh well, that's not something you can dictate. But a woman like that—it makes me dream a little. For one thing, she must certainly cook better than I do.

45

SPECULUMS

You lay your pen down on the grid-lined index card. You smile at me. "All right, let's take a look. If you'd please undress, I'll examine you. Keep your top on."

You pick up the two telephones, you lay the receivers down on the table and, while I undress, you walk to the other end of the consulting room. Perpendicular to the wall separating this from the waiting room, to the right of the entrance, there stand two tall shelf units of varnished wood filled with books and magazines. That wood-and-paper barrier acts as a screen and shields the gynecology examining table from the rest of the room.

You stand at the faucet and pour liquid soap into the hollow of your hand.

"Can I keep my socks on?"

"Yes, sure."

While you soap your hands, I draw near with some hesitation. At this end of the room a rolling table, a tall stool, and a plastic drawer-chest are lined up beneath the window. A small refrigerator hums in a corner. On top of that stands an autoclave in chrome metal; on it is a yellow sticker saying, "Contents sterilized." You point to the stepstool.

"Sit on the edge of the table there."

I climb backwards onto the step. I set my buttocks on the paper sheet of the examining table.

You take a metal bowl from the rolling table. You turn on the two faucets, hot and cold, with a fingertip you test the warmth of the water coming out, you hold the beaker beneath it, you half-fill it. You pour in a bit of yellow liquid from a plastic bottle. You open the autoclave, you take out a big metal box and set it on the rolling table. Then you turn to me.

You have me lie down, put my feet in the stirrups that rise at the end of the table. The padded surface is firm, and chilly despite the paper cover. Beneath my head you set a small cushion. You seat yourself on the tall stool, you light the mobile floorlamp behind you, you aim it between my thighs, you open the big metal box lying on the rolling table, you take out a speculum, you hold it between your hands for some ten seconds. You dip it in the bowl, with two fingers of your left hand you spread the lips of my vulva and you slip the speculum into my vagina. I stretch my neck to see, but your face has vanished between my thighs and all that shows is the crown of your head draped with brown hair that could use a good shampoo.

"This all right?"

"All right. I don't like it much…"

You spread the blades of the speculum. "Your cervix looks healthy."

❋

You spread the blades of the speculum.

"Mmmhh… How long have you been itching?"

"For about… four or five days."

"I see. And your husband? Does he itch?"

"Uhh, no. I mean, he hasn't said anything to me."

"He's going to have to be treated too. I'll take a smear, a sample, to be sure it's not something else than a yeast infection. But I don't think so."

"Oh, that's good… Will it hurt?"

"The smear? No, it feels like a slight scraping."

"Oh."

From a box on the rolling table, you take a long cotton-tip wand sealed in a plastic tube. "You've never had a smear taken?"

"Umm… I don't think so."

❋

You pull the speculum out. "Anyway, your coil looks to be in the proper position. I can see the strings."

"Oh, you see them? That's reassuring, I had the feeling it had shifted."

"When you bled yesterday, was it heavy?"

"No, but it was just after we'd had intercourse, so naturally it worried me… and my husband too, of course."

"Did you have any pain?"

"Uh—a little. It was like a spasm… Good thing I had the coil in, because it felt like contractions—you know, the kind you have at the beginning of a pregnancy…"

❋

"Have you had any contractions?"

CLINICAL EXAMINATION (MONDAY, NOVEMBER 18)

"None at all, everything's fine since I went on maternity leave, except that for two days now I feel it moving less…"

Your head comes up from between my thighs, you look at me with a frown. "Less, or not at all?"

"No, no, it's moving! But less than before."

"Do you often feel the urge to urinate?"

❀

"It doesn't let up! It itches and I'm always running to the toilet!"

"And during intercourse, does it bother you?"

"To tell the truth, I haven't had intercourse for two weeks, it burns so much I didn't want it!"

❀

"It must bother you during intercourse."

"Oh my yes!"

"At the moment of penetration, or after?"

"Sometimes during, sometimes after. It depends…"

"On what?"

"Well, on if he's in a rush or not. You know how men are…"

"Mmmhh."

❀

"Actually, it's mostly when I'm tired. Or tense."

"But not all the time?"

"Yes, nearly. Actually, it's never really enjoyable. But that's been true since the very first relations I ever had. This didn't just start lately."

"Were you very young?"

"I was fourteen."

❀

"And even so, you were able to get a prescription for the pill?"

"Yes, at Family Planning. And besides, you could work something out with girlfriends."

"Still, it couldn't have been very easy…"

"No, but it was that or not have sex, and you looked dumb if you didn't have sex!"

"Really?"

"Yeah, that's how it was. I knew one girl at the lycée—she was pretty, tall, slim, all the guys hung around her, but that's all they did: she didn't have sex. Back then, everyone said she was dumb, that she'd never know how to choose when the time came if she didn't sample what was out there. Now—"

"Yes?"

❋

"Now I'm sorry I sampled as much as I did. And back then there was no AIDS yet, either! Is it true that there are more and more sexual diseases these days?"

"Not more diseases. But people infected, yes."

"And for protection, there's nothing but the condom?"

"No. There's abstinence, too. And fidelity."

"Oh yah sure. I don't believe in that—it never goes both ways. You know how guys are..."

"How?"

❋

"Guys—like, it's not their body, they don't give a damn if it's a pain in the ass for *you* to take the pill. As long as they get laid!"

"Mmmhh. To hear you talk, it sounds like you'd just as soon drop the whole business..."

"Ah, sometimes, yes, really, I think I should just pack my bags and take off. But with two children..."

❋

"With two children, the varicose veins I got from the pregnancies, and then I smoke almost two packs a day, I decided I better find some other way..."

"And what made you decide?"

"The conversation we had last time. Really I was sick of the pill, I was always forgetting to take it. When you showed me the IUD, I saw how tiny it was... I thought I'd be less nervous with that."

"Okay, all over, it's in."

"Already?"

"Yes, that's it, I'm just trimming the filaments... not too short, of course, but you can rest easy, it's very rare that the thing shifts... There now, I'm taking out the speculum, it's all done."

***

"It's done."

"All over, I can get dressed?"

"Yes—if you want to put on your lower things and take off your brassiere, I'll examine your breasts."

46

DRAWINGS

The door opens, you appear.

I stop drawing. Papa stands up, you give him your hand. "Hello Monsieur Michard."

Papa waves at me. "You wait there, kiddo, I won't be long. Finish what you're drawing."

Papa goes in, you go in after him, the connecting door closes with a click and I hear the inside door slam.

I look around me. I'm alone in the waiting room.

I take a breath, my mouth crinkles up, my eyes get wet and I start howling.

❋

"So, tell me, do you know why you cry at night?"

"Because I'm having a nightmare."

"A nightmare that scares you?"

"Yes. A horrible nightmare."

"Are there monsters in it?"

"Yes."

"Do you think you could draw them?"

I nod my head yes.

❋

You lean down to the briefcase at your feet, you take out a big sheet of paper. I reach for the pencil-mug, you take out three felt-tip pens, a red a black a green, you hand them to me. I climb onto the chair, I'm just about high up enough to draw. You stand up, you get a thick book from the shelves, and you sit me down on top.

"Here, little bug, this should help."

While Mama gets undressed and heads for the other part of the room, I draw the sun, a tree, a house and three people inside it.

❁

I didn't finish yet. Mama did talk for a long time, but my picture took long to make. Now she's standing up, we have to go.

I lay down the felt-tips. I don't let go of the picture. I look at Mama, I look at you.

"Can I take it with me?"

"Sure you can, it belongs to you."

I hold the picture tight against my chest.

❁

The door opens, you appear. "Yes?"

"Excuse me, Doctor," Mama says, "but my little girl—she insisted on coming by—she wants to give you a picture."

"Really?"

I hand you my picture, it's red and blue and yellow and there's a doctor in it with his white coat and his listening thing hanging out of his ears.

You take it, you look at it, you nod your head.

"Thank you, bunny."

"Are you going to put it up with the others?"

"Absolutely. You want to show me where?"

I nod my head.

"I don't want to take your time," Mama says.

You shake your head no, you bring us in. "Show me where."

I point to the wall. "There."

"Next to the lion?"

I nod yes. "Did Virginia make that lion?"

"Yes, Virginia did it. Do you know her?"

"We sit next to each other in lunch."

You hold my picture against the wall, you take the thumbtack, and you pin it up. I stand up, I look at the wall.

You smile. "Are you looking for your other picture?"

"Yes."

"I moved it over, there were too many. There it is." You point up a little higher, to the left. "Do you remember what you drew?"

"The ocean."

"Is that the red thing?"

"No, that's the wall. The ocean is behind it, you can see a wave coming over, right there."

"You want it back?"

"No. I know where it is. You're not going to throw it away?"

"I never throw pictures away."

47

A LITTLE NOTHING

"I'm here to see you—oh you'll laugh—it's just a little nothing but see I've got one nostril always clogging up and it makes me snore at night and that bothers my husband, so I was wondering if you could..."

"I'm coming in for not such a big thing, it's just that my daughter doesn't eat and I'd like you to give me some vitamins to put in her soup because that's the only food she'll take, but I don't want her to know so I didn't bring her with me."

"I won't bother you for long, I just want you to make me out another prescription like last year, you know? I just got in from Malaysia and I leave in a week for Senegal and of course they've got nothing at all down there. So I'd need thirty boxes of sterile compresses, twenty rolls of adhesive tape, six months' worth of quinine, twenty boxes of acetaminophen—chewable, since it's better not to take things with water there—and then also ten or twelve tubes of Balsamo ointment, that's good for all those sunburns and stings and bruises, I don't know why they don't reimburse for it but okay it's not too expensive. And oh, yes! I nearly forgot: gauze bandage—three-, six-, and ten-inch wide. That's not reimbursed either but even so the pharmacist insists on having a prescription slip for some reason. I'm awfully sorry to waste your time like this but you see it's not a big deal. Is that all right?"

"Madame Renard sent me, she has none of those green capsules left. She told me to tell you that you should just pass by her house when you leave tonight after you're finished, to give her the prescription and because she's got this tiny little thing to ask you but she saw there were a lot of people in the waiting room a while ago and she didn't want to bother you for so little."

"I don't know how to say this, it's such a small matter, but I've got to get it off my chest, I just wanted to ask you a tiny question. I know I could have called, you've told me that before, but I was afraid of disturbing you, so I thought it was better to come in but I don't know if it's worth having you examine me, it's such a small matter. Only it does bother me a bit and I don't know what to think about it, but I think you'll be able to clear me up on it because I'll feel better even if it does seem a little silly. I'm sure you're going to laugh at me you know how it is we make a whole mountain out of nothing but still it keeps turning over in your head and until you see somebody you just can't rest so this is it: my hair's falling out by the handful and I was wondering if it's something in the water."

"I'm here to ask you a—a favor... it's not a very big thing... The lady at the pharmacy sent me, because she told me I'd need a prescription... Yes, for anesthetic jelly—ya know, the kind of stuff you put on your skin to numb it before you get a shot? yeah, that's right... No, no, I don't need a shot, it's—it's a little touchy to explain, but the thing is, my wife—how can I say this? My wife likes it—No, no, not the jelly! I mean she likes *it*... ya know what I'm sayin? We do it a lot, every day, sometimes two or three times in a day... She's always ready for anything, and me... well, I'm not gonna say no, whaddya think, I know guys at work, theirs always have a headache, so I'd look pretty stupid complaining, but... what can I say? Some days it hurts real bad. I mean it burns, like. I'd like to slow up a little, but she's really fierce, you know? if I say I'm a little tired, she makes a big scene, so okay, so it burns, but I don't say anything. And then the other day, I hear about this jelly thing, there on the TV, so I says to myself if they can use it on kids that means it can't be dangerous, and maybe I could put it on my... Just so I hurt less, ya know what I'm sayin?"

"I don't want to take too much of your time, there's people waiting, it's just to get a form. You're the one, aren't you? who went about my son the other day, when his tractor turned over on him in that steep field? The firemen told me—it was a pretty ugly sight... I did tell him to be careful locking the cab back on, he took it off just while he cleaned out the stable, and he didn't put it back on right away. And that's what happened. This morning I got a letter from the insurance, about the loans he took out for the farm and that weren't paid off yet naturally. They're asking me what he died of and I thought you could tell them... But really, what I want to know myself is... is whether he suffered."

48
_____

PHONE CALLS

The grey telephone rings.

"Excuse me a minute—Hello?"

From where I'm sitting, I sometimes hear a voice shout, "Hello, Edmond, is that you, Edmond?," and you answer, "No Madame you must have a wrong number" and you hang up. But more often, I hear nothing and you answer, "Yes, hello Madame," you reach for the appointment book, you open it. You flip the pages. "Mmmhh. When would you like to come in? I see patients here until five o'clock and then I leave on housecalls. Yes, in the evening, that'll be easier... After six o'clock... six-thirty?" You pick up your black pen. "There, it's written down. You're welcome. Goodbye, Madame."

❀

The telephone rings. You pick up.

"Hello? No, sorry, ma'am, this isn't the Provincial Credit Bank..."

You hang up.

❀

The telephone rings. You shake your head, you look at me apologetically. "Please excuse me."

"Of course."

You pick up. "Doctor Sachs here—Hello Mother... Yes... no. No, I'm with a patient, I'll call you back... Yes—yes, I will call you, but right now I really can't. Fine, talk to you later."

You hang up curtly.

❀

The telephone rings.

"Doctor Sachs here—hello?... Hello?"

You hang up.

❋

The telephone rings. You freeze. It rings once, twice, three times. You fling your pen onto the table, you pick up.

"Yes!"

You sigh. You search (Just a moment—) for your pen among the books and you don't find it, you take another from a pencil-cup, but it doesn't work. You finally pick out a black felt-tip. (Go ahead.)

You take down some figures (Yes) one after another (Yes) on a sheet of paper (What did you say? Yes) without looking at me. When you've finished writing (Go on) you tap on the sheet with a fingertip (And how much more did he take?) you look up (Last night or this morning?) you look at the wall where the children's drawings are tacked up (Has he eaten anything?) you look down again, you lay down your pen (Yes, he should take a little more...) you scratch your ear and I see that the the skin on your fingertips is peeling in bits, as if you were shedding scales.

❋

The telephone rings.

You pick up and you put the receiver back almost immediately.

"One... two... three..." You pick up, you listen for the dial tone. You lay the receiver down alongside the phone. "Now no one will bother us. Go on."

❋

There's a busy signal. A few minutes later I call again. Busy again. I hang up. I call again a little later. Still busy! It's been busy for a good half-hour now, that's strange.

I wait another little while and call again. Ah, this time it's ringing. Once. Twice. Three times. It picks up.

"Doctor Sachs here!"

"Hey there, little cousin! It's Roland!"

"Yes—hello, Roland."

"Oh boy, you sound exhausted! Didn't you get any sleep last night? I'm not bothering you, I hope?"

"No, no, but the telephone hasn't let up all afternoon."

"Ah, that's why I couldn't get through! But that's good, fella, that means you've got patients!"

"Yep… What can I do for you?"

"You're sure I'm not bothering you? I'll only be a minute…"

"Go ahead, I'm listening."

"Okay. It's Jackie, our youngest. He's just getting over a case of bronchitis. And since he's supposed to go off on a class ski trip, his mother's worried—by the way, how's your mother doing?"

"Uhh—she's fine, fine. I had a quick conversation with her an hour ago, she was fine. You could call her, she'd really like that."

"Oh no, you know, I don't want to bother her, I just wanted to know how she's doing, because I was talking about her with my father the day before yesterday, he asked if I'd heard any news of her and I told him that it was a long time since I'd called you so I didn't know, but that the next time I did I'd ask you. So she's doing all right then? That's great."

"So, the boy is going on a ski trip…"

"Yes—did I already tell you that? Oh, yeah, I just did, that's right, I don't know which end is up. And of course his mother's making a big stew about it—you know how mothers are, you see enough of them every day, I bet!"

"…"

"Ever since he got this bronchitis, she's on my back every day to call you, she's scared it'll start up again down there, and I said okay, okay. Myself, I didn't want to bother you, you've got plenty of patients who call you every other minute, so if the family starts in besides! Although it's true, when it comes to family, aside from your mother, my father, and me, you haven't got much left, huh, you poor guy? Ah, they're all gone now, it's too bad… Anyhow, my wife told me to ask you if the boy could go on the trip, but if it would be better if he stayed back in the ski lodge afternoons instead of going out to ski with the other kids…"

"It's a class ski trip, right?"

"Yeah…"

"Well, if he's not allowed to ski, I don't see the point."

"Exactly! That's just what I thought, and I told Mireille, but she wouldn't listen to me, she told me Call your cousin, and so there it is, when there's some medical problem, never mind that I've got the Health Encyclopedia in twelve volumes at the house, it cost me plenty even buying it in installments naturally, but so what, I still have to ask my cousin. I gotta say, when it comes to medicine Mireille doesn't trust anybody but you! Never mind that we live two hundred miles away—there's always the telephone! How many times have I said to myself Good thing we've got Bruno! If you weren't around, I don't know how we'd manage— and at that we've only got two kids, and Françoise is grown up now, she's a young lady, we don't have to take care of her anymore—well, I mean Mireille doesn't.

Myself I never got too involved—girl business, that's not my department... So you think we can let him go skiing?"

"Sure. Anyhow, I already told Mireille that. She called me last week, or two weeks ago, when he was sick..."

"Oh really? She called you? Well, I'm sorry—she didn't tell me! You see how women are? I told her, Call Bruno! Call him, I'm telling you, he'll reassure you! No, no, she said, it'll be okay, I'm not worried—actually, it's me she didn't want to upset because when she's upset I can't stand it, you know? And she called you anyhow, without telling me! What does that make me look like, huh? Well, if she calls you back, don't tell her you told me, okay?"

"Told you what?"

"That she called you!"

"No, of course not. You know I'm silent as a tomb. In fact, I shouldn't even have told you."

"What?"

"That she called me. Since she didn't tell you..."

"I adore you! I know I can always count on you. I'm always telling your mother that—Bruno is the soul of discretion!... I've really gotta call her, because it's been a long time, but you know how it is, you're working you finish late, you don't think of it and when you do think of it, it's too late at night to call. Anyhow, I did right to phone you, you're done by this time, aren't you? You're done with your day?"

"Yes... No... I have to run an errand and I'm coming back in, I have appointments later..."

"Oh, you're not done, well then I won't pester you any more, thanks again, you've made me feel better. He's gonna be glad, Jackie, here he thought he'd be spending the whole afternoon in the lodge, he wasn't too happy about that. And then his mother'll be relieved, you know how she is, Mireille!"

"Yes, she's like my—like all mothers."

"You devil, Bruno, there you go! So long now, hugs!"

"Me too. So long, Roland! Kiss Mireille and the children..."

"Yes... You I don't ask—you're still a bachelor, huh?"

"Yes..."

"Can't wait too long, you know, a man shouldn't be by himself. Look at me, I got around to it late, but I'm sorry I took so long. When you're fifty and you've got a ten-year-old son you do worry about the future—still, though, it's better than not having a child at all. Of course there was Françoise already and she loves me a lot, but I'm not her father, it's not the same, lucky Mireille was still young because otherwise I'd never have had the experience. So you've got to find yourself a little lady too, you're still young, you're what, thirty?"

"Thirty-four pretty soon..."

"Yeah, that's the same thing—thirty's not forty, you'll see when you're my age... There must be a few single women over there where you are, no?"

"Oh, for sure... Excuse me, Roland, I've got to go..."

"Sure, sure, go ahead—ciao!"

"Ciao, Roland."

I suddenly have another thought. "Hello, Bruno? Bruno!"

But you've already hung up. How dumb—I forgot to tell you, the next time you talk to her don't forget to give your mother a kiss from me.

49

THE PHARMACISTS

The automatic door opens with its usual hiss. I look up from my screen. You come in, smiling.

"Hello, Doctor!"

"Hello, Madame Lacourbe. Looks quiet here." You shake my hand.

"Yes, very quiet, for November. But the weather's good for now. Apparently the flu is on its way."

"Is that so?"

"Yes, I heard it on the radio. And then the vaccine company man came around to say we could start mentioning it. Well, he told us that in August, but of course as long as the good weather holds, there's not going to be much demand."

"Mmmhh…"

"What do you need, Doctor?"

"Well, I have no more injectable morphine left, and a few other odds and ends—here, I've made you a list."

"Shall I make up the whole order right now?"

"No, I'll come back tomorrow. Today, all I need is the morphine. I'll fill out a controlled-substance order."

"I'll go get that for you…"

I step into the back of the shop and I knock at the office door.

"Yes?"

I open the door, put my head in. "Madame Grivel, it's Doctor Sachs, he'd like some morphine hypodermic, can I get the cabinet keys from you?"

"Certainly. Do you need me?"

"No, it's fine, things are quiet."

I take the keys from the right-hand drawer of the little desk, I open the high-security closet, I pull out a box of injectable morphine. There are five vials left in it.

From the rotating display stand, you've picked up a toothbrush and three packs of licorice gum.

You give me a controlled-substance form, I write your name and license number on the big register with the data from the package and the required administrative information.

You're practically the only one in the district who comes in regularly for morphine. Early on, that surprised me a little, it even disturbed Madame Grivel, because we thought you were ordering a lot of it compared to your colleagues. Sometimes, especially when you started your practice, you looked so sad that we thought you might be taking some of it yourself. One day I asked you if you had a lot of patients who needed it, and you looked startled; you said No, I don't use much. So then I went back and counted and it was true: you would come in for four or five vials every two months, which is actually very little in fact, but we just weren't used to it: your colleagues never ask for any. And then I noticed that you were also asking for other painkillers, and Madame Leblanc explained to me that the drug companies wouldn't always send you samples of those. And then, people talk: oh, Doctor Sachs came over last night because my father was in terrible pain, he gave him a shot and that really helped him, or: If Doctor Sachs hadn't come and given me a sedative I don't know how I would have gotten through the night. Mothers call you Doctor Aspirin, the old folks call you Doctor Relief. You never leave a child suffering from fever, you never leave anyone in pain. That must backfire on you sometimes—I know there are people who'll call in a doctor because they're afraid they're going to be in pain, even before it hits them—young folks these days are so soft, so insecure, so worried over the least little thing. But for every four people who are more scared than they are miserable, and who already feel better just from seeing the doctor walk in the door, there's a fifth one who's writhing in pain, who can't figure out a position, because it's torturing him in the stomach or in the chest or someplace, and it's unbearable. If those people are dealing with some other doctor, they won't get relief very soon (how often have I heard people tell me they'd been left to suffer, them or their father or brother, with the doctors saying there's nothing they could do, that above all you mustn't mask the symptoms, that pain is useful because *it lets the doctor know what's happening*— you get the sense that they're annoyed to see patients get better); but if they're lucky enough to fall into your hands, they'll get through the rest of the night in comfort. It doesn't irritate you when patients don't suffer.

One day, we had a visit from a regional medical inspector from Tourmens, who felt that a lot of morphine was going through this shop compared to some others, but since he wasn't seeing any sign of it reflected in the patients' prescription forms, he wondered where it went. When we opened the registry to him, yours was the only name on the pages, of course. I was about to explain that you're often on night duty and that you use a lot at those times, but I didn't get a chance. When he saw your signature he said, "Oh, I understand." He said he knew you, that he'd been in school with you, he added something else I didn't catch, and he left smiling. Personally, though, it worried me; I kept thinking maybe there were some other drugs than morphine to use for people in pain. And then, one day—by then you'd already been here several years—Madame Grivel's mother broke her hip getting out of the car; there were loose pebbles underfoot, she wasn't too steady, she slipped and that was it. You weren't their doctor but it was a Sunday, they were on their way home from Mass when it happened. I live right nearby, so Madame Grivel called me to help her, her mother was howling with pain, and I told her to call the firemen and the ambulance but she was completely helpless, she didn't know what to do, if you moved the old woman the slightest bit she would howl even more, so we just held her there, half-sprawled on a stair, me standing, her crouching, we didn't dare let go of her. A neighbor saw us there and called you. You came very quickly and you didn't hesitate—a subcutaneous morphine shot and a pill beneath the tongue, some drug that wasn't out in the pharmacies yet but that you got at the hospital. In three minutes—it's no lie, five at the most—Madame Grivel the elder could bear to be lifted up and transported into the house. She was a little knocked out of course from the morphine, she was saying, "It still hurts but much less than before," they laid her out on a couch and she waited calmly for the ambulance. And you stayed sitting right by her, you held her hand and explained to her that they'd do an operation on her, that she'd walk better than before—that is, you kept her spirits up.

Since then, whenever her mother comes to visit, Madame Grivel calls to invite you to dinner. You've always refused nicely, saying that you weren't awfully good company, and that you spend your free evenings with your mother, who lives in Tourmens and is unwell. They still invite you from time to time, they do want it to happen. Madame Grivel the elder tells everyone she owes her life to you. So anyhow, as far as we're concerned, you'll never lack for morphine, and I never let our supply run out. Other druggists keep telling us that with all these robberies, it's a real risk to keep it on hand, but Madame Grivel and I are in complete agreement that it's worth that risk. The other day on the radio, the Minister of Health was saying he's decided to set up a special teaching program on pain management for medical students, and I said to myself it's about time, at the end of the twentieth century! He's got it wrong, that minister. We already have everything we need for treating pain; it's the will that's missing, that's all. Most doctors just don't care. Once they go out the door and start the car, the pain's not their problem anymore.

"We've only got five vials on hand, will that do?"

"That's fine."

You put the package into your pocket, you shake my hand. "Goodby, Madame Lacourbe."

I hear steps behind me.

"Oh, Mr. Sachs, I was afraid you'd already gone!"

"How are you, Madame Grivel?"

"Very well. And you? you look tired…"

"I was on call last night."

She hands him a paper bag from beneath the counter. "Here, Mr. Lessing left me this last week—he wanted to replace what you used for him."

You open the bag, you take out two suture threads in sterile packaging, and a bottle of antibiotic syrup.

"Oh, yes, I see," you say. "Thank you very much. Is your mother well?"

I move away, I know she likes to talk with you. She told me she was sorry she couldn't make you her doctor. I asked her, "Why not? You have no obligation to keep using Doctor Jardin your whole life!" She answered, "That's true, but Doctor Sachs—it's not the same, I couldn't."

Sometimes I think she must feel awfully lonely, on rainy Sundays in her house behind the pharmacy. At fifty-two years old, it's not very easy to find a husband.

You shake her hand, she holds onto it a little, you don't take it back, you wait until she lets you leave. You wave to me from the doorway, you go out chewing a stick of licorice gum.

"Goodbye, Doctor!"

On the little book where we write what the doctors owe us, I mark down the morphine vials, because I must. But not the licorice gum or the toothbrush.

50

IN THE WAITING ROOM

I set down the book. I rub my eyes. Outside, it's begun to rain. Beside me, a woman suddenly starts, mutters, opens her purse, digs inside, rummages, digs some more, grows agitated. I hear her scold herself: "It can't be, it can't be, I didn't forget it! How could I? Oh, of course: I left it on the bureau, I must have, because I took it out to give the girl money to go get me some bread… Ohlala how awful how awful how awful but I can't go back to the house, I'll lose my place and it'll take me another hour… He won't scold me I'm sure but I'll look like a… You just don't do a thing like that!"

She closes her purse, opens it, rummages inside again just to be sure, shakes her head (That's where I left it, that's all it could—) then closes it again and clutches it on her lap. She looks around to see how many people are ahead of her, she looks at me—and I can't help smiling, I'm remembering something, and rather than meet her gaze I leaf back through the pages.

51

FEES

Some people never know the fee.

Some people—old folks mainly—always want to pay the exact sum in change, in the coin of the realm: "I got some at the grocery before I came, that should help you out too, with all these people waiting."

Some people give a little more, so they can say "Keep the change, please," and then watch out of the corner of their eye to see what you'll do.

Some people pull out a bundle of big bills, "How much?" as if they were giving a tip. And they tend to look twice under SIGNATURE CONFIRMING PAYMENT (COLUMN 12): "Well look at that! Is that all it costs?"

Some people smile, "If you haven't got the change never mind—you can give me back the five francs next time I have to come."

Some people the minute they walk in pull out their checkbook, set it on the desk, like, "Look, I'm paying so I want my money's worth."

Some people are embarrassed, "Because my wife went out shopping and took the checkbook with her."

Some people send their children in alone with a folded bill.

Some people take a signed check out of their wallet, "You don't mind filling this out for me? Because me and writing, you know…"

Some people pay when they come in, "This way it's all taken care of" and leave without taking their prescription slip.

Some people pay after twenty minutes to show they're in a hurry to get out, and then hang around an extra hour.

Some people stop in, "I'm here for two seconds, just to show you my test results," and it takes only fifty seconds, but they still want to pay, "Well yeah, really, it's only right otherwise how you gonna earn a living?"

Some people will pay next week.

Very few people never pay at all.

Some people offer you coffee, "In this house we take it with a little drop, but a doctor, I dunno!"

Some people don't know How to thank you Doctor do you like strawberries/green beans/tomatoes/walnuts/cherries I've got a garden full of them.

(Some people leave a bulging sack in the waiting room. You've got to dig down to the bottom of the sack to find their name written very tiny in pencil on a torn shred of envelope to figure out who it came from and if you haven't done that, then when they run into you in the street they tactfully call out "So, how'd you like the plums?" before you've even had a chance to say hello.)

Some people dedicate their self-published book to you—the account of some adventure, a tribute to an adored father, a memorial to a child departed too soon: "This may interest you, you can read it if you have time, you'll see it's not very long, I'm glad I did it, it was hard but it made a difference to me."

Some people offer you their bodies, but you mustn't touch.

Some people learn about a rise in fees before you do, "I heard it last night on TV, you didn't know?"

Some people say, "I have no money and my parents don't know I came in."

Some people stand up in the waiting room, "I left my money home can you take me anyhow?"

Some people check each medication on your prescription slip, "Do they reimburse for that one I should hope? Because these days never mind that we paid in, they don't give much back anymore."

Some people, "My, it's gone up a lot! Of course I'm not sick very often, the last time I came in was ages ago!"

Some people give a nudge, "So pay the Doctor already, you can see we're taking up his time and there's a load of people waiting!"

Some people don't look like much

Some people "With what he's cost us"

Some people "I'm sick of being a money machine"

Some people "I don't know if it's worth it"

Some people "I'm no good for anything anymore"

Some people pay for the rest of them.

52

WIPES

You stand up, you walk to the other end of the room. I sob. You understand, doctor, I can't sleep since my dog got this tumor in her teat (you take a tissue from the dispenser on the glass table) I'm worried and the veterinary says she hasn't got long to live even if he operates (you come back over) and I believe him you know, he's not one of those vets who operate for no reason (you hand me the tissue) "Thanks," but it's torture for me I'm telling you it's torture and I don't sleep anymore because of it (I wipe my eyes and you sit back down in your rolling chair.)

❀

You stand up, you walk to the other end of the room. I sigh. See, Doctor, things aren't easy these days so I don't know if I should take on more debt (you pour some liquid soap) or if I should stay where I'm at obviously I've got to make a choice but I say to myself (you soap your hands) that if I take on a little more debt, okay fine there's the insurance, but suppose something happened to me (you take a paper towel from the dispenser on the wall) what would become of my wife and children? (you wipe your hands) because if I change location the whole point would be to expand of course but that means more stock which means more work and I don't gross enough to hire somebody (you come back over) my wife already puts in practically the whole day to help out but I can't put her on salary it's too complicated that would change our tax bracket (you sit down again) two children isn't enough but no way (you write on a white file card) we can have any more, my wife wants another one or two—you know how women are—but I tell her No way how do you expect us to manage (you look at your ink-stained fingers, you stand up, you walk to the other end of the room. You take a paper towel from the dispenser on the wall), I heave a sigh.

❀

You wipe the tip of your pen.
    You wipe up the ink that just spotted the white table surface.
    You wipe your fingers.
    You wipe your forehead.
    You wipe your glasses.

❀

You stand up, you walk to the other end of the room. I try desperately to limit the damage. You see, it's like this day after day, it doesn't help for me to put thickener in his cereal, I put in twelve teaspoons when the box says put eight (you come back over) I give him the drops they prescribed at the hospital, I know it's nothing serious, I lay him down on his stomach with his head raised but it still keeps happening and I'm (you hand me the paper towels but I don't know what to do with them when I've got the baby in my arms) I'm sick of changing his sheets four times a day. They keep saying it'll get better as he grows but it's been two months now and it's not getting any better (you take back the wipes and you clean up the vomit that spattered the floor as soon as I sat down with him on my lap) I just wonder if he should have an operation after all (you take the baby from me, "May I?" you lift him up you weigh him you put him back in my lap you give him the transparent rattle with the colored balls that go up and down inside and the baby says Dadaadaaaa?) my husband doesn't want it, it scares him for a six-month-old baby, but he's not the one who does the laundry, you know how men are (the tears start pouring down my cheeks) Excuse me would you have a tissue?

❀

You walk past me and go to the other end of the room. I don't move. You take a paper towel from the dispenser on the wall, you come back over to me, you detach the electrodes from my torso and you wipe off the slimy contact gel smearing my skin and sticking to the hairs, or the tears from my cheek or the drool running from my lips or the snot from my nose or the shit from my behind.

CLINICAL EXAMINATION (MONDAY, NOVEMBER 18)

53

THE INEXPRESSIBLE

You're sitting at your desk. You don't move.

From the side, your body describes a kind of *S* seated/scrawled on the rolling chair, a long heavyish reptile leaning forward onto two arms, the hands nearly joined at the far reach of your gaze.

Your left hand lies flat beside the sheet of paper. The pen is suspended in your right hand just above the page.

On the page, you've written

The body does not exist. Encased in the white coat, the clothing.
The hands, just barely. When they have no gloves on.
The eyes stare from behind those damned greasy glasses.
Greasy hair, nose gleaming like a beacon light.
Can his howl be heard, from the outside?
Touching everything, grudgingly.
Answering everything, grudgingly.
Rolling up the sleeves doesn't strip one naked.
To be naked at last he'd need to

You're hunting for the right word, or perhaps you've got misgivings.

$$54$$

DANIEL KASSER

Breathless, distraught, she bursts into the studio. "He called me! He called me! He found an excuse and he called me!"

"Who did, my darling daughter?"

"Him! You know who I mean—the doctor at the hospital, Bruno Sachs..."

"Sex?"

"Oh, please! *Sachs.* I told you about him! I went back for an examination today, and—"

I lay down my tools and look at her. I go over to her, I take her by the shoulders, I sit her down, I sit beside her. "Tell me."

She stands up, she can't stay still, she circles about, she can't think what to say, how to start.

I stand up myself. "You want coffee?" Without waiting for her answer, I push her toward the kitchen. There's still some hot coffee in the thermos jug. I pour her a big cup. "It's very strong."

"Yes... All the better."

She takes the cup of steaming coffee. She clasps it in both hands, as if to warm herself. She stays standing, leaning on the door.

"I couldn't—I couldn't pull myself away! Even though I felt so awfully stupid!" Her voice has grown very soft now, almost inaudible.

"It was a follow-up visit, see... I mean, you know, there's nothing amusing or intimate about those, they're more like... But he's—he's not... He wasn't a doctor this afternoon. He was... him. He talked to me, he talked and I didn't even listen, I just stared at him, and I don't remember a thing he said but he talked to me a long time... I stayed almost an hour and it was too short, I wanted it not to end... Finally he apologized, said he was talking too much, and I—I wanted to tell him no he wasn't, that I didn't mind at all, but he stopped, he asked if I had any questions, and I said No, I can't think of any, and then he said, "That's really too bad.""

CLINICAL EXAMINATION (MONDAY, NOVEMBER 18)

He seemed… sorry that it was ending and I—I felt like a complete idiot, I didn't know what to say to keep it going, to keep him talking to me…"

She stops. She sighs, she drinks a mouthful of coffee, she looks at me.

"When I left, we looked at each other, it was just for a second, the time it took to leave the room… I didn't want to go away and I sensed that he didn't want me to, he never took his eyes off me…"

She begins moving about again, she sets down the cup and starts striding back and forth across my tiny kitchen. "And then just before, as I got home from my office, the phone was ringing and it was he, I recognized him right off, I recognized his voice I couldn't believe it, he was stammering these excuses… And hearing him I started laughing—he must have thought I was a complete idiot—but I was happy, I was hoping… I knew he would try, that he'd find some way, some pretext… because I hadn't made another appointment. You're supposed to come back in a few weeks, and when the receptionist suggested it I said no, I'll call in, and as I left I said to myself There, now I've done it, I'll never see him again— And now here he's called me tonight! he was stammering out all kinds of excuses, how he'd forgotten to tell me something or other, some precaution I should take—but it was a pretext, just a pure pretext, it made no sense at all, he just wanted to call me!"

"Did he say that?"

"No! He didn't say anything… I don't even know what he said, exactly. He didn't say anything. He wanted to talk to me, but he didn't say anything, he sounded terribly flustered and I—I didn't know what to do!"

She sighs again, she comes over to me, she clings to me. "You think I'm idiotic…"

"No, not at all, daughter mine." I hold her tight in my arms. "You're going to see him again. You'll make an appointment…"

She pulls away from me, she shakes her head hard, her eyes closed.

"No."

"Why not?"

"If I make another appointment, once that one's over I won't have any more reason to go back. And besides… I don't want to see him at the hospital."

"So then what?"

"So," she says, "so… I don't know."

CATHERINE MARKSON

There they are, the three of them—Ray, Bruno, and Diego.

They're talking, haranguing, cracking up, as if everything was perfectly all right. Bruno's sitting in the armchair, Diego's at the end of the bed. Now and then, to emphasize something he's saying, he puts a hand on Ray's feet, where they're bundled under the covers. Or else he reaches out his open palm, and Ray and Bruno slap on it together and they laugh even harder, while the blood pours through the tubing attached to Ray's arm.

Bruno hasn't looked at me since he came in with Diego. Ray is in heaven, it's been weeks since they spent any time together all three of them. It's a very long time since I've seen Bruno. He phones Ray, he runs by the house like a gust of wind—only at times when I'm out, as if by chance. On the telephone, he talks to me, but always briefly, always a little curtly.

Tonight he's as lanky, as thin, as stooped as he was fifteen years ago. He still needs a shampoo and a haircut, he hides behind his glasses. He's greying a little at the temples. He's less talkative than when we first met. There's a kind of anger to his silence, a kind of hatred to his words. Ray's the only person who can still get him to lighten up, I think.

Diego, now, he hasn't really changed. He's going bald. He's maybe a little calmer, a little more reserved, a little more at ease with himself. He doesn't look at Ray the same way he used to. Or me either, of course. I've never dared ask Ray if he knew, if he guessed. And I never will ask him, it's all too long ago, it doesn't matter any more. I think. And yet. Would the three of them be so close if there hadn't been a lot more between them than just childhood memories, Bruno's year in Canberra, the hell they raised when Ray came here... and me?

I don't even know whether I count. When they're together, nobody else exists. Ray is their big brother, their mentor and their protegé. When he got here he was thirty-eight years old, he was still a virgin, and he didn't speak a word of French. They taught him everything—the country, the language, women. He taught them world history, geopolitics, philosophy. And that's been going on for fifteen years, they talk for hours, they yell at each other, comfort each other, love each other. What the hell was I ever doing with them? What the hell am I doing with them now?

How much longer will it last? The doctors are evasive, Bruno doesn't answer my questions, and Ray himself never stops telling me that doctors are all nincompoops, as if that should make me feel better.

They burst out laughing again, but Ray starts to cough. He's thinner and thinner and because of his anemia his skin is livid. His freckles look like a centenarian's liverspots. He won't let anyone cut his hair right now, so his thick ginger mop is scraggling all over the place. He coughs harder and harder, Bruno and Diego stop laughing, Bruno leans over to him, Diego lays a hand on his back, Ray is crying, I see his eyes redden, he cries with pain when he starts coughing. I'm about to ring, to call a nurse, but suddenly it quiets down.

"*Hey, that's some nasty thing, that*—what do you call it in French?" he says, in that mixed-up lingo of his.

"What?"

"That fungus thing—the stuff they found in my lung. Grilled-Asparagus-something?"

"Aspergillus."

"Yeah, that's it! When I was in theology *grad school*, I never would have thought I'd wind up spitting out asparagus in Tourmens!"

He throws Diego a sidelong glance. Diego returns his look, murmurs something as he nods, a smile hovering around his lips. "You old jerk!"

"A little respect, *young man*. Or I send you back to review your Wittgenstein. Hey, Kate, what do you think? You think we could make him do his *ole Witty* over again?"

"I don't need any review, asshole teacher mine. 'The world is all that is the case. The world is the totality of facts, not of things...'" And Diego goes on to recite the opening paragraphs of the *Tractatus*.

"Hey! You still know it! What about you, Nox?"

Bruno picks up exactly where Diego left off, but he gets stuck after a few lines, and with a grin he scans Diego's face.

"Nossir, I'm not helping you out—you just should have studied harder!"

"When you recite that, it sounds like you're saying Kaddish," Ray murmurs. "You can say it for me when I kick off..."

Bruno doesn't answer, he looks at me, lays a hand on Ray's arm and finally says, "It takes ten men to say Kaddish... The two of us won't be enough."

"Right," says Diego. "And I'm not even Jewish..."

"So what? Neither am I, but I've got a right to my Kaddish, don't I? A prayer for dying that doesn't say a single word about dying—everybody has a right to that, correct?"

Bruno takes a very deep breath. "Quit your dumb talk… Still, I'm convinced that when he was working on the *Tractatus*, Ludwig had his grandfather in mind. He didn't just write that book, he chanted it."

"Say, Professor Markson," Diego interrupts in a shy little voice I haven't heard from him in ages, "is that why you had us memorize this damned text? When some joker would open the wrong door at school and discover your little grouplet in the midst of a loud recitation, we sure looked smart!"

Ray draws himself up on the bed, fulminating, the tawny lion about to whack his cub with a good strong paw.

"You little jerk! Doesn't a person know a thing better, more *intimately*, when he's learned it by heart? Doesn't he remember it *forever*?"

"Yessir!" says Diego, raising his arm to shield himself. And all three of them start laughing their heads off again, and I start to worry that Ray's going to start coughing again, but no—they laugh and he leans toward them and they've got their arms around him now, smacking each other on the ribs, their laughter charged with all their memories, all their tears, all their late-onset adolescent highjinks, lived out so long after their actual adolescence—does anybody ever get to be an adolescent at the right time?

And just then, I feel so alone, so desperately alone, so torn up with sorrow and pain that my tears start pouring in floods, rolling down the length of my face, dangling at the tip of my nose, but I don't move, I don't say a word, I don't even get out a handkerchief, I don't make the slightest gesture for fear they might turn to look at me, they're together, close and happy, and I don't belong here, I don't want to break into that, I don't want to drown their delight with my tears…

I see that they're crying too, and that they're laughing at the same time.

I look at Bruno, he's laughing too, his face brightens, he opens out as he laughs, he grows larger, he is handsome and good, he becomes once more the Bruno I met before I met Diego, before I met Ray, and I start longing to huddle in his arms, I start to tremble with longing so hard for him, for all the nights I never spent with him, all the nights I implored him to stay and he said no… I say to myself, This time I won't let you tell me no, you don't have the right. Pretty soon we'll be leaving the hospital, Ray will tell me to go with the two of you, he'll ask you both to take me to dinner and a movie, the way the four of us used to do, or the three of us when he'd be off in Australia visiting his mother, that's how he knows about films I've seen with him and without him, sometimes I'll say, "That reminds me of the scene in that movie, remember?" Ray looks at me and says, "That wasn't me, that was two other guys." When we leave I'll tell you—*you*— exactly what I want. Diego will understand, he already knows, I'll say Bruno, what I

CLINICAL EXAMINATION (MONDAY, NOVEMBER 18)

want is you, I'm sick of suffering, of crying at night next to that living corpse of a Ray I've loved so much but who's never been able to love me the way a man loves a woman, I'm sick of waiting for you to take me in your arms and love me, I'm sick of you being afraid of everything, of me, of other people, of your own shadow, of whatever. I'm sick of it, I can't do it anymore and this time I'm not going to let you go.

SOLO DIALOGUES

III

THE SESSION

I cross my legs and I write the date: December 10.

He's silent for a good while, then he heaves a big sigh.

"Nox came into the bookstore Saturday. I hadn't seen him for a month.

"It was busy, so he waved hello and went to browse through the books. He's always been like that...

"...Nox. At medical school, the students used to call him *Nox* because he'd always be knocking on doors and heads, lecturing them all the time, so they'd go after him. He used to go around the school sticking up fliers that said things like "Doctor's Orders: The New Order?" or "We Are All Nazi Doctors." He scared the bejesus out of the medical students. They thought, stupidly, that he was as aggressive as his posters. One day he admitted that very few people actually read what he wrote and that the ones who did paid no attention, especially the administration—he'd been dreaming of getting called in to the dean's office so he could spit in his face, but the dean probably didn't even know he existed. So he quieted down, he stopped pasting up fliers, he turned into a guy who was kind of glum, kind of taciturn, kind of snarly with everyone, nothing like when we were kids, back then he was timid, he was scared of a fight, he kept to himself—when I remember him in grade school, I wonder how we ever came to be so close...

"His mother cooked very, very well. Not as well as mine, but still. We'd spend the whole afternoon together reading comics or science-fiction books. He had a great big easy chair in his room, big enough to fit the two of us side by side.

"When he came back from Australia, I knew he was going to do medicine. He didn't have much choice—beloved only son, his parents expected nothing less.

"As for me, I went to work almost right away in the bookstore. Before, Moses ran it all by himself, but he was getting old, and since I was always hanging around there, since there was nothing else I wanted to do—for me books were all I cared about...

"When Moses had his stroke, I found him very early in the morning, lying at the bottom of the staircase, freezing, paralyzed down one side but alive. He couldn't say a word. I would talk to him and he would squeeze my hand with his good hand, to show me that he heard, that he understood—one squeeze yes, two squeezes no, like when you're a kid. I asked him if he was in pain, he said no. I asked him if he was afraid, he said no. I asked him if he wanted me to keep him at home, and again he said no. And I didn't understand that: he'd always sworn he didn't want to die in the hospital. So I asked him that same question again several times, but he kept answering no, no, no. And then when I asked if he wanted me to call an ambulance, he squeezed my hand once, very hard, he blinked his eyes one time, to tell me YES...

"He didn't want me to be taking care of him. He knew I'd stay with him in the apartment, but he didn't want that. If he was living alone, he would let himself die, but he didn't want that to happen in front of me.

"I went with him to the hospital, and who do I see in a white coat at the door? Nox, who I'd hardly seen at all for three or four years. He never left the hospital anymore, he worked extra shifts, and at my end I never left the bookstore. We'd give each other a ring now and then but that was it—and he's the one we landed on.

"It was Nox who told me it was hopeless...

"If it had been anybody else, I would've spit in his face, I wouldn't have let anyone tell me there was nothing more to be done... In fact, he didn't say that. He said, 'It's a lousy break.' He looked at Moses: 'You understand what I'm saying?' And Moses signaled yes by squeezing his hand. Of course he understood. A person knows when he's dying.

"If Nox had already been in practice at the time, we could have worked something out between us, we could have arranged for him to die at home...

"After Moses died, I didn't feel much like seeing Nox. I'd think of Moses whenever he came by. I would say I had work to do, book business to take care of.

"One day—I'd been on my own there maybe six or eight months—into the bookshop there comes this big red-headed guy, talking French that was very correct but with a heavy accent, and he asks me if I have any books on Australia. I say, 'I know a guy who lived a while in Australia,' he goes 'Oh, really?' sounding not very interested, and then we talk, we get along, he tells me he's been living in Tourmens for a couple of weeks, that he doesn't know people yet, and he invites me to come have dinner some night with 'one or two other acquaintances.' I accepted, naturally.

"... I liked him right away. He was good-looking, he was brilliant, he was funny, he talked like a god, he knew more than all the little profs I meet in a year, he was goodhearted, he was clumsy and puritanical... I don't know why I'm talking in the past tense, he's not dead...

"… And so there I am at his house one fine evening, there were half a dozen girls… and Nox. Of course Ray and he did know each other; he'd wanted to surprise both of us.

"We talked all night, and at seven in the morning we were still at it. The girls had left, since it was turning into an oldtimers reunion, they felt superfluous. Except for Catherine, of course. She was studying philosophy, and as soon as Ray arrived in town she'd signed up for his seminar. She'd known Nox for several months already, he'd taken care of her mother in the hospital, and they'd… become friends, let's say. Nothing happened between them, Nox was much too rigid. But she was in love with him from the start, you could see it a mile off.

"… Ray and Nox started singing songs from musicals—*Porgy and Bess, South Pacific*, and especially *Kiss Me Kate*… From that night on we never called her 'Catherine' again.

"… She was writing a dissertation on Wittgenstein. Ray and she began talking about him. They didn't see eye to eye, they were throwing quotations at each other. I was having a ball, Nox was trying to follow the argument.

"… Eventually Kate scored some point, and Ray started laughing with that Homeric laugh of his, he said she deserved the most coveted title in contemporary philosophy: 'Wittgenstein's Mistress.' Everybody laughed harder yet, Kate blushed as red as a peony, and Nox was staring at us with his eyes like saucers. Finally Ray, who was practically choking, tapped him on the shoulder and said to him, 'You prob'ly didn't know old Wittgenstein was… ' but he gagged, he choked, he couldn't get his breath so he looked at me and I said 'Queer as a three-dollar bill!'

"'Wittgenstein's Mistress'—didn't she just wish! Never saw a woman so torn! Here she was still in love with Nox, she fucked like a lunatic with *me*, and Ray's the one she married… The day after his wedding, Ray was still a virgin.

"And this dumb lug Nox just went right along as though nothing was up, we'd all see each other once or twice a week, we'd have dinner together at their house or lunch, the four of us, at the bistro across from the Mall Bookshop, and every now and then he'd tell Kate she looked beautiful, that marriage suited her, that she'd be lovely pregnant—What a jerk! He's not the one who was always picking up the pieces afterwards—it would shatter her. Nox has never understood a thing about women.

"Kate never did manage to get him into her bed, but not for lack of trying. A week before she got married, she turns up at his house, she tells him she wants him, that she never wanted anyone but him, that there's still time, that Ray would understand—and that imbecile throws her out!

"She told me that. He never said a word about it. He must have thought it would be a betrayal… I could see he didn't love her. I thought for a long time that he'd never be able to love anyone. He didn't know how to love, he'd never learned. In his house, people didn't love, they possessed. Rule Number One there was: 'I

SOLO DIALOGUES III

love you, that gives me rights over you.' He got that in the belly every day, that 'Darling do this for your mother, it'll make me happy.' 'Son, do that for your father, it'll give me such pleasure.' Every single day. He avoided them like the plague, but that's all he knew. And still he had to make a couple of bad moves before he realized. Once he nearly fell into the clutches of some woman, a bank clerk. Bad dresser, awkward, unhappy. Not pretty. A victim—you know, '*A sad li'l girl whose name was Irma, didn't have no mama didn't have no papa...* ' Well, actually, this one did; she was the last of a big litter. Five brothers and three sisters. Very good family. The boys were an engineer, a CEO, a lawyer, a priest, and an army captain, naturally; the sisters grew up to be one a nun and the other a bigshot arts-patron type. And then this one was a bank clerk. And a chronic depressive. She hadn't found herself a husband—shameful. And she wasn't even a regular employee, just a temp—here one day, someplace else the next. I don't know what Nox saw in her. She must have spotted him coming. One day he goes in to make a deposit, she gives him her mournful smile. 'Hello Doctor... Well, are you seeing lots of patients? You know, in a way you and I are in the same line of work. People entrust you with their most precious possession, and us too—we listen to them, put their minds at ease, buck them up... But who takes care of you and me? Sniff sniff... ' And so on. And I can just see one thing leading to another, she probably invited him to come have tea in her little pad.

"He must have been feeling very lonely around then.

"That lasted a few months. Later she fell out of the loop, I don't know how he got rid of her. And then next there was the teacher. Not exactly the same style, but this one was also a victim. He always had a weakness for victims. They move him. And they can smell him out ten miles off. This one ate like a horse. Three times a day. Right out of a refugee camp. She even managed to get herself invited home to mother, and that was a record—Mama Sachs must've really gone downhill.... Anyhow, that one didn't last either.

"Now and then I'd know he had somebody because when I went to visit him— Ray and Kate would come by at closing time to pick me up and take me over to his house for dinner—the place looked different somehow, there'd be cigarette stubs in the ashtray or a pair of pantyhose tossed in the garbage.

"But then for a long time there was no one. His damned job, the nights on call, his department meetings, the classes he was teaching for the medical students, the articles he was writing for that damn magazine, and nothing else.

"When Ray got sick, Kate started to act up. And Nox began to pull back into himself. He could sense that the thing was hanging in front of his nose, that she'd waited long enough...

"One night, last month, he and I met up at the hospital in Ray's room. Kate was there, of course, and while we were horsing around, I could feel her examining us each in turn, Ray first with his skin and bones and his hair all tangled, then me (she must have been trying to remember how it was when we'd spend whole after-noons screwing her to *con-soul* her for having a historian husband who'd rather make it with Wittgenstein...), then Nox, the love of her life, the inaccessible, you could see it like the nose on your face, she was devouring him with her eyes.

"When we left the room, it was eleven-thirty. The night nurse kicked us out because we were making too much racket. Outside it was nice, you would have thought it was May. Ray's window was the only one lit up and he was waving to us through the glass, he'd gotten out of bed and he was holding the sheet in front of him. Kate took Nox's arm. She said, 'Shall we drop Diego off and you take me home?' And he goes, 'Uhh... ' I didn't feel like hearing what came next, so I said I was going to walk.

"The next morning, he told me he'd spent the night with her. He said some-thing terrible: 'I did it so she wouldn't feel so bad... And because Ray is still alive. I couldn't have done it on his grave.'

"He couldn't find an excuse to give her, but he was still looking for one for himself. 'I did it so she wouldn't feel so bad... ' I bet he really believed that, the stupid ass!

"Against all the odds, Ray did finally come out of the hospital, his goddamn pneu-monia got better thanks to some experimental antibiotic or other. He vomited blood and guts, but he got better. From the pneumonia, anyhow. The leukemia's still there.

"Kate is no better, she's withdrawn into herself. She looks after Ray, she cod-dles him, he's not doing badly, he reads, he writes, he plays the piano, now and then he goes out, he walks with a cane, and they come over to the bookshop. But he gives her his arm as if she were the one who's ill.

"Whenever I called Nox, he wouldn't have time to talk, he was always busy. Kate didn't see him either, she said he wasn't talking to her anymore, though he would phone Ray three times a week, and send him prescription slips if he needed something. But he didn't go by to see them. Maybe he was worried Ray would read something in his face.

"And then Saturday, I see my crazy friend come in, looking grey as death. I think to myself, He must have stopped by the hospital, because it was five in the afternoon and that morning I'd talked to Kate on the phone: Ray had gone back into the hospital, he was bad again.

"Anyhow, Nox comes in. It was a little crowded, Saturday is my busy day, so he just waves to me—he raises his hand to face level and wiggles his fingers, like this—and he starts trailing around the counters, he picks up some books, leafs vaguely through them, how many times have I seen him do that and then start bellyaching, 'Oh, there's too many books published, who needs them, bunch of phonies, waste of time, flash, garbage... ' The Mall is the only place he can do that, of course. When he started medical school, he used to go to the Book Market too, downtown in Tourmens, or to Narcejac's, and he got himself thrown out because he'd tell the bookseller to his face that he was selling crap… a first-class drag!

"Saturday, what with prowling around like a dog on a chain, he ends up finding something that catches his interest, he hunkers down like he always does in the cranny there between the reserve shelf and the spiral staircase, and he starts reading. I've got customers, so I stay put, I figure things will quiet down and we'll talk later.

"And then it doesn't quiet down, I don't know what's going on but in come eight, ten, twelve people one after the other, some I know and some I don't, asking for books I have or don't have, but they stay on, rummaging, poking around. I'm taking orders back to back and I hear a voice say Hello.

"I'd only seen her once, but I remembered her perfectly, she'd had a slightly sad look, legs slightly too white as they went up the staircase, curly black hair pinned up at the back of the head, a few grey hairs. Kind of tired-looking, features drawn, but beautiful, I'd thought. This time, though, last Saturday, she'd changed—she looked cheerful, she had a short haircut, a narrow nose, a very red mouth, and she smiled at me: 'You told me to come back on December 7. I was looking for a book for my godson, remember? You said your nephew would be here… '

"Right, I had said that, yes, I remembered, and my nephew *was* in on this Saturday, he'd gone out to get me some change and he'd be right back. And just then, as I'm speaking, over there at the rear between the shelves and the staircase I see Nox look up and stiffen, the book falls from his hands, his eyes go wide and he stares at me as if he's going to swallow me up, but no it's not me he's looking at, it's her, she has her back to him and I get the feeling he's waiting for her to turn around, that he's imploring her to. She does turn around, but she doesn't see him, she reaches toward a table, she picks up a book, she reads the cover copy, puts it down and picks up something else, and my Bruno goes on drinking her in, he's devouring her, he doesn't move, it's as if he were seeing an apparition—or a ghost, rather—but he doesn't do a thing, he stares at her.

"It was very fine out on Saturday, full sunshine early in the afternoon, I'd lowered the awning so that the book covers wouldn't fade, but now it was after five, it was starting to get dark, so without taking my eyes off them, I began rolling up the awning.

"That's some noisy awning," she said, and she raised her head. Back in the corner behind the staircase it was dark, but she saw him instantly. And he—I saw his shoulders slump, as if he were letting out a long breath. At first he didn't move, nor did she, they just stayed still, looking at one another, it seemed to last an eternity. Suddenly, he moved toward her; when he was very near he began a gesture, she reached out her hand, he took it, they held one another like that without moving for a split second, she said nothing and I could see him babble something but

THE CASE OF DR. SACHS

of course from where I stood I couldn't hear it because of that stupid awning, she nodded Yes, she turned to the door, he opened it for her and they went out. He pointed as if to show the way and they began to walk slowly, she smiling, her eyes lowered, one hand in her jacket pocket, the other grasping the strap of her purse, he walking and talking and waving his arms.

"I thought something dumb—it's got nothing to do with anything, but it keeps coming back to me since. When she came into the bookstore that other time, it's strange—I was talking to Bruno on the phone...

"I don't know how to explain it... but seeing them go off, I thought to myself, 'They've found each other.'

"Fine," I say, laying down my pen.

FURTHER INVESTIGATIONS

(Sunday, February 29)

And he that increaseth knowledge
increaseth sorrow.

Ecclesiastes

56

THE NEXT-DOOR NEIGHBOR

The telephone rings. I wipe my hands and pick up.

"Hello?"

"Martine? This is Germaine. Did that doctor leave home yet?"

I take a quick look out the window. "Uhhh—no, his car's still here."

"What the hell is he doing? We called him two hours ago and his wife said she'd tell him! Did he go out at all this morning?"

"Well, no, I don't think so, I didn't see his car move. I don't even think he got called to go out during the night. She parked her own car right in front of the gate, yesterday, and she hasn't moved."

I can hear Germaine talking to someone behind her. "Blandine! Leave him alone! You leave him alone, I'm telling you! Pierrot, you gotta keep Blandine from bothering the cat, last time she closed him into the storeroom he peed all over the potatoes! Right—put him outside. And get her out of here too, you can see I'm on the phone!... Martine? Are you still there?"

"Yes."

"Oh, dearheart, if you only knew, she's killing me! Oops, gotta go, here come the cousins. The minute you see him go out, that darn doctor, let me know, I'm not calling him again. Although it's really too much—if it wasn't a Sunday I'da called somebody else. And on top of it, the newspaper had it wrong, I hadda call the county police to find out who was on call today!"

She hangs up.

I don't understand why he hasn't left yet. He didn't hardly do anything Saturday, his car never moved. Last night I thought I heard an engine start up but I must have been wrong because her car is still in the same place she parked it yesterday. I don't know what she was up to, she kept going and coming the whole afternoon.

Still, it's not right he doesn't step on it a little more than that. I have to say, since she turned up he's not the same. For one thing, her car's almost always

FURTHER INVESTIGATIONS (SUNDAY, FEBRUARY 29)

parked in front of the gate. Fine, she leaves early in the morning, but meanwhile the back end sticks out into the street and Roger has a hard time getting his tractor past it, to me that's not right. And then, they go out nights a lot, they take her car, I call his house and nobody picks up, but before, ten o'clock at night, he used to always be there. Or else there's a busy signal for hours, I just wonder what people do if they're sick… Before, he was always on duty, nights. But now, if he's leaving the phone off the hook all night, I don't see how he could be! And it's been like that for three months already…

Anyhow, it's just not right it takes him two hours to get over and see about my aunt. I know it's not exactly an emergency, but still!

57

THE SERVICE OPERATOR

It rings. Once. Twice. Someone picks up. It's a woman's voice, as it was yesterday.

"Yes?"

"Umm—this is operator 24 at the answering service, I have some calls for Doctor Sachs…"

"Hold the wire, please, I'll get him."

I hear her lay down the telephone, then nothing; she must have pressed the "hold" button. He never used to do that. Before, when he was on call on the weekend, if he put the phone down I would hear music or the TV (we were often watching the same station, he likes Westerns) or the kettle whistling. Since yesterday, every other time I call she's the one picking up. And another operator here told me that the two previous times, she was already there…

"Hello?"

"Hello, Doctor, sorry to disturb you—I've had four calls for you. One's a fairly urgent house call, and two less so."

"Go ahead."

"Well then, first there's an appointment, a girl who wants to get a vaccination; I told her to see you in your office."

"Mmmhh. What time did you give her?"

"Eleven o'clock, is that all right?"

"Fine."

"Next, there's the emergency housecall—an older man who's been short of breath since last night, he's having trouble breathing, his wife said, and he has a bad heart. It's pretty far away."

"Okay, let me guess—it's over in Sainte-Sophie?"

"Right," I say, laughing, and I give him the address. "He called five minutes ago, I told him you'd get there as soon as you could…"

"You did right."

"Then, there's a young man to see at Deuxmonts, a soldier at the army post who's got flu. And the last one is a death in Saint-Jacques, this morning—a woman was bringing her mother breakfast and found her dead in her bed. She called at seven-thirty to get you to sign the burial certificate, but since it wasn't an emergency, I let you sleep."

"That was very nice. I'll go by there coming back from the first two calls, it's on the way, and then I'll go into the office for the appointment. If you get other calls, tell them to phone me later at the Play office, that'll be quicker."

I give him the two last addresses, he takes them down, he hangs up.

He's always nice, but we don't talk much anymore.

Yesterday already, he was very busy all afternoon. I figured he didn't have much time to talk. Actually, I think he just doesn't feel like it anymore—simple as that.

THE NEXT-DOOR NEIGHBOR
(Continued)

I'm peeling the last potatoes when I hear music. There he goes now out of his house, I look up at the clock—ten-fifteen, he sure took enough time!

She comes out after him, she's wearing some kind of cream-colored jumpsuit, she opens the gate for him, and I think now she'll be moving her car, but no! He gets into it! He's taking her car! Well now, that's new! Sure it's bigger than his, and it's gotta be neater, probably doesn't have all that mess he's got in his back seat, sometimes when he's parked in front of his gate and I'm going into the village for bread, I take the bike but I don't get on it right away, I walk it past the car and I look inside, it's not so wonderful! Lotta times I say to myself he really needs a wife, but I never thought he'd be getting the use of her car out of it too! He opens the roof, he's right the weather's good, you wouldn't think it was February, he opens the window, she leans in to him, very close, what else could they have to say to each other, and he still doesn't look like he's in any rush. Oh, doctors! You could be dying, they take their own sweet time!

Now he's gone. She waved hard from the roadside, like he was leaving on some big journey. She's walking back, I see she's smiling. I'm thinking she's about to go inside, but no, she bends in through the house door, picks up some rubber boots, puts them on and walks toward the kitchen garden—well it's years since it was a kitchen garden, back in old lady Camus's time you'd still see tomatoes, string beans, lettuce, cabbage, carrots, parsley, but once she took sick nobody minded it anymore, acourse, and since the doctor took over the house, he's not the gardening type. I did tell the Camus boy, "Don't rent it out, you never know who you'll get in there, then when you decide to get rid of them you won't be able to." But he didn't listen to me and now see, I told him so, and when the tenant's a doctor it's hard to tell him to get out just like that all of a sudden.

I put the potatoes into water, I turn on the gas, I wipe my hands and I pick up the phone to call my cousin.

"Hello, Germaine? This is Martine. The doctor just left."

"Well, he took enough time! You sure?"

"Yeah, yeah, I just saw him, this minute. And he should get there soon, being how he took the big car, his wife's—I mean, that belongs to the lady who's staying there, whatever."

"That's new?"

"Yeh, well not exactly, three months now, maybe more, Iowno, I can't be standing by my window all the time to see what he's up to. And besides, he had somebody else before, but like just passing through, cause I never saw the same one twice. This one, though, she looks like she's sticking around, she came over a coupla times and then it was pretty quick, in a week she brings over her suitcase and now she spends the night there every day, except the weekends, but him neither."

"Still that's no reason not to come see about Mama! If it wasn't a doctor I'd give him a piece of my mind! I mean now, with everybody here, I'm not gonna say anything, but that don't mean I don't want to! It's really awful!"

"Yeah... Hey... hey! what's she doing?

"What? Who?"

"His lady friend... Well, there's something you don't see every day!"

"What's she doing?"

"Well... she's out in the vegetable patch, digging!"

"She's digging?"

"That's what I said!"

"Well, now, you're right—you don't see that every day!"

59

A CONVERSATION

The telephone rings. Once, twice.

"Yes?"

"Hello, Bruno."

"Hello... I knew it was you."

"How did you know?"

"I knew it. I felt it. The telephone doesn't ring the same way when it's you..."

I smile. "That's because you're in love."

"Whatever gave you that idea?"

"I don't know. My feminine intuition, maybe."

"Mmmhh. That's an impressive weapon—I'll have to watch out. Or ask you for advice."

"Advice?"

"I could really use some feminine intuition in this job..."

I say nothing.

"I'm awfully sorry, I have one more patient coming in, someone just called as I was about to leave."

"Don't be sorry, nothing you can do about it... How do you feel?"

He laughs softly. "Mmmhh... A little tired, actually! What about you?"

"Very good. I even did some gardening!"

"You're not exhausted, after last night? You didn't have to come along..."

"No. But you were in no condition to drive."

"Mmmhh. When that happens to me, I open the windows all the way and wake myself up by driving... But you did wait over an hour for me in the car."

"It didn't kill me. Your patient was a lot worse off than I was..."

"Mmmyah. And it's still not a sure thing it'll work out. The hospital didn't phone? No, that's right—the service is taking the calls."

"Next time I can take them, if you want."

"Absolutely not. You'd be stuck in the house. Now, at least, you can go out for a walk, if you want…"

"A walk? Without you? Never. Does it bother you to have me stay here?"

"That's not what I meant, but…"

A silence, then he goes on: "What about you—doesn't it bother you to sit there waiting for me without knowing when I'll be coming in?"

"Of course not. I have things to do. And besides, you're working, I don't hold that against you."

"Yes… Well, a Sunday on call—that's not much fun."

"Not for you either. So we might as well be on call together, no?"

He answers Yes, very tenderly. Then, after a silence: "I jumped when you called. This telephone doesn't ring often. It never really did ring much. No one knows the number. There was my mother… and then Ray and Diego… But they never call me in Play. Only at the house."

"Do you mind if I use it?"

"No! Absolutely not! That's what it was for, originally. So my—well, so someone could always get me on a personal line, here or at the house. But actually, I never gave the number to many people."

Another silence. "What's dumb is that it makes me uncomfortable to have two phones that could ring at the same time. When I'm stitching someone up, or doing a GYN examination. So I take both receivers off the hook. But it irritates some people when they can't get—oh, here comes my patient."

"Yes, I heard the bell."

"Well then… so long."

"Yes. So long, Love."

THE ATTACK

I ring and go in. At the other end of the room I see a closed door, I lean against the wall, my heart's pounding, my head's aching, I know my lips have gone blue and I'm colorless, I saw it in the girls' eyes, and my chest is wheezing as bad as it's ever done. I open my raincoat—it feels good in here, the heat's on, it's nice out today, the sun is bathing the garden that's visible outside the two big windows.

I stay on my feet, it's harder to breathe if I sit. On one of the chairs I see an open book, laid face down, as if the reader had left it just to step out for a moment. It's got a thick plastic cover on it, I can't see the title. It's a fairly thick book. I turn it over, it's open to page 227. I lay it back down, I don't feel like reading. I'm having too much trouble breathing, it's been like this for hours already.

I expected the doctor to come out to meet me, but no, he's staying put. Yet he did tell me that he was alone and waiting for me. As I came in, I thought I heard a phone ringing.

After a moment, I go back to the door and ring again.

A few seconds later, the door opens at the end of the waiting room.

He's tall and dark, and wearing a white coat. He shows me in. I look vaguely around. The examining room is rather dim: he hasn't opened the shutters, probably because today is Sunday.

❋

"Have you been having trouble for long?"

"Since... yesterday. Actually, for the past two weeks... it hasn't been good... and nothing helps me much anymore when... I've got bronchitis on top of it..."

Just then I start coughing violently, sweating, suffocating even more. He puts a hand on my arm and has me sit on a seat covered in black fabric. I'd been afraid he would ask me to lie down; most doctors don't know that makes it worse.

He looks at me and nods. I believe he's about to speak, but no, he opens the little chest at the head of the cot. He pulls out a pocket inhaler and a plastic nebulizer. He points to the latter. "You know what this is?"

I nod yes. I've got one at home but I never use it.

He hands me the inhaler; it's not a drug I'm familiar with. He insists I use the nebulizer, and take several puffs. I do it.

Then he asks me to take off my shirt, sits down beside me, takes my blood pressure and listens to my chest, one hand resting on my naked shoulder.

"Sounds like a little less wheezing, you think?"

"Not… quite yet…" I start coughing again, I'm sweating great drops.

He rummages in the drawer, takes out two glass vials, stands up to prepare an injection.

❈

He sticks me painlessly, finds the vein right off, injects the drug very slowly, and we stay seated there, face to face, for a long time—ten minutes, a quarter of an hour. He keeps quiet, listens to my chest, watches me.

"You must have been in a bad way for some time…"

I don't answer.

Little by little, my breathing loosens up, there's less and less wheezing, I'm not perspiring any more, my heart slows down a little.

He pulls the stethoscope out of his ears and lays a hand on my arm. "Your skin is very dry… And you've got some eczema. Probably since you were a kid…"

"Yes. But compared to the asthma, it's pretty much secondary… Ummm—I have a terrific need to urinate…"

"Go ahead, please."

❈

The bathroom is outdoors, along the side of the building. Whitewashed walls, a bench equipped with a simple plastic seat, spider webs. I piss quarts—he warned me I would, it's a side effect of the injection.

When I step back into the waiting room, he's left the two doors open. He's sitting at his desk, a big wooden surface painted white, and he's writing. As I enter, he turns his head, offers me a chair beside him. "How're you feeling?"

"Better. A lot better… I haven't felt this good in two weeks."

"Mmmhh. I like that better. I was this close to putting you in the hospital."

"Really? I've been in that condition several times before, and I always stayed home."

"I don't know if that's wise. A bad asthma attack is actually fairly… you were very cyanotic when you came in, pretty near to asphyxiating…"

"I know. Sometimes there are moments when I start—floating. At times like that, I know things are bad, but—how can I say it? It's as if it doesn't much matter. Everything seems a bit futile… It's not unpleasant. It's the lack of oxygen, I guess… I shouldn't drive when I'm that way… And then after a few hours it gets better, or it gets worse… and then, well, I really have a rough time."

"You came here alone, in your car?"

"Yes, but the house is only two minutes from here, on the Deuxmonts road… I'm a widower, and my daughters don't drive yet."

"Mmmhh. They're waiting for you right now?"

"Yes. I told them I'd be gone a half-hour and—(I look at my watch)—I've already been here for over an hour."

"Here," he says, sliding the phone over to me. "Call them and tell them you're okay."

❋

I stay with him another half-hour, talking—about my asthma, my eczema, about movies and novels; he takes my blood pressure and pulse every now and then, between chest soundings. Toward the end, he asks what I do for a living. When I tell him, he makes an odd face. "A lawyer! Well! And the asthma doesn't get in your way when you're pleading a case?"

"I never have an attack when I'm pleading a case."

He smiles. He nods. He takes off his glasses. He lays them on the painted wood surface. He looks at his hands. His palms and fingertips are peeling; strips of dry skin trace ragged lines. I get the sense he's laughing gently.

"All right. I'm going to put you on antibiotics and cortisone for a few days, to get rid of the infection. But next time," he says, pursing his lips in sorrow, "don't wait till you're in that state to get help…"

"I was that bad?"

"Mmmhh. Let's just say it's a good thing you came in… If you start feeling lightheaded this evening, call me right away. Otherwise, keep taking this, strictly on schedule. (He hands me a prescription slip.) Here, take this inhaler too. The pharmacy on call today is the one over in Marquay. Do you know how to get there?"

"Yes… I know every pharmacy in the area. I never have time to see a doctor during the week, so I often find myself in this condition on weekends."

"Doesn't that kind of wreck your family Sundays?"

"Sure does…"

I wait for him to say something more, but he nods his head, that's all.

❋

When he opens the connecting door, he offers his hand. I take it, hold it, and say, "Thank you. Thank you very much."

"For what? For giving you some relief? That's my job."

"Thank you for not bawling me out. I always wait till the last minute. I tell myself it will pass. I empty my inhalers but, after a certain point, I know that it's going to get worse. When I go to a doctor, it's because I can't manage anymore. And each time, they bawl me out, they say I'm really insane, that I could drop dead, that I'm a bastard for doing this to my daughters… I know it's true, but that doesn't help me. And it doesn't give me much taste for going to a doctor. But you… you didn't lecture me."

He laughs gently. "Lecturing is even more suffocating than asthma…"

I laugh too. It's nice to be able to laugh without choking. I hesitate, then I say, "My wife… She died of breast cancer, two years ago. We were already living here, but she had a doctor in Tourmens. I'm sorry we didn't know you then. That would certainly have been less hard on her. She always worried terribly when I got like that. It would have comforted her to know that I could call on you. But that"—I point to the telephone—"even just doing that was a comfort to the girls."

My eyes fill. I'm still holding his hand in mine. He puts his other hand on top of them. "I'm very glad you're feeling better."

He's about to say something else but I hear the waiting-room door open and I see him looking past my shoulder. I turn around. A woman is there, her color bad, her hair disheveled. She looks sad and weary.

"Are you… still taking patients?" she asks.

I say, "I'll leave you now. Goodbye, doctor."

"Goodbye, Monsieur Perrec'h."

As I leave the waiting room, I slip my hand into my pocket and clutch the inhaler.

61

A LOVE STORY

I go in. I look around me; the room is dim, he hasn't opened the shutters. He points me to a seat, then to the telephone. "Excuse me, I have to call my—call home."

"Yes, of course. I can wait outside if you like."

"No," he says, smiling, "no, please, sit down."

He settles into his rolling deskchair, picks up a grey telephone receiver hidden by books and magazines. "This is Bruno… Yes, I just wanted to tell you I have another consultation to do. You're not getting impatient? (He smiles.) Yes… no. No, of course not… That's fine. See you soon… Me too. Goodbye."

He hangs up. He swivels around on the caster chair and turns to me. "What can I do for you, madame?"

"I'm sorry… I saw in the paper that you were on duty, I took a chance and came by… I didn't know where your office was… I don't even know why I'm here… To tell the truth, I was hoping you wouldn't be here…"

"When I'm on duty, I do have to be here, after all."

"Yes, of course, but I mean, not *in*. I thought you might have gone out on a house call… At this hour, it must happen often, I imagine…"

"Yes, fairly often… although between noon and two, people are often busy with other things…"

❄

I realize that I was looking at his hands, which were still flat on the desk. I raise my eyes and I see him smile, attentive and puzzled.

I take a breath and I say, "I came because I needed to talk. I'm not sick… that is, not sick like the sick people you see, I'm a little ashamed, I think I'm taking up your time. You don't have a housecall to make?"

"Not that I know of. I'll have some later, certainly."

FURTHER INVESTIGATIONS (SUNDAY, FEBRUARY 29)

I'm having trouble breathing, my throat tightens. Tears rise to my eyes, I open my mouth but nothing comes out. "Excuse me…"

He waits patiently, and then, seeing that I don't manage to put forth a sound, he murmurs, "It seems to be quite hard."

"Yes… And at the same time… it's so unbelievable and so… banal, both!"

"Mmmhh."

"I'm—I'm single, but it's as if I were married… and I have a lover. That is, there's just him. I mean, I have only one man in my life… if you can call it a life… and sometimes I see him every day, and sometimes I hardly see him at all for weeks… He's both very present and very absent. And I… I can't take it anymore."

"Because today's Sunday—that's why you're not seeing him today?"

"No, no, that's not why. I do see him Sundays, I see him a lot, even. He—he works it out. His wife… often goes away. She doesn't work, she plays bridge. She plays tournaments. She takes advantage of the money he earns, she'd be wrong to deprive herself… Today I won't see him, he's… they've gone to her family, to keep up appearances. A birthday dinner, I don't know, I don't want to know. When he does that, I hate him, I want to kill him, I'd like to kill the two of them, and have it over with!… I run into her sometimes in town, I see her in expensive shops, she spends an absolute fortune… I find it very hard not to say something insulting…"

I look at him. He doesn't say a word. He nods as if he understands.

Yes, I believe you do understand.

❁

"He… he can't leave—or he doesn't want to. I don't know what holds him. He never touches her anymore, they sleep in separate rooms… anyhow, so he tells me. But what do I know…"

"Do you think he's—leading you on?"

"No!… no. He's too unhappy, too… I know it's complicated. He has a daughter. At the beginning, when we first met, she was only eight. He couldn't just leave, suddenly. She wouldn't have understood… And her mother is too—she can't do a thing, that woman, she's a parasite. I think early on he was afraid she'd take revenge by going off with the child… or worse…"

"Mmmhh. How old is the daughter now?"

I look at your hands, they're joined in front of you, resting on your thighs. Your legs are folded back and crossed beneath the caster chair.

"She's seventeen."

❁

"Now she goes to the lycée in Tourmens. Mornings, her mother drops her there, or she takes the bus; evenings she gets home around seven, and since he doesn't finish work early himself, he doesn't see much of her…"

"But he has time to see you, still?"

"Yes. It's easy. I work at home. I live in the 'Barracks,' that apartment complex at the factory, at Saint-Jacques—you know the place?"

"I have some patients there."

"It's enormous, and there are several different entrances, so he can come and go unnoticed… and anyhow, it wouldn't be strange to see him in the stairwells there, considering his work…"

You raise an eyebrow. "He's a salesman?"

I smile. I sigh. "Umm… not exactly." You can see that I don't want to say more about it.

※

"I—(I'm laughing and sobbing at once)—I realize that it's a little scattered, what I'm telling you, and I know you can't do anything about it, but today I couldn't take it any more, you understand, he called me earlier, he calls me even when he's home with his family or at her parents' house, he goes out saying he's going to buy the Sunday paper, or cigarettes, and he calls me from some booth, he tells me he can't bear it, that he can't go on making believe, acting like a nice stable bourgeois couple—husband with good job wife with lovely home daughter with promising future guaranteed—it all makes him sick. But he goes anyhow. And when he goes, I detest him, I want to kill them, I tell myself that it's finished, that I won't answer when he calls, and then when he calls I pick up anyhow, and I hear him talking to me, he's so sad, he's… But for me, you see—sometimes I can't bear being at his beck and call that way, stuck in my house waiting for him to come or not come. I can't bear making lunch for him at noon knowing that he'll be having dinner at night with that cow and their daughter, and that even if they don't sleep in the same bed anymore, he spends the night there, there in their petit-bourgeois house *de merda!*"

I slam my fist on the white desk, so hard that the little gray receiver falls off the phone. "Ah, *scu*—pardon me, I am so sorry…"

You put the phone back, you nod your head. "Doesn't matter. But—may I ask you a personal question? You have an accent?"

"Yes… I'm Italian. But I've lived in France for a long time…"

"Your accent came out when you got angry."

"Right now, I can't control myself anymore, that's why I came to see you… He called me this morning, he's been gone three days. He's not coming back till Monday… I hate weekends and vacations. I never take vacations, I have no desire to, what would I do on vacation all by myself? Summers, I send my son home to

FURTHER INVESTIGATIONS (SUNDAY, FEBRUARY 29)

my parents at the seaside, because summer here it's grim. He doesn't want to go, but I know he's trying to take care of me, he wants to act like a little man. But it's not his job to keep me company. He's got a right to live a child's life, not have to be anything else but my son."

"He knows you have a man in your life?"

"…I've never told him. And when Jé—when my… friend comes to see me, it's during school hours—or else because he's got some good reason for coming openly…"

"And… you think your son doesn't suspect anything?"

"No—well, yes. He does suspect. I know from certain remarks he makes, questions he asks. For a long time, he used to ask me if I'd have a husband some day… and I'd answer that I didn't know, that things don't always go the way you want them to. One day he said, 'Anyhow, to get a husband you'd have to spend time with a man you like, and you can only do that when I'm at school, or when I'm asleep.' It wasn't a question, he said that in a very serious tone, and when I asked him what he meant, he didn't answer, you know how children are, they blurt something out and then go right on playing as if nothing happened, they don't even remember what they said if you raise it later. One night I was putting him to bed, he asked, 'Mama, when you have a husband, can I get to call him Papa?'"

❀

I was already twisting my wet hankie, when you saw the tears pouring down you stood up, you crossed the room, you brought back a big box of tissues and put it down on the painted desk surface, next to me.

❀

For a long time I said nothing. You looked at me, you said nothing either. My tears eventually ran dry.

❀

Finally, I sighed, I tried to smile, I straightened up, I said, "I won't burden you any longer, I should go home. My little boy is at the neighbor's… Her son and mine are in the same class. I—I wanted to thank you for listening, but I feel a little awkward…"

"Awkward? Why?"

"I—because I came and took up your time… even though I'm not sick…"

"No, but you're in pain."

❉

When I get out into the courtyard, I see that my hand is clenched around my Social Security form, and I realize that you didn't make out a file, you didn't take any notes, you didn't even ask my name.

62

THE BAKER'S WIFE

The little bell jingles. Jony throws his plate on the floor. His father gives him a smack. I get up, I leave the kitchen. The doctor from Play is in the shop, he's looking at the chocolate éclairs.

"Hello, ma'am. I'd like a country bread and three or four croissants, please."

"Three, or four?" I say, laying the baguette on the counter.

"Well… (he smiles) make it four."

I stuff my last four croissants into a paper bag and I tap out the receipt. "Twenty-two francs ninety."

He digs into his wallet and puts the exact sum down in front of me. Then he takes his bread and croissants and leaves. "Have a nice Sunday."

He's in the big green car again. His girlfriend's.

She's been here already. These days, she comes in often, almost every afternoon, except Sunday. Sundays I never see them. I'm surprised to see him today, I guess he's on duty. I look at the clock, it's quarter to two, yes, that's it, he must be on duty today. I go back into the kitchen. Jony is sniffling over the plate his father has stuck back under his nose.

"That was the doctor from Play. I wonder where she came from, his girlfriend."

"What girlfriend?"

"You know, the one with the great big car, the other day she had the roof open and she was wearing sunglasses—looked like she thought she was some movie star."

"Maybe she is," Jean-Yves answers without taking his head out of the newspapers. "Shit! I shouldna played seven…"

"What's the difference, you always lose."

I clear the table. I know Jony won't eat any more, now. Anyhow, he doesn't eat a thing, that kid. I don't get it, how come he's not worn out, with the little bit he eats! He doesn't like bread, even. When I think how when I was little I spent my whole time swiping cakes or warm bread from the shop.

Sometimes I think I should take him in and get some doctor to look at him. And then I'd get a chance to talk about me and Jean-Yves. Because really it's not right how he doesn't make me come when we have sex. It's not right that it just gets started and it's over already. He says it's because I put on weight from being pregnant, that it turns him off, though he does manage to sleep just fine after. And anyhow, it was like that from the beginning, when he was apprenticing with Papa—the first time, we did it on the kitchen table one Sunday morning. Papa had just went to bed, Mama was in the shop, she called me to come help her, I was never so scared in my life, but seeing how short it took, I didn't have to worry. After, when we'd go dancing Saturday nights, we'd do it in the car. Even when we were engaged, my parents didn't want him to come see me at night at the house, so we'd do it wherever we could, even in his friends' houses... He was always saying people should really get to know each other before they got engaged. And it never took very long, so I couldn't say no. My cousin, at that same age, with her and her boyfriend it would go on forever, one time upside down next time right-side up, she had to do it every whichway! Jean-Yves, though, he's the speedy type. No more time than it takes to boil an egg—I know because once... Well anyhow, when Jony was on the way we had to decide, and I was against abortion. So all right, Jean-Yves wasn't too pleased, but I told him, if we know each other enough for him to get me pregnant, we know each other enough to get married...

I thought doing it in our own place it would go better. But right away the wedding night, we got to bed so late I just wanted to go to sleep. Him, he was big on making a video of it with a camera his army pals rented for him. He set the thing on the table in the hotel room so it would shoot the bed, but he didn't know how to aim it right so all's it shows is the wall up above with a hunting picture, and you hear Jean-Yves going Huh huh huh (me, I was too worried somebody would hear us so I didn't make a sound). The counter at the bottom of the picture says it lasted two minutes and twenty-two seconds, and then nothing, after that you hear him snoring. It was a three-hour cassette. After, that's the whole movie: the hunting picture and Jean-Yves snoring.

Okay so, when I tell him I don't think it's right that he starts snoring after three minutes, Jean-Yves says It's your fault, Marie-Claude. First it was because I'd be having my period, then it was because I was pregnant, later it was I was taking the pill or I was a few pounds over. I'm kinda fed up with the whole business. Now, since we took over the bakery, it's better. He goes to bed at five o'clock, he's knocked out, he leaves me alone. Except Sunday nights, because on Monday we're closed. Then I know that after the movie on Channel One I'm in for it. Still, some day I got to take Jony to a doctor, and then I'll talk to him about it.

But there's no doctor right close by here, and the one over in Play, I don't like him. He doesn't appeal to me. His girlfriend neither.

63

PHONE CALLS

I pick up and I hear, "Hey there, baby cousin, this is Roland!"

"Yes?"

"Hello?"

"Yes, hello—whom do you want, sir?"

"Ah, this isn't Bruno Sachs' house?"

"Yes, it is, but Bruno isn't home yet—Oh, if you'll wait just a minute, I hear his car."

I set down the receiver, I run to the door. Bruno closes the car door and heads for me, smiling, with the bread and croissants in his hand.

"I love the way you greet me at the door," he says as he gives me a kiss on the lips, a kiss he tries to prolong.

"...Excuse me, but there's someone calling for you. Cousin... Roland? is that right?"

Bruno opens his mouth, closes his eyes, and sighs. I relieve him of the bread and croissants and point to the phone. "Go ahead! I'll take care of these."

He picks up the receiver and drops into the big armchair. "Hi, Roland," he says, rolling his eyes to heaven. "What's up?"

❀

"Hiya, boy, you're good?"

"Okay..."

"So, what, you're on duty today? That can't be much fun, huh, with all the sick folks there are out there! But I won't bother you for long—I'm not disturbing you, I hope? You weren't the one who answered, so at first I thought I had a wrong number, I almost hung up, but the young lady told me you were just coming in— I mean, I say 'young,' but what do I know, I never saw her, right?... Anyhow, she has a really pretty voice! But don't you tell her I said that, okay? I wouldn't want her to think I'm some kinda yokel!... I'm not disturbing you? You sure?"

"No, not at all... What's up?"

"Because if I'm disturbing you, you tell me, right? I'll call you back later, tomorrow or day after, if you want..."

"No, no, no Roland, really, I'm glad to hear from you. What is it?"

"Ah, you're nice, to say that... Okay, well, for once, I'm calling about myself! See—lately I've got some pain bothering me in my left shoulder, it comes in the morning, it comes at night, it comes any old time, and when it comes I don't know which way to turn!"

"What kind of pain?"

"Well, a pain, that's all. I don't know how to describe it... it starts from the shoulder, you know, that pointy bone up on top you can feel under the skin..."

"Yes..."

"And then it goes down to the elbow, and I can't move my arm."

"Does it last long?"

"No, a split second, barely, but does that hurt! After, I can't do a thing anymore, I'm too scared it's gonna start up again, nossir!"

"Have you taken anything for it—aspirin?"

"Well, you know, I never thought of it! By the time I'd think of it the thing would be over, anyhow!"

"And does it happen often?"

"No, not too often. Eight or ten times a day, but it goes away fast, you know, like lightning. That's it! It feels like a lightning flash going down my arm and naturally that worries me, at my age..."

"Oh yeah? What are you thinking?"

"Well, a heart attack, of course! With all the smoking I did when I was young and all my worries, on top of getting old!"

"Oh! I see... Listen, I can reassure you—a heart attack doesn't feel like that, it's even more painful and when it hits it doesn't let go. In my opinion, what you've got is some tendinitis."

"But I thought—I mean, I don't know where I read, or who told me—that a heart attack makes a pain in the left arm... Oh, I know! It was the brother-in-law of Mireille's brother-in-law, you know who I mean? Albert!"

"Mmmhh. Do I know him?"

"Sure you do! The husband of Josiane's sister-in-law—you know, Josiane, Mireille's sister! Anyhow, what it is is, he had one, a heart attack, and his left arm was hurting for three weeks before, he kept rubbing in these liniments, he thought it was tendinitis, right, and then whaddya know, he goes to his doctor, the doctor lays him down, puts the stethoscope you know where and he turns green— the doctor, not Albert! He does a cardiogram then and there, and the tape wasn't even finished coming through before the guy's on the phone to the EMTs! And at the hospital they told him—told Albert—that if his doctor'd called five minutes later, he could've just said Bye-bye to his widow! So I was thinking I might have the same thing as him…"

"No, Roland, really I don't think so. Tell me, does the pain come when you make certain movements?"

"Movements? Well you know, in my line of work, I make plenty of movements, but if you think I could tell you what they are—I don't know, I'd have to pay attention… So you say it's nothing serious? It's not a heart attack?"

"No, I'm sure of it. Try taking aspirin in the morning when you get up, to see if the pain doesn't ease up."

"Nah, I'm not gonna bother—it's bearable, you know! I'll forget, anyhow. Now that you put my mind at rest, I won't feel it anymore. I mean, as long as it's not a heart attack or angina, fine, it's just the heart I worry about, everything else is in good shape… Still, it's a good thing we've got you! Granted you're not right nearby, but it's worth spending a little extra in telephone bills, you calm me down, specially Mireille and me we do tend to get worked up! In a way, it's probably better you're not right nearby, we'd always be running over to see you, I'm sure. Especially Mireille, she's so anxious!"

"How's she doing, Mireille?"

"Good! Good! Thanks for asking. In fact, she sends her love. Well, right now she's gone out, but every time I call you she asks if I told you she sends her love, and every time I forget, and then she yells at me. So this time, for once, I've done my job! She's over at her sister's, I didn't want to call while she was here, since I hadn't mentioned anything to her, I didn't want to worry her. Now when she comes back I'll be able to tell her I called you, I'll tell her I was worrying and it'll reassure her to know that you told me it was nothing, but you know her, that won't stop her from getting worried herself, in retrospect."

"Yes… it's nice to worry retrospectively. You can scare yourself all you want, you know it's over nothing!"

"Hahahaha! What a joker! You're some guy, Bruno! I'll really have to pass that one on! Ah, you really are Doctor Feelgood, huh? I guess they have a good time, your clients—I mean, your patients… When you can't cure them you can at least see to it they die laughing, right? Your mother used to tell me that all the time, how you made her laugh… Such a sad thing that she's gone, her too! Ah, life, such misery…"

❈

Bruno hangs up. He takes off his glasses, rubs his eyes. "What a nut! Whenever I hear him, I want to laugh and cry at the same time!" He looks up. "Have I told you about him?"

"I don't think so."

"He's the only family I've got left, or just about. His father is still alive, ninety-four, my mother's second cousin. When she died last year, it must have been forty years they hadn't seen each other, but they did talk on the telephone four times a year. Roland I see once a year—in June, in Paris, at the synagogue."

"At the synagogue?"

"For my father's memorial service. I used to go with my mother when she could still walk. That's how I met Roland. When he saw her he flung his arms around her, she didn't recognize him: the last time she'd seen him he was fifteen years old and she wasn't in the same condition. When she told him I was a doctor, he said, 'No! Oh gosh wow, that's great!' He asked her for my address, and ever since, he calls me whenever something bothers him. Generally, he tells me he hasn't told his wife about it, that I shouldn't mention it if she phones—and generally she's already called me the night before to warn me that he's reached crisis level, that a phone call is imminent, and she makes me swear I won't tell her husband she called me! In short… Anyhow, I reassure them, we exchange platitudes, and that's it. Sometimes I get three phone calls in a week; sometimes I don't hear from him for six months. But in the end he always calls. When we meet at the synagogue, he never talks about his health, he tells me his memories of my parents…"

He looks up at me. "Every year, at New Year's, to thank me, he sends a bottle of port, or chocolate cherries. I've never dared tell him I don't like them…"

I burst out laughing. "Now I understand why you have six bottles of port in the storeroom!"

"Yes… the chocolates I give to Madame Leblanc or Madame Borges—their husbands adore them."

"You must really calm him down."

"You think so? I get the sense that he calms himself down, just like he doesn't need anyone else to start worrying. He isn't a hypochondriac, but every now and then he gets a kind of huge fit of anxiety, and when his wife asks what's wrong, the milk boils over (here Bruno beetles his brows, twists his mouth, and starts talking with his hands): 'I've got responsibilities, you know! What would become of you all—the baby and your daughter and you—if I died suddenly? If I died without leaving you a cent, I'd be ashamed the rest of my life.' Anyhow, he'll say he's going to get a checkup, but his wife doesn't want him to, she senses her man is getting frail and she's afraid that some day they'll find something really serious wrong with him… She's the type who says, 'Anyhow, doctors don't ever tell you what they think, they tell you Oh, it's nothing, we'll fix you right up, good thing you came in, and before you know it you die on the operating table and your widow's got nothing left but the eyes to cry with. So for me, doctors, the less you see of them, the better off I am!' The day we met, he introduced her as we left the synagogue, and from the way he said 'This is Fanny's son, you'll never guess what he does—he's a doctor!', I saw Mireille's face light up, she insisted on taking my mother and me to dinner, and ever since then, I'm their compromise: he gets a doctor's opinion without having to go in and be examined... It calms them both down. Since I'm part of their freaking family, even if it is at long distance, they're convinced that Bruno *cannot* lie to them."

"And you think they're wrong to believe that?"

He shrugs. "So far, it's been true. But if someday... he has something serious, what'll I do then?"

"When that day comes, he won't be just your faraway cousin, he'll be a patient. And you'll talk to him the way you do to patients, won't you?"

"Yes... probably. Still—the act of calling me may reassure him, but it doesn't protect him."

"Well no! You're not God Almighty. You're only Doctor Sachs. Which is already pretty good!"

Bruno gets up, he puts his hands on my arms, his forehead against mine. "It doesn't bother you to hang out with some Doctor Feelgood?"

"No. If I was hanging out with some Doctor Feelbad, it would mean I was a masochist. With you, there's not a chance I'd hurt for more than forty seconds. Me neither, my love—you have no right to let me down either."

"You're a hard woman!"

He takes my face tenderly in his hands, puts his lips on mine, and the telephone rings.

64

RAY MARKSON

The telephone rings. Once. Twice. Three times. I hear him yell, "Yeah!"

"*What's up, Doc?* Am I disturbing you?"

He sighs. Apparently I've called at the wrong moment. I hope they were only at the foreplay stage.

"Ah, hi, Ray... No, no, not at all. How are you?"

"Me? I'm full of beans, man. I've been fine since they put me on—what do you call it, this *ecumenical* medicine, whatever, that stimulates the white cells *and* the red cells and everything else. Okay, so apparently it'll only work for a few months—that's what your pal Zim tells me—but you know the story about the guy who jumps off the top of the Empire State Building, don't you?"

"Uhh... No, I don't think so."

"Sure you do! I told it to you a hundred times! You know, as he drops past each person leaning out a window, he yells—"

"Oh yeah, it's coming back to me..."

" 'Fine so far!' Hahahaha!"

I hear him put his hand over the receiver and say "It's Ray." I laugh even harder. I start coughing, but it stops soon.

"But I didn't call to talk about my health, *buddy. Happy birthday!*"

"... Oh! You're a sweetheart, Ray. Outside of Diego and you, nobody ever wishes me happy birthday."

"Really? You astound me! What about your Juliette, there—What's her name again?"

"Uhh—Pauline. I don't know if she knows the date..."

"Yeah, well, I don't want to mix in where it doesn't concern me, *and you're a big boy now*—what are you, thirty-seven? Thirty-eight?"

"Uhh, no, not yet... thirty-four."

"*Whaddyaknow! You're just a kid!* Kate swore to me you were older. Just shows how wrong you can be, *hey?* Anyhow, listen to the advice of an old Puritan who's seen enough of them: a girlfriend who's not instantly interested in your birthday, your zodiac sign, and your shirt size—you gotta ask yourself some questions! I don't want to make trouble between you, but… you understand that for Kate and me, it's important. We don't want you falling into bad hands."

I'm having trouble keeping serious. Kate throws me a disapproving look.

"Uhh… You're very kind, Ray, but I don't think you have anything to worry about. Really."

Bruno's voice has turned hard; I decide I better not press it. "Okay, okay! In any case, we wanted to send good wishes today, it's not nothing, especially for you, with a birthday only every four years!"

He gives a little laugh. "Yes—I could even consider that I'll never die, since three years out of four I can't even be sure I was born!"

"Hey now, always the philosopher, huh? Why did you study medicine, *for Pete's sake?*"

"Dunno. To make Mama and Papa happy, probably."

"Jackass! Doesn't matter how old he gets, he still spouts bullshit!"

"Fine, so you called to insult me, is that it, or to wish me happy birthday?"

"Both, *mon capitaine.* We wanted to come over and see you tonight, but Kate remembered you're on call, *right?*"

"*Right.* And it could get real busy, there's a mumps epidemic at the moment."

"*Mumps? Watch your balls, bud!*"

"Don't you worry, I already had it when I was little."

"Oh, then I won't say anything to your—Pauline? Is that right?"

"Thanks so much!"

"But tell me, when are you going to introduce us?"

He hesitates, then fidgets again. "Uhhh… it's just—the right time hasn't come up."

"Diego's seen her twice for five minutes, so he knows what she looks like, and he's pretty impressed, but when it comes to chicks he's not the best judge—"

"Oh, and you are?"

"Whoa there, you little jerk!" He starts laughing. "Okay, I won't press it, but you know what I think. And anyhow, if one of these nights we feel like stopping in without warning, you won't throw us out, right?"

"No, of course not… We'll set something up. I'll call you this week, okay?"

"*Suits me fine.* Meanwhile, I send a hug. And I'll give you to *the one and only Wittgenstein's Mistress. Bye!*"

I hand the phone to Kate, who looks daggers at me. And while she's talking to Bruno, I leave the room and burst into laughter.

65

PAULINE KASSER

He lays a hand on mine. "That was delicious." Then he lowers his eyes, sighs, frowns.

"What is it?"

"I'm really sorry you learned about it that way—my birthday."

"What does that matter? And besides, the subject never came up. We didn't celebrate mine either."

Still holding his hand, I stand up, circle the table and come to sit beside him on the wooden bench. I put my arms around his neck. "Anyhow, this weekend wasn't ideal for a birthday. Sure, if I'd known, I could have made you a better meal."

"Impossible!"

"Oh, you—you're just in love."

"Yes. You aren't?"

"This isn't about me."

"Sometimes," he says in a faintly suspicious tone, "I find that you have a strong tendency to avoid answering a question."

"Ah, and what is it your teacher, and nonetheless friend, the good Professor Lance always says? 'When you ask questions…'"

"'…all you ever get are answers.' Mmmhh. You already know too much."

"Well then, there's no point in discussion." I plant a kiss on his lips and stand up to make coffee.

In search of some final trace of sauce, Bruno wipes a last bit of bread over the inside of his plate, then stands up and clears the table. I see him lean, deep in thought, against the wall near the window, and scan the landscape. Finally he says,

"In December, two years ago, this whole area woke up to two feet of snow. Ever since I learned how to drive, I've had a unholy fear of snow. Here, with the ditches, the narrow little roads, the steep farm trails, it's hell. Usually it doesn't last

FURTHER INVESTIGATIONS (SUNDAY, FEBRUARY 29)

long, the weather's too mild around here. But that year, just before Christmas, it turned very cold. In the cities, the homeless were dying like flies. I told Madame Leblanc to leave the office door open at night on weekends, and to put the word out. I didn't want anyone dying of cold at the door of a place that was empty but always heated... It was ridiculous, because there aren't any homeless people around here. There are people who are utterly destitute, or very backward, sometimes living in unbelievable shacks way back in the woods, or even right in a village, but everyone has a roof over his head... Christmas Eve, coming home from the clinic, about three hundred yards past the bridge over the Tourmente, I was rolling along, I saw a fellow staggering in the other direction, in shirtsleeves, cigarette stub in his mouth, some awful bag over his shoulder. He had to be coming from the café at Saint-Jacques and walking home after closing time. I kept on another few hundred yards and then I thought, the bridge railing is pretty low, the walkways are icy, and down below the Tourmente is frozen. What do I do? Do I keep going, or do I turn around to satisfy myself he doesn't break his neck in the dark? I made a U-turn—he was halfway across the bridge, leaning over the railing, he was swaying back and forth like an old Jew praying. I stopped, I lowered the window, I asked him where he was headed. He didn't answer, so I got out. I asked him if he was going home, and where he lived. After a bit, he babbled something incomprehensible, he was muttering, waving his arms, he was blind drunk. He finally did tell me he was going 'that way', and pointed vaguely. I got him to sit in the car, I asked him to show me how to go... We drove two or three miles on roads I'd never been on before, or that I didn't recognize because of the dark and the snow. He wasn't in great shape, he was talking by signs, and since we couldn't go fast, it took a while. I was thinking we'd never find our way, and that I'd have to bring him back here. And then all of a sudden, he signalled me to stop, he got out, he pushed open a gate, and pointed to a wooden shack a little way off, I could see a thread of smoke coming out of a stovepipe on the top of the roof. He kept making me these confusing signals, he was getting excited, spluttering because I didn't understand. It turned out the road was a dead end and he was trying to get me to turn around there in the front area so I'd be able to leave. As soon as the car was facing the other way, he knocked on the window, and said—distinctly, this time—'You're a nut... case.'"

Bruno paused a moment, then resumed. "That was the night it was ten below, remember? The next morning, two people in the area had died of cold: an old lady with no family who'd been without heat for a week, and who nobody was looking after... and a baby whose mother had stuck him in the garage because he was crying too loud and keeping everyone else up. She'd put him on a folding bed a yard away from the heater, thinking that would do fine. When I went over there, she couldn't believe me when I said he was dead. She howled, she cursed me, but she didn't believe me."

I come closer, I slip my hand into Bruno's, I lay my head against his shoulder.

"Over the next few days, I looked for my drunk's house; I never managed to find it. All that winter, and even after, whenever I crossed the bridge I would stop and look over the rail to make sure no one had fallen into the water or onto the rocks…"

He turns toward me, a mournful smile contorts his lips. "He was right. To do this job the way it should be done, you've got to be nuts. Nuts are the only ones who want to save people's lives, without realizing it can't be done. People who pretend to believe otherwise are bastards."

66

IN AN OLD JOURNAL

Life together, most often, isn't life as a couple, it's a life of trouble, a life of trumps and chumps. I've seen so many ill-matched couples, hating and accommodating at once, for whom the main issue was power—determining the color of the couch and the bathroom tiles, choosing the children's names and the way to dress them, refusing pleasure in the name of duty, sneaking pleasures in the name of personal freedom, rejecting the partner's desire in order to vindicate one's own frustrations, letting him fuck around right and left in order thereafter—in a display of magnanimity and understanding—to enslave him the more by forgiving him.

In the common mythology, living as a couple, marrying, having children, is "creating the true family we dreamed of and never had." In reality, it is mostly reproducing the bad family we came out of, restoring in caricature the same goddamn family we used to spit on, giving a semblance of legitimacy to a dubious bond—of circumstance or convenience.

I've seen infinitely more marriages of convenience than abortions of convenience.

Most couples detest one another and are determined to do nothing about it. Dependence—material, symbolic, social, emotional—is such, for both parties, that they refuse to separate because they know that what they cannot manage to pull off together they will be incapable of pulling off singly. Living in a couple is so much more convenient than living alone. It makes it possible to have a house of one's own, a car for work and another for the weekend, to travel to sunny places with the gigolo or whore you sleep with every day (it's so dangerous, so uncertain, to fuck at random!), to get low-cost loans, to frequent other couples without arousing pity or dying of jealousy (at least not immediately), to produce children, to look socially correct, normal, like everybody else.

And therefore, settling down is often a matter of settling issues, sparing yourself. You marry a blonde with big tits and a big behind to avoid knowing you're homosexual, you pile up professional burdens to console yourself for never having shown a painting or finished a novel, you take out a big life insurance policy (double indemnity in case of death by road accident) to cancel the guilt of not loving the old lady and kids enough.

Marrying means grabbing the neck of the bottle and sliding right inside it, into the formaldehyde flask where you'll end up an aborted foetus, an unfinished person, stifled, sealed up, forever mummified, a stranger to love, forever exiled from life.

Everyone talks about love, and all there is is arrangements. Separate and sometimes irreconcileable hopes writ between the lines on the joint wedding wish-list. Outsize expectations which each one knows the other could never fulfill.

Everyone talks about trust, and all there is is fakery, counterfeits, disguises, lies. Inside the couple, it's every man for himself. Which is to say, it's war.

And the strongest sentiment is often contempt.

I grasped this a long time ago, one night at work when I was learning to deliver babies. I saw war, ruthless war, between a man and a woman.

The man was standing by the labor table; it wasn't their first child, but it was the first time he was present at the birth. I've never understood why fathers are required to be present at childbirths, as if all of them are equipped to manage it. This one was obviously in agony. It hurt him to see his wife pouring sweat, suffering, writhing. The more time passed, the more he resented her, the more he hated himself for resenting her, the poor parturient on her bed of pain. I could read it on his face. The woman, for her part, felt things weren't moving ahead, she was haranguing everyone, and him especially.

They already had three daughters, and he would have liked a son, that's understandable, but she was heartily hoping for another girl; she had told us that several times, while staring hard at him as if to say "You don't carry them, you've got nothing to say about it."

During the delivery, the husband was having a terrible time, he was trying not to look at that area of his wife's body he'd certainly never seen in that condition—distended, deformed, monstrous, unfathomable. The midwife presented them with the baby, saying, "It's a beautiful little girl." And at that moment I saw the wife turn to her sheepish, clumsy, unshaven husband—her husband who during that whole previous hour was probably yearning to be somewhere, anywhere, else, disappointed now but still very moved—who was reaching out tenderly to take the child in his arms and lay it on his wife's belly. Before he could touch it, right under his nose she snatched the baby out of the midwife's hands, clutched it to her flowery nightgown, and with a look of triumph said to him, "HA!"

Life can't be happiness. It can only be never-ending misery and troubles. And when you're two people together it's twice the misery.

FURTHER INVESTIGATIONS (SUNDAY, FEBRUARY 29)

Everyone pretends to forget that whatever happens, living equals suffering. The body is much more suited to pain than to pleasure.

How long does it take to reach orgasm? An eternity. How long does it last?

How long does it take to feel pain? A split second. How long does it last?

In any case, loving or not, beloved or not, sooner or later a person suffers. Willy-nilly. That's what the body is made for. To suffer and to reproduce. In other words: to perpetuate the suffering of the species. This is not a moral concept, this is not a religious concept, it's a biological reality. My body suffers to remind me ceaselessly that the world is hostile. That fire burns the fingers, that snow freezes the toes, that billions of micro-organisms, when the fancy takes them, can just slap me with a case of meningitis or septicemia in a flash, and that's all, folks!

The body suffers because the body lives. Suffering is neither redemptive nor punitive, it is consubstantial with life. The body is not fragile, it is hypersensitive, irreparable, biodegradable. The body is a goddam sensation machine and most of its sensations are unpleasant, because every passing second hastens its deterioration. Even for newborns, pure pleasure—just suckin'n'sleepin'—is not the whole story, as we'd like to think. With the first suck, pow! the first colic. With the first kissy, pow! the first cold. With the first summer, pow! the first convulsion.

The top cause of death in newborns is compromised intrauterine development, from women drinking, smoking, using drugs, or not eating. In infants and toddlers, it's accidents in the home—He fell off his changing table; in older children, it's car accidents—No seatbelt on; in adolescents it's suicide—We never would've imagined.

That being the case, who's got the nerve to say that the family environment isn't lethal?

Life is a hell. You don't see it right away, you learn it in your body. And when the partner's body gets involved, if there's no love, or love no longer, the hell is double.

I've seen women with their thighs pressed tight together and their purse parked on top, spitting forth their hatred of a husband who—when he's not out sleeping with tarts—dozes off during the TV movie, then slouches up to bed and, when she finally joins him after hanging out the third wash and putting a suppository up the little girl who won't sleep, rolls over to her without even opening his eyes, mashes his muzzle against her face, pushes up the nightgown—need I say more, Doctor? *You know how men are...*

I've seen men murmuring, as they write out their checks, how they would really have liked to get back to soccer or start building models again. But Saturdays it's impossible, there are errands to do at the supermarket and my wife doesn't drive, or she hasn't got the patience for it, or she wants me with her to pick out the doormat color. And Sundays it's not possible either, there's the bike to grease, the table to fix, the car to clean, the lawn to mow, the pipe on the built-in stove to replace because the in-laws are coming to lunch and the oven has to heat up at least an hour beforehand; and in the afternoon, if it doesn't rain, the women always want to take a walk along the banks of the Tourmente up to Grandpa's cabin, since he died the flowers need to be watered in summer and the roof checked for leaks in winter... So soccer—really can't get to it, the models—really no time, and anyhow I've got no room for a workshop so I'd have to do it in the living room but that's always annoyed her to see me carving balsam wood with a razor blade or glueing on my sails with tweezers, she says if I took that much care with everything it would be wonderful! It doesn't help to put down newspaper, she hollers because it leaves marks on her oilcloth, and if ever a drop of glue falls on the floor she jumps all over me, but when it comes to bed, I don't have to tell you. She always says she wants me to be tender, say sweet things, talk to her, but actually what she wants is for me to let her talk, talk, talk, you know what I'm sayin, *You know how women are...*

67

PAULINE KASSER

I put down the journal.

Seated at the table, Bruno looks at me. "You're going to tell me I'm a sonuvabitch, writing that and making you read it…"

I shake my head no. I kneel beside him, he bends and lays his head on my shoulder, I say in his ear, "When you talk to me, I listen to you. When you have me read something, I try to understand what's behind it… the way you do with the people you see. You spend your time listening to what people confide in you, and you shouldn't have the right to write?"

He lifts his head, he looks at me. "You're not scared?"

"Scared! Scared of what? Of what you think? What you write? Your outlook on life is one thing. Your looks, your words, your touch on me, that's another. I know who you are. You're the man I love and who loves me. What you write can't do me harm."

His throat tightens. His eyes mist. "Do you think writing —writing heals?"

68

STABBINGS

The telephone rings. I pick up. "Hello?"

"Madame Benoît?"

"Yes, this is she."

"Good morning, madame, this is Doctor Sachs, from Play. You asked me to call…"

"Oh, yes, good morning, doctor, Thanks for calling back, I'm sorry to trouble you on a Sunday like this, but you know my husband and I have a store, we're very busy during the week. I wanted to speak to you about my brother…"

"Your brother?"

"Yes, you know—Georges, he lives with our mother, Madame Destouches."

"Yes?"

"It's a little hard to explain, but… my sisters and I—there are four of us—we're very worried over the question of Georges. Actually, mainly for our mother, who's old, after all, and has these leg ulcers—of course you know all that, how do they look to you these days, her ulcers?"

"Mmmhh. They come and go. She's very old, she's not able to form scar tissue easily."

"I can certainly believe that, it's been going on for so long! I will say, though, that since she moved she's much better off than in the cottage where the two of them were living, they slept in the same room, it was damp. Now at least she's got her own room. But actually, that's not what I…"

"Yes…"

"You see, doctor, my sisters and I feel it's wearing her out to live with Georges, in fact she says so, she's tired, and he really doesn't make her life easy…"

"What do you mean?"

"Come on, you know very well he drinks! Everybody knows that, you've gone to pick him up on the road just like we have, he's nearly gotten himself run over, he's taken a lot of falls and he just about froze to death in the ditch, I don't know how many stitches he's had—you know all that!"

"Well, and what?"

"Well, it can't go on, that's what! I'm sick of seeing Mother live with that—that drunk, that good-for-nothing, seeing her waste away, it can't go on this way, that's what! And besides, he's filthy, he never washes, he smells bad, it's unbearable to live with him! Something has to be done! He has to—he has to go!"

"Mmmhh."

He doesn't speak for a moment, then he goes on: "I've been taking care of Madame and Monsieur Destouches for years, and their life together hasn't always been easy, but your mother doesn't seem to want him to go. At least, I've never heard her say she did. Quite the opposite. She's even very attached to him. And he—"

"Well of course, sure she's attached to him—to that ball-and-chain! I never did see why! Whenever he finds a job, within three days they throw him out, and now ever since his accident, not only has he turned into a wino but he hasn't had to lift a finger, because he gets this disability benefit! My sisters and I have to work, break our backs on the job, we have children to raise, and him—he just sits there, he does nothing, he smokes, he drinks, and on top of it he's spending our mother's retirement money, and we don't know if she's got anything left to live on!"

"Come now, I think you—"

"So, you see, we've discussed it and we've come to a decision. And since you're Mother's doctor, I'm calling you so we can work together—"

"Work together?"

"Yes, we've decided Georges has to go into a rehabilitation program, because enough is enough! He's going to turn dangerous, and there'll be trouble. The other day, in fact, when I went to see Mother, he got almost aggressive with me because I was trying to convince her to go back into the hospital to get the leg-ulcers treated! Really, you know, she can't go on this way—I don't mean you're not taking proper care of her, but the skin graft did do her good the first time, so I don't see why it shouldn't be tried again, and besides, while she's in the hospital she won't have to deal with Georges!"

"Wait a minute, I'd like to get this straight. What would be the purpose of hospitalization, in your mind? To treat your mother's ulcers, or to separate her from your brother?"

"Well, that's just it, that's what I was coming to, Doctor. We know very well that Mother would never let Georges go into rehab while she's home. But if she's in the hospital, we could tell her that it wasn't working out and we had to take him away!"

"Take him away? Where?"

"Look, you know what I mean—to a sanitarium, of course! We just have to get him committed, and that'll do it!… Hello? Doctor? Are you there? Hello?!"

"I'm still here, Madame Benoît… What is it you expect from me, exactly?"

"Well, I talk to Mother often about her ulcers, and so do my sisters, we talk about it every time we go see her or speak on the phone, I have a feeling it won't be long before she'll agree to another skin graft, so we thought since you're the doctor for both of them you'd be in the best position… Once Mother's in the hospital, you'll make out the commitment papers for us. And then, since you go often to the hospital, you'll be the one to explain to Mother, when it's all done. Coming from you, she'll accept it, because she trusts you—"

"I see… You know, there's a strong likelihood that they wouldn't keep him in—the psychiatrists have something to say about it, and the facilities are always very crowded…"

"Ah, I know, I'm aware of the problem—my younger sister is a practical nurse at the hospital center in Tourmens. But she's already spoken to the doctor there, she knows him well: he takes care of her son and her husband. And she called me this morning to say that he agrees to keep Georges for as long as necessary, until we find a solution—"

"A… final solution?"

"Well, I mean, some kind of solution! Because I'm not gonna kid myself—Georges is just unsalvageable, there'll never be any way to stop him from drinking, and even if they managed to, he's a parasite anyhow, you can't do a thing with him, all he knows how to do is live off Mother!"

"He's got his disability benefit…"

"He drinks it all up, his benefit! He doesn't contribute a cent, and when she sends him out to do errands for the house he buys wine, so it's got to stop! You understand?"

"Yes, Madame Benoît, I do understand. But I won't commit your brother, and I won't hospitalize your mother to make it easier for you."

"But—but—"

"Goodbye, madame."

And before I can say a thing he hangs up. I try to call back for a while but it keeps giving a busy signal. Damn phone system—never works when you need it.

69

TWO HANDWRITTEN PAGES

When I was a resident in pediatrics, there was an eight- or ten-year-old boy on the ward who constantly shit in his pants. Not because he couldn't retain it but—on the contrary—because he retained it too thoroughly. He never went to the toilet. He'd held it in for so long that he could no longer feel the stuff piling up in his rectum. So, from building up like that, it would come out on its own, sometimes in a flood. Efforts were made to re-train him, by making him go to the toilet regularly—every morning, every noon, and every evening after dinner. To check whether or not he'd emptied his rectum, you had to put a finger up his hind end every day. And, of course, it was always full. And of course, he was always frightened at the sight of one of us coming into his room with a rubber sheath on the index finger.

I loathed doing it to him. I would warn him a quarter-hour in advance, as much to prepare myself as him, and I asked my chief not to make me the only one to do it. He answered, "It's your patient, work it out." So, one time out of three, I didn't do the examination, and I'd write just anything on the record sheet.

He was a very gentle, fearful child, whimpery, clinging. Always looking to be cuddled. The nurses on the unit adored him because he'd follow them around like a little dog. He smiled all the time, like a happy idiot, but he was neither one nor the other.

He'd stay in pajamas all day because that way, when he soiled it would show right away, and it was easier to change him. For lack of any success at teaching him to go shit where he was supposed to, we tried teaching him to change himself, but he wasn't even aware that great packs of shit were filling his pants and sliding down along his legs.

Ever since he was born, his mother had been putting diapers on him.

One day, I asked the psychologist on duty if anyone knew why the boy held it in like that. He told me that "encopresis" (the word itself is very constipated. And it doesn't tell you anything!) was often the result of a disastrous relationship with the mother.

I refused to believe that. Until the day I saw the mother.

She never came in the morning; I wondered why. She would drop by to see her son at eight in the evening, when there was no doctor left on the ward. And even so, she came hardly more than once a week.

But she did come once in the morning because she was forced to: we had called a planning meeting to decide what to do with him after the hospital. He had been there for three months without a bit of progress. It would require the mother's consent to release him (nobody in the place knew the father). Actually, we suspected she was quite content not to have the boy on her hands anymore, and didn't much want to bother with him. What had brought her to hospitalize him was that as long as she could put him in infant things, the constant changings were all right with her (he wasn't really awfully big), but now he'd started growing; she had to buy him the adult-size diapers, and that cost too much.

She had some nondescript boyfriend with her, who stayed out in the hall for the five minutes she spent in the boy's room (the nurses had told me about him) and whom the kid detested with all his heart (he's the one who told me that).

I was at the door of the treatment room. The kid—I can't for the life of me remember his name—was in the hallway, dressed in pajamas that were slightly too large (since he soiled himself two or three times a day, we had to dress him in whatever we had on hand), and he was playing with another hospitalized kid. The little ones adored him, because he was completely docile and absolutely incapable of brutality.

Just then, I saw a woman come in—medium height, blondish short hair stuck to her neck, a suit that was too short and ill-fitting, expressionless face, pinched lips, a strange mix of coldness and vulgarity (I think I recall high heels). This lacquer-haired guy with a little mustache, spindly and buttoned up in a tight suit, followed right behind her, a raincoat over his arm. The woman called the child sharply by his first name. "What are you doing out here? Don't you stay out in the hall, you're in people's way! Go into your room!" The boy had turned as she walked in, and started toward her. When he heard this he stopped short, his eternal smile vanished for a split second, then he began playing with his friend again and they went into the room. She hadn't made the slightest gesture toward him—nothing that might indicate that she was his mother, that he was her child.

As she walked past me, I heard her say, "I told you they wouldn't do a thing for him!" and her boyfriend nodded like a dashboard doggie, his lips pursed in contempt beneath his mustache.

That day for the first time I had a terrifying sensation, the same one I felt just now before I hung up the phone on another miserable turd—an uncontrollably powerful feeling of hatred that leaves me trembling whenever it surges up in me.

257

That day, I almost did a very stupid thing. Seeing the way that woman spoke to her son, I wanted to spring on her, punch her, fling her to the ground, slam her head against the tile floor and strangle her to death—a hideous death, lips blue, tongue bulging out, eyes glazed.

I believe the reason I forget the child's first name is that his name, as the mother had spat it out in the hallway, was drenched in all the hatred she felt for him, hatred she probably felt for all men through him.

Good God, how some women hate men. And how they make themselves hated back.

70

SUTURES

You rinse your hands. "Well now, young man, how did you manage to get yourself into such a state?'

"He climbed the cherry tree and he fell…"

You take two or three paper towels from the dispenser, you dry off and you come back to me. "All right then! Come closer, so I can have a look."

Standing in front of you, with my mother holding me by the shoulders, I'm sort of shaky, I feel like crying. You roll the desk chair over to me and you sit down. Your face is just at the level of mine. "If I hurt you, tell me."

My wrist hurts and I support it with my other hand. You put your big hands delicately on my arm. "Can you turn it?"

I try. I can't, it hurts too much. I shake my head. Your fingers slowly feel along the bone beneath the skin, inch by inch. Suddenly the pain starts up again. Tears rush to my eyes.

"It's broken, I'm afraid," you say.

You stroke my cheek and the back of my neck. "Okay, now—we're gonna send you over for an X-ray, and you'll have something to draw on at recess tomorrow."

"Is it serious?"

"There's certainly a fracture, ma'am—you see here, the bump he's got just above the wrist, that's the bone overlapping there. But at his age, these things mend very well in a few weeks. I'm going to put his arm in a sling until he gets the cast."

"Oh, gosh! That forehead's really bleeding—and what've you got on your knee, young lady?"

"I banged it Friday."

"What? Friday? You waited three days to come in and get that stitched?"

With your hands on your hips, a little paunchy in your white coat, you give me a wrathful look.

"No, no, Friday was the knee! The forehead I just did now, I was playing with the kids in the square and me and Annette crashed heads…"

I refold the piece of blood-soaked cotton and press it back to my eyebrow. You take the cotton from me. "Leave that alone, silly, cotton sticks to wounds. You've got to use gauze pads. Or a clean handkerchief. You press hard for a few minutes and the bleeding stops. Come over here."

You point to a white chair near a sink. On that side of the room, hidden behind very tall shelf-cases backed by some cloth with broad green stripes, there's a high examining table with a plastic sheet. I sit on a stool near the basin, facing the table.

"Does it go real deep? Do I need stitches?"

You pour water into a little metal bowl, liquid soap into the water. "We'll see. What about your friend—did she get hurt?"

You dip a sterile pad into the antiseptic liquid and move toward me.

"No, she's okay."

"Lean your head back." You wipe the pad over my forehead. "Does that sting?"

"N-no, it's okay."

❀

You throw the gauze pad into the garbage can lined with a blue plastic bag. You dip another gauze pad into the warm water and go to work again. You rub a little harder. Lying on the table, I raise my head to look.

"See, cotton sticks to it… And you've got lots of tiny bits of gravel in the wound—where did you skid, on your bike? In the square at the town hall, I bet… Am I hurting you?"

"Not too much."

While you're throwing one pad away and taking another, I feel something trickle on my thigh. "It's bleeding!"

"Don't move, it's nothing. Press hard on it, it'll stop."

You apply the gauze pad to my leg and you set my index finger on top. When I press it hurts, but I'm scared it might start bleeding again, so I press hard.

"Good! Well, you'll need a couple of stitches, on top there."

"Really? Will it hurt?"

"Horribly! But if we don't do it, we'll just have to cut off the whole—"

I look at you—you're smiling this wicked smile. "Okay, go ahead."

*

You lean over, you take a metal box from the bottom shelf of the rolling table, you set it next to me on the stone edge of the sink and you open it. It holds metal instruments, scissors, a scalpel, I don't know what-all. My heart skips a few beats.

"Is it deep? Can you see the bone? I didn't even hit that hard…"

You reach into a small chest of drawers and get a tiny plastic envelope, you peel it open and you drop its contents into the instrument case.

"When the skin is cut right through at that spot you'll always see bone. Are you frightened?"

I don't answer. I'm not feeling too well. I'm hot, I'm dizzy, my eyes fog over a little. "I'm dizzy, I feel about to fall…"

"I see. Come lie down, monsieur, you'll feel better."

I stand up, but my legs give way, I feel like a sack of cement. You support me, you lift me up, you lay me on the examining table.

"It'll pass."

You take my pulse, look at your watch. My mouth is dry, but I think I'm a little less dizzy.

"It's silly, a man my age passing out…"

"There's no special age for passing out."

*

I moan, I open my eyes, close them. I bring my hand to my forehead. I mop it with the little tissue that I'm still clenching from earlier. I hear you cross the room, then come back to me.

"Once you're lying down, there's nothing more to worry about, ma'am. Here, this'll be more comfortable." You lift my head and put a firm little cushion under my neck. "There now! Shall we start?"

I open my eyes. I sigh. "Do we have to?"

You push the rolling stand over to the examining table, you pull up the tall stool and, before perching on top of it, you bend over and then straighten up with a long packet in your hand. You peel it open and pull out two gloves. You put on the left one, then the right; you tug at the cuffs and they snap into place.

"Well, yes, we do. It's not very deep, but it's big, and if we don't sew you up, at your age you could develop a leg ulcer…"

"Good Lord! Is it going to hurt?"

"I'm going to give you a local anesthetic. You won't feel anything but the shots. Are you vaccinated against tetanus?"

261

FURTHER INVESTIGATIONS (SUNDAY, FEBRUARY 29)

"Good Lord—years ago! You realize, at my age! Is that dangerous?"

You take a syringe, a needle, a little glass vial filled with translucent fluid. "As far as we know, no... If it's over ten years, you should have both the serum and the vaccine."

"Good Lord, all that!!!"

You set down the vial. You point the syringe toward the ceiling and press the plunger. A drop beads at the tip of the needle.

"All set? Here comes the shot."

I clench my teeth.

❋

"Do you feel anything?"

I feel the fluid fill out the web of skin between my thumb and index finger, I turn my head, I crane my neck, I see swelling at the spot where you've injected the drug. You pull out the needle. I'm sweating heavily.

"A little..."

"I'm going to do it on the other side, too, so the area gets completely numb."

"Go ahead—that'll teach me!"

Now you part the index finger from the middle one and you push the needle into the web between them. I clench my teeth.

"Soon you won't feel a thing."

You press the plunger. After a few seconds, I no longer have any sensation in my finger. I heave a great sigh of relief.

"That must have been one hell of a pain!"

"Oh yeh, and it's my own fault—I tried to take it out with tweezers, but I'm right-handed, obviously, so of course I couldn't really pull. Then I pushed instead, but that was worse: I would've had to force it out the other side, but that hurt too much. When I think how I usually take one of those things out in two shakes, it burns me up!"

"It's always easier when it's not on yourself. But tell me..." You look me straight in the eye. "I've never fished, so I don't quite see—How does a person put a hook into his own finger?"

71

IN THE SMALL LOGBOOK

Sunday housecalls:

Jules Gavarry, Deuxmonts (Dr. Boulle)—sciatica: *Saturday night/Sunday morning. I gave him an IM shot of anti-inflammatories, but he was absolutely determined to leave very early in the morning for some trade fair, so you probably won't see him this week, I hope he doesn't have too bad a time, he did have to travel four hundred miles*

Armand Duras, Sainte-Sophie (Dr. Jardin)—attack of cardiac insufficiency: *I asked his daughter to call you Tuesday if he isn't any better*

Arnaud Belletto, Marquay (Dr. Boulle)—flu

Janine Daudet, Saint-Jacques (Dr. Jardin)—death certificate

Lucienne Darrieussecq, Langes (Dr. Carrazé)—abdominal pain: *I don't know what to think, I can't find a cause for the discomfort she experiences during evacuation, but on examining her abdomen I found it hard, I wonder if her colon ought to be explored*

Sunday office visits:

Norbert Ferry, "La Robertine" (Deuxmonts): Asthma attack

Madame ?? (Saint-Jacques)

Mathieu Valabrègue (Play): suture

André Alferi (Play): removal of fishhook

Roselyne Mémoire (Marquay—Dr. Boulle): *You know who she is? Oh, you know the family? This child is in a mess beyond belief. I'm very, very disturbed because somebody has got to take charge of this situation. She seemed to want me to keep this to myself, but it shook me up so badly that I thought I've got to discuss this with—*

FURTHER INVESTIGATIONS (SUNDAY, FEBRUARY 29)

72

IN A NEW JOURNAL
4:25 p.m.

I'm waiting for a patient to call me back to say how long ago he had a tetanus shot.

Last night, eleven o'clock, a fireman phones me, he wasn't on duty, he was at a family dinner at his parents' house. His little girl was playing dolls with a slightly older cousin, they'd gone beneath the dining table among the parents' legs, it's so much better for playing under there. As they got ready to leave, the parents look for her, finally find her, but the kid doesn't want to go, she's happy there, she wants to stay. "Come on out now! We're leaving." "Nooo, I wanna play!" The father's exasperated, he grabs her, the youngster wriggles, he tugs, she twists away, she lets out a scream, her arm goes stiff, and the mother yells, "Now he's done it, pulling on her so rough with his big paws, now he broke something!" The child's not moving the arm, can't touch it no way, she hollers if anyone comes close. "Take her to the hospital?" "Well couldn't we maybe go to the doctor's first?"

When they come in, the fireman father is embarrassed, he's holding his daughter tight against his chest, she's simpering and whimpering but she's also keeping an eye on whatever's going on, she's perfectly aware that she's got him by the nose, this big lug who's done her wrong.

She wasn't three years old, she was cute as a button, big brown eyes, when I saw her I thought I would've loved to have one like her, if I hadn't ruled out that whole business.

She looked at me full of suspicion, I looked back, I went into my number as this fellow who only cares about grown-ups, and while the father was confessing his crime in minute detail I was fiddling with the fancy multicolored-triple-ball rattle, the one nobody can resist when it's lying on the edge of the table, not even the mothers-with-big-families, who've certainly seen plenty of rattles. In twenty seconds, the child reaches out her left hand, she grabs the rattle and turns it every whichway, that's what it's made for. Her right arm doesn't move, the wrist flexes a little, but that's all. As the father is talking and the child is playing, I put my thumb on the fold of her elbow, very delicately I take hold of the right wrist, I turn it, I fold back the forearm, I feel the snap of the dislocated bone moving into place, the child gives a little cry of surprise and jumps off her father's lap, darts away and doesn't even realize that she's now playing with both hands again. Cases like that I'd be delighted to have every Saturday, every day even. But that would be too nice.

At 11:45 this morning, a girl—blonde, impassive, silent, eighteen or twenty years old, walking so slow you'd think she's been hit over the head or she's got something pressing on her brain. She's come in for a follow-up vaccination: she holds out her health booklet and pulls the package from the pocket of her car-coat. I show some surprise: a vaccine, on a Sunday? Her bulging stomach and chest are unmistakeable; I say "How far along?", but she looks at me blankly, so I feel very foolish, I think I've goofed, I've said something dumb, I flush, I take her health booklet, she's sixteen and a half but seems a lot older, her hair is dirty and she looks tired, I tell her that first I'm going to examine her, "Keep your slacks on, lie down," and she does. Her breasts overflow her brassiere and with the stomach she's got on her, the brown line, the extruded navel, I know I wasn't dreaming. I lay my hand on her belly, nothing's moving, I take the obstetric stethoscope, I listen, I hear, the heart's beating, it sounds right to me, I move my hand again over the belly and I feel an arm sliding under there and I look at her, she says nothing, she remains expressionless, passive, silent, off somewhere else.

And finally I say, "I don't think we'll do your vaccination now."

"No? How come?" in a monotone.

"We don't give this kind of vaccine to pregnant women."

She looks at me with that same absent gaze, she doesn't speak. I don't get the sense that she's thinking, but rather that my words are coming to her from very far off, and don't matter to her. I do nothing, say nothing, I don't move, I wait, but she goes on looking at me with the same fixed air of someone waiting, someone with all the time in the world. After a long, long silence, she says, "Can I get dressed?" I say yes, I wonder what she's going to do, what she'll ask me, she gets dressed, she takes back her health booklet and her vaccine, puts them into the left pocket of her car-coat, pulls her wallet from the right pocket—"How much is it?"—and, dumbfounded, I say, "You haven't registered your pregnancy yet, have you? Would you like me to make out the papers?"

She shakes her head violently. "No."

"You don't want to?"

"No." She opens her wallet. "How much is it?"

I didn't want her to pay me, she wouldn't leave without paying me. She stood there, immobile, obstinate, a bill in her hand, she didn't budge, all I could do was give her the change. She said thank you and she left. I know her name, I know where she lives, I know who her family doctor is (I could see all that in her health record booklet), but I didn't know what to do and I still don't.

FURTHER INVESTIGATIONS (SUNDAY, FEBRUARY 29)

73

CONSULTATION: IMPOSSIBLE
(Fourth Episode)

The baby's still grumbling, she hasn't been walked enough to put her to sleep. Maurice is pushing the carriage, he's stronger, it makes a smoother ride. There aren't many cars on the road, it's early, the weather is nice, it's still full daylight, people don't want to go back into the house when in weather like this. It is a little cool, yes, but for the season that's not really surprising.

We're passing the door to the doctor's office. The shutters are closed, but there's a white car parked in the blacktop courtyard. Mr. Troyat's, probably—it's getting to be a habit, he thinks it's his place because he lives right next door, and sometimes even, when he's got family visiting, all of them park in there. Fine, on Sundays it doesn't matter because you're not in the office, unless you're on call, but today I know that's not the case—yesterday's paper said it would be the Lavinié doctor. Actually, I'm surprised not to see him going by; usually when he's on duty he's running the whole time—the district is big, and a lot of people take advantage of the Sunday to call in the doctor because they can be sure he'll come over that same day, no need to wait around at his office. There really are some people who have nothing better to do than call the doctor on a Sunday.

Your sign's tarnished. It should get a good wipedown, what with all the cars going by. Over the long term, of course, the metal does get dark. And the screws have rusted. The baby is crying, a little gust of wind has flipped back her blanket. I tell Maurice to cover her but he doesn't hear me. He never does hear me when I talk to him. And anyhow what's he doing, walking so fast? He still doesn't know I have a bad knee? I catch up to him, make him stop. I vaguely hear the sound of a car door slamming, an engine turning over, behind us. I fix the baby's blanket so she doesn't catch cold. Her cheeks are real red but her hands are icy; good thing I put on her woollen bonnet, can't have her catching cold, the daughter-in-law would scold me for not keeping her covered well enough.

The white car comes out of the courtyard, drives past us, and at the wheel it's you. I just have time enough to recognize you, you wave like you always do even though I've never been a patient of yours, and you're already gone, you vanish at the corner, on the road to Lavinié.

Well, then! So it *is* you on call, after all! Just can't count on the newspaper, they always get things wrong. And even so, how could I tell you were in? If you'd opened the shutters, I would have understood and I would have come in, I've meant to for such a long time, I would have told Maurice there was something I needed to find out about for the baby! Oh, nuts! she's sneezing. I knew it, I knew it, I knew it. And the daughter-in-law said they'd pick her up at five o'clock exactly. It'll be like the other times—they'll come by in a rush so they can get home before dark, and you can bet she'll be on the phone at dinnertime to tell me the baby has a fever, that I shouldn't have taken her out, but it's sunny, even if it *is* a little cool. If only they were picking her up later, she'd already have started her fever at my house. Then I could have called you, Maurice wouldn't have said anything—our son has good family coverage. Anyhow, whenever a doctor comes over about one of the children Maurice never budges from in front of the TV; I could have taken advantage and talked to you. If he knew it was about me, I'd never get rid of him, he wants to hear everything. So the one time I could have had the doctor over to the house without Maurice on my back... just my luck!

74

PAULINE KASSER

I hear a car door slam, I open the door, I run up to you, I leap at your neck, I kiss you, you drop your briefcase, you wrap your arms around me.

"Mmmhh... what a welcome!"

I look at you. You're tired, I see it in your eyes. I bite my lip.

"I'm so sorry—another call just came in."

You look at your watch. "The well-known five-thirty fever?"

I smile, shake my head no. "What do you mean?"

"Sundays, it's nearly always at five-thirty that someone calls me about a child who's got a fever. In general, the kids were fine in the morning, at noon they have lunch at the grandma's or the aunt's, the afternoon they tear around the garden or watch TV with the cousins, and then, at the end of the afternoon, they start complaining, headache stomachache, they shiver, they throw up in the car, and because there's school the next morning, someone calls the doctor..."

"No, this is something else... A woman across the bridge..." I see you stiffen.

"Mr. Guilloux—he's not well?"

"That's it. His wife wanted to ask your advice..."

"Ah... I'll go see her, it's not far."

"No, no, she didn't want you to go over, only to telephone. She doesn't want to bother you."

"Okay... She called here at the house?"

"Yes, I was surprised, but she told me you'd given her the number."

"I told her she could call me at any time, if she needed to... These are people who never ask anything. They never want to be a bother. I've never heard Guilloux complain, and yet he's in really terrible shape!"

I take your briefcase, you lay an arm over my shoulders, we walk toward the house.

"He's got cancer of the larynx. The first time I saw him, I thought he was going to die in my arms. The next day he had a fibroscopy and three days later, they operated. Since then, he can't talk, he breathes through a cannula inserted in his neck… He wasn't doing badly—he lost weight, of course, but he went on puttering and tending his garden. Last week, he got bronchitis, and he's congested. He stays in his armchair, because he's very short of breath, and his phlegm has to be drawn out through a plastic tube threaded through the cannula…"

I've started to shiver. You clasp me to you. "I shouldn't be telling you all this."

"Oh, no, of course not! Censor yourself—that'd be much better!"

We go into the house. You head for the telephone. You put a hand on the receiver, read the number written on the pad, look up. "Maybe I will go see him after all… Would you mind awfully?"

"Well I should say so! You'd rather spend your time with a sick man than with me—it's a scandal! And leave me here waiting for you, like an idiot. I would've done better falling in love with a bank clerk."

You look at me, uncertain. I take your hand. "Call Madame Guilloux, Bruno."

I go into the bedroom, put the briefcase on the chair. I take some corduroy trousers out of the closet and hang them from the window handle; a shirt, socks, underpants, and a sweater I lay on the bed.

I come out of the bedroom. You're just hanging up the phone. You keep your hand on it. You look up. "She's having a lot of trouble aspirating him, it makes him cough and that frightens her a little, she's afraid she's hurting him. And still she doesn't want me to come. She says she'll manage."

"Did she ask how to do it?"

"No, she knows that. But when you aspirate a person, it sometimes provokes frightening reactions—you feel like you're tearing out their lungs, they turn blue from the pain… Monsieur Guilloux would never say a word, he lets her do it, but it hurts her as much as it does him. She wanted some reassurance. I don't know if I gave it to her."

"She would have asked you to come by, wouldn't she?"

"Mmmhh… no. Yes. I don't know."

I walk over to you. I lay my hand on your cheek. Your face is tight, tense. "You should go have a shower and change your clothes."

"You think? I might get another call…"

"I know. What then? Life is full of risk."

You smile, you nod. I pull off your sweater, you let me. I unbutton your shirt. I push you into the bedroom. While you finish undressing, I turn on the water and adjust it to a good temperature.

75

THE NEXT-DOOR NEIGHBOR
(Final Installment)

It's ringing at the other end. Twice, three times—well for heaven's sakes she's taking her time.

"Hello?"

"Germaine? This is Martine."

"Oh, good!"

"Everything okay?"

"Ah, don't ask! Old Aunt Jeanne and Uncle Antoine just left."

"What? *They* came over?"

"Well yeah, never would've figured on that, huh? With all this time them and Mama weren't speaking!"

"How did they act?"

"Almost nice. But I think they were here mostly to find out what notary's handling the estate, seeing how Mama's the one inherited grandpa's land, and they're next in line—I mean, except for you and me, since your mama's already dead and since our Blandine doesn't understand anything anymore so she doesn't really count…"

"What'd you tell them?"

"That we'd see each other at the notary. Because I don't guess we'll see them at the funeral…"

"I see."

"Anyhow, that's how it is. But I'm sick of the whole thing! She was my mother, but she's giving me trouble right up to the end! If she didn't decide to die on a Sunday, I wouldn't have all these people parading through the house!"

"Yes, and besides you wouldna had to wait for the doctor…"

"Ah, don't get me started! You know what time he turned up?"

"Yeah, you told me before—ten-thirty, something like that!"

"Yeah, I didn't tell you the rest, because since then it's been nonstop—people are very nice, but we're not burying her until Wednesday, they could've waited to come tomorrow or the next day. Well course not! They had to come today, like she was gonna fly away! Yeah, while she was alive, there wasn't a lot of folks rushing to visit her, but dead, they all come around with their gloomy look! Like she could see them!"

"And so—what about the doctor?"

"What? Oh, yeah, the doctor, so he gets here at ten-thirty, almost quarter of eleven, he looks real perky getting out of his car, like he just won the lottery, to me that was a little annoying, seeing how long we were waiting for him, so I don't have to tell you I gave him a piece of my mind. I says to him, 'Well, just take your time, why don't you! A person can die and it's not an emergency any more! Especially when it's not a patient of yours!'"

"What did he say?"

"He gaped at me, he didn't know what hit him, it was some act, I swear! But that got to him, let me tell you!"

"So then?"

"So then he asked why I was talking to him like that, I thought he was about to get up on his high horse the way they always do, but no, he stayed just as meek as a lamb—"

"He must have felt like he was in the wrong!"

"You bet! He even told me it wasn't his—his whatever, the woman, there—who took the call, that it was a phone service, that they only gave him the message at nine-thirty, who knows, he had some story, I didn't exactly get it, but he was certainly trying to weasel out of it..."

"Certainly!"

"And so then he asks why I'm so mad, claims he had other housecalls to make before coming about Mama, and so I says I don't like it for people to tell me stories, that I knew very well it wasn't true, and if you saw his face when I said, 'My cousin lives across from your house, she saw that your car didn't move all morning until you left to come over here!' So then he didn't say another thing, he asked to see her, and I told him he was lucky it was a Sunday and my regular doctor wasn't available, because I woulda thrown him right out..."

"And anyhow you wouldna called him in the first place!"

"Course not!"

"So then?"

"So then I says I want him to make out the death certificate right away because we still had to get her dressed and if we waited much longer it wasn't gonna be easy to do! I actually don't know when she died, Mama, during the night I did hear her get up to pee, but I don't know what time that was, so to figure out when it happened... All's I do know is she was still good and warm when I found

FURTHER INVESTIGATIONS (SUNDAY, FEBRUARY 29)

her, I even didn't believe it, you know, it was like she was… she was… sleeping-waaaahhhhh!"

"Oh you poor girl," I say. "You loved her so much, your mama…"

"Oh, don't even talk about it. These last months it was terrible, she didn't understand a thing anymore, she was arguing with me all the time, always on my back, like when I was a kid, You didn't do this, You didn't do that, That's not how you're supposed to do it, That's no way to keep house, You poor girl what are you doing, You poor girl… She was always calling me Poor girl! But when it was our Blandine, if Blandine'd knock over a pot or she'd find the sewing shears and cut up a curtain, Mama wouldn't say a thing, she'd tell her Darling little girl you don't know what you're doing but never mind, you're my darling little girl…" She sobs even harder.

"Oh, you poor g— Poor Germaine…"

She sniffles. She blows her nose. I wait a little, then I say, "And then what?"

"What, 'what'?"

"With the doctor…"

"Oh, yeah, well so he doesn't say anything, he takes his bag, he goes into the bedroom and he closes the door, I even thought what's he going to do with her? Of course she didn't have to worry anymore, but these doctors you never know what they're gonna come up with!"

"You're right, there! Last week I was in the post office and I heard old Madame Gallo talking to the mayor of Lavallée, and whaddya know but she's telling him how her husband just went into the hospital for his stomach, and how the doctor told him they'd have to operate—come to think of it, it was this same doctor, the guy next door here—and so anyway he said they'd have to take out two-thirds of the stomach cuz he had a prefferated ulcer, that it would bleed, that it could turn into cancer, long story short, it had to be done, and so she's telling the mayor that if she could get some extra hours of a nursing aide in the house for her grandma, that would be some relief for her. And then whaddya know, Madame Gautier—she was just finishing up buying stamps—she gets into the conversation and she says, 'Well I don't understand, I've got my brother-in-law uses this same doctor, from Play, and he told him he had a stomach ulcer but it should absolutely not be operated!' So naturally that makes you stop and think…"

"Yes, that's really something, seems like it depends on the patient!"

"And so then what happened?"

"Well he comes out of the bedroom after ten minutes, I was wondering what he was up to in there and I was chewing my nails, I was thinking how I'd be having to dress Mama and if she was to get too stiff on me, it'd be impossible! It was worrying me, worrying me, you can't imagine. I remember when we found grandpa dead, that had to be several hours after for sure, cuz he was already all stiff, and he fell down in between the bed and the wall so he had one arm sticking up and the other bent behind his back, and getting his shirt and jacket on—believe me!"

"Well yeah, I know—I'm the one who found him!"

"Yeah? You sure? I thought it was Mama and me…"

"Oh no, no. In fact I was taking him in his clothes that I just finished ironing, and it really gave me a shock!"

"Yeah, well, me too, it gave me a shock, that's why I thought… Anyhow, if you're sure it was you… Well so with Mama, I was afraid it'd be like that and we'd have to really sweat nails to get her dressed, I wanted her to look presentable, I didn't want people to say I didn't take care of her, it's not my fault she wouldn't put on anything but her raggedy old nightgowns, she made a big scene every week about changing them, good thing she'd put on a bathrobe over, that would hide… But dead, now—no problem."

"And so?"

"So, after ten minutes, almost a quarter-hour, he comes trotting out, he looks at me, and *me* he doesn't say a word to, he turns to our Blandine and he asks *her* to come in and help him!"

"No! He didn't know she can't understand anything? You can see it, though!"

"Well I guess not! He didn't catch on! But what really got me is, she went!"

"No!"

"Yes! I did try to stop her, but he closed the door, and I heard them making a racket inside. And I says to myself, what are they up to in there, and then all of a sudden I think: I just hope to God he's not abusing her! If he's mad that I talked to him that way and he picks up that she's simpleminded, you don't think he could decide to take it out on her! And being a retard like she is, she might never tell us!"

"You're crazy! You didn't go in there?"

"Nossir! I didn't dare! Mama always told me that when the doctor is in with a dead person, you're not supposed to disturb them! So I tell Pierrot to go in, he knocked, he went in, he closed the door behind him, and then *he* didn't come back out either, but there was no more noise, I decided if there was anything funny going on, Pierre would do something."

"And so? And so?"

"And so, after a good twenty, twenty-five minutes, they all come out. Pierrot shows him to the bathroom, and the two of them go to wash their hands."

"What about your sister?"

"She was in the bedroom still, sitting on a chair, she wasn't talking."

"And your mother?"

"Wellll… She was still on the bed, but they had her dressed. Pierrot told me it was the doctor who did it, but I don't believe that, doctors never dress the dead, and that one especially, he was too not nice. Supposedly him and Blandine got her dressed together—can't you just see that? She can't even pick up a cup without breaking it!"

"She was all dressed? Your mother?"

"Yes! In her good clothes, the ones she wanted to be buried in, she always told me—'Germaine, when I die, open the bottom drawer, take out what's in there and dress me in that, that's how I want to go.' But I don't understand how they knew what to put on her, seeing how the doctor couldna known, and Pierrot never paid any attention to that stuff."

"Well then, that's really strange, because it couldna been Blandine who told them!"

"No, not with the three words she's got, no way!"

"Well then really, that's really strange!"

"Hah! You can say that again!"

"And so? And so?"

"And so, well… that's all."

"That's all?"

"Well yeah."

"And did you ask him, the doctor, if your mother's Extended Coverage would pay for his housecall? Because on Sundays it's not cheap!"

"Uh, no, I didn't have time. He signed the certificate, I asked what he was putting down, he says 'I'm putting down what needs to be put down,' and he closes the envelope, he seals it with his stamp, and gives it to Pierrot. And then he went into the bedroom to shake Blandine's hand, he came out and shook Pierrot's hand, he nodded goodbye to me, and he left."

"And how much did he charge you, for that?"

"Well, I didn't even have time to ask him, he was gone. After, Pierrot told me that for a death certificate, that guy never charges."

"Ah, heaven's sakes, that's strange! He'd sure be the first one like that! Because the doctor from Lavallée, you ask him for the littlest scrap of paper, you pay, even if he hasn't got time to take your blood pressure! Last month we called him to come see old man Nadeau because he fell over in his yard, he was dead as a door-nail, well this guy didn't lose a minute, he made out the blue form and since it was the neighbor who called him and old man Nadeau has no family left, he goes into the corpse's jacket, pulls out the wallet, and takes his own fee!"

"Well this one, see, he didn't charge… But it must be because he felt ashamed for not coming as soon as he was called!"

"Well, really, that's strange! But y'know, seeing it from this end it's strange too. Thing is, all day long he took her car—I mean his… that lady's. He came and he went, and it doesn't make much noise, that car, so sometimes I'd see him coming back when I never seen him leave, sometimes I'd see him leave and even if I listened for it—I can't spend all my time at the window, I have other things to do—I wouldn't hear him come back. That really annoyed me, not to know if he was home or not! And then the lady, his—lady friend—this morning when I saw her digging in the garden, I says to myself, 'She doesn't know the first thing about it, five minutes and she'll quit, she'll get tired out.'"

"And?"

"Well, believe it or not, she spent *two hours* at it! She got the ground ready for peas—she didn't plant them, seeing how the moon's on the wane, but I know it was for peas cuz she put up trellises—and she planted onions and shallots and garlic too. And that's all!"

"I don't believe it—she's moving in!"

"You're telling me! But the funniest thing is, they're not even all alone in that house!"

"Really?"

"Well yes—this morning, you know, when I saw her digging? I said to myself, If somebody calls with an emergency, she's never gonna hear them! So I dialed the number and I was really surprised, somebody answered right away, the same voice as this morning, but it couldn't be *her*, cuz I could see her out digging in the garden!"

"Well so who was it?"

"Well Iowno! Anyhow, so I hung up, I dialed again to be sure, I asked if the doctor was in, the person answered that he was on a housecall, so I hung up."

"You don't think he could have *two* of them, could he?"

"Well Iowno, but you know, with what goes on these days!" Anyhow, from the voice, it wasn't his mother! And maybe there's a whole army of people in there, cuz I called back again a little while later when the girlfriend went inside, but this time it was a man answered, and it couldna been the doctor, seeing as how his car—I mean her car—wasn't back yet."

"I just don't get it!"

"Yes, and listen to this—a little while ago some other car pulled up in front of the house, driving very quietly, it was dark already, it musta been six or seven o'clock, it turned off the headlights, and these three men got out, in raincoats, they didn't look too up-and-up, they crossed the yard like they didn't want anybody to hear them, and they just went inside—without knocking."

"Without knocking?"

"I'm telling you! And they didn't come out yet!"

"What could they be doing, turning up with no warning at the doctor on duty like that, on a Sunday?"

"Well, I dunno! I mean, some people have no shame, they have this idea that, you know, they're paying for it so they can do whatever they want!"

76

PAULINE KASSER

You stand up from your chair, you come over to the bed. You hand me the pages you've just written. I close my book.

"Thank you, Love..."

You pull off your T-shirt and cotton trousers, you slip into the bed. You lay your head on my shoulder and a hand on my belly while I read.

March 1, 1:17

When I came out of the bedroom, the first thing I saw was the table, the five place settings, the candles, the flowers. Without thinking, I said, "What are we celebrating?" and I heard people laughing and singing

Happy birthday to you...!

and there they were the four of them, Ray and Diego laughing like crazy Kate a little tense but smiling, Pauline beaming, she'd dressed up while I was showering, and I felt the tears rushing into my eyes, I wanted to snarl at them, tell them to get the hell out!

I said, "What the hell are you doing here?"

Ray answered, "Coming to meet your Pal-ine! You wouldn't show her to us, so we decided we weren't going to ask your permission!" and he was really laying on his accent.

Then Diego: "You see, Ray? I told you we'd be intruding. I say we all go to a movie!" and he turned to Pauline: "Will you come with us?"

She smiled and shook her head. "Not tonight, I'm on duty here. But you're not going to leave with an empty stomach!" and she handed me a glass of champagne.

I said, "You invited them over without telling me... But it was my place to introduce them to you!" and Pauline said, "Then introduce me..." Whereupon Diego: "It's a good thing you came into his life. He's a real bear, we never get to

276

THE CASE OF DR. SACHS

see him anymore. But you—you're adorable, I have a feeling we're going to spend a lot of time with you!"

And then we had dinner, and I haven't had so much pleasure talking to Ray for months, maybe for years. Diego was in brilliant form, he was sitting between Pauline and Kate, he was making them laugh, it was ages since I'd seen Kate laugh like that and I thought she'd be very beautiful if she weren't so sad. At a certain moment, Diego made some joke, the two women started weeping with laughter and they each took his hand at the same time, they were beautiful the three of them, Diego imperial, Kate the way I remembered her, Pauline more desirable than ever. Ray leaned toward me and said, "She's spectacular." I nodded, I said, "Yes, you're a very lucky man," and he jabbed his elbow into my stomach, "I'm talking about *your* woman, not mine, *you nincompoop!*" and at that same moment Pauline took my hand and we were all gathered together for the first time and happy together...

I lay my hand on yours.

At the end of the meal, Pauline and Kate went to make coffee, Diego and Ray and I started talking—about Australia, of course. Ray declares to Diego that the fauna of Australia is among the least known in the world; he turns to me:

"Hey, I bet even you, when you were down there, I bet you never saw a *padmouse...*"

"*Padmouse?* Whazzat?"

"Oh, yeah," Diego chimes in, "Ray was telling me about it in the car, it's a little animal with a very long tail, it eats practically nothing, it's very easy to train. It reproduces a mile a minute. In the early eighties, the Americans—you know them—they imported some to the States, and they've spread like wildfire, now you find them all over the world, it's a real invasion!"

Just then Kate and Pauline came back in, one carrying the coffee, the other a cake, and somebody put two packages in front of me, the first the size of a fat paperback but lighter, and the second as big as a one-volume encyclopedia. I picked up the smaller one and shook it next to my ear. Pauline started laughing. "That one's from the three of us," Kate said. The wrapping was black, the ties gold and silver. Inside it was a white cardboard box with the words *The Original Australian Padmouse* written in Ray's hand.

When I opened it, in a great mass of absorbent cotton, I found a mouse. With two buttons. Decorated with an Australian flag. I looked at Pauline, and the three others laughed at my expression. I said, "You're crazy! You're an absolutely crazy woman!" In the large package was a laptop with a built-in printer.

In a daze, I stood up, I embraced them all one by one, I didn't hear what they were saying, and then I took Pauline in my arms, I wanted to give her the most passionate, the longest kiss in the whole history of foreplay—but I couldn't, I was all choked up, I gripped her by the shoulders, I said, "Why?"

FURTHER INVESTIGATIONS (SUNDAY, FEBRUARY 29)

"What do you mean, 'Why'? You won't use it?"

"Of course—but…"

"It's too much? You don't *deserve* such a gift?"

"Yes… I mean, no! I mean—I don't know! I'm not forty, that's a gift for a fortieth birthday, or for—"

"Sure, I should've waited for a good round number! And until then you could always buy disposable ballpoint pens…"

She kissed me, sat me down, invited me to blow out the candles, and handed me a knife: "Instead of splitting hairs, how about splitting the cake for the five of us?"

I feel your head slip onto the pillow, you've closed your eyes, you're breathing more deeply, you're falling asleep.

When I type on this keyboard, the words line up on the screen faster than on my Selectric, and above all without that racket. So here we are: I'm writing, you're in the bed behind me, and you're reading. Tonight I think I understand what it is to be whole, fulfilled, and enfolded—despite Ray's illness, despite the shadowy spaces between Kate and Diego and me, despite everything you still don't know about me but thanks to what you already do know—ah, how you do know me! How close you are, and tender and loving! And although I sit here before this jewel which I'm discovering as I use it, which registers words faster than I manage to think them, I still don't know what to say, I don't even know what to write, because there's too much to say and write and because I know both too much and too little about it.

Now you're snoring softly. I pull one of the pillows out from under your head and you turn toward the wall, in fetal position.

I get up, I put the three pages on the desk, I turn out the light, I lie down along your body. My fingers touch your skin, seeking out the pits, the small swellings, the hollows, the scales. Since the day I first laid my hands on your back, I've known what you were. I saw the scars of an old acne, not entirely dormant, that periodically goes into eruption, raising sinister red volcanoes with purulent crests, sensitive, painful, explosive. You let me touch them, bandage them, care for them, you rid yourself of the shame you felt the first time I made you take off your shirt so I could swab one of those bleeding wounds. Day after day, I learned to decode your body, and if I know you, if I see who you are, what you feel, it's partly because my fingers find their way by the marks you carry on you permanently, inscribed on your flesh like a Braille text, invisible to those who do not know you, incomprehensible for the women who, until me, refused to read it. I love you, Bruno, with your wounds and your scars, and with everything you cannot say boiling just beneath the surface.

I cling tight against you, I slide my hand along your belly and, very softly, I bite your shoulder. You let out a long sigh, you turn to me, an arm encircles my hips, a hand comes to rest on my nape, your lips seek mine, and I smile as I say to myself that the longest kiss in the whole history of foreplay…

"Hey! So you were only half-asleep…"

"Mmmhh. You know how men are."

SOLO DIALOGUES

IV

THE SECRET
(Soft Version)

Annie—oh, Annie's doing well. Very, very well. For six months now, she's been a real angel... Yes, I took her to see the doctor in Play, didn't I tell you about it? I went very reluctantly, but I couldn't manage any more: she was irritable, hostile, insolent, and Dominique advised me to go see him... Ah, no, Annie was definitely *not* willing. The first time, we had a long wait—there was a huge crowd—and when our turn came, she dragged her feet. I told her, "Come on now! Look, you're holding everyone up," she answered "You give me a real pain in—" but still, she did go in. I was so ashamed, if you only knew! Well, the doctor gave us a very odd look. I took a seat, Annie slumped down with her hands in her pockets and never looked at me. That's what hurt the most—the way she acted as if I didn't exist. I *am* her mother, after all. I was doing it for her own good! In fact, everything I do is for her, she ought to see that. No, darling, at the time she was still too young, too immature. And yet I always got on very well with the other students in her class. I wonder if she wasn't jealous—or anyway jealous of Camille, a former student I like a lot, I've had... some very good times with her. We still get together now and then—she monitors classes at the school, and sometimes we meet for lunch at the brasserie, or I have her over for dinner at the house, and I think Annie didn't like that. Back then, she used to throw enormous tantrums, she'd tell me I cared more about my students than about her, can you imagine? when I always spent all my free time with her—I'd take her to the movies or we'd go visit Mama or Nicole and her girls. The rest of the time, I did have to correct my student papers! What more did she need? I couldn't split myself in four, I had to keep food on the table! Anyhow, that day, the doctor looked at Annie without saying anything, but clearly he was concerned to see her so withdrawn, and I said: "I'm bringing you my daughter because she's not eating!" And immediately Annie jumps on me—Yes! Yes, I assure you—she starts shouting "Stop it, you're talking complete bullshit!" That's what happened! I just went on telling him the story—

that for one thing, she didn't eat, that she hadn't gained any weight for six months at least—she was still wearing the same shirts even though the year before she'd grown six inches in the one year (*that* was pretty disturbing, I didn't want her shooting up into some five-eleven beanpole like her father, what a catastrophe!) And can you imagine, the doctor smiles and says, "How beautiful—a tall young woman…" Yes indeed he did, my friend! I just sighed politely, to show him that that wasn't what I was asking him, and I went on: "I brought her in so you can examine her, send her for some blood tests, find out what her trouble is, maybe you could also tell her that leaving for school in the morning without breakfast isn't smart!" Especially since at fourteen she still didn't have her period, although I'd told her that if she didn't fill out a little she'd *never* be able to bear children.

All right, he must have seen that Annie's condition was disturbing. So then he asks me, "What is it that you're concerned about exactly, Madame?" And I answer, "Everything! She doesn't eat, she won't talk to me, she doesn't let me kiss her goodnight, she sulks when I take her to school, and here I went to such terrible trouble to get myself a job at Sainte-Jeanne's so I could be with her! In fact, she's always sulking, she never helps out at home! When I was her age I wasn't like that at all, my sister and I always helped my mother set the table! So I don't understand why she acts like that, I am her mother after all, she owes me some respect and she's supposed to obey me—(That really is true, you know! She does have certain duties toward me! And up to the age of eighteen, I have full legal control over her. Yes, and even after that, actually! Her grandfather left her some money, but she'll be too young to spend it, she'll need someone to advise her! You're right, everybody's got problems with authority. What worried me the most was that she didn't eat! Nothing! But nothing, I tell you! She'd say it wouldn't go down, that she had something stuck in her throat. So there in front of the doctor, I told her) Go ahead, Annie, tell the Doctor, tell him how you can't get it down! Annie? I'm talking to you!" Then I said to the doctor, "You see? She won't even answer me when I talk to her! And the worst is that, in school, all the other teachers tell me she's wonderful, that she's a good student, but in my class she's unbearable, she talks all the time with her pal Sarah, I can't just send them to the principal's office after all, she is my daughter after all, what would that look like?" (Oh, yes, you're absolutely right, it really is not an easy thing to be your own daughter's teacher!) And then the doctor asks, "You have your daughter in your class?" And I say, "Of course! I've always had her, ever since first grade! I was the primary-school teacher at Langes, above Lavallée. The class there combined several levels, so she was with me right on through! But since my—well, her father— didn't have steady work, I couldn't always count on making it through the end of the month, so I trained for my junior-high teaching certificate—it's a good thing there *is* such a program! and a good thing you can do it over the school year and not during vacations, because with all the work it takes, and the nervous tension,

I really need my vacation time—a lot of people call that special privilege, but they should just put themselves in our shoes! (—What was I saying? Oh, yes... I tell the doctor that when I became a junior-high school teacher, for French and for history-geography, the timing was just right: she was going into sixth grade.) And so one way or another I had her with me for the next four years. In seventh grade it was marvelous—I had her class in both subjects. Of course there was a terrific woman heading the school (yes, Dominique Dumas!); we had a great deal in common, unfortunately she too had... troubles with her husband. You know her! (He certainly does know her, he's practically the person who advised her to throw her husband out!) And when Annie moved up to tenth grade, and I... asked her father to leave—I mean, things hadn't been good between us for a long time, in any case he never did a thing for the child, no matter how much I told him he could maybe make a little effort for his own daughter, I even suggested going to a psychiatrist together, he didn't listen... Yes, I still resent him for that. When I think how I gave him the best years of my life—"

And at that point I hear Annie sighing and saying, "*Mo*ther!" So I say, naturally, "Well, will you look at that! Got your tongue back now, have you! The minute I mention your father, you wake up! I do have the right to talk about him, after all I'm the one who had to take—I mean, who put up with him all those years! You, of course, you never saw a thing! Anyhow, I know he gets you worked up against me! Whereas I—I've never said a thing against him! And I certainly could have!"

At that, the doctor stood up, opened the door, and said, "Mademoiselle... could you please leave me alone with your mother?" and he showed her out. He came back to me, he sat down, and there we were by ourselves, I was so overcome, you can imagine! I wasn't sure exactly how to proceed—you can hear how just talking about it now I've got tears in my eyes. And I said to him, "Yes, I was telling you about her father, but that's not what I came for, of course. It's Annie who worries me. I don't know what to do with her. She... she ran away, last week."

And he says, "Ran away?'

I say, "Yes, she left school without saying where she was going. Usually she waits for me—we live over at Langes, so naturally we have to go home together. I go early to drop her at school every morning at eight o'clock, even though sometimes I don't teach until eleven! (Yes indeed, my dear! she doesn't realize how lucky she is! Anyhow, to go on with the story:) You see, ever since I've been teaching at Sainte-Jeanne's... I should tell you that when her father left like that, all of a sudden (Yes, yes, of course I'm the one who threw him out! but I wasn't about to tell this man everything) he left me with nothing (No, I don't mean things—actually he didn't take anything with him, that would have been the last straw! But since he never brought in a cent, I always paid all our expenses out of my salary, so I see no reason why he should have taken anything at all along with him, you know what I mean!), I didn't know what to do, I nearly went into a serious depression, luckily Dr. Boulle (that's the doctor at Deuxmonts, the one I usually went to) put me on a long leave of absence from work and since it was January, I managed to hold on like that for the rest of the school year. I didn't want to ruin Annie's year—she was always a very, very good student (I always saw to that!)—I'd collect myself, I'd take her over to school and pick her up, it was hard but I did it anyhow (Oh la la, if you only knew, I was exhausted!)... After a few weeks, I said to myself that I couldn't let her move up to the lycée without going with her, what would become of her? we'd always been together! So I asked Dr. Boulle to help me, and the autumn she started ninth grade, he put me on a therapeutic half-time schedule, so that way I was able to work toward my license for teaching at the lycée level; I got it (and since Dominique had just been named director of Sainte-Jeanne's, of course I got a position right away.) That was two years ago, and ever since then..."

And can you believe, right there he breaks in! "You mentioned running away, earlier..."

"Yes, excuse me, I lost track, I'm so upset to see my little girl in this condition, she's got nobody else but me, and I have no one but her!"

"But—what about her father?"

(Well, I was outraged, you can imagine!)

"Her father! Her father! He'll never set foot in my house again!"

At which he says, embarrassed, "No, I meant—doesn't your daughter see him?" (Well then I really did have to explain—that for months he didn't accept getting thrown out, so he was always turning up—supposedly to see her, he'd go pick her up after school, he'd bring her home, he'd come in with her, hang around, sit down, act right at home! When he never gave me one penny for her! He left because supposedly I was preventing him from living, sure, but he didn't spit on my money when it came to dressing Annie or feeding her, you know? What—No, no, what are you saying! I couldn't have him thrown into jail, really! I wouldn't have gained anything by that, and then can't you just see how it would look to the people I work with? Anyhow, I did tell the doctor that ever since he's with this—this *woman*...)

"Oh, absolutely! Of course she sees him! But as little as possible! Before, he used to take her whenever she was sick, but for a year now it's been alternate weekends, and half the vacations, and that's all!" (I felt like crying then, and the doctor saw it, he gave me a tissue, and then he asked me again about the running-away business...)

"Anyhow, that day I didn't see Annie anywhere when school let out, so of course I got worried. I asked Dominique's—Madame Dumas'—secretary if she'd seen her. And she told me Annie had left! You can imagine my worry! I was beside myself, I thought, What in the world got into her? And just as I was going out the door, wondering if I should call the police, the secretary waved me over,

THE CASE OF DR. SACHS

there was someone on the phone for me. It was Annie! She'd finished early in the afternoon, she had no more classes, and since I was supervising a quiz she didn't want to wait around in study hall, and she went home by train! (I swear! She took the monorail that runs out of Tourmens and stops at all the little villages. She got off at Lavallée, and hitch-hiked home from there! I could never have done that at that age! My parents would have forbidden it!) And you know what the doctor said? He looks at me kind of bewildered and he says, "Mmmmhh, that's not really running away…" And I say "I beg your pardon! When an adolescent disappears for three hours, I call that running away!" And he says, "Mmmmhh." (Yes, he does that *Mmmmhh, Mmmhh* all the time, after a while it gets on your nerves. And he goes on:) "Mmmhh. What about the poor appetite?" And I say, "Ah, don't even talk about it! I don't know what to make for her, she doesn't like anything, she keeps asking for unbelievable things! It's her father and his—that *woman*—giving her these ideas…" And he says, "Does she seem tired?" And I say, "Tired, no! But for me it's exhausting! She's always nasty, she closes herself in her room and starts crying, I go to comfort her but she won't open the door, and that—that just breaks my heart! My little girl! What's happening to her, what's happening to us? And yet I don't refuse her a thing, I don't know what more I can do to please her, she has *everything* she could want for being happy…" (Oh yes, it was very hard, I tell you!) And he says, "Mmmhh. Since when did you notice she was eating less?" And I say, "Since the last school break. Because actually, it started when she came back from her father's. I'm sure that went badly, his—that *woman* may try all she likes to buy her love, by giving her clothes and little presents, she's still not her mother! And then I don't think things are going so well over there: last month she spent the first half of the vacation with her father and when she came home she looked as if she was at a funeral, I couldn't get her to say what was wrong, she started crying. Since then, she's been eating practically nothing, so obviously I worry, I think that maybe something happened, if it turns out she's having some… problem… with her father (there I had a sob in my voice) I worry so much, I wonder if she—might turn anorexic on me" (and on top of it, you remember, it was just at the time when the daughter of that actress—what's her name? Yeah, that's the one!—She got anorexia very young, she went from one psychiatrist to another; her mother, poor thing, what a disaster, I put myself in her place but I'd rather keep mine, having a daughter like that! And after several years, when there were no more signs, she thought the girl was cured—she'd even written a book about it and the two of them went on TV—with no warning the girl threw herself out the window!) and I say to the doctor, "You know, for a month now, I've started watching whether Annie is secretly bingeing on cookies, and when she uses the bathroom I go in after her to make sure she wasn't vomiting in there. (No, no, she never did, what do you think—if I'd seen that I would have put her right into the hospital!) In fact I also asked Camille, my former student who's the monitor at Sainte-Jeanne's, to keep a quiet eye on her, but she told me that noontimes in the lunchroom Annie was eating normally. All right, so I was imagining things—still, here at home she wasn't eating)... Well, you know what the doctor had the nerve to ask me? You'll never guess! He says, "Does she eat when she's at her father's house?" (Well, that really made me laugh, you can imagine. Because, fine, apparently his... *woman* cooks very well. But from Annie's face each time he brings her back here, I'd be surprised if she eats a thing the woman makes. When I took her to the doctor, she wasn't even eating her favorite dishes. Not even semolina pudding! When she was little, if I hadn't put my foot down she would never have eaten anything else, every single day! But six months ago, if I decided to make semolina pudding, she wouldn't touch it! Oh, yes, it was truly painful.) So I say, "I don't know about that, but in any case she doesn't go to her father's very often, so what she eats there wouldn't make up for not eating in my house! You think you'll be able to do something?" And he says, "Mmmhh, there's always something we can do, Madame. I'll examine your daughter and then we'll decide on a course to follow. But if I understand you correctly, I don't believe she's in danger. To look at her, I'd say she's going through a bad patch, and she needs some help, and so do you, I think..." And I say, "Oh, Doctor! It's good to hear that! If you knew how hard it is! I never complain, not to anyone, and I'd never say the slightest word against her father! Yet with what he did to me, I'd have plenty to say!"

And then he stood up and opened the door, saying, "If you'll allow me, I'll bring Annie in now to examine her... I won't be long."

Yes, yes! he sent me out! What could I say? He's the doctor, I couldn't tell him no, true she was only fourteen-and-a-half at the time, but Dominique had told me he was very good with children, and I thought it wouldn't be bad to have him set her straight a little without me in the room. And in the end, I was right: if I'd stayed, she would certainly not have listened to him, while as it was, you *would not* believe your eyes! But wait, there's more... So: Annie was standing in the waiting room with her hands in her coat pockets, and when I came out, she gave me that stubborn look she used to get when she was little. She didn't move, so I took her by the arm. She snatched it back violently, but the doctor waved her in, she hesitated but finally she went and he closed the door again. I stood for a long while because the room was full, with not a chair free. At first, I thought he might have some trouble with her, and that by the end of five minutes he'd be sick of it... A country doctor, what do they know about adolescents? In fact, if Dominique hadn't recommended him I wouldn't have gone to see him, nossir! And after all, Annie was a bit young to be taken to a gynecologist, it would have shocked her!... Yes, I do too, I use a woman GYN—I won't let a man touch me again! Mine is very good, very proper, she was married to a psychiatrist but she left him because he was impotent... Yes, that's who it is. Really, you know her? What, you go to her too? Oh, that's really funny! Tell me, is it true she's Jewish? Oh well, nobody's perfect, and in a woman it doesn't show, right? HAHAHAHA! Well, I wouldn't have been comfortable taking my daughter to her. Still, at the time, Annie hadn't started menstruating yet and at fourteen-and-a-half, I have to admit I was concerned. I wasn't able to have another child after her, and I wouldn't want her to have any problems. It's true she came a little early—but once she was there, I was very happy. And then later, I would never have wanted more children with her father! Dominique, now—she would have liked four or five, but it was her husband who refused. Yes, it's too bad for the children that she left him, but she did have to live her own life. And besides, as it turns out, the children are in fine shape. We manage to do very nicely without men, right? HAHAHAHA! See now, that's something I'd like Annie to know—I'd like to be able to tell her that they can't be trusted. What do you expect—I try to protect her, but it can't last forever, whatever happens, I *am* her mother, and what's closer to you than a mother? Right? Right? With a father, a person never even knows for sure if it really *is* the father, right? And then sometimes when you're pretty sure he is, you'd be very glad to forget it! HAHAHAHA!... Of course, for Annie, I *am* sure, since there was nobody else before him. I really gave him everything, *everything*! Ahlala! If you only knew! Lately she's so sweet, so attentive, so close, I've been thinking that one of these days I'll tell her the whole story.

But six months ago, she understood nothing about anything, and I couldn't keep living in such anguish. Well, believe it or not, after he'd kept me with him a half hour, he kept Annie in there *a full hour*! I swear! When he opened the door again I was so embarrassed—the waiting room was jammed, and he took me back inside! He was very clear, very firm, he said, "We've got to be serious now. Your daughter and I have talked for a long time about the situation. Right?" And at that, Annie nodded. She was smiling—I don't know how to describe it, she was *a changed person!* I couldn't believe my eyes! And then he handed me two prescription slips. "I asked her to take a little blood test." And I said, "But—she's willing?" And Annie: "Yes, yes, I'm willing!" And then he says, "And I've ordered a little tonic for her—at her age, with the exams to study for, she has good reason to feel under stress. You know all about that, I suppose?" And I say, "Yes indeed—all those tests to correct, it's a lot more stress for the teachers than for the students." And he says, "And I've asked her to come back in three weeks to discuss all this again." And I say, "Of course, and for the blood test results." And Annie nods her head, *smiling!* I was stunned! I'd never seen her like that... Ah! I don't know, I can't tell you a thing, he didn't explain—first of all, that day there was such a crowd waiting, there was no time; and ultimately it doesn't matter, what counts is the result! Now, I will say, he did charge me for two consultations plus an extra fee because the whole thing went on so long, but it was well worth it! Anyhow, I always get the full amount back from the teacher's co-op insurance.

And that's the whole story! Annie has changed completely: she doesn't answer me back anymore, she doesn't tell me to go to hell, she always goes home with me at five o'clock except when she has no late classes, and on those days she's asked me to arrange for her to leave school early, she goes over to the Tourmens library to study and she meets me when I'm done. At night she sets the table, she cooks... She was already a good student, but now she's even better, she's certainly going to get very good grades on the French lit baccalaureate exam—that's coming up soon but she's very calm, she tells me "Don't worry Mama, it'll all be fine," and I believe her. She's doing extremely well in everything, I'm very proud of her now, all my colleagues sing her praises to me, I was right to have her skip two grades, her father didn't want it but now I ask you, who was right? In fact she doesn't want me to mention her father to her anymore. One day she said, "Mama, I'd rather you didn't mention Papa to me anymore," and I understood that she'd distanced herself there... Of course, she still goes to visit him, every other weekend and half her school vacations, but now when she comes home she's not a wreck anymore, the way she used to be. She's even fairly cheerful these days. Really, that doctor has just transformed her for me, I don't know what he did! Three months ago, we went back for a last visit, she was doing very well, so he said there was no need to come any more, and now my mind's completely at rest! But my, what I went through! With children, you never know what you'll run into! Anyhow, now, the worst is over, I'm much calmer. I mean, it's true men are bastards— you can't trust them, turn your back and they pull some dirty trick on us—but that doctor, I've got to admit he really did set things right for me. I feel better. And Annie is so good these days, I have a hard time realizing that this is actually my little girl—she'll be fifteen soon but she'll always be my little girl. We're real pals now, even away from school... And fortunately, she's not interested in boys. But she does take an interest in what I'm doing, she confides in me—and I do too, I can finally tell her things a mother longs to tell her daughter, you know, woman things... Anyhow, nowadays things are going really well, I think I haven't been this happy since—oh, for years. Not since—since you and I were in teachers' college together... I mean it, you know. Yes... me too. Yes... You know, we ought to get together, it's been so long. I know, poor dear, he gave you a hard time... Well, at least yours coughs up! You did right not to agree to Mutual Consent. If he wanted to get back his freedom, all he had to do was pay for it—HAHAHAHA! Tell me, what are you doing this weekend? Really? Really? You'll come visit me? Oh, my darling, that makes me so *happy*!

THE CASE OF DR. SACHS

DIAGNOSIS

(Saturday, March 29)

Know the difference
between God and a doctor?
God doesn't think he's a doctor.

Law & Order

77

CLINICAL PICTURE

The alarm clock drills into my eardrums. I've got a sticky mouth, a clogged nose, a head like a big melon. I'm sure my breath stinks, it always does that on rainy mornings, but that doesn't stop doctors from insisting flatly, with a contemptuous look, that the weather has no effect on health.

I set a foot on the floor. It hurts, of course. For the past three, maybe four months now. Before, it was my shoulder; before that, the knee; I wonder what it'll be next time, if there is a next time—before it gets better I've got plenty of time to die.

I get up. My head's spinning, goddam sinusitis. Shall I drink coffee this morning, or tea? These days coffee doesn't go down too well, and every time it's the same thing: if I take it cold, it comes back up on me; if I take it too hot, it burns my tongue. And I can't have bread-and-butter—that starts me sweating for an hour, I'd like to know the reason why but nobody's ever been able to tell me.

In the mirror, I have an ugly mug, greasy nose, dirty hair, I can shave twice a day and I still look like I haven't done it for a week. I stick out my tongue, it's white at the tip and yellow in back—anyone ever has me say "ahhh," watch out—white settlers up front, yellow peril behind! contagion! quarantine! spray disinfectants!...

A muscle twitches under my left eyelid. I feel it flutter. It doesn't hurt but it's annoying. And also my foot hurts, that bugs me. I know it disappears after an hour, when I start walking I don't feel it any more, and that's why I don't take anything for the pain—I can't see how it would help—but it does wear me out.

This morning I shave with the electric razor, I'm sick of cutting myself. The cutting head is full of gunk, I must not have cleaned it last time, I blow on it kind of hard, the hairs fly up into my eyes and nose, I weep and I sneeze and now I'm spitting and scrabbling blindly for a handkerchief to clean myself up, I'm sick of this and my foot hurts.

I step into the shower and I just about break my neck, who's the idiot kid who left the soap on the floor? I twist a wrist trying to catch my balance by grabbing the faucet, and since the hot water's already on, naturally I scald my hand.

I yell. For a few seconds, it's like my hand's just out of a frying pan, but at least I don't feel my foot anymore.

I soap my torso, arms, then the belly and the balls, why do they cling to the thighs in the morning, for a while now they've seemed like hanging bags, like they're worn out, I'm not in my andropause yet as far as I know, but they do seem to be withering, drooping like old socks or those eroded tits on old African women, what was it I read about male hormone treatments?

The sound of running water gives me a terrific yen to piss, this morning it's fine, the stream looks right to me, it's not like some days when it doesn't turn off, sometimes it keeps running in my underwear for ten minutes after, it's awful.

I soap my cock with a bit more care, kind of seeing if it still responds, a long time now it hasn't done any business and these days there's no tentpole under the sheets in the morning, when you don't get that during your sleep anymore apparently it's an early sign but I'm not going to do like what's-his-name, I'd never go to a sexologist, I'd hate to get felt up by some pervert—don't see how a person could do that kind of work if he's not.

I soap my asshole with the other hand, don't wanna mix the two things, the other day when I had trouble shitting I touched there and I thought I was laying an egg, it was round and stretched and it hurt like hell, I put a mirror on a stool and I straddled it to see, without my glasses I had a hard time, and then besides it's all hairy around there—who knew! There was kind of a pinkish-red ball there, to the naked eye it wasn't much bigger than a cherry-pit though to the finger it had felt as big as a billiard ball, but when something hurts, it can fool you.

I didn't do anything, just took an aspirin and clenched my teeth, can't let anything show, it finally eased up. Now I don't feel a thing. Yeah, I do—my foot. But that's got nothing to do with this.

I do a serious soaping in the crannies because I hate stains on my underwear and it's never clean around there.

I come out of the shower. I dry myself everywhere, especially between the buttocks because of the yeast infection that gave me such a pain last year, I have to wonder why I got that, apparently when you don't dry yourself real well, fungus likes damp places, and in there between the buttocks, down in that fold I can feel with my finger, there's like a little hidden pocket—that's where it started. First it itched a little, then I started scratching harder and no matter how hard I'd rub with the towel, it burned like crazy, I couldn't keep from scratching, even through my trousers, and it began to bleed, it was staining my underwear, I was determined not to let my wife know, so I'd put them into the machine myself. And then I remembered there was a tube of cortisone cream somewhere, I used to put it between my toes when I got athlete's foot, I finally found it and I smeared my crack with it. The first two times it felt like someone was putting a red-hot poker to me; the next day, though, I was already feeling better. Since then I've learned my lesson, I wipe myself twice instead of once, and when I feel that's not enough I use the hair-dryer.

I don't tighten my necktie, since the shirt-collar just hits the boil that started up yesterday morning, today it's huge, if it doesn't burst by the end of the day I'll have to lance it again tonight with the needle, it must look kind of sloppy.

Then last I make fresh coffee. Yesterday's is bitter, even if I add water, and the microwave I don't trust. You never know if it's breaking down the molecules into heavy water that'll give you cancer before your time.

The bread's hard. I scrape the roof of my mouth on the right, and goddam, the left side's hurting too, I guess I didn't brush my teeth right last night—I wasn't in such good shape, I shouldn't have mixed Scotch and white wine—and some stuff must have been stuck under the gum, now I've got a sore. And my foot hurts.

Just as I'm leaving, I get a stomach cramp, goddamn! bad timing, I'm running late, luckily it goes away, I leave the house, I get in the car and it hits me again, fuck! And then it disappears, it comes and goes like that the whole trip, it isn't anything I recognize, appendicitis I've already had and it's not likely I'm getting my period, oh well I'm only a little worried, anyhow there's no time to feel sorry for myself but it's a bad start, usually when I leave I don't feel my foot anymore at all but today the slightest tap on the brakes and I'm in pain, this is a big help I swear! Once it starts up like that I'm in for a day of it.

Traffic's bad, Friday natch, everybody and his brother in a rush to warm up their cars for the weekend, gotta add your bit to the pollution, have I got an inhaler in the glove compartment? Jesus shit christ no! S'all I need, have an attack before I get in, I can already feel my heart pumping and I try to talk myself down because—Hey, schmuck, if you could just move your jalopy over by one hair, I could pass you and make a right, but fuck you!—I already feel it tightening up on me and I start sweating like a pig, my foot is hurting even more, the boil's swollen to three times the size, I decide to fart, that'll make me feel better, I pick up one cheek, and suddenly the guy opens the lane, I swerve out onto the avenue, where there's stoplights I'm okay.

When I get to the office I breathe better, but naturally I still hurt, I'll have to take something, anti-inflammatories always give me the runs I don't find that prospect enchanting, but hell I can't go on this way all day, who knows what's waiting for me when I get in, I can see it already, my secretary looking frantic, "The phone's been ringing off the hook for the last hour, I tried to reach you at home but you were already gone, the salesman called to say your cell-phone is fixed you just have to go by and pick it up, what a drag it fell out of your bag, since you got one things have been a lot easier, but those gadgets when they don't work,

DIAGNOSIS (SATURDAY, MARCH 29)

and I'm sorry to tell you you've got a full day there's already six housecalls to make, this afternoon's appointments are all booked but I had four other people call who absolutely have to see you today and—Something wrong, Doctor? You don't look too well…"

MADAME LEBLANC

I bike into the courtyard of the medical office. It's raining. I look at the time. I speed up. It's just as I thought: the office shutters and the waiting-room door are still closed. In the courtyard there are already a couple of cars, and people standing about. They watch me pass by on my bicycle. I should have brought the key.

For the past several months you've had much more work. That makes problems on Saturday mornings, since I don't go in then. This morning you must have been called out to see a patient and not had time to come by and open the waiting-room door. I've told you many times, though, that you could phone me and switch calls to my house if you had to be out, but you said you didn't want to trouble me. Still, I can't help it, I don't like to see the patients waiting outside, especially in the rain.

I go to my house, I drop the bread in the hallway, I take the office key and I go back to open up. When I arrive there are seven or eight patients at the door, and two or three in their cars. It's not raining much anymore. Two children are jumping in puddles.

Seeing me come up, everyone smiles and greets me.

I open the outside door and the one to the waiting room, I bring them inside. A little girl asks if you can go by to see Madame Renard after your office hours. I warn her that it could be late, probably not before one o'clock.

The wall clock says five to ten. The patients settle in, chair-feet scrape on the floor, the children tromp around, the raincoats drip onto the tiles. You've got a long morning still ahead of you.

CONSULTATION: IMPOSSIBLE
(Fifth Episode)

I leave my house around nine-forty, to get there before you do. In the courtyard three people are already waiting. One is standing, the two others are in their cars. The entrance door is still locked. Anyway, it's not raining, that's something.

Five minutes go by, now we're a half-dozen and it does start raining. Then Madame Leblanc arrives and opens the waiting-room door for us. At ten exactly, your car pulls into the courtyard. You come in, you greet us each in turn. You cross the room, you go into the examining room, leaving open the two connecting doors. You soon come back out, carrying two large wooden panels which you stand against the wall across from the secretary's desk. On the back of one I read, "Garden, left." Three minutes later, you come out again with two more wooden panels and set them against the first two. On the back of one I read, "Courtyard, left." You go back into the examining room and the connecting door closes. A few moments later, a loudspeaker attached near the ceiling begins to play music. Twelve minutes later you come out again, you say, "We can begin." One of the two men who were there before me stands up, with his wife's support. You step aside for them, and you close the inside door as you follow them in; meanwhile the connecting door shuts with a click by the force of the closer mechanism.

I wait. I keep a calm eye on the wall-clock hanging between the two windows. A quarter-hour goes by, a half-hour, forty-five minutes. Other patients have come in after me. Several times, through the wall, I've heard the telephone ring inside your examining room. It's already past eleven and the children get out of school at a quarter to twelve. The other gentleman has finished reading his paper. He looks at his watch. He rummages among the magazines piled on the low table and finds nothing to his taste. He crosses his legs and his arms and waits with a sigh. Two women, who came in at the same time, are talking louder and louder. One of them—a heavy woman, older—says it's always like this at the doctor's, gotta be patient. That it wasn't like that at the beginning, of course, she lives three steps away and she was awfully glad to get a doctor right on her street, and that at the beginning, you weren't seeing huge numbers of patients, naturally, so she felt a little sorry for you, she'd come in from time to time to have you take her blood pressure, it wasn't a big deal since the insurance paid for it but at the same time she kept using the doctor in Lavinié for her hypertension treatments and the diabetes and the cholesterol and the varicose veins. And then one day she had you come to her house because she wasn't feeling well, not at all well, she was hot she was cold and she kept on like that for three days and she'd waited, thinking it would go away, and then when she called her old doctor he wasn't there or else he couldn't come for another two days, and when you came you saw right away that she was really sick you gave her a thorough examination and you found she had gallstones and you sent her right in for an operation. She didn't want to go to the hospital, of course, and you told her that she could do as she pleased but that she already had jaundice and she risked getting septicemia too so of course she said yes and when she got to the hospital they told her "Well dear lady you just about lost it that young doctor saved your life," and the day after the surgery she was still practically in a coma and she heard somebody calling her name she woke up and who was there at the foot of her bed? The young doctor, who came to see how she was doing. So naturally she thanked him and he modestly said it was nothing but when she saw what they'd taken out of her gall bladder she couldn't get over it: three dark brown rocks as big as pigeon eggs that they'd put in a little bottle and gave her as she left, if Madame had a few minutes after the doctor she could show them to her. So naturally, that creates a bond. And since then she always used him. But that at the beginning a person almost never had to wait: she'd ring, she'd come in, she'd sit down and she was hardly in her chair when there he was coming out of his examining room because he was alone in there—waiting for patients, probably—and he'd take her right away and he had time for conversation. Whereas nowadays, naturally, people are pleased with him and they keep coming back, it's not like in the old days when you had to pay the doctor and the medicines were expensive, these days what costs is getting to their office. When there's no doctor nearby and you have no car, you've got to ask somebody or other and naturally they can't always do it when you need it, so when there's a doctor right nearby it's a lot easier, especially for these young mothers who've got kiddies and they're not too sure what to do when the baby runs a fever or starts vomiting, they go to the doctor easier and I hear he even keeps some medicine in his drawer for if a person needs something at night and that way you don't have to ask somebody for a ride to the pharmacy the next day, oh yes he sure is awful useful, my little doctor, and then you know I got my husband he lays hands on me, he stops the fire, but he never does stop the fire for me as good as my little doctor does and still I suffer so much ohnomygod how I suffer, the fat lady is saying just as I hear the doorknob turn. The connecting door opens before the gentleman who was the first in line, and he comes out—not very quickly, dragging his feet, breathing with difficulty, he really doesn't seem to be in very good shape, I can see why you kept him so long, but what strikes me odd is that I don't think he was in such bad shape as this before he went in. The second gentleman goes into the office, I look up at the wall clock hung between the windows and I read twenty to twelve—no! It's already time for me to go pick up the kids at school—I don't believe it! Good thing I didn't have an appointment. For once I decide to go to the doctor early—just my luck!

80
———

INKJET

CANCER(S) 1576-1645: adenoidal, anaplasic, anogenital; colon (*see* Colon, cancer of); diagnosis; etiology; evaluation (clinical, stage); hemorrhage (intracranial, etc.); incontinence; larynx (*see* Larynx, cancer of); liver (*see* Liver, cancerous lesions of); lung (see Lung, lesions of; metastases to); metastases (*see also* Metastases); Melanoma (malignant); mouth (*see also* Mouth, cancer of); pharynx; pleura; skin (*see* Skin, cancer of); stomach (*see* Stomach, cancer of)...

LARYNX Abscess of...; Biopsy of...; Cancer of: Physical examination: anemia; biopsy; chemotherapy; classification (physiologic, stage); screening for; diagnosis; clinical signs and circumstances of discovery... .

Cancer of the larynx manifests by local signs and symptoms linked to tumor growth, by signs of invasion or obstruction of neighboring organs (particularly the esophagus), by regional adenopathies through invasion of lymph pathways, and eventually by the distant occurrence of metastases by dissemination through the vascular system... Secondary signs of tumor growth in the parenchyma or endobronchi are coughing, hemophthises, wheezing and stridor, dyspnea or pneumopathy (with fever and expectorant cough), resulting from the obstruction of respiratory pathways... *Extrathoracic metastases* (*see* this term) are discovered upon autopsy in more than 50% of cases of epidermoid epithelioma, in 8% of adenocarcinoma. At autopsy, metastases are found in nearly all organs. For this reason, most patients with larynx cancer will at some point require palliative treatment.

81

MONSIEUR GUENOT AGAIN

The door opens.

I stand up, my cap in hand. I pick up my wallet from the low table, the health booklet with my prothrombin record, the Social Security form, and the prescription slip I brought along. You offer your hand. "Hello, Monsieur Guenot."

"Hello, Monsieur—uhh, Doctor."

"How you doing?"

"Well I come about my prothrombin…"

"Mmmhyes, every month."

I open the envelope and take out the results of the last blood test, I set my cap on the chair.

"It went up since last time…" I say.

"Did it? Let's see… thirty-six percent. Last time you had thirty-one—that's good. Between twenty-five and thirty-five percent, there's no problem…"

I take off my jacket, my vest, I undo my belt. "Fine, well you could maybe have a look at me. Should I get undressed?"

"Yes, please…"

I take off my pants, I lay them on the chair. I take off my undershirt. "Socks off too?"

"If you want."

"Lie down?"

"Yes, please."

You swivel around on your chair. "What's new since last time?"

"Oh, not much, but I have no more of that syrup, got to get me a renewal, you never know. And I'm supposed to get my tetanus booster."

"Mmmhh. I'll give you a slip, we'll do it next month."

I give you my right arm, you strap it into the gray armband and, without dropping the rubber pear, you lay my arm gently on the edge of the bed. With your right hand, you pick up a stethoscope, you slip the listening-plugs into your ears, you set the cup of the instrument on the pulse inside my elbow, you squeeze the rubber pear.

"One-thirty over eighty—that's good."

"Last time I had one-forty…"

"Mmmhh… same thing. It's still normal. And your wife, she's well?"

"Holding up… We're not getting any younger, you know."

"Don't I know it! Sit on the edge of the bed here."

You test my reflexes. "Perfect."

"So then? The old horse ain't about to drop dead?"

"Far from it! In fact, you seem to be in good shape."

"Can't complain, holding up… But at seventy it's not like at twenty! Heck! Gotta take care of yourself."

"Come over here so I can weigh you."

I step up on the scale. "Did I lose any?"

"No, no change since last time."

"I should get dressed?"

"Mmmhh."

You go back to your chair. Meanwhile, I put my socks back on, my trousers, my shirt, my shoes. I see you take a prescription pad. I pull out my wallet and I see you write my name on top over on the right, same line as yours, with the date right underneath, then, carefully, in capital letters with a little dash before it, the name of the medications you've been prescribing for me since the first time I came to see you. There are only two of them; you say that should do, although it really surprised people in the beginning, they'd say, "I guess he doesn't have many patients, he doesn't prescribe much, and the pharmacists say they don't make much from anybody who's a patient of Dr. Sachs," but acourse, for those fellows all's they care about is the money. It's true, though, people do expect a doctor to order them lots of medicines, they've paid in enough on the health insurance, and even myself I thought that was strange in the beginning, but since it worked fine for me, why go change to somebody else? Except that doesn't suit everyone, and people talk, they say things, like for instance that our doctor doesn't live alone anymore, that he's got hisself a ladyfriend, that she's very nice really and they're living together and it wouldn't be a big surprise if one fine day we hear he's going to leave. But I been hearing that for a long time and I just say, "Why would he come here and set up practice if he was going to leave all of a sudden?" So I don't put too much store in it, and yet I know there's people who ask you the question, but to me I think that's crazy—there's always rumors, and if you were going to leave, we'd know about it, in fact when I hear that, I just ask Madame Leblanc, quietly, I say to her, "I know it's just rumors, but the doctor's really not leaving, is he?" and she looks at me surprised and she answers, "I certainly hope not! Anyhow, he hasn't said a word to me." And if you were going to tell anybody, you'd tell her.

On the prescription slip you put the blood test to be done by the nurse, next month, for the prothrombin.

I stand up, I point. "You're not forgetting to write 'home visit'? Otherwise they don't pay it back…"

82

THREE SHEETS FROM A THICK PAD

Sheets 1 and 2

"Hello, Doctor? This is the ambulance squad from Saint-Jacques, you forgot to sign the transport requisition for that gentleman the other night and also we're calling to tell you that we're on our way to the hospital to pick up old Madame Doubrovsky, your patient from Deuxmonts, and take her back home, could you stop in to see her this evening, that would help the family feel a little more secure…"

"Hello, Doctor? This is the nurse. Am I really supposed to do three injections a day on Madame Benoziglio, because fine, it's okay with me, but she's in a lot of pain, and that medication is very thick, it takes me at least ten minutes to inject it—Oh, it wasn't you? It's the hospital prescribed the injection form? I thought so. Yes, it's an antibiotic… Well yeah, that's just what I told her, 'You know Madame Benoziglio, there must be some way to take this by mouth'… Yes, that would be more comfortable for her. It's no trouble for you? She'll be relieved, for sure. Fine, I'll tell her grandson to go by your office and pick up the slip…"

"Hello? Good morning, Doctor, this is Monsieur Sulitzer, from the Provincial Credit bank, I heard you had rather old office space, and I thought you might be considering a change soon… or maybe buying a house? or even building, so I'm taking the liberty of calling to offer you a mortgage plan we've created especially for professional offices…"

"Hello, Doctor? This is the gendarme headquarters in Lavallée. Pardon me for disturbing you. Two nights ago—you were on duty, I believe—did you by any chance treat a patient for bullet wounds?… Yes, sure I know you're pledged to confidentiality, but it's no good telling that to my superiors, they insist we have to call you anyhow... Actually, up here you and your colleagues never tell me anything, but I remember once, I was stationed down south, a doctor answered me, 'Yes, I did see a suspicious fellow yesterday, he'd been stabbed and he asked me to stitch him up, I thought it looked fishy, and now that you tell me this, I'm not surprised—he never did pay me!' and he gave me the name and address, he must have been pretty annoyed getting woken up at three in the morning! Well, believe it or not, the guy in question, when we went to arrest him—it was a payback, he stabbed the boy who raped his sister—he got his lawyer to sue the doctor for violation of professional confidentiality, and even though he was in jail, still, that lawsuit against the doctor—he won it anyhow!"

"Hello Doctor? This is the secretary at the town hall, I wanted to let you know that measles vaccine came in, you remember? You're supposed to come give it to the children the end of this week, and you asked me to remind you..."

"Hello, is this the doctor? This is Madame—*Tsee-heehee!*... Madame Cocteau, I'm calling to ask if you install contraceptive IUDs... and diaphragms? And—*tse-heehee!*—And what about sh—shock absorbers! *Heehee... Hahahahaha... .!!*"

"Hello, Doctor Sachs? Montrond Laboratories here. I'm reporting test results on Monsieur Huysmans René 13 Route de la Grange-aux-belles in Play: erythrocytes four point two million, hematocrit thirty-seven percent, leukocytes twenty-five thousand, polyneutro thirteen, eosinophils four, baso ten, mono eight, lymphocytes sixty-three, young forms two percent. Commentary: follow-up verification recommended in a few days electrolytes—you with me? I'm not going too fast?"

"Hello, is this the doctor in Play? This is the Lavallée social worker, I wanted to talk to you about Madame Musset, you had her as a patient when she lived in Forçay and now she lives in the Boizard housing project—yes, that's right, since three weeks ago. She's applying for some hours of a Home Health Aide, I wanted to find out if that's justified because of course I'm no doctor but she doesn't seem very sick to me what do you think?"

"Hello, good morning sir, sorry to disturb you, I'm doing a survey for the AAA Company I'm sure you've heard of them—kitchen equipment/encyclopedias/frozen foods by home delivery..."

"Hello? Edmond? Is that you, Edmond? Oh, this blasted thing never works!... Hello? Hello? Edmond? If you're there, answer me! Edmond!"

Medical discourse is like cancer. It proliferates. Each disease name refers to multiple meanings, allusions, extensions, implications, variants all the more numerous because any single disease almost never has just one characteristic, it has *forms*—forms which are more or less frequent, "typical" or "unusual", and which are defined by various striking signs they might cause, but never by the person who's suffering from them. In this country, diseases, like syndromes, are named after the doctors who first observed or at least described them. They are never named after the persons who suffered them. Which demonstrates nicely the degree to which disease *belongs to* the doctors—to a caste, a group which alone benefits from it. Professor Thingamajig's Disease, Doctor Whatsis's Syndrome—why is it never "Destouches's Acute Renal Failure," or "Deshoulières's Malignant Liver Syndrome," "Guilloux's Choking-Ulcer Cancer"? Giving a disease the name of a doctor makes all its victims into a kind of appendage of the knowledge, the power, the glory of the damnfool doctor who's stuck his lousy name onto some hideous monstrosity.

How can a person take pride in putting his name to a hideous monstrosity?

People—patients—don't give a good goddamn. They don't have "Lapeyronie's Disease," they've got a cock that bends sideways. They don't have "Dupuytren's Disease," they've got hands that don't open. They don't have "Charcot's Disease," they've got a creeping paralysis, their muscles melt down, their strength deserts them, and by the end they can't breathe anymore so we stick them into an artificial respirator because their thoracic muscles have melted along with the rest. People don't have some Whozit's Disease, they have pain, they suffer, they lose weight, they throw up, they don't sleep, they cry, they die an endless death...

We remember Charcot's name but not the names of the people who've died of the abomination he gave his name to. Charcot himself didn't die of it. And even so, the doctors' names are only a hypocritical cover to avoid having to say what we're talking about. "Kaposi's syndrome" sounds less ominous than "Kaposi's *sarcoma*." "Charcot's disease" sounds nobler than "Amyotrophic lateral sclerosis." "Down syndrome" is more glamourous than "mongolism."

Meanwhile, Monsieur Guilloux hangs in there. Today, I was supposed to go see him and he insisted on coming to my office instead. His wife brought him to Play in the car. I remembered a skeletal body, but today he looked like a deep-sea diver whose wet-suit bottoms had taken on water. His legs, his thighs, and his genitals had tripled in size. Last Sunday I wasn't on duty and he didn't want his wife to phone me at home so he called in the woman who was covering for Boulle. She must have seen he had edema in the legs, and she knows what he's sick with (I leave the file at his house so whatever doctor sees him can consult it.) But she didn't do a thing. She didn't even put him on diuretics for a couple of days, to try and bring down the swelling. She must not have given a damn. She said, "It's nothing, it'll get better." Stupid bitch! I phoned her to ask for an explanation, she stammered, she didn't know what to say, idiocies like: "Diuretics are contraindicated when the cause of edema is unknown" and I said: "What about your head—what do you use it for? Did you see the amount of morphine he's getting? He has an invasive cancer, IN-VA-SIVE! What were you afraid of? Of killing him? Was it better to let the skin on his legs explode all over the room? Didn't you see that his balls are so swollen he can't get his shorts on? Do you think you're gonna keep him alive longer by doing nothing? Quality of life, you know what that is, you stupid bitch?" And I wound up by saying that if she had to come down with ovarian cancer to understand what Guilloux is going through right now, she should just go into another line of work. She took a lofty tone. Mediocrities don't get it when you tell them that's what they are. That night, Boulle called me back, he was pretty stunned, he hadn't believed her when she told him the story but I confirmed it word for word. And I added everything I hadn't thought to tell her at the time. The anger hadn't subsided. I ended by saying that she was far too stupid for him to keep using her as his substitute. Boulle said, "The thing is, you worry much more over your patients than I do over mine..." His voice was curiously sad. I said I didn't think so, it was just that he and I have different ways of expressing things, that's all. He didn't comment.

A little while ago, Madame Guilloux phoned. She told me her husband has practically no edema left but he's exhausted. He's not getting up right now. For three days he never stopped urinating, he keeps a flask constantly within reach, empties it into a bucket alongside the bed. And, as always, he's listening to his radio and puttering, in bed; he's fixing a lamp or gluing a broken trivet, but he doesn't complain about a thing.

83

IN THE WAITING ROOM

My nose is stuffed. I put down the book and take out a paper tissue. I blow and try not to make too much noise. The little boy looks up, then goes back to his blocks. The little girl turns to me and points to the stuffed animals lying on the floor, saying, "Sshhh! the bears are having a nap." The pregnant woman looks drowsier by the minute. She holds onto her belly as if she were afraid of falling.

Beside me, the teenager and her mother keep needling one another. Or rather, the mother is needling the girl, with her "You'll see, I'm going to tell him. We can't just leave you like this. It can't go on. I'm doing this for your own sake, you know! After all, I *am* your mother." And the girl answers, "Stop it! Stop it, you're driving me crazy!" and keeps sighing endlessly.

The door opens. The man with the cap comes out: "Good, well can't take up your time! People are waiting for you! So okay good-bye then, Doctor, see you in a month!..."

"Goodbye, Monsieur Guenot."

You turn toward us. The mother stands and steps forward. The daughter sighs, then she gets up too, and goes in sullenly. I look around me. I didn't think it was their turn, but maybe I'm wrong.

The connecting door shuts behind you with a click, by the closer mechanism. Behind it, you can be heard firmly shutting the inner door to the consulting room.

I put the tissue in my pocket and pick up my reading again, leafing back and forth a bit because I've lost my place.

84

VIVIANE R.

It's four o'clock. She's been sitting on the terrace for nearly three hours. When she got here, it wasn't too nice out, there was some wind and I would have sworn it was going to rain, with the leaden clouds moving by up there. But she sat down anyhow at their usual table, and pretty soon the wind dropped, while I was taking orders inside the clouds disappeared, the sun started getting warm, she took off her suit jacket.

She's waiting for him, certainly. They often come here early Saturday afternoon, most often she arrives before him, she pulls out a cardboard file from her bag and she reads. At the beginning, I thought it was student compositions, there are a couple of teachers who come here to correct papers. But this one isn't a teacher. I've run into her before, where she works—in an office, or some public agency, but I can't quite remember where, maybe the town registrar, or the prefecture. There are lots of people in those places. It intrigues me, I'd like to know a little more. Him I know—I mean, that's an exaggeration, but I've talked to him long enough, last year when he was treating me at the hospital, to know the kind of man he is. At the time, somebody or other told me he lived alone, and I found that surprising: a bachelor, not bad-looking, kind and intelligent, and a doctor besides—that's not so common. And I knew he wasn't the kind who prefers men—that would come through too—although one day I did see him hug the guy who runs the Mall Bookstore—that guy I do believe is that way, but they were hugging like two brothers, that's all.

And then one day, I never thought of him any more (I don't actually think of him very often, it's just that he used to come here even before he started coming with her, he'd come on Saturday afternoons, he'd sit down and write in a journal or read a book, in winter right inside the street window, in summer outside but mostly in the shade) and there he was, walking toward her (she was sitting on the terrace and I thought she must be waiting for someone but it never occurred to me it would be him), she looked up, he leaned down to her, and I'd never seen a man kiss a woman with such tenderness, or a woman close her eyes like that to receive a kiss, it didn't last long, but it was as if time stopped.

Since that day, I've never seen either of them come alone. Most of the time they come in together, or she arrives first and he joins her. When they're together, they talk. They talk a lot, they sometimes talk for a long time. A lot of times he's upset when he gets here, it's rare you see him smiling. He comes over, she smiles, she gives him her hand, he takes it, he leans over, she receives his kiss, he sits down, and he starts to talk, about his patients often, I hear bits and pieces. He begins, "You know what happened this morning?" and she says, "Tell me…" She listens to him; after a while he relaxes, he's calmer, they order something, often some espresso. And sometimes they talk about what she was reading before he got here.

It's months now that they've been together. It shows in the way they talk to each other, in the way he'd help her put on her coat this winter, the way she takes his arm when they go off… They never look around them when they're sitting on the terrace, whereas in a lot of couples, there's one who talks and the other who looks around, to see if he recognizes someone, or out of fear of being recognized.

You'd think they'd been living together for years, and they still say "vous" to each other. It's odd. Actually, it's no stupider than with American movies that're dubbed into French, when the couples use "vous" for the whole first part of the movie and "tu" after the first kiss or the first sex, whereas in the original language nothing changes, since there's no "vous" and "tu" distinction in English. In *Bébé Donge*, when they're in bed, Danielle Darrieux says "tu" and "vous" alternately to Jean Gabin, because she's trying to keep her distance.

It's as if they've found the right distance. They're in love, and it's lasting. As if it's never going to stop. It shows in their eyes, in their way of looking at each other, of laughing or being serious. He used to be gloomy a lot, and he's less so as the months pass. It may be my imagination, but that kind of guy wouldn't stay with a woman who doesn't make him happy, he wouldn't treat her the way he does, he wouldn't tell her he loves her smile. I know some men who can never get free of their lady-friends' claws, I've got to say there are some huge bitches out there and when they get hold of a good man, they don't let him go, they'll drop two, three kids p.d.q and the man is stuck there—nice guy fall guy.

But her, she never irritates him. Sure, it's true I'm not always right there in their lap, but I dunno, you can feel it. When he's in a bad mood—with all the misery he must see, he's got a right after all!—she doesn't mother him, she doesn't make nice, she just puts her hand on his. And sometimes, when she's the one who seems to be having trouble, he's right there too.

They're always there for each other.

They give me a pain in the ass, loving each other so much.

They give me a pain, with their happiness and their talent for sharing problems without ever getting irritated, without ever resenting each other, without ever feeling swallowed up or closed out.

They give me a pain, being so much in love, smiling at each other, kissing, touching each other as if they were in foreplay all the time, as if they could suddenly stand up, pay the check, leave, go down the street arm in arm, walk into her apartment house (I've seen her several times coming out of the public housing over by the Mall), climb the steps four at a time, throw open the door, kiss like maniacs as they close the door, he takes her by the back of the neck, their mouths devour each other, she clutches him to her and slips her thigh between his, and in a minute they're undressed and flinging onto her bed, she probably has a very big bed—a woman like her sleeps sprawled out—even if she doesn't always sleep there now, even if she spends most of her time with him, still the bed is always ready, with a spread in some good dark gray or nearly-brick red, the corner of the quilt is always turned back, open, on the side where he slept the first time, and they're in there clasped to one another, him on her, or her on top of him this time, she likes him to hold her, she likes to impale herself on him while he holds her, his big hands set on her hips, and she likes him to look at her while he digs in deep and makes her dance, and she—it drives her insane when he holds her and stares at her, he tells her she's beautiful, how beautiful you are, how good you are, I love you—how he loves her! He gives himself, he fills her up, she takes him in, receives him and sucks him into her, yes, they're in ecstasy, and saying "This is good" isn't saying a thing, because it's *all* good between them, in them, because they have each other.

They give me a pain, with all that desire, that pleasure I read on their faces. They give me a pain, I'd like to tell them it gives me a pain seeing them so in love, so close—whether they're happy and gay or sad and down—seeing them so united.

But I won't say anything. Because they're the only sun I've got in this jail. Because the world is gray, everybody's ordinary, people are cowards or idiots. Everybody's miserable, bored out of their skulls, they spend their time hating—men hating women, women hating men, men killing each other, women robbing each other. Everybody's worthless, and nobody believes in love.

Me neither—for a long time I believed it didn't exist. I believed that the alliance, the proximity, the complicity, the silent understanding I see in those two—those things couldn't exist. Except in movies. In cheap novels. In fairy tales.

But I also thought that if people made so much fuss about love, maybe that was because it really does exist. Maybe some people do experience that.

Which is why I keep my mouth shut. I don't want them to move to some other café terrace. I don't want them to stop coming here. I don't want them to disappear. I want to be able to watch them, to hear scraps of their conversations, catch sight of their smiles and their movements, watch him talking loud, waving his arms and mimicking people to tell some story, and see her smile, and hear him laugh, with that Homeric laugh that flings his head backwards, see him take off his glasses and rub his eyes to wipe away the tears.

I don't say a thing. I watch them. I drink them in with my eyes, while they drink my coffee. They give me a pain, but they're all I have. So I take good care of them.

85

INITIAL OBSERVATIONS

The first time I felt a breast tumor, it was in the breast of a woman I was making love to.

❋

I was a new trainee in a medical unit, they asked me to do a gynecological exam-ination—or more precisely, a vaginal palpation—on a girl who was slightly retard-ed. It was the first time for me and for her both. I wrote on the file that I'd done it, that it was normal, but actually I hadn't touched her. I felt slightly guilty about that, until I realized that the resident was just hazing me.

❋

During my first week of practice here, I listened to a man recounting his life to me; what struck me most was that throughout his whole childhood, his mother used to call him "My little turd," and from adolescence on, his father'd always told him, "You're just a piece of shit!"

❋

One night, in maternity, I was ordered to stitch up the episiotomy of a woman who'd just given birth. I had observed gynecologists do it, but at a certain moment I realized I was stitching the labia together.

❋

When I was still only in my first or second year, the grandmother of a woman friend told me the story of her life as an exile between the Black Sea and the Atlantic. She made me promise that if some day she were paralyzed, I would give her what she needed for dying. I did promise. When she died, she was in a hospitalized in a mental ward. She had Alzheimer's Disease, or some dementia of the kind. She was no longer in condition to ask to be killed.

I'd set up practice a few months earlier, when someone called me to a house where a child had something wrong. He was three or four years old. He couldn't stand up. He reeked of wine. He'd swilled down half a bottle, but his mother swore up and down that it wasn't so. She had the facial structure of an imbecile and so did this boy, but the other three children were very beautiful.

When I covered for Boulle, I'd sometimes go to treat the children of a single mother who lived out on the Lavallée road. She had maybe six or seven of them. One day she came in to say that she was afraid she was pregnant and that she couldn't handle it, I'd absolutely have to abort her, that otherwise she'd never manage, etcetera. I examined her; her uterus was enlarged, but not very much. I asked for a pregnancy test and it came back negative. Later, Boulle explained that she'd had her tubes tied four years earlier, but that she pulled this on him regularly. The first time, he went along. Thereafter, he refused to run the tests just to satisfy her delusion. She took advantage of his absences to ambush his substitutes or his colleagues. When I set up practice, one Saturday when Boulle was away her call got passed to me, and apparently she didn't make the connection, because when she opened the door to let me in I saw her start to do the same number she'd run on me a few months earlier; then, recognizing me, she stopped, and instantly found some other pretext for having phoned.

One night when I was on call, the answering service told me that a woman wanted me to come way the hell out somewhere (probably Sainte-Sophie) to prescribe her some laxatives. It was like half-past midnight. I wasn't sleeping, I was watching a foreign-language film on the TV, and I really didn't feel like moving. I phoned her. She answered in a trailing, faint, whiny voice, she said she couldn't stand it any longer, that I absolutely had to come by, that she needed a laxative. Sensing that I wasn't much disposed to travel twenty miles back and forth to prescribe a medication that she wouldn't go out to fill before eleven the next morning, her voice started to swell, to hiss, to scold. Finally she yelled, "Oh! You're just like my husband!"

DIAGNOSIS (SATURDAY, MARCH 29)

The first article I published was in *Utopian Medicine,* a journal run by activist doctors. It was a broadside exhorting doctors to use the check-ups they do for athletic permits as an occasion to give men thorough examinations. At the time, I knew for a fact that doctors never hesitated to examine women's breasts, but rarely checked what might be going on inside men's shorts. We must remember, I wrote sententiously, that not only were there organs down there to be examined and treated, there were also things to be explained, and anxieties to be allayed: testicular cancer of course, but more often hypospadias, undescended testicles, phimosis, swollen scrotum, cysts, twisted testicles or hydatids, trauma, fungus growths, venereal infections, herpes, vague pains, pubic hair going white—Is that normal for my age?—some inflammation of the glans or the foreskin, skin discolorations, decreased sensitivity in the penis for more than a few months in a twenty-five-year-old guy who's just been circumcised for some reason… Reading over this list a few days ago, I said to myself, "Who in hell would want to go into all that?"

❋

When I was a child, I firmly believed that any catastrophe I could think up (my father's death in a car accident, for instance) was less likely to happen if I imagined it down to the last detail. Real catastrophes—ones that would actually come to pass—would be the ones I hadn't foreseen.

One year, at medical school, I proofread a medical textbook edited by one of my professors. I reread the whole thing from beginning to end, night and day over a period of weeks, except during training stints. (I'd already finished my coursework by that time.)

The description of all the illnesses in the catalog passed before my eyes, and I got the idea that if I memorized the symptoms of every fatal disorder, and if I recited them regularly in my mind, that would immunize me against them. Much later, I came to understand that the disorders in textbooks are themselves only artifacts produced by an arbitrary system. In the real world, people don't die the way it says in medical books.

❋

One day when I was working as a nurse in a small hospital, there was a guy there thirty-five, thirty-six years old who'd been operated on for a brain tumor. He was a farmer, he had three children. He was something like six feet tall and weighed nearly two-twenty. He yoyo-ed up and down. He giggled constantly. The nurses' aides never wanted to get him out of bed, because he was heavy, but also because the minute he saw a woman he'd start masturbating furiously with whichever of his huge paws he could still move. Obviously, they always wanted me to go take care of it instead. When he saw me coming, he'd take my hand and say, "Li'l Bear Li'l Bear Li'l Bear," and he'd cry. One day, I came in to give him his medicine and his mother was there. She was stroking his head with her hand, and saying, "Li'l Bear Li'l Bear Li'l Bear," and she was crying.

❊

When I was in Med School, I saw Dalton Trumbo's movie *Johnny Got His Gun*. That night I put together a poster that summarized the movie and urged my fellow students to go see it. I taped it onto the door of the auditorium the next morning. Two hours later it was gone.

❊

One of my first training supervisors, a forensic surgeon, invited me and two other students to come observe an autopsy he was to do. The body was that of a woman whose companion had killed her with two loads of buckshot, one in the abdomen and one in the temple. In the elevator, coming up from the morgue, he told us that his assistant (who as we watched had scalped the woman, then cut away her skull with a little electric circular saw, and whom we saw weighing her liver, her heart, and the various organs in a butcher's scale as the forensic surgeon extracted them one by one from the cadaver) had a few years earlier been the woman's lover.

❊

That same supervisor, who was in charge of a unit for people they used to call "bedridden" and now call "terminal cases," decided to show us how to do a vein strip on an old man in a deep coma. This involved dissecting a thick vein in one foot to install an intravenous catheter. I asked why he was doing it, since the patient didn't need it (he was perfectly well hydrated; his arms had very good veins). The doctor answered that he was doing it "for pedagogic purposes."

❊

Each year, all through medical school, I gave blood. The blood collection crew would set up once a year in the corridors by the faculty cafeteria. They'd arrange portable partitions and put brochures on the tables, along with sandwiches and fruit juices for the donors. They stayed only the one day, generally, but it was impossible for a student to walk by without seeing them. Once I asked one of the nurses drawing blood if they did this in all the different divisions of the university. She told me yes, and added that the medical and pharmacy students were the ones who gave least.

❋

One day, standing in for someone, I went out on a housecall to a couple on a miserable farm in the depths of a forest. They were both over sixty. She was paralyzed from a stroke, bound to her wheelchair, her mouth drooping, drool hanging from her lips, incapable of a single word. He seemed a little younger, he was jovial; he'd give her her medications, make her eat, put her on the toilet, wipe her, and he explained to me that she didn't communicate very much, but she did a little, and that he could understand her. Good thing he was there, he said—otherwise, he didn't know what would become of her. And he was careful about her hypertension medicine because he really didn't want her to have another stroke. When I was leaving, he asked me to check his blood pressure. He had something like 200 over 120. I took it twice. For some reason, I told him it was normal and I didn't prescribe anything. A few months later, I asked their regular doctor for news of him; he said, "Poor guy, he died of a stroke," and he blamed himself for never having thought to check his pressure. Frozen, I managed to say, "He never asked you to." That didn't seem to console him.

❋

When my father fell ill, and they told him what he had, I was so upset that I asked him to tell me about it. It was a disease he didn't know, because it was rare, and very remote from his own specialty. I looked for some article on the subject. I found one, which had just been published. I brought it to him. A few days later, he asked me, "Did you read that article?" I said I hadn't wanted to do that before he did. He said, "Just as well, it's a poor article," and he didn't give it back to me.

86
VIVIANE R.

She drops the sheaf of paper onto her lap. She looks kind of perplexed. She raises her head, looks at her watch, but she's not worried. She goes back to her reading. From time to time, she makes a pencil mark in the margin, so delicate it hardly shows. Sometimes, even, she picks up the pencil, then thinks better of it, and writes nothing. Sometimes, like right now, she stops. I get the sense she's finding it hard to go on. She asks me for something else—coffee, lemonade. She's catching her breath.

When he joins her, often as soon as he's seated, she goes back to reading the page she's started. He looks around for me, he orders something. He picks up the pages she's already gone over, he looks at the notes, he pulls a black fountain pen out of his pocket, he makes changes, he writes along the margins or even on the backside of the sheet. Or else he watches her, he doesn't speak, he waits.

Right now, she's gazing at the street. Past the terrace go a couple, a very old woman leaning on a cane, her other arm linked to a man of fifty with a mongoloid face. The two of them are walking with tiny steps, and it's not clear who's supporting whom.

87
_____

A LOVE STORY
(Continued)

Somebody rings the doorbell. Mama strokes my cheek, gets up, and goes out into the hall. I hear her open the door.

"Hello, Doctor."

"Hello, Madame Calvino."

"Thank you for coming… It's for my son. Doctor Boulle is away just now, and he told me I could call on you. We already met, you and I—one Sunday, a few months ago when you were on duty."

"I remember. And I recognized your accent on the phone."

Mama laughs. This man comes in. I never saw him before. Mama told me it wouldn't be Jérôme, but that this man was nice too. He's tall, almost as tall as Jérôme, but he has black hair, dark glasses, and he looks like he didn't shave this morning. He's got a leather jacket and a big bag, and he's fooling with his keys. He smiles at me; one of his teeth on top is chipped.

"Hello, little guy."

"Hello…"

"So what's going on with you?"

I don't answer. He puts his bag on the table and sits by my feet at the edge of the couch. He looks at me, he doesn't say anything. I look at Mama. She looks at me.

"Answer, darling."

I don't answer. I don't know how to talk to him. With Jérôme, I know how to.

"I'm so sorry, I had to argue all last evening and part of this morning to get him to let me call you. With my—with Doctor Boulle, of course, it's always easy, he's known him since he was born, he's not afraid of him, but when he goes away, it's always hard. And by some bad luck it's often during vacation time that he gets sick…"

I hear the sadness in Mama's voice, but I hear something else too. I hear that she talks to this man with the same trust she does to Jérôme. So I put my hand on my neck and I say, "It hurts here."

"Mmmhh. When did it start, little guy?"

I turn to Mama. She answers: "Three days ago. I've been giving him aspirin when he got home from school, and it would pass. Last night, he started a fever. I wanted to wait for... Doctor Boulle to get back. Usually, I don't wait so long. But this time he went for a week and he won't be back until Monday. It looked like we were in for a long weekend..."

As Mama talked, he was listening to her and still watching me. Once I saw his eyebrow go up, but he didn't say anything.

"And apart from the fever? Is he eating? Drinking?"

"Yes, but it hurts him to swallow. And he's listless and pale—I haven't seen him like this since he had the mumps, when he was three."

"He hadn't been vaccinated?"

"No, Jé—Doctor Boulle was about to vaccinate him but the mumps broke out before he got to it. That started on a Sunday, too. He had a hundred-and-four, he was delirious, he cried constantly—I was so worried that I called Doctor Boulle at home. I never do that, and he wasn't on call that night, but since he knows us well... He knew I wouldn't call without a good reason, so he came over. The boy had a hundred and four for nearly a week, the doctor came in morning and night... Later on, he told me that he'd probably developed meningitis from the mumps, but that he hadn't wanted to hospitalize him because that kind of meningitis is always benign and he didn't want to put him through all the examinations, the spinal tap, and so on..."

He's watching Mama and nodding his head. "It's true, it wouldn't have helped any. And having a child in hospital is no laughing matter. You know when he goes in but you never know when he'll get out."

"Yes. That's what he said..."

The man turned to me. "Would it be okay with you if I examine you, today?"

"Will you do it like Jérôme does?"

He smiles. "Mmmhh. If you want. You just tell me how he usually does it. Where does he start?"

I pull up my pajama tops. "Okay, doc."

He pulls a red stethoscope out of his bag. He warms the end of it between his hands. He listens to my heart. "What do I do next?"

"My stomach."

I lie down on the couch, I push my pajama bottoms down a little. He crouches next to me and he lays his big warm hand on my stomach.

"Mmmhh. And next, do we look at the ears or the throat?"

"Ears. The throat comes last. The spoon makes me feel like throwing up."

"Well now, you know something? I don't use a spoon."

"Really?"

He looks in my ears, and then he asks Mama for a mirror. She brings a little square one. He hands it to me. "Open your mouth wide, stick your tongue out, and tell me what you see way in the back."

I stick my tongue out and he aims the beam of a pocket flashlight straight into my throat. At the back of my mouth, I see two big white round things...

"Say AAAAhhh..."

"Oooooaaaa—byuuuch!"

"Not so awful, huh? You've got a strep throat, little guy. Your mama did right to call me. You would have had a rough weekend, so would she, and I'm sure your... doctor will be glad you didn't wait to treat it till he got back."

He turns off his little light, puts his instruments away, and pulls out some prescription slips. He starts writing. "Okay, I'm ordering syrup, antibiotics, aspirin, and—you like ice cream?"

"Oh, yeah!"

"What flavor?"

"All kinds," Mama says.

"But best I like lemon..."

"Ooookay. So—I prescribe lemon sherbet for the next three days."

I look at him, I'm wondering if he's joking me. He says, "No, no really, I'm serious. Your tonsils—you know, those big round bulbs in your throat—they're infected, and the best thing for soothing the pain is ice. You've got some on hand, I hope?"

"Yes," Mama says. "Always."

He goes on writing. Mama goes to find her purse, to pay him. When she gets back with her checkbook, he just hands her a prescription, raises his hand, and starts to say, "Please..."

She looks at him, she looks at me, she insists. "Yes, absolutely, I must!"

He shrugs, sighs, then takes an orange paper out of his bag. He fills it out and gives it to her. She sits down at her table, at the other end of the living room, and pushes her keyboard aside to make room for writing her check. He looks at the computer screen.

"If it's not indiscreet—you work at home?"

"Yes," Mama answers. "I'm a translator."

"And what do you translate?"

"Oh—a bit of everything. Manuals, sometimes a novel, catalogues, cartoon strips..."

He points to a bookshelf. "So *The Good Little Girl,* translated by Flavia Calvino'—that's you?"

"Do you know it?"

"I sure do. That's no children's cartoon…"

"No, but I'm happy to have it to translate. It's a regular job. For me, that matters."

"I find it very well translated. It's an… acrobatic sort of work. And you do great things with it!"

Mama gets all red. I never saw her like that, except once, when Nounou was bringing me home from school and Mama came out of her bedroom with Jérôme.

She gives him the check. He slips it into the pocket of his jacket, he sticks out his hand. She shakes it without saying anything, then very softly she says thank you.

He turns to me. "Take good care of yourself, fella."

"Are you gonna come back to see me next week?"

"I don't think I'll have to. You're going to get well real quick. In two days you'll feel better. You can go back to school next Thursday. And besides, if you don't feel good, Doctor Boulle will come see you. Tell me, though, what's your name?'

"Jérôme. Like Doctor Boulle. And when I'm big I'm going to be a doctor, like him. Like you."

He smiles, he runs his hand through my hair, he tells Mama goodbye, and he leaves.

I watch him open the door to his car, toss his bag in back, close the car door and start the motor. Just as he's leaving, he looks up in my direction. I wave to him, like I do to Jérôme when he goes, but I don't know if he sees me, because of the curtain.

88

MADAME DESTOUCHES

I hear a car stop at the house. A door opens, and slams. Somebody knocks.

"Come in!"

The front door opens and then closes.

"Come in, Doctor, I'm in the kitchen."

I pull my walker close, I lean on the table to stand up. You come into the kitchen, you set your bag on the table, you offer your hand. "Stay sitting, Madame Destouches."

"Hello, Doctor."

"Excuse me for coming a bit late, but the office was very busy this morning."

"Not at all, doctor, I understand. Anyhow, I've got plenty of time, as you know. It's only that on Saturday afternoons, the pharmacy is closed…"

"Today it's the pharmacy here in Play that will stay open—Madame Grivel."

"Oh, good. She's very nice. She always helps me out when I need something. She says she arranges it with you…"

"Mmmhh. Well now, what's up?"

"Oh, not much, doctor. The visiting nurse came by this morning to change my dressings; the ulcers don't disappear, they're no better and no worse. At least, they're not hurting me the way they did. But I'm about to run out of gauze pads and saline solution. Here," I say, handing you my little list, "I wrote it all down."

You pull the stool out from under the table, you sit down beside me. "Okay, but I'll check your blood pressure, anyhow."

"It's probably not very high…"

You take out your blood-pressure equipment and your stethoscope. I give you my right arm, you wrap the band around it, you tighten the knob and start inflating. It tightens. with your fingertips, you slowly loosen the clamp. It hisses.

"One-thirty over eighty—that's good."

"Really? Last time it was one-twenty, as usual… Why is it going up? Should I change the dose?"

"No, no, absolutely not, it's nothing dramatic, you know, at your age, to have one-thirty. In fact it's even desirable…"

"Really? How?"

"Well, you see, in people who're… getting on—"

"Please, doctor, I'm eighty-three, don't try to spare me!"

"Well, at your age, the arteries of the brain are a little stiffer, they've lost some flexibility, so when the medication takes the pressure down too much, the blood circulates less well and the brain gets less oxygen…"

"Oh, I see. It could go soft, and I'd turn into a potted plant."

I look at you. You don't smile.

"Speaking of that, doctor—I meant to ask you…"

"Yes?"

I hesitate. I don't know how to tell you this. "You know…" I look around me—the white-walled kitchen, the mica cabinets, the curtain at the window, the perfectly clean sink. "It still strikes me odd, living here. Ever since we moved out of our little house, I feel a bit lost."

"It's more convenient, I imagine…"

"Yes! Oh, yes! That, no question. Down there I only had the two rooms, and of course the coal stove wasn't awfully healthy, and in summer the place was very hot. But, you know—it was home, I lived there with my husband, all my children were born there, except the oldest, I gave birth to her in my husband's wagon… The older ones slept in the main room, on benches that we'd fold up in the morning, and there was always a baby at the foot of our bed, naturally! It didn't belong to us, but the rent wasn't high. I don't know why the owner wanted me to leave. It was his mother who rented it to us, and she never made any trouble."

"But you were relocated here…"

"Yes, as far as that goes, the mayor was very nice. As soon as they started planning these apartments, he came to tell me right away that there'd be one for us, and they're built specially for old people like me, and for young folks who don't have much money yet. But…"

"But?"

I sigh. I look at you, then I look at the sink, the clean ashtray on the shelf. I raise my head but I don't hear anything from the living room.

"I don't know… It's not really home. And I'm lonely now."

You lean toward me, you lay a hand on mine. "You miss Georges."

I pull out a handkerchief, I wipe my eyes. "Yes… I shouldn't be telling you this, I know that you were against it. But what can I say, you have to understand… He drank so much at the end there, he was always drunk, he snored all day long, it was impossible to move him when he was on the bed, sometimes he'd slip off and of course with only the one arm he couldn't pull himself back up, and there was just no way I could help him… So yes, when my daughter told me her idea, I

DIAGNOSIS (SATURDAY, MARCH 29)

was shocked, and in fact I was glad you came to Georges' defense and said you wouldn't sign the papers… But in the end it just got to be impossible, he was smashing up everything in the house and he started fighting with people, smashing their bikes or their rear-view mirrors, and of course they'd come to me afterwards, and it was costing me a lot… When my daughter put it to me, I was exhausted, I said to myself, If he goes around smashing everything in the apartment like that, they won't let me stay, or else it'll cost me a fortune, and with my pension I can't afford it. And then what would become of me?… You also told me it was complicated, these days, to get a person put away. But my daughter found a way, she knew someone who worked in a mental hospital, thirty kilometers the other side of Tourmens… Georges has his disability benefit, so that goes to pay his way, I put in a little something too, not very much of course. I hear the place has beautiful grounds, they can go walking there… But he's always saying he wants to come back here. My daughter told me they've had to go searching for him in the woods twice already. Naturally, he tries to get out, but there's a wall…"

"Do you want him to come back?"

"Oh, my lord, no! He put me through too much! Besides… my daughter would never agree. And… her husband threatened to stop bringing my grandchildren over if Georges kept on living here. But you understand, he's my son. I miss him. He was company, in spite of everything. For years, before he started to drink so much, he used to help me a lot, even with his handicap; he'd do the shopping, he'd paint the shutters, he'd chop wood. And then when his stump began to give him pain, he couldn't…"

"Have you heard from him?"

"Not often… It's complicated to call him to the phone, and when he gets there he doesn't say much…"

I start to sob. "Actually, he doesn't say a thing. He won't talk to me. He's mad at me, I'm sure—I let my own son be locked up… You know, doctor, if he hadn't been in the house I wouldn't be alive today. The first time you came to see me—when you sent me to Doctor Lance, and he operated on me for that infected kidney—it was Georges who got me to call you. My regular doctor was Doctor Jardin, but with him, you always had to wait three days for him to come, he never took us seriously, and I'd already been sick for three days before that, I had a hundred-and-four fever and I wasn't eating, and Georges—if he could have dialed the number he would have, but I wouldn't let him do it, the telephone was next to me and he didn't dare try. Then, after three days, he ran into Madame Leblanc in town, and he told her I was sick, and Madame Leblanc sent you over… But really, if it'd been up to me, I wouldn't have seen any doctor. I'd already had enough of living, you know… It was a relief to me, the idea of dying… I wasn't afraid… I'd had more than enough…"

I can't talk any more, I'm sobbing. You get up, you rummage in your pockets and pull out a packet of tissues, but I've already got my soggy handkerchief out of my smock pocket.

"I didn't know that, Madame Destouches…"

"Of course not, I never told you, because it's thanks to you and Doctor Lance that I'm still here. But Georges is the reason I didn't die…"

And we stay like that for a long moment, without talking, you holding my hand and me crying over these years my son gave me that I didn't want.

89

THE ACCOUNTANT

Beneath the mail slot I find a large brown-paper envelope, a note from Doctor Sachs. The final bills for the past year. The documentation on his outside income. The checkbook stubs I was missing.

Now I can finish up his tax return.

At the bottom of the envelope, there's a folded sheet I hadn't seen.

Dear Monsieur Scribe,

I plan to take on a substitute once a week—Thursdays, I think. Of course, I want to guarantee him suitable compensation, even if he does little work at the start. Could you work out one of those "simulations" you have the knack for, and tell me if this is at all conceivable at the present time, financially speaking?

I'll call you in a few days. Thank you in advance.

Kind regards,

Bruno Sachs

This boy is going to scuttle his practice. If he pays his substitute the way he does his secretary, he'll put himself three years behind. He would certainly see things differently if he had a wife to support and children to supply with jeans and scooters and school.

90

VIVIANE R.

I was behind the bar when he got here. It was a quarter past four. First I saw her look up and smile, and then he appeared. He looked a little done in, he slumped onto a chair, he shook his head from left to right, he sighed, shook his hand as if to say Oof! and laughed at the same time, pointing to his mouth. I set down the glass and the rag and went to take his order. Seeing me coming, he smiled the way he always does and said, "Hello—you're well?" And I answered, "Fine. What can I get you?"

He looked at her, she made a face that meant, "I don't know what you're allowed to have," and he said, "Mmmhh—he didn't tell me not to drink, but anything sweet seems like a bad idea," and he asked for a sparkling water. She took another espresso.

While I was clearing the neighboring table, I listened to them talk.

"He told me I shouldn't eat jam anymore…"

"My poor love. Well then, I won't make you any!"

"Oh yes you will! It took me twenty-five or thirty years to kill off my molars, it will certainly take another twenty to kill off the rest of the teeth—I'm not going to deprive myself for that… But when he was scraping my teeth with his little hook and he pulled out these crumbling bits saying it was all decayed enamel, I felt like I was already starting to rot—to rot in the mouth… Yuck! You should change boyfriends!"

"Oh yes, absolutely! And look for one who's got teeth that can stand up to my jams. So how do I recruit them? Classified ads? and put them through testing?"

He burst out laughing, and I went back into the bar.

When I got back with the sparkling water and the coffee, he'd opened a little notebook on the table and was writing names and numbers while she went on reading. As I was uncorking his bottle, she put the pages down on her lap and said, "The section on the hospital is very… rough."

"Really? Is it that badly written?"

"Not at all! I mean it's rough to take in!"

"Oh. I was afraid it would seem sentimental."

She stared at him with a mixture of stupefaction and disbelief.

They stayed like that for a long time, without talking. She went on reading, and he went on writing things into his little notebook, leafing through it, sometimes staring at it for long moments the way people do at those pocket bibles with the text written very tiny. I watched them from behind the bar, stacking glasses, thinking back over my day. Around five o'clock, a lot of people came to sit on the terrace, and I went out to them. I took an order from one table—the father had already decided but his little daughter went back and forth endlessly between ice cream and a no-alcohol cocktail—when I heard the doctor say, "Hey! Hello there, mademoiselle!" I looked up. There was a tall girl of fifteen or sixteen standing at their table. He reached out his hand: "How are you?" She answered, "Fine." She looked very, very cheerful, she pointed and said, "I'm living with my father now." A little way off, near the fountain, a couple were reining in a small boy of two or three who seemed to be trying to stick his arms into the water. Just then the man turned around—to look for the tall girl, probably—and Sachs leaped to his feet. The man's jaw dropped, I saw his lips shape something like "It can't be!" he ran over, the small boy and the woman followed him. Sachs stood frozen, his mouth gaping, as if he'd seen a ghost. The man stopped smack in front of him and said something like, "Is this bizarre?" and he said, "Unbelievable!" And the man went on, "Annie told me what you did for her—for us! It's getting to be a habit with you!" and Sachs said, "I didn't do anything…"

The woman came over, the little boy clung to his father's trousers, the man picked him up, the four of them stood staring at him, smiling, not saying a word. Finally, he put out his hand to the man. "Annie is an… amazing girl." The man couldn't talk, he gripped his hand a long time, then he took off with his little family.

Sachs stood there as if he were paralyzed, then finally he turned to her, he stammered apologies: "I didn't even introduce you—it's a long story," she took his hand, and just then I heard another customer call me, the telephone rang, and the little girl ended up choosing a chocolate milkshake—which is to say, the thing I most detest making in the world, goddamn shit hell.

91

THE SIGNATURE

❁

You wrapped me in your arms, you pressed yourself to my back, my hips, my but-tocks, you were tender and enveloping. You laid your chin on my shoulder, and I heard you sigh. "My love…"

I nodded softly, I heard you drop away, and I drowsed off.

❁

When I come out of it, you're lying on your back, my head is on your shoulder. You look at me.

I see the time on the alarm clock. "Already seven-thirty? I was sleeping…"

"You certainly were."

"You too?"

"A little. I was thinking about the office. I don't know how people can want to come in to talk when they have to wait an hour and a half for their turn. I told you about the couple I saw this morning?"

I climb out of bed, I take you by the hand and draw you with me into the bathroom. "Keep talking, I'm listening."

"The young man I've been seeing for some time. His name is José. He has two older brothers, happy-go-lucky party-boys; he's the youngest. I've always known him to be withdrawn, always a little gloomy. One day, some years ago when he was still at the lycée, he came into the office ahead of everyone else, at nine-thirty, to be first in line. He had classes that day, but he hadn't gone in. He wanted me to get him excused from physical ed for the year, but he couldn't bring himself to tell me why."

I turn on the water, I adjust it to the right temperature, and I shove you into the bathtub. You sit down in it. I hand you the shower-head. You hold it against you to warm yourself up, while I soap your back.

"And finally, after much beating about the bush, he ends up telling me they'd be going to the swimming pool all trimester and that it was real torture for him to undress and take his shower with the others, because he was probably homosexual."

"'Probably'?"

"That's what he *felt*, without ever having actually done anything. And as far as I was concerned, I was really at a loss: I couldn't excuse him from physical ed for homosexuality! So I went over everything he had in the way of little problems, and then I wound up telling him I'd get him excused from the pool for a month on grounds of a lingering sinus infection, but that I couldn't do much for him beyond that…"

You wet your hair, I pour shampoo onto it.

"Of course, he was only half satisfied, but I told him that if I did anything more, it could draw attention and that might not be exactly what he wanted… But he must have thought I was about to fix things for him once and for all."

"He hadn't run into any other boys like himself at school?"

"No. I think he must have been too inhibited, too private for anyone to approach him, and maybe he was ashamed. When he went back into the waiting room, there was another patient of mine, Monsieur Duhamel, a math teacher at the lycée. They said hello, Duhamel said something like 'Gosh, José! You don't look like things are going too well!' and put his hand on the kid's arm. Then José left, and I brought in the teacher, who told me that José was a student of his, that he thought he was enormously intelligent but he was sorry to see him always so sad. And with a smile he added that he'd really like to help him out somehow.

"I didn't see either of them again for months. Until one day when Monsieur Duhamel came in, for some little nothing, something so innocuous that I wondered why he bothered to show it to me. And then, just before he left, as I had my hand on the doorknob, he told me, "Doctor, I wanted to thank you…" and he told me that the day he'd run into José in the waiting room, he'd seen him hitch-hiking on the highway on the way home. So he stopped to pick him up. It was the first time they'd ever talked outside school."

As I rinse your hair and the water runs down over your face, you smile, eyes closed: "This morning, they came in together to see me. They've been living together for five years."

✻

You hadn't shaved for two days. You do it now after your shower. You're tense. Naturally, you slice yourself up. Constellations of tiny bloodstains dot your neck.

"We're going to be late…"

"Bruno! It's a book-signing, not a night at the opera!"

"Yes, but Diego really wanted us to come, and if he doesn't see us there…"

332

THE CASE OF DR. SACHS

"Well then, phone ahead, if that'll make you feel better!"

"No, no. I don't want to bother him…"

❊

At the bookshop, there's a bigger crowd than I expected. A couple is seated behind a table, signing, while a half-dozen people gather around them with books in hand.

"We shouldn't have come," says Bruno.

"Oh for heaven's sake, don't be dumb!"

Diego's already seen us and is heading over. "Hi there, you gorgeous young thing!" He kisses me alongside my mouth. Then, noticing Bruno's dazed expression: "What's wrong with you? Are you still jealous?"

Bruno doesn't answer. He is paralyzed. His jaw clenched, he stares at the couple. "Why did you ask me to come?"

"So I could introduce you. Come on now, stop behaving like that! You don't even have to talk to them if you don't want to. But I invited them here, and, like a good little provincial, I introduce them to my customers, my best girlfriend and my buddy the mongoloid medic!"

He drags us over to the table. When the last reader has gotten his books signed, Diego waves to me and, gripping Bruno by the arm, says, "Danièle, Claude, I'd like to present Pauline Kasser and Bruno Sachs—I've told you about them."

The man and the woman rise, greet us. They are about sixty. Danièle is smiling and beautiful, Claude is bald and kindly. And forthright. He lights a cigarette and says to Bruno, "Aha! So you're the doctor who writes!"

❊

You watch Danièle and Claude vanish into the hotel.

You take my arm and we walk toward the car.

"I'll drive," I say.

As we pass the bookstore, you murmur, "Actually, they're very nice… What are you smiling about?"

"You never stopped talking through the whole meal."

"Oh sure—you mean I didn't let them get a word in!"

"Not at all. They're big enough to take care of themselves. And besides, I think they had a good time…"

"That sonuvabitch Diego didn't tell me he'd asked them to have dinner with Ray and Kate and us…"

"He knows you, you would have made some excuse not to come!"

"You really think that?"

"Absolutely. You would have said you didn't belong there."

"Did I belong there?"

"Ah, Bruno! I love you, but sometimes you give me a real pain! Did you belong there? There was Diego, Ray, Kate, and me, and we were having dinner with a charming, intelligent, friendly couple. If you didn't belong there, would you have enjoyed that dinner so much?"

"Ah... you could see it."

"Your enjoyment? Noooo. Your friends are so used to seeing you smiling and happy that they certainly wouldn't have noticed anything different. As for me, I'm incapable of recognizing pleasure on your face. But that's understandable—all I ever do is stare at the ceiling..."

"Bitch!"

The car crosses the bridge. The Tourmente is so still it looks frozen. You fall into thought. After a while I say, "Ray was tired..."

"Yes. Kate told me he was making a big effort tonight, but that he isn't eating much these days. But I wasn't thinking about him. Would you..."

"What?"

"This morning, after office hours, Madame Guilloux telephoned. I was tired, I still had three house calls to make, I didn't have the strength to go see her husband... So I told her I'd come by tomorrow morning. I know it's Sunday, but— I'm so sorry, I should have mentioned it to you."

I slow down, I glance into the rear-view mirror and make a U-turn.

"Where are you going?"

"Out to your cottage. I'd rather we were staying nearby, I don't like knowing you're on the road. Unless you'd rather sleep out there alone?"

"Um—no. But you—maybe you'd rather stay in Tourmens tonight?"

"Dope. Nozzlehead. Donkey."

You stiffen; then, after a moment, you unbuckle your watch and lift it to your ear.

"Bruno... Why do you do that?"

"Do what?"

"Your watch. Why do you listen to your watch whenever you're worried or tense?"

"When I was a kid, if I was sad, if I'd hurt myself falling, my father would always take me in his arms. I could hear the ticking of his watch as he comforted me... It's an automatic, it winds itself as you wear it. When he got sick, he stopped putting it on, and I'd pick it up from his night table and wear it through the night... I never did let it run down, but he died anyway."

THE CASE OF DR. SACHS

92
_____

LAMENT

Saturday, Saturn Nights, saturnine night-to-write… Doctors write, doctors wrong, doctors write all the time, but flyscratches on unreadable prescriptions, scribbling, spitting ink, for two or three copies gotta press hard on the penpoint or it doesn't show, doesn't write, they almost write, they prescribe, they proscribe, t hey record observations, reports, cases, they file them away in rusty dusty drawers, jammed with details they register without meaning to, without trying to, without paying particular attention, drawers and drawers, drawers as far as the eye can see, organized not by alphabetical order but by the order things happened, from the longest ago to the most recent, along a corridor where you don't turn back, can't even stop, just barely move forward without looking around, drawers without files or letters from specialists, without test results, drawers for bits and pieces, all jumbled, not in order, not classified, pulled arbitrarily into loose little piles, remote similarities, linked ideas… they're all there: all the times they came in, all the good reasons for coming, all the lines they said, the clues—real or false—they laid out on the painted-wood desktop, on the examining table or on the threshold, with a hand already on the doorknob—the gestures of weariness, of anguish, of frenzy, of hopelessness, of bellyful, of grief, the faces (the mouth, not the eyes, because when they talk to you it's always the lips you look at, as if your eyes were trying to aid your hard-of-hearing ears), the scowls, the uneasy smiles, the sulky mouths twisted with what won't come out, the toothless gaps, the whisperings, the silences, the sighs, the frantic glances, the hesitations, the shaking heads, the sobs, the breaking voices, the sniffing noses, the closing eyes, the mouths gasping for air—an air of what—their body shapes (the ones you recognize, the ones you get wrong, even when they're not a bit alike or sometimes no longer alike, of course—what did it matter if you wondered as you sat him down whether the man in your office was Monsieur François Stevenson or Monsieur Jacques Stevenson, his twin brother? Impossible to rely on the body shape, early on they looked the same, it was only when François began to lose weight from the monstrosity growing in his gut that you could recognize him for sure. Later on, he never left his house anymore, so you knew for a fact that it was Jacques standing at the window of your waiting room. But what did

DIAGNOSIS (SATURDAY, MARCH 29)

you feel in that split second when, catching sight of Jacques in the street, you thought you were seeing the ghost of François, by then two years in his grave, and said to yourself, "No, it can't be…"? And what did you feel when François' widow called you in to look at Jacques, whom she'd married after her husband/his brother died? What did you feel when, from the depths of the bed, his shrunken body croaked out, "François and I did all the same things, but I always took my time about it…"), the emaciated bodies, obese bodies, pustulent bodies, bodies flaking with eczema or patterned with patches of psoriasis, sweating bodies, bloated bodies, plump bodies, desirable bodies, deformed bodies, bodies covered with filth and smelling of woodsmoke, white bodies beneath sunleathered faces, nauseating bodies, mutilated bodies, bodies slashed every whichway by surgeons, pockmarked bodies, bodies contorted with pain, slick bodies, flaccid bodies, sticky bodies, tense bodies, bodies shivering on the icy sheet, heavy bodies, burned bodies, moaning bodies—and the blood, tears, shit, snot, purulent eardrums, throats clogged with diphtheria membranes, breasts stretched lopsided by tumors, balls engorged with fluid, genitals dripping milky clots, anuses swollen with hemorrhoids, lips split by fists, eye-sockets shattered by hard heads, fleshless knees chewed up by asphalt roads, parchment strips hanging from the shins of old ladies attacked by their coffee-tables, cut tongues, crushed fingers, scalped skulls, stabs in the abdomen, bullet wounds, ribs crushed by overturned tractors—and the drunks, the cripples, the beaten, the breathless, the amputees, the senile, the endlessly embittered, the jobless, the sorrowing mistresses, the orphans

THE CASE OF DR. SACHS

93

THE TURN

"Watch out!"

You grab my arm. I brake. The car skids, stalls, and freezes on the shoulder. You peer into the darkness.

"Sorry—I thought someone was coming from the other direction and was about to—"

You open the car door and get out. It's chilly, I pull my raincoat tight and get out as well. Standing, leaning against a steel pylon, you're looking up at the top of the hill.

"This is the most dangerous turn in the district."

You point to the spot where the asphalt shows, a little farther up, and your finger traces a trajectory through space and lands against the pylon.

"There've been twelve accidents here in seven years. Always the same scenario: young people from the city, coming back from the nightclub in Lavallée at three or four in the morning, Sunday. They cut through Deuxmonts to get to the Tourmens road, they don't know the area, they've been drinking, they're having fun, they speed, their car comes tearing down the hill, they see the turn too late.

Since my cottage is right nearby, I'm always the one the firemen or the police come looking for. I hear knocking, I see the blue flashers through the cracks in my shutters, and I know instantly what it means… Sometimes I would have dreams about it, I'd wake up with a start thinking 'There's another one!'"

You turn to look at me. "But I haven't had the dream since I met you."

Your eyes are two dark wells. "For a long time I used to think it would be a good way to go… I have life insurance. The amount doubles for death by car accident. I thought that if it should happen… that would give Diego some security for a good while. But now…"

"Before you met me, you wanted to die?"

"Of course I did. Who doesn't want to die, now and then? Those young jerks who slam against this pylon—don't you think they're looking to die?"

I take your hand.

"I don't want to die anymore now, because you're here. But I can't rid myself of the idea that I don't really have the right to be alive, when my father's dead."

I don't answer.

"…I always had the illusion that he couldn't die. That he couldn't leave me without having told me everything, without bequeathing me his knowledge, his wisdom, his humanity. Without having taught me how to take care of people the way he did…"

"But you do know how to take care of people! You do it constantly! Where do you get that, if not from him?"

"No, I don't know how to do it. If I did, I'd have taken care of him. I would have gone with him when he died, but I didn't know how to. I resented him for being sick, for having been so strong, so large, and then getting sick in such a stupid way! And on top of that, I tried to be a smart-aleck, I wanted to show him what I knew. That article… after he died, I found it in his desk, under a pile of books. It described exactly all the stages of his sickness. From start to finish. I didn't take care of him—I showed him how he would die!"

Headlights blind us, a vehicle emerges from the turn and stops behind our car. Two men climb out. "Your papers, ma'am-sir?—Oh! It's the doctor!"

"Evening, sergeant."

"Sorry, Doctor, I didn't recognize you. You having car trouble?"

"No, not at all, we stopped… to talk."

"Uhhh—Right here isn't too safe. I'm not telling you anything you don't know…"

❋

I wake up, you're not in bed. The living-room light is on. You've fallen asleep sitting up, your head resting on a big sheet of drawing-paper covered with writing, spread out on the round table. Ray gave it to you earlier, at the bookshop, rolled up in a cardboard tube. He said, "Here, buddy. A piece of incunabula…" You pulled it out, unrolled it, and when you saw what it was, you were speechless, your throat knotted up and your eyes swelled with tears. Still holding the sheet, you moved away from us, you climbed the wooden steps of the spiral staircase to take refuge on the upper level. Ten minutes later, I went up to join you; you were sitting on a pile of cartoon albums, your glasses in one hand, your ear pressed to your wristwatch.

Hearing me come, you stood up, you pulled me to you and kissed me with a power and a despair I'd never felt before. Then we went back down. At the bottom of the rickety stairs, Ray looked tenderly at you and Diego said, "Pauline, I thank the heavens I kept that staircase in the shop. From here on in, I'm always putting your books up there."

You put your arms around Ray. Your eyes—yours and Ray's and Diego's—were brimming with tears.

I watch you; you're sleeping deeply, tears have run onto the broad sheet. It bears a long text, in your handwriting.

I read a title—*Johnny Got His Gun*—and a sentence: "*The world is all that cries out.*"

SOLO DIALOGUES

V

THE SECRET
(Hard Version)

My mother—I could have killed her. No warning, and she drags me out to see some guy I don't even know! Oh, I could have killed her! I even dreamed about it after: I get up, I go into the kitchen, I take the cord and the corkscrew, I go into her bedroom, she's snoring, I tie her arms to the bedposts, I twist the corkscrew into her mouth and I pull out her tongue. She howls, but I howl louder than she does. "Guess the cat's got your tongue, huh?" I snarl, and then I give her tongue to my cat, but the cat just sniffs it, looks up at me, and says, "You treat me like a dog! I don't eat forked tongues or dead tongues either."

I could have killed her. I loathe her, I cannot take her anymore. She's stupid, ugly and disgusting. One night—Papa had already left long before this—instead of saying "yes-Mama-fine-Mama" (she was asking me to set the table and telling me how she always used to help her mother do it), I answered back—I said that was a stupid lie because before Grandpa left they used to have a maid, and when she got married she didn't even know how to lay out the tablecloth. That was the first time I ever answered back, she stood there with her mouth open, I saw her turn green, and then she started to bawl Boohoohoo, she rolled on the floor howling and writhing around, and then she stopped moving, she just moaned. That scared the hell out of me, I thought maybe she was having an epileptic fit, like one of the girls did at school, and that she might die, so I started crying too. When she saw that, she stood right up and got all clingy: "Oh my little darling girl don't get upset it's all right!", she slobbered over me and popped me into her bed. That shut me up in a second, I hate her to touch me, when I was little she was always hanging around begging "a kissy, give me a kissy, don't you want to give a little kissy to your little mommy who loves you so much," I felt like I was her teddy bear! So I made believe I was asleep. After a minute I got up, she was on the phone. She spends the whole night on the telephone with her buddies or her mother or sister, telling stupid lies about Papa, or about Rachel—she calls her "that... *woman*" and she'll let out a big sigh, the poor victim, like "Oh lord! I'm managing but it's really hard, I deserve a medal!" I didn't dare go back up to my room—I'd have had to pass through the living room and she would have grabbed me. So I lay back down but as soon as she came to bed herself and I heard her snoring, I went back to my own room.

Since I was sulking and I wouldn't eat what she cooked, she got it into her head that something was wrong, and she took me to see the doctor in Play. It was him or the doctor in Deuxmonts, and him I can't stand, he always takes her side and they go on and on about her pal Dominique, who left her husband to go live with some other woman and who I can't bear she's such a jerk, no wonder they get along so well. I was determined I wouldn't open my mouth, so at first, when I went in, I didn't even look at him. But then while she was blabbing away with the usual stuff—Annie won't eat, Annie's sulky, Annie ran away, Annie talks fresh to me her mother who loves her so much and who does everything for her little daughter I'm so miserable boohoohoo—I watched him. He was going *MmMm-Mm* while she talked, it sounded like he was snoring, with his two hands folded on his belly—he reminded me of my cat. I was sick of it, I kicked myself for not staying at Papa's house the other day... When I got there, he told me, "You can't stay here, she'll raise all kinds of hell!" but Rachel was saying they should call a lawyer, if I didn't want to go back to my mother's house nobody could make me, and I was hanging onto her and crying, I didn't want to leave them, Papa and her and the baby. We talked for a long time like that, the three of us, Théo was napping but Rachel finally went to wake him up and when he saw me, he stood up in his crib, he yelled "Nannie!" It just broke me up, he's so gorgeous that little guy! And then Papa finally said we had to go, and he drove me back to Langes...

While my mother was talking to the doctor and doing her routines (she always says the same things, it's always, "Oh, it's so awful, I don't get along with my beloved daughter, and here I do so much for her." And of course because Papa left (if I was him I'd have left sooner! I can't understand how he lived so long with her, she stinks so much!) everybody feels sorry for her and calls him a bastard. First of all my grandmother, naturally, she'd told her often enough not to marry him! And now she says, "Oh my poor girl! I told you so but you wouldn't listen! Oh, a woman makes one mistake and she pays for it the rest of her life!" And the same thing with my aunts. You can see why—there aren't any men left, in that damn family. All there is is these ladies who can't stand the sight of a guy! Grandpa's dead, Papa took off, and look at Nicole—my mother's older sister—she claims her husband went out one night and just "disappeared," but I know it's a lie—he took off for America to be with a woman chemist who was doing the same research he was, they'd been writing to each other for years. One day, he had just about enough of Nicole's face and he went to join that woman. They even have children, and Nicole had always said he couldn't have any! When Papa told

THE CASE OF DR. SACHS

me that, I began to see that all those dumb women just lie all the time. My grand-mother, for starters! Her name was Ginette, but during the war she changed it, she called herself Raymonde, she thought it was classier! To me, it sounds just as cruddy! And my mother lies all the time too! She always told me that Nicole's husband went out to buy a pack of cigarettes and was never seen again. She always told me Papa didn't give her a penny for child-support, and then one day I asked him about it and he showed me all his cancelled checks to her since he left. My mother lies constantly, she always says, "Oh, men, you just can't rely on them. Either they die or they abandon their wives and children." One day, I yelled, "You're lying! Papa's not dead, and he left you because he was sick of you, and he hasn't abandoned me!" so she started to cry Boohoohoo, the minute I contradict her she starts crying, or she'll say something like, "Oh, a person can't talk to you, you always have to have the last word, like your father!" It's a smart idea, it stops the discussion, but ever since then she does wait till I'm out of hearing to say that stuff.) I watched the doctor, he wasn't talking, he just sat there with his arms crossed, he looked as if he was going to drop off, I couldn't see his eyes because he has dark glasses and the sun was very strong that day, but finally I understood. His *Mmmmhh, Mmhhh,* that was to make her think he was listening when really he was watching me. And he must have seen that I couldn't take much more because, just as I was about to explode and spit in her face that I was sick of her lies, that I wished she would die, he got up all of a sudden, he took me gently by the arm, and he sent me out of the room.

There were people in the waiting room, and I had to cool off. There were two children with their mother, the little girl was playing school with the stuffed ani-mals, the little boy was playing with a car. The car rolled up to my feet, the little boy didn't dare come over so I handed it back to him, and he took me by the wrist to get me to play with him. He looked like Théo—I mean, bigger, because Théo had just turned two at the time, he was only beginning to talk—but they had that same little pieface, the same smile… I want so much to watch my little brother grow up.

…After a while, I heard a voice behind the door and the doctor sent my mother out and had me come in alone. I was very suspicious. I didn't want him to touch me, I didn't want him to look at me, I didn't want to look at him. After a time, he said, "You're angry."

"Oh, boy, you can say that again! Am I ever! I'd just like to know what you plan to do to me, you know?"

"I'm not going to do anything to you."

I shrugged my shoulders. "You just spent a half-hour with her, you must be going to give me pills to calm me down and teach me a lesson. I bet she told you lots more of her stupid lies about Papa!"

He crossed his arms and answered something funny: "If you're asking a question, I can't answer that."

"Why not? I'm too young? I won't understand?"

"Oh, sure you would! But I can't reveal what some other person said to me…"

"Phooey. That won't stop you from telling *her* everything. But I don't have anything to say to you."

He looked at his feet and said, "If I told your mother what you told me, or didn't tell me, I wouldn't be a doctor. I would be… a dirty pig."

He'd taken off his glasses and was rubbing his nose. I remembered what Sarah had told me. "So it's true?"

"What is?"

"About the secrecy. A friend of mine, Sarah Féval—you know her, we go to school together—she came to see you because she wanted to get the Pill. When she told you her parents shouldn't find out, you told her that you're pledged to confidentiality."

You smiled then, and it was the same smile as when Papa, Rachel, and I go to the movies and afterwards when I say I understood this or that about it, they look at each other and Papa gets this proud look, he puts his arm around my neck, he kisses me without saying anything and he smiles.

"I can't discuss your friend, but what she said about confidentiality is absolutely true." He pointed to the floor. "What is said in this room doesn't leave this room. In fact, anything a person tells me on the telephone or in the street—same thing. For a real doctor, privacy is absolute."

So I just started in—what did I have to lose, anyhow?

"My mother… everything she told you about Papa, it's not true. Papa left because he was sick of it all. Sick of being her dog, sick of getting yelled at because he didn't earn enough money, sick of being treated as incompetent and lazy by my grandmother and my aunts, sick of living with a prude who stinks and gives us the same things to eat every single week—Monday stuffed omelet, Tuesday beets, Wednesday soup with two leeks two carrots a potato and a turnip (by then I was imitating my mother's voice, sometimes I even try to do her smirk-thing, but I can't exactly get it—her lips stay pinched in the middle of her mouth and they open at the corners, like the Greek mask of comedy—and I copied the way she'd say "Turnips give such flavor!") and every Saturday, without fail, a chunk of some kinda meat with cubes of half-fried potato around it! Papa left because he was sick of it, and he was right! And when she says he abandoned us, she's lying! I don't feel abandoned by my father, I feel like I'm being held in jail at my mother's! But that's not the story everybody tells!"

"What story does everybody tell?"

"Lies! They all say it's Rachel that made him leave!"

"Rachel? Your stepmother?"

"She's not my 'stepmother.' She's my father's wife. I love her more than my mother, and she loves me better than Mama does. But she's not clingy! And when they say she's the reason he left, they're lying! He didn't even know her! He left, and then he met her three weeks later."

"You think your father was right to leave?"

"Of course he was! They were always fighting, anyhow. I'd hear them fighting at night and I'd cry so I wouldn't hear them, and I'd hear them mornings when I got up. Well, not every morning. Sundays, my mother never got up before ten or eleven, and she snored so that would wake me up, and I'd hear my father get out of bed. So then I'd get up too, I'd make him coffee and bring it to him, and I'd stay with him in the studio."

"The studio?"

"The room where he paints. I like to watch him paint. Weekends, I spend hours watching him paint."

"And that doesn't bother your—Rachel doesn't mind, that he spends hours painting?"

I shrugged. "Well no, why would she? She loves him, to her it's natural! And besides, he works hard all week, he certainly has the right to paint on Sunday!"

"Where does he work?"

"Now, at home. Before, he used to work in a cookie house."

The doctor started laughing, and so did I. Whenever Papa says that, I can't help laughing, and I was glad to be making somebody else laugh, on my own. "Yes, yes! He was a designer in a cookie factory."

"Okay, now it's a little clearer…"

"When I was little, I'd watch him design the packages—he made games to go on them: crossword puzzles, cut-outs. When they were printed, he'd bring them home for me, and my mother would grouse at him for bringing home empty boxes. Well of course, he wasn't bringing them so I'd have cookies to eat! He was bringing them for me to *play* with! I remember he did a whole series with a cut-out doll and clothes that went on her, you know… First he'd draw them with a pencil and felt-tip, and then he'd finish them off with water-colors. And then one day he bought himself a computer and a drawing table, so that besides his job at the factory, he was designing things for customers right and left. Eventually, he got tired of the cookies and he quit. He left his wife and the factory the same day, and he went out on his own. He's full of ideas, so naturally he's got lots of commissions! But he works all the time! So he certainly has the right to paint when that's what he wants to do! But my mom could never stand that. She couldn't stand that he wouldn't be right there for her, but her—when she's correcting her damn compositions, she's never there for anybody. Sometimes, Papa would be working late at the factory to get some project done on deadline, and when he came home she'd tell him, 'Your dinner's in the oven, I have papers to correct.' So he'd eat alone, and then afterwards he'd go paint. And that she could not stand.

SOLO DIALOGUES V

She'd go in and pester him constantly: 'What are you doing? Can I see? Did you finish that other picture, the one you were doing last month? Can I see it? Will you show me?' and when he wound up showing it to her, it was never right, 'Why didn't you do this, why didn't you do that?' She didn't understand that he went into the studio to keep from seeing her or hearing her!

"What I would do, when he was painting, Saturday afternoon or Sunday, I'd sit on a stool beside him, I'd watch him without talking, and he never threw me out! Now and then he'd start to talk while he painted, and after a while he'd stop painting, he'd stand up, he'd step back to me, he'd put an arm on my shoulder and he'd say, 'See, when you're here and we're talking, I don't think about the picture, it paints itself without me, I just watch it happen.' I've even seen him painting with little tiny Théo on his lap, and Théo would hold out his arms and say A-da-daaa and Papa would go on painting! Mornings, when Rachel goes to work, he takes care of Théo, he dresses him, he feeds him, he takes him to the sitter. In the evening they go together to pick him up, they bathe him, they put him to bed... One day I was sick, my mother didn't want to use a day's leave to watch me, so he came over to get me and took me home with him. That day, Théo was sick too, he had a cold and Papa just decided not to take him to the sitter. When I saw Papa changing him I asked him, "Did Rachel teach you how to do that?" He laughed and said, "No, monkey, you did!" And he told me that when I was born, for six or eight months he wasn't working, because of his accident, and he took care of me. And I was stunned, because my mother was always complaining that he never took care of me when I was little! When I saw him taking care of Théo like that, I knew that she'd lied to me, because he picked up the baby, he put his mouth against his ear, and he went Wowowowow very softly, and when I heard him do that, all of a sudden I remembered the sound in *my* ear when I was tiny—it was warm, it buzzed... I got the shakes and I felt like crying... And then, from the way he was holding Théo, who was very tiny at the time—a few months—it reminded me of something else. When I got home I looked at the picture album from when I was little. There aren't many pictures of me in my father's arms, my mother always said he wasn't ever around, but actually, the reason is because *he was the one taking the pictures!* There was one with him, with a thing wrapped around his arm. I don't know why, I had always thought it was a cast—that when I was born, he had a broken arm from his accident. This time when I found the picture again, I was stunned—the shot wasn't very good, and it was taken from far away, but I could see very well that what he had on his arm wasn't a cast; it was *me*, this little shrimp, lying flat on my belly on his forearm the way I saw him doing with Théo now. And then I was even angrier at my mother, because when I would ask her if Papa took care of me when I was little, she would never answer, she'd just raise her eyes to heaven and make a sobbing sound: 'Oh, it's so painful to me that I can't tell you a thing!' That slut!

"She's too stupid! She doesn't want me to have a father, she doesn't understand that I've got a little brother, the one time I tried to talk to her about him she spat out, 'He's not your brother, he's your half-brother!' And I told her she had a nerve, seeing how she had a half-sister herself: Grandma had Nicole *before* she married Grandpa, but when I said that, she gave me her Greek-mask grin and sighed, 'Yes, but you and this baby haven't got the same *mother*!'"

Telling all that to Doctor Sachs, I felt like crying and screaming at the same time, and I banged the table with my fist.

He put his hand over mine, and he said, "What do you want to do?"

"I don't know." And I started to cry.

Right then, I was thinking I would never get through it. Once, my mother had told me, "Until you're eighteen, I have full legal control of you!" If I was gonna have to stay with her till I was eighteen, I'd die!

I said, "I—I want to leave, I want to go live with Papa... I asked him if I could come live in his house. I'm sick of living alone with a mother who's always moping, when I could have a family life with Papa and Rachel and Théo! I want to watch my little brother grow up. Whenever I visit there he knows how to do some new thing, and when I don't see him for a week or two we have to get acquainted all over again... My mother knows how I feel, once when she was asking me to set the table because she was having some of her pals over to dinner, I said I wasn't her maid, and she started hitting herself, she does that all the time when I resist her, she'll slap herself and start crying! She said, 'Anyhow I know you want to go live with your father!' It never occurred to me that was a possibility, and I thought to myself, 'That's true! A father counts just as much as a mother—why couldn't I go live in his house?'"

"And what did he say?"

"He said yes, he said he'd discuss it with my mother, but..."

"He didn't do it?"

I sniffled. "Yes. But she—she's a lousy bitch!"

"Tell me what you mean..."

"Papa went to talk to her. But when he came back, he told me it couldn't be done. That it was better to wait. And that it wouldn't be good if we tried to force things. I didn't understand, I was mad at him, I didn't understand why it couldn't be done. But Papa was completely beaten down, he didn't want to talk about it anymore. Later, Rachel explained—she saw that I needed to know. She told me my mother knew certain things about my father, that she would tell them to the judge if ever he asked for custody of me, and that that might make trouble for him, but especially for Rachel and Théo, and that there was nothing he could do about it... From that moment on, in fact, as if by chance, my mother stopped letting me go to his house when I'm sick or when I have no classes. She even made me go along on a study trip with her so she wouldn't have to ask him to keep me at his house while she was away."

"So now you see your father less than you used to?"

"Yes—except for vacations, I only go to their house five days a month. Two Wednesdays and two weekends. My mother tells everybody he doesn't want to see me anymore, that I don't get along with Rachel, that I'm jealous of the baby, but of course she never says it in front of me, so I don't get to tell people that's bullshit…"

"What do you do now, when you don't have class?"

"Last week, I got fed up… I cut school. I was passing by the secretary's booth, I asked her if she'd seen my mom leave, she said no, so I said oh, she must have gone home ahead of me, and I walked out with a big smile, Bye-bye Madame! She didn't suspect a thing! I went to Papa's house on the bus, it was Théo's birthday, he was turning two and I wasn't supposed to see him till ten days later, can you imagine? Ten days for a kid that age—it makes a big difference!"

"What about you, how old are you?"

"Fourteen and a half."

"Yes… For you too, ten days is a long time. And three years is even longer."

"Anyhow, there's no point telling you all this, and I'm not sick. She's the one who's sick."

"You're right… you're not sick. And you haven't asked anything from me. Your mother's the asker."

"She's always asking! She doesn't know how to do anything for herself. And she moans so much that people feel they have to do things for her. There's some nail she needs hammered in, she stands up in the teachers' lounge—I know, I've seen her do this—she puts on her poor-stupid-little-me face and she says, 'What'm I going to do? How can I manage?' And of course there's always one of her pals who'll pipe up and say, 'Oooh, who can you ask?' Big shaky sigh: 'Well, nobody, you know perfectly well!' 'But that's terrible! We'll find you someone!' And the pal turns to the first sucker who walks in and says to him, 'Hey you, c'mere, we need a hand!' And what does the poor guy do? He goes and nails in the poor lady's nail! And once he steps into the house, he doesn't get out without nailing in everything else there is to be nailed! And it's like that all the time! One day the clothes-washer broke down, and I said, "Come on, let's go buy a new one!" She tells me, "No, you don't know anything about it!" And what does she do? She calls her mother! And Grandma, at age seventy-five, takes charge of the whole business! She phones the store near her house, she has the washer delivered, and she pays for it!"

He put his hand on my arm and said, "You could try to find out what your mother threatened your father with. And when the time is right, go see this man (he wrote a name and address on a slip, and handed it to me), use my name, tell him the whole story. He'll help you. But to do this, you've got to learn to put the enemy off her guard."

He told me he'd order a simple blood test on me to satisfy my mother, and he'd give me something he used to take going through his medical school exams— some orange-flavored vitamin capsules. They're not bad, actually! Then he brought her back in, and while he talked to her, explaining about the blood test and all, I thought about what I could do to put her off her guard. I looked at her; she was soft and flabby like a cow, with her look—whiny and stupid at the same time—and her way of sneaking glances at me as he talked to her. And looking at her, I understood that she was scared of me—that she was hanging onto me that way because I was validation for her, and that the more I closed myself off the more pity she'd get. So I sat up straight, I looked right at her, and I smiled. And ever since then, I look grown-ups in the eye, I smile, I answer politely, and I say as little as possible. At the beginning it was tough, because it took everyone by surprise, especially my friends. And then it turned into a game—I was seeing and hearing a lot more things. I realized that it made me seem older. And since I'm taller than my mother, I sometimes feel that I'm the grown-up and she's the little girl. It's like with the name—when she finally agreed to the divorce, she kept Papa's name. I'm sure she figured, "If his paintings turn out to be worth something down the line, I should hang onto his name," it would make her look good. One day I asked her, casually, "How come you still use Papa's name? I mean, I bear my father's name, that's natural! But you—you're not married to him anymore, and you're not his daughter! If a guy left me, I certainly wouldn't want to keep calling myself by his name!" And I guess that got to her, because gradually, she went back to using her own name again.

And bit by bit, she started to change, too. She began telling me stuff, as if I was her sister—or worse, her bosom buddy!

Not too long ago, one of her friends came to see her, somebody she'd been friends with back in school and hadn't seen for fifteen years, since just before I was born, I think. When this lady came in, I thought it was a man. Short hair, big body, taller than me. They drooled all over each other weeping, it was sickening, and from the minute she got here, the two of them acted as if I didn't exist. And I just acted like I didn't notice a thing, I listened to them rant away about men. And then suddenly they start talking about money, and my mother tells her friend, "You know, everything her father owns goes to Annie! That *other woman* won't get a thing!" And she walks into her bedroom, she comes back out with a wooden strongbox, she took out some papers. I was making coffee in the kitchen, but she went right on as if I wasn't there. She explained that when she "threw Papa out," he'd taken along the furniture they had from his parents, he had some very good pieces, she was sick about it, with all she'd given him, the best years of her life, she certainly deserved to have it! Then one day when she was cleaning her closet, she came across a paper he'd made out once that said, roughly, that all the furniture, the paintings, the rugs—the things he'd taken away—belonged to her. She said how she'd been scolding him at some point for not really loving her, and so Papa, to prove that wasn't true (he must have still believed he did love her, at the time) had written out that document. "The bastard—he carried everything off with him, but when Annie sets up house she'll get back what belongs to us." Hearing her say that, I wanted to strangle her.

Her chum had brought a bottle of champagne, and the two of them drank up the whole thing themselves. It was the first time I ever saw my mother drink. She's even uglier and stupider when she drinks—good thing it doesn't happen very often!

I went to bed, but I didn't stop thinking about that paper. I couldn't believe that that was the reason Papa couldn't ask to take custody. He doesn't give a damn about furniture, and neither does Rachel. But I wanted to go see. I got up without making any noise, they were sleeping in the same bed, snoring in chorus like a couple of ten-year-old cousins. She had left the box open on the table, with the paper inside it. Beneath it there were two bundles of letters, I recognized Papa's handwriting. Around one of them there was a pink ribbon; I thought those must be the letters he wrote her before they got married, and they were. And then there was another packet. This one was even thicker, bound with two elastic bands and wrapped in a plastic bag. Those were older, not in Mama's handwriting, they began with Papa's name and "my darling," and going by the date, it was way before they would have met. And I thought how it was really shitty of my mother to be keeping those letters. And then, beneath those, there was this big cardboard case with elastic clasps, with Papa's name on it and a whole bunch of his drawings inside. I wanted to look through them, but I put everything back in place and got into bed again.

That happened two weeks ago.

Last night Papa came to pick me up. My mother had a meeting and I had no classes in the afternoon, vacation was starting today. I'm supposed to stay at my father's for the beginning of this vacation, so she thought I'd want to go there directly from school but I said no, I want to get my stuff together, I'll go home by train and he can pick me up there. She looked surprised for a sec, but she said, "Whatever you like, dear," she slobbered over me, and that was it.

I called Papa to tell him to come get me at Langes. Actually, my things had been ready for a long time. I'd already moved almost everything to his house. What's left at hers, I don't care about, everything I love I took.

When I got there, I hugged Rachel and Théo, I was so happy! I took the two bundles of letters out of my valise. Papa couldn't get over it. He cried. I realized that what Mama held over him was in the letters he'd sent her. But that wasn't why he was crying, it was about the other ones—he'd thought she had destroyed them, he never imagined he'd see them again. He took the letters written to my mother and burned them up in the fireplace. He couldn't talk. Rachel said, "You know, you did a very important thing for him—but for me and Théo too!" She had tears in her eyes and she embraced me in a way she never had before and we all started to cry. I don't know why, for a moment there I thought I heard chains falling—but it was Papa stirring the ashes with the poker, and I could hear him breathing hard, like you do when you're coming up from underwater.

And then I pulled the cardboard case out of my valise, and gave it to him. He opened it. There were drawings, watercolors, sketches, but way down at the bottom there was an envelope, sealed and banded with several layers of brown sticky tape. He said "No! It can't be!" and he started laughing and couldn't stop.

I asked him what was up.

"It's a gift from your grandfather. Your mother's worst fear. And she didn't even know she had it right under her nose!"

He laughed all evening long, he laughed looking at the envelope and then cried looking at the letters, and finally he turned serious and he said to me,

"I'm going to ask for custody. Now she can't do much about it anymore."

When I answered that I didn't want that, of course he was startled. Rachel, no, because I'd already talked to her about it and she knew I'd made an appointment. So there you are—I'm awfully sorry to have taken so much time to tell this whole thing, but I wanted you to really understand. I told Papa that I didn't want him to get involved, he was always the one to take the punches, but he doesn't have to anymore. I'll be fifteen in three days, and I'm the one—I alone—who made the decision to come here; I don't want to go back to my mother's house, and I did what Doctor Sachs said, "When the time is right, go see Monsieur Perrec'h, he'll help you."

So here I am.

TREATMENT

(Friday, April 4)

The captain eyed me and,
setting his hand on the butt of
his pistol, declared haughtily:
"Doctor, I kill a man at fifty paces."
Baring my teeth, I replied,
"Captain, at point-blank range,
I don't miss anyone!"

Abraham Crocus, *Vanished Words*

94

THE SECRET
(Original Version)

Once upon a time there was a medical student—we'll call him K. He was a brilliant fellow from every standpoint, but very troubled, very rebellious against the establishment and against life. Very fragile, basically. We lived in the same dorm, our doors were across from one another; he was a little younger than I, but occasionally we studied together, because several times we'd borrowed the same books or articles at the same time from the library, and that was odd enough to bring us together: most of the students never went to the library. He was so brilliant that when we studied together he almost always taught me something. He drew wonderfully, freehand—three-dimensional illustrations of histology cross-sections, or anatomy figures. Sometimes he'd knock at my door, to lend me a book, show me a drawing, pass along a question he couldn't answer, and we'd go on late into the night. These were just pretexts. He'd come because it gave us such pleasure to talk together.

One day, during review week—it was very warm out, I was working with the shutters closed—I hear someone running in the street, climbing the stairs four at a time and charging onto the landing, a sound of keys, swearing, someone drumming on my door.

I open up and I see K., collapsed on his knees, unable to speak. I bring him into my room, I sit him down, but before I manage to ask him anything, I hear a police siren. Through a slit in the shutter, I see a squad-car pull up short at the building and three cops jump out. K. throws me an exhausted look and shakes his head. Without thinking twice, I stick a bath towel and a shampoo bottle into his hands, I pull him along to the other end of the corridor, I stick him into a shower stall, I wet down my own head in the next one, and I step back out into the hallway. At his door, the three cops are waiting, pistol in hand, for the building concierge—a retired cop—to open up with his pass-key.

TREATMENT (FRIDAY, APRIL 4)

"Doctor," (he always called me Doctor though I was still only a student), "they're looking for Monsieur K. He just got into some weird business."

"Really?" I said, with a big smile. "What did he do, steal the exam questions? He's in there, taking a shower."

The cops stare at me, suspicious. The concierge, though, believes me: one day I told him to take his mother or his aunt—I don't remember which—to see Professor Lance, and Lance straightened out her problem. He turns to his colleagues there, tells them he's surprised they'd be looking for K., he's a good quiet boy. He says, "If Doctor Sachs says Monsieur K. hasn't been out in three days, then it's true." Just then, K. comes out of the shower room, his hair dripping wet. I turn and say, "Feels good, huh?" and signal him to shut up. And the concierge says, "See, he was in there! If he went out today, I'd have seen him go by!"

The cops mutter something, ask to check his room, find nothing, ask us a few questions—Where were you this morning, where were you yesterday?—finally the concierge takes them off to the side, they talk, they wind up leaving with apologies to us.

K. hung out with a pseudo-grouplet, little jerks who liked to come on as the Red Brigades of the area, but whose goals had nothing political about them. They were spoiled kids from rich families, and they were majoring in burglaries of whichever university departments they were enrolled in, to pay for their drugs and their weekends. Hearing K. talk about them, I gathered they manipulated him, that he functioned as their ideological alibi: he was the only working-class boy in the group. And the only one who'd read the master-thinkers they spouted.

A few months earlier, at the medical school, the biochemistry labs had been burgled. The thieves had taken off with some equipment that was worth an insane amount. Since the lab had neither adequate locks nor an alarm system, the insurance company was refusing to pay out for it. The dean had been contacted by the thieves, who offered to return the equipment against a ransom, and the school had calculated that it would cost less than buying everything new. I'm sure K. had given his pals the idea. I knew he was heading for trouble with them; I told him so, and he told me to mind my own business.

When the cops left, he tried to tell me what had happened, but I refused to listen. I had exams to study for, I wasn't interested in what he'd done. It all came clear the next day, when I read the newspaper.

Three characters in doctor's coats and Mickey Mouse masks had held up a small bank branch on the outskirts of Tourmens. Unfortunately for them, the cops had been alerted, they set up a trap, and—as was frequent at the time—fired happily into the tangle. The three robbers were killed, along with a young woman who worked at the bank.

K. was probably supposed to be their chauffeur, because he drove very fast and very well. He'd managed to escape, I don't know how, as the carnage was going on. But the cops must have known he was involved. When they didn't find him at the bank, they came to look for him at the dorm.

He stayed cloistered in his room for the next three weeks, leaving it only to go to his exams. I passed by one of the auditoriums where he was working on one. He was sitting in front of his white paper with a vacant stare. When the grades were posted, he had zeroes on every test. And then one day he disappeared. Going up to take him his mail, the concierge found the door hanging open, the room empty.

Several months later, in a movie theater at the other end of town, I see a couple in the back rows. The girl I don't recognize; the guy, yes. He's shaved off his beard and cut his hair, he's wearing horn-rimmed glasses and a corduroy suit, but I recognize K. I walk toward him, he sees me, he stares hard and shakes his head no, so I stop and pretend to be examining the publicity shots from the film. The girl with him was pregnant up to the gills.

❁

When I moved to Play, Madame Borges, who'd cleaned house for the previous tenants, offered to go on doing it for me. We would talk, we'd discuss some medical broadcasts, various disorders of her great-nephews or her grandparents, but I never had her as a patient. One morning, though, she phoned to ask me to come see someone whose house she tended in Langes. "This man lives alone, he's very sick, his doctor is away, and I thought of you, Doctor."

I get out in front of a kind of manor house in the middle of the woods. Madame Borges, very worried, is watching for my arrival on the doorstep. "He's very, very sick, but he doesn't want to go to the hospital, even though his doctor has been urging him…"

The instant I saw him, I realized that this man was carrying an enormous burden of guilt. He had cancer of the breast, very rare in a man. His tumor was bursting through the skin, it was oozing, there were endless secondary infections, and he had a huge bandage over his thorax to hide it. His house was superb and perfectly maintained; he was himself always impeccable, elegantly turned out, Madame Borges told me, but he had always refused to have his cancer treated. He bandaged his wound himself, morning and evening. It was the first and the last thing he saw, touched, smelled, every day, and the pain of it never left him for an instant.

That day, for the first time, he had not got up from his bed. He was white. His wound had bled profusely during the night, but he refused to be hospitalized. He had authorized Madame Borges to call me after making her swear that I would not put him in hospital. All he wanted was (I recall his words), "Something... to lessen the pain just a little. It's come to the point where I really can't bear it..."

I gave him a morphine shot and, of course, he went quickly to sleep. As he slept, I changed his dressing: his wound was truly dreadful. I coated it with antibiotic ointments—as much use as a hot-pack on a wooden leg. It was inoperable, his liver was full of metastases, and he had others in many areas of his skin. He weighed ninety-five pounds. He was letting himself die.

That evening, the telephone rang as I was leaving the office; I had just switched on the answering machine. He asked if I would please come back to see him, as he hadn't paid for the morning visit, and he was concerned to take care of it. I told him it could wait, but he insisted, and I realized there was something else.

He was waiting for me, seated in his living room; he had shaved and dressed.

He thanked me; he was in less pain, he asked if I could prescribe morphine for him, he knew how to give himself subcutaneous shots. His doctor had refused to give him the drug, in fact he had none in his trunk. "Is that usual, Doctor, for a physician not to carry morphine with him?" I smiled and nodded.

"I would understand if you refused. I'm not a client of yours..."

"I don't have 'clients.'"

I gave him nine of the ten vials I had in my bag, and told him it wouldn't be necessary to inject them. He could swallow them in water or in fruit juice. I don't know why I gave him so many, I could have left him three with a prescription for the rest.

As I was about to leave, he invited me to have a drink with him. "Unless you're expected somewhere?"

He sat me down by the fireplace, and served me an old brandy. Then he began to talk.

When I left him, it was five in the morning. I had nearly fallen asleep a number of times, and sometimes I lost track of what he was saying; then he would break off, the silence would rouse me, and he'd take up again. At the time, I believed that if you listened to people for long enough, they would eventually hand over the depths of their hearts.

It's not always true, of course. But it was true for him. And, a strange thing—around three-thirty, four in the morning, his story began to stir something in me.

✸

Once upon a time there was a man—we'll call him Monsieur de B. His family had a great deal of money. Just after the war he had married Raymonde, a girl of modest origins. Monsieur de B. had never been really in love with his wife, but she had lived through a dreadful event: her first fiancé, Abel, was a Jew. In

February of 1944, he had been arrested before her eyes by the French police, and deported.

Abel and Monsieur de B. were friends. They had met Raymonde together, in the moviehouse where she was an usherette. Abel was immediately attracted to the young woman, and his friend, as a man of the world, had kept a discreet distance. When Abel was arrested, Raymonde clung to him in her despair. Monsieur de B. did all he could to get Abel set free, but in vain. After the war, when it was clear that Abel would not return, he felt morally obligated to marry the young woman, in memory of his friend. They had several daughters. The last—call her Blanche—was born late in their life. At seventeen, she fell in love with a medical student. Monsieur de B. liked the boy very much, but Raymonde wouldn't have him in the house: he was of modest background like herself, and she couldn't stand him. She had in fact always concealed her own origins from her daughters. On top of it, Blanche's young friend was a rebel: he talked about practicing a "different sort of medicine," he was willfully provocative, aggressive. Monsieur de B., who'd never had a son, liked the way the boy stood up to him, he liked the discussions they had together. "At times," he told me, "I felt, selfishly, that he'd come to dinner in order to talk with me, not to see my daughter…"

When he said that, I felt my throat tighten. The more he went on, the more I was convinced he was talking about K. When he finally mentioned his name, I had great difficulty holding back my tears.

One day, Monsieur de B. sees his wife come in, furious. "Blanche is pregnant! Pregnant by that scum! What are we going to do?"

Monsieur de B. was an upright man. He heard out his daughter, who wanted to marry K. He received K., who was prepared to marry Blanche. Monsieur de B. then made it clear to his wife that such would be the case, and that there was nothing more to be said.

They married in early summer, just after K.'s exams. The next day, as the two youngsters left on their wedding trip, Raymonde began screaming with rage and blaming Monsieur de B. And she spat forth what she knew about K: his friends were criminals, he'd recently taken part in a bloody hold-up, he just barely managed to evade the police.

"How do you know this?"

"Blanche told me about his 'friends.' Three months ago she heard them planning a robbery. I didn't want her involved in that. I warned the police."

"You warned the police?"

"Yes! Sooner or later, those hoodlums would have gone after Blanche. Or us! But don't worry—I didn't give my name!"

Of course, she had swallowed her tongue the day after the holdup, when Blanche announced she was pregnant, and when it was clear that K. himself had escaped the police. Since she could not tell Monsieur de B. what she'd done, and since she could no longer inform on K., whose side Blanche now never left for a minute, she had kept quiet until the marriage. Until the moment she saw her darling daughter departing *"with that little shit kike."*

At those words, Monsieur de B. slapped her for the first and last time. As frightened by his reaction as he was by the thing that had roused it, he took his wife by the shoulders.

"How can you say that? And how could you have done such a thing? How could you inform on him?"

"You poor idiot!" spat Raymonde. "What do you think I did to get you to marry me?"

❊

Abel hadn't been arrested by chance or by bad luck, but by denunciation. In Raymonde's view, Monsieur de B. was a better prospect than a penniless Jewish student. She knew that breaking with Abel would not bring her closer to the young aristocrat. He would never ask her to marry him, because he didn't love her. She didn't belong to his world. But if their mutual friend disappeared under dramatic circumstances, he would stand by her because he was a loyal young man.

"When Abel was arrested," Monsieur de B. murmured, "Raymonde was pregnant. When the child was born, she could no longer be given her father's name. So I recognized her, I married her mother, and I raised the child as if she were my own daughter. Out of loyalty, you understand? He was my friend. My dearest friend. My brother."

❊

The night he learned of Raymonde's double infamy, Monsieur de B. left his home in Tourmens to live in his Langes house, and told his wife that he wished never to see nor hear from her again.

Later on, probably at the instigation of both Blanche and Raymonde, K. paid a visit to his father-in-law. Monsieur de B. received him very warmly, but he refused to explain what had transpired. He was a man of honor. He declined to reveal what he had learned and thereby become an informer himself.

For several months, he did not see K. He thought with shame that his daughter might have purposely got herself pregnant, as her mother had, and he could not bear to meet the young man's gaze.

K., too, was a man steeped in moral consciousness. That same moral consciousness that had spurred him to revolt he now turned against himself. He wasn't at his comrades' side when the cops cut them down, and he felt deeply guilty for that. Indeed, he had avoided jail, but, married to Blanche, he was expiating his crime in another and sturdier prison. Raymonde and Blanche must have believed that he would be forever at their mercy. He was expected to take the makeup exams, he was expected to become intern and then senior resident, he was expected to develop a career, he was expected to earn a good deal of money. They would do very well with him.

But life is strewn with imponderables. Two weeks before Blanche gave birth, K. was run down by a pickup truck as he crossed the street. Cerebral concussion, coma, life support. Monsieur de B. went to see him daily. Raymonde and her daughters were concerned only with Blanche and the expected child. If K. should die, a new husband would surely be found for the young widow; a gynecologist would fill the bill perfectly.

The child was born. It was a little girl. They named her Annie.

✸

Monsieur de B. was talking very low in the dark. He was suffering, but not from his cancer or his open wound. He was suffering because his life, which he would have wished to be simple, worthy, uncomplicated, was instead a web of lies and ignominy.

After twelve days, K. came out of his coma, with residual memory loss. His medical career was over. Blanche and Raymonde were left stuck with a cripple, a parasite, who could not be blamed because his condition was accidental.

K. was unable to see his daughter for several weeks. He was in rehabilitation, and Raymonde was zealously protective of the mother and child. Learning this, Monsieur de B. went to Tourmens, demanded his daughter hand Annie over, and took her to see his son-in-law.

Time passed. Annie grew up. K. handled much of her care because Blanche preferred to spend her time with her mother and sisters. For six or seven years, he brought the child regularly to Langes to visit Monsieur de B. On her seventh birthday, Annie asked Raymonde why her grandfather wasn't coming to her party with the rest of the family. From that day on, Blanche and Raymonde refused to let her see him.

Blanche apparently decided to turn her hand to something, and she became a schoolteacher. Her mother drilled her for all her exams. K. began to draw and paint again. He had been aware of his talent, but he had never considered making a living at it. Tired of staying at home, he eventually found a job as designer in a cookie factory.

When Monsieur de B. fell ill, he sold nearly all his holdings and donated significant sums to organizations for concentration-camp survivors and to orphanages. One day he arranged to meet with K., Blanche, and their daughter at a bank.

He had established a trust fund for his granddaughter, and deposited (he startled me with the expression) *a load of dough* in it, which would come to her at her majority.

That was the last time he saw Annie. She was ten years old.

Six months later, Madame Borges called me to his bedside.

✹

He sensed it was the end. He needed to tell the whole story to someone he felt could carry out a mission.

"In the past, I would probably have asked the priest. But I haven't believed in God for a very long time. Madame Borges has often spoken of you. She trusts you, and I trust her."

He handed me a packet which I was to mail from Tourmens after his death. It bore K.'s name and business address. He said simply, "When I'm dead, I don't want that boy and his daughter to stay in the clutches of those women. The day he's had enough and wants to leave, this will make it possible for him."

He rose with difficulty, thanked me, walked me to the door, and watched me leave. It was five in the morning.

At about nine-thirty, Madame Borges phoned me again, in tears. She had found him dead in his armchair. When I arrived, the notary was already there, Madame Borges had called him. According to Monsieur de B.'s instructions, he took inventory of the household. After the funeral, he called the family together and read them the contents of the will.

Monsieur de B. no longer owned anything but the two houses—the one in Langes and the one where Raymonde lived in Tourmens, a very large town house.

His daughters inherited the Tourmens house and various pieces of furniture. To Annie he left the Langes house, whose cash value was far less but which was very dear to him, as well as all the keepsakes that came to him from his family. He had detailed the list in his will before two witnesses. Blanche was permitted to live in the house with her daughter, on the express condition that Raymonde never set foot there.

He also bequeathed Madame Borges a tidy sum that could free her from the need to work ever again. Still, when I asked her if she could find me someone to replace her, Madame Borges looked at me slyly. "You don't want me anymore, Monsieur?" I didn't press it.

The day of the funeral, I went to Tourmens and mailed the packet.

95

MADAME DESTOUCHES

"Goodbye, Madame Destouches."

"Goodbye, Doctor."

I stand up; you look surprised. It's no use telling me, "Don't move, don't move;" I stand up anyhow, I lean on the edge of the table, I clasp your hand.

You bow your head, as if the handclasp weren't adequate, and then you draw the door shut behind you and you leave.

I fall back into my chair.

I watch you through the window. You open the door to your car, you toss the black bag into the back seat from the front, you climb in, you roll down the window. You were parked in the sun, so it must be hot inside. With one leg still outside, you turn on the radio, you look for some station. Finally you slam the door, you start the engine, and you go.

❁

I look at the room around me.

On the oilcloth Madame Barbey cleaned this morning, the ashtray is empty. It's always empty, now. I wonder why I keep it. In the kitchen, she's left my noonday meal. Grated carrots, creamed cucumber. I only need to warm up the veal blanquette.

I'm not very hungry.

I see my reflection in the television screen. My daughter insisted on giving me her old set, I watched it for two weeks and then it irritated me. It's an assault on my ears; these people talk and they don't say anything. They must have very little to do in their lives, if they're willing to spend their time exchanging such empty chatter, or listening to stupid questions and then applauding themselves with foolish smiles when they give the wrong answer.

TREATMENT (FRIDAY, APRIL 4)

Today is Friday. My granddaughter will be coming over around two o'clock, she has no school this afternoon. She'll chat with me, she's darling, but after a while I'll tell her that I'm going to lie down, that I'm tired and want to take a nap.

I never take naps, but I know she comes because her mother told her to, and I don't want my granddaughter wasting her afternoon with an old wreck. Today, though, I'll be glad to put my arms around her…

She's a nice girl, my little Lucie. Georges used to like her. She was never afraid of him, and he was always gentle with her—he who was always so clumsy, and sometimes so rough.

I go back to what the Doctor asked me before—whether I'm too bored, whether I feel too lonely.

I said no—that I had company almost every day, that it's rare I spend two hours without seeing somebody.

First there's Madame Barbey, who comes in to work her two hours three times a week, and who often does more than that, since she also stops in Sunday mornings on her way to Mass—supposedly to say hello, but she always uses the occasion to tidy this or that, or get something out of the fridge for my lunch.

And then there's Madame Queneau, the nurse, who comes every morning to change my dressings, or else it's Madame Matiouze, her associate, who covers for her when she's on vacation or like last month when she had a baby.

Lately, I see the mailman a good deal, he always has some registered letter he needs me to sign, or a tax document, or maybe just the newspaper, and he invites himself in to have coffee when Madame Barbey is here. They seem to enjoy chatting together.

And there's the notary. He knows I can't go out, so he comes here, or he sends his clerk—a very good, very nice young woman, who explained everything quite clearly, it's so complicated. She reminds me of the doctor, she's always checking to be sure I've understood.

And then there's my daughter. She comes almost every evening, just before dinner. She comes with her husband, but he stays in the car. He doesn't really want to come in, and to tell the truth I don't really want to see him.

My daughter I don't much care to see either. But I don't say that, because if I do she throws a fit, she cries, she whines, and I hate that, sometimes I wonder where she gets it.

Whenever she pulls up, I turn on the television at random, and when she comes in and kisses me, I pretend to be absorbed in the program. We don't talk much. She hasn't got much to say to me. And I don't want to talk to her. She's my daughter, yes, but she's also the person who took Georges away from me. And he would never have done what he did if she hadn't had him locked up. She never speaks of it, because she's too afraid I'll blame her for it. But I won't say a word to her. She wouldn't understand, anyhow. She's… she's not like me. She does look like me, though—she's clearly my daughter, when I see a photo of her I'm seeing myself at a younger age—at forty-seven she looks the way I did in the photograph at the wedding of her father's cousin, and yet I was only thirty-two then. But in my time, people aged faster.

I don't want to talk to her anymore. I won't talk to her anymore. It hurts me too much to see her coming over every night as if she's trying to win a pardon for herself, when she knows very well that it won't bring Georges back.

I did tell her he wouldn't be able to bear it. I said, "Georges is the way he is, but he won't survive being locked up. If he's locked up, he'll let himself die." I knew it; he was my son. But she couldn't understand that, she didn't live with him and he wasn't like a real brother. His sisters never got along with him. They always did everything together, just the three girls. And sometimes, family feeling doesn't count for much.

Except when a person is a little bit simple. Like Georges.

Georges never had anyone but me in life. He was never able to find himself a woman, of course, so the only person who understood him was me.

And I actually think he was the only person who understood me, in his own way.

But he probably didn't understand how I could let him be locked up without saying anything.

And as for me, I can't understand why he did that. I don't understand *how* he did it, with only the one arm—he's so heavy, and he could never even manage to tie his shoelaces himself.

I know I never could have done it, I wouldn't have the courage, the idea of strangling frightens me. It would be better to go to sleep and never see a thing again.

When my husband got his cirrhosis, he never slept, he was holy hell, at the time the doctor gave me pills for him, they just barely made him drowsy, but at least he wasn't smashing things anymore. They were strong, those pills. The doctor had said that he shouldn't take too many, and so he didn't sleep completely at night and he dozed in the daytime.

One night, though, he finally did go completely to sleep, and he didn't wake up.

I kept the pills. Just in case.

Sure, by now they must be stale, but for what I want to use them for, it probably makes no big difference.

TREATMENT (FRIDAY, APRIL 4)

96
_____

MONSIEUR RENARD

Mother don't quit her walking back and forth, sticking her head out the door, watching for her little doctor. She wears me out. It's always like that. You'd think she was waiting for God. It's me he's supposed to be coming for today, but I know she's not going to let me talk, she's way too wrapped up in her own self—Ohno-my God I hurt here, Ohnomygod I've got a pain there—on and on she goes like that. And her chest pain, and her legs swelling up, and her Can't sleep took two capsules they don't work no more by now probly.

In the old days there wasn't no doctor in Play, when we got the farm here there was the fellow in Lavallée but it was during the war, he did his calls on a bicycle, anyhow he wouldna went all over the place like they do these days, and no way she'd ever call him, for one thing it cost plenty and she was tough or anyhow she counted every penny, but nowadays.

Nowadays you get the money back, she don't give it a second thought.

I don't know when this-all started. Sometimes I try to remember—I know when we were young folks we didn't bother about things, we worked hard, there was the kids, I mean five kids, they had to get raised. I didn't hear her complaining none back then. After... after, some time, she started to feel not so good anymore, a little bit change of life, little bit rheumatism, maybe since our boy took over the farm and we come to live in town. Course I kept on helping out with the cows, so I used to be over there all the time, and Mother was always trying to go mix in on the daughter-in-law's business, until one day she tells her it's their house now and Mother couldn't be always around. So course she didn't like that one bit and I'd hear about it—I should talk to our boy, I shouldn't let her get away with... Finally, I told him it'd be better if he hired somebody, with her it wasn't gonna work out, me going over there.

She wasn't so bad when we was young.

❂

When we was young we worked a lot.

She was still scared of me, back then. She wasn't easy, even so, but still you could find some way to stop her when she went too far.

And then I think it started going bad when our boy and the daughter-in-law told us they were quitting the place. I mean, I sort of expected it, I knew he could do better for hisself. And anyhow, farming's too hard for young folks these days. And I used to hear his wife saying "We might not stay here our whole life."

Now we see a lot less of em, acourse. Well sure, his work's different, what he has in Tourmens he's got a regular office day. He wanted to get ahead so he took school at night and he kept working right on through too, so he didn't have too much time.

When we went to visit at the house they bought, three four years back, I could see he was getting to do what he wanted. But that means he's always busy…

And also, the daughter-in-law—I think she's not too fond of having us over to supper, so…

It's a little sad our girls have gone off, too. We don't see them much either. And I'm no good on the telephone.

I don't even know how many grandkids I got, I ain't kept track.

For a long time I used to still go back in the woods to clean out brush there, or pick up chestnuts, or hunt with the dog—it would keep his legs moving even if he was old… It was a grief to me when he died. To our boy too, seeing's it was half for him I bought the dog in the first place. Well, the mutt was thirteen by then, after all…

Mother keeps getting up and sitting down, she's driving me bats and I can't say nothing. Anyhow, no way I could have the last word, or even the first one, since she's always right. And if I keep trying she starts moaning, "You're so mean to me, Marcel!" and sniffing, I hate that even more, specially when she starts doing it in front of people. That's the thing, that's what I can't stand, with her. I never could stand it. It's always her the one suffering. Other people never. And if she's not suffering, you don't have no right to. And when there's people around, she's always complaining, she's suffering, she's miserable and I don't understand her, and so naturally the people look at me funny. Or else they just plain holler at me, if one of our girls comes over once in a while to visit on a Sunday, I know what I'll get: Your father did this to me, your father did that to me, I'm so miserable Ohnomygodyouwoudnbelieve a person could be so sick…

I remember once when she did that to the doctor, at the beginning when he just started here, I didn't want her to be calling him every minute, it was for some stupid thing again, she asked the little girl who comes to clean to go tell him to come, and as soon as he comes she tells him how I'm cruel, how I wouldn't let her telephone him, that I didn't care if she was suffering or not, Ohnomygodyouwoudnbelieve and the whole business. She told him she must have a hundred-

TREATMENT (FRIDAY, APRIL 4)

and-four fever, that she's freezing and she's burning up at the same time, and I don't know what else.

And him, he doesn't say a thing, he sends her into the bedroom, he makes her get undressed and lie down naked and wait a little before he takes her temperature, and then he comes back out and he sits down at the table and he looks at me:

"Must be rough, huh?"

And right off I could see she didn't put anything over on him.

He told me, "If you need to see me, stop by and ask Madame Leblanc, she'll tell you when you can come in so we can talk by ourselves."

He knew that a couple of times a week Mother goes into Tourmens with a grand-niece of hers, I don't like her but the two of them they get along fine, they leave about two o'clock, quarter after, and then until five, five-thirty, I got my peace and quiet. Before this business, that's the times I used to go into the woods.

Well, when that come on me, I went to see him, and I told him what was wrong—that I wasn't digesting good, that it felt burning sometimes when I drank coffee, that my stomach was full the minute I started eating, when it used to be I ate like a horse.

And then he sent me for some tests, and then for an operation, and when I asked the surgeon what he found, he said, "A kind of ulcer," and I saw what was up right away, I'm not stupid.

When Mother went to ask him he told her the same thing, and in a way it was good because if she knew she woulda made my life miserable, she woulda hollered around to the whole neighborhood and our boy specially our girls, and there would be this big parade through the house, I could hear it already: "Come see your father before he goes, Ohnomygodyouwouldnbelieve the bad luck I have!" I didn't feel like I was dying, the Doctor told me, after, that they caught it early and at my age there was a good chance it would heal, and he's not the type who tells you stories. And he was right, it's six-seven years now, and it never did come back. Two years ago, when I went for my follow-up and my regular exam, the surgeon told me I didn't have to bother any more coming to see him every six months, once every two-three years would do fine.

And I'm still here, not in great shape, sure, but anyhow… and meantime the surgeon died. Heart, they tell me. When she heard that, you wouldn't believe, Mother kept moaning instead of me: how he took such good care of her Marcel, how he was such a fine gentleman, how it was really bad luck, such a young doctor—Well, don't go overboard, he was fifty-five and he smoked a lot, when I'd go in to see him it would sting your eyes the room was so smoky and he never put out one cigarette without lighting the next one from it. People said he held off smoking while he was operating and then he had to catch up after.

In one way I was glad he didn't tell Mother what I had, but in another way, it wasn't so great, cuz he said I had an ulcer, and so then she used that to keep me from eating things I liked. It didn't help that the Doctor would tell her there wasn't nothing I couldn't eat, she wouldn't listen. No fat, no pastry, no red meat, no wine without water, no drop of something in the coffee. And it didn't matter if I argued, nothing doing. What it took was, one day she does this whole number on me in front of the Doctor, to sound so smart, like, "Doctor, tell him he's not supposed to eat this, not supposed to eat that." Bad luck, she ran into trouble. I remember he looked at her without saying anything, he looked at me, and he asked her what things she didn't want to give me to eat, and when she told him the list, he started practically yelling, "What's the matter with you? You trying to kill him?" And boy, I never did see Mother like that before, she didn't say another word, she just stood there without moving, you'da said she was some pillar of salt, well sure, her little Doctor scolding her in this loud voice, she did not like that one bit, and I didn't hear a peep from her for a good two days after, when people would come see her and they asked why she wasn't talking, I told them she lost her voice.

She got even with me.

In the old days, I used to heal people, laying hands on them. If some person skinned his leg on the road falling off a bike, or some kid got burned on the woodstove, they'd bring him to me and I'd stop the fire for him. After, it would heal up its own way, nature would take over, but at least it didn't burn anymore. Well acourse Mother used to be very proud of me for that, seeing how in those days there was no doctor next door, and it cost a lot to go. People would come from all over town, sometimes even from other towns around Play, and I didn't charge, because my grandfather told me that I had the gift but if I ever sold it for money, even once, I'd lose it. Still, people were pleased, acourse, and they would want to return the favor, so I'd say all right they could give me something if they felt like it, but not right away, later, when I forgot I ever saw them. And some people would come back six months later, when things were good, with baskets of cherries or with a pheasant, and they'd give them to Mother when I wasn't there. And acourse she would go make a big fuss: "Lookit what they give me to pay back my Marcel! He really did them good, I'm real proud of my Marcel, oh, if only he wasn't so mean to me sometimes."

Nowadays, it's not "sometimes" I'm mean to her, it's all the time, according to her. She don't quit her talk. Says whatever comes into her head. She's jabbering all the time. Summertime, she leaves the door open, she sits in the shadow just inside on her chair there, and the minute she sees somebody go by she'll start the jabber, and just watch out if you stop, you'll be there all afternoon.

She could see that little by little I was having more trouble walking and holding onto things, she saw how I was shaking and I couldn't eat any longer. And the worse I get, more she calls me mean, and acourse that gets me mad when she'll say that to just anybody, and there I go, I get mad and I tell her shut up and then

TREATMENT (FRIDAY, APRIL 4)

she goes, "You see that! Ohnomygod I'm so miserable!" or else maybe I act like I didn't hear anything and she'll turn to me, "You should be ashamed, acting mean to me like that, Marcel, in fact I think you *are* ashamed, cause you're not talking," and the other person looks at me funny, like they're saying, "That's not nice."

She knows I'm no good for anything anymore, that I can't even go for a walk, I gotta take a cane, and that makes me worried. I almost can't get over to the Doctor's office, and she never lets me go anymore by myself. She don't like me to talk to him alone, and I can't tell her to leave, because then after, when we get home, she hollers at me, she says, "If you're gonna be like that I'm not making you anything to eat."

I'm going deaf from her! She wears me out.

I don't know how long this'll keep on. Pretty soon I won't be able to walk at all. They'll have to send me to the hospital to die, or else they'll put me in an old-folks home, because Mother won't be able to help me get up anymore, or do anything else. Even now already I gotta call her when I'm on the toilet, sometimes I can't stand up after by myself.

Still, I've worked hard, I've seen a thing or two, but this, really—this is no way to live.

Sometimes I just suddenly start crying, without meaning to without even feeling sadder than usual, it just hits me, it pours out and I can't stop. And that's even worse. She hollers at me even more, how I got no guts, how I'm not good for nothing anymore, and what's going to become of her with a man like that?

❁

There she goes again. "He's late…"

"Sit still will you!" I go. "He has sick people to see. Real ones."

"Oh, you're so mean, Marcel! You know I'm sick. You know I'm not putting it on, such a long time it's been! And besides, you should know! You're the one used to lay the hands on me before we got our little doctor…"

"Yeah."

That's really the one thing that consoles me. Used to be, with Mother, when she would get her pain, I could stop the fire for her. It didn't help for very long, but it lasted for as long as it lasted. And then, after a while, it stopped working so good, and then lucky thing her little doctor started out here. So then she told him about her heart pain, and he told her fifty times it wasn't her heart, it come from her back, a nerve that's pinched up behind there and it hurts in front. But she just would not listen, even though I explained to her it's like the sciatica, it's pinched up in the back but it can hurt way down in the foot, but you think I got anywhere? Sometimes I can see it drives him crazy too. When she calls him, he tells her he'll come at, say, ten o'clock, and then he comes at noon. She's already half-undressed at a quarter to ten, but here's this big drafty house, her teeth are chattering even with the layer of fat she got on her. And then when he turns up and he examines her, she's whining about her godawful pain in the heart, and he gets behind her and I hear him say, "How about here—does this hurt here?" and Mother yelling "Yessaow!" And he doesn't let up: "How about here?" And she goes "YeaOwwwwiiee!" And I'm thinking real hard, "Go ahead, fella—show her!" and I get this feeling he's making it last, that he's pressing as hard as he can, and believe me he's strong, the other night when I fell out of bed and he come over to put me back he just put his arms underneath me and picked me right up... And hearing Mother yell Aiee! Aiee!—it makes me laugh, because if it was me doing it to her she'd call me all kinda names, but her little doctor course she don't dare say too much.

So, I get a little revenge, see her come out of there all red, laughin an groanin both, from the pain. For once it's real.

97

MADAME LEBLANC

The phone rings. I pick up: "Doctor's office, Play…"

I hear, "Hello, Edmond? Is that you, Edmond?" and then the person hangs up abruptly, without even letting me say a word. She hasn't called for a long time.

I stay by the phone a moment, but she never calls twice. I look up at the wall-clock. It's eleven o'clock, that's always the time she calls.

There's something odd about her voice. Tired and stubborn at the same time. As if she had something important to tell him, her Edmond. As if she never did manage to reach him, in all the time she's been trying.

I pick up the phone again, I punch Doctor Boulle's number, in Deuxmonts.

It rings. Once, twice.

"Hello?"

It's a voice I don't recognize. "Hello, madame—this *is* Doctor Boulle's office?"

"Oh yes—the Doctor is out on a housecall, what can I do for you?"

"This is Madame Leblanc, Doctor Sachs's secretary. Doctor Boulle sent us some test results that came to him by mistake—that often happens to us too, because the secretary at the laboratory mixes up the addresses, we get his tests and he gets ours. But this time, when he slipped them into the envelope, by mistake he also stuck in a letter of his own, some insurance document, and Doctor Sachs wanted to let him know not to hunt for it, he'll leave it in his mailbox tomorrow. It's a letter from Tourmens Insurance."

"Very well, thank you, I'll tell him. Goodbye."

"Goodbye, Madame."

I hang up. I put the sheet into an envelope, I write "Doctor Boulle" on it and tuck the envelope in the appointment book. A little while ago, when the mail came and I saw Doctor Boulle's letterhead, I was surprised to find this thing underneath two laboratory results. It's odd that he would put this document in without realizing it, but when you're in a hurry, you don't pay close attention.

I was going to put it in an envelope and give it back to the postman when he stopped back to pick up out outgoing mail, but you came in. You looked at the document, you read it, you frowned, and you said you'd take it to him yourself.

I change the sheet on the cot. I put back the little bolster and the big pillow with its striped green cover.

The office has changed—it's brighter, cleaner, since you repainted it white with Madame Kasser and your friends. Madame Kasser made some double curtains and pillow-covers, and hung a matching fabric down the back of the tall shelves, to form a screen. It still takes me by surprise, because it's very recent: I discovered it when I came in on Tuesday morning, you used the Easter weekend to do it, and you really got a lot done in three days.

I go back into the waiting room and I look at the appointment book. You already have a good many appointments for this afternoon, and I'm concerned, because I don't know how you'll feel when you see that, after your housecalls. This morning you were really in a very bad mood. And then a lot of people called to ask if you'd be having office hours this afternoon, and I said yes, so you're certainly going to have a heavy session, and I'm afraid that will irritate you still more.

I don't understand why you're like that. You're so changeable. On certain days, you seem very cheerful, very happy, and on others it's as if you were sick, you're so gloomy. A few months ago, I thought it was because of your mother's death, but I don't think that's it. The night she died, you told me you wouldn't be in the next morning, you had to make funeral arrangements, but you did come in for office hours that afternoon. And over the next few days you looked sad, of course, but sometimes you'd heave a big sigh and then suddenly start laughing. I was sorry when she died. She was always very nice to me, she would ask after my husband and my children, she even invited us to come to tea at her house in Tourmens one Sunday when you were there, without telling you, as a surprise…

It's terrible, how these things can happen to a person. A bad cold that turned into pneumonia, and even though you sent her to the hospital, it didn't help; in a few days it was all over.

She never met Madame Kasser. That's sad. They would certainly have liked each other. I know how your mama felt about that. She didn't say much, but I understood. She wanted you to find a woman who'd take good care of you because she'd say that you didn't do much to look out for yourself. If she'd lived, she would have seen how you've changed. You're much better dressed, you change every day, your hair isn't long anymore the way it was. You never used to have time to go to the barber, but now that Madame Kasser cuts it for you, that doesn't matter.

And you've put on a little weight, I think. Your white coat doesn't hang so loose on you as it did just a few months ago.

People even say you're different. They find you more patient, less jumpy, less

TREATMENT (FRIDAY, APRIL 4)

sarcastic than before. More attentive. Quicker, too. You don't spend hours with everyone who's got a problem. You're less talkative.

But I don't know, at the same time, you seem—I don't exactly know how to say it—more distracted...

You spend much less time on the telephone, but much more working on your little computer.

And on top of that, there are more and more patients.

You realize that. For several weeks now you've been talking about opening up the office on Thursdays, and taking on a regular substitute doctor to fill in. You talk about it, and I think it would be a good idea, but I have a feeling you're not in a big rush to do it. It seems to weigh on you.

Still, people do ask for it. And I don't find it easy, on that day, to tell them to call someone else.

I raised it again this morning, and you told me you were thinking about it, but that a substitute was hard to find. And then you changed the subject, I could see that it irritated you.

Actually, I don't know how it would work with a substitute. People are used to you, and so am I. A substitute would have to adjust to our ways, and people adjust to him. The other day, you asked me whether I saw any problem with it being a woman. Makes no difference to me, as long as she's nice.

98

THE ELECTROCARDIOGRAM

You undo the armband and lay it on the little cabinet. You set the cup of the stethoscope against my chest and you grip my wrist between your thumb and middle finger.

You listen. "Breathe deeply."

You move the stethoscope a few inches, to the left and then the right, around the palpitating area on my chest. Occasionally you leave the cup resting on my skin and lift your hand off it. The cup jumps to the rhythm of my heartbeats.

"Do you feel anything?"

"Yes, I feel it skipping…"

"Your heart is… very irregular… Do you smoke?"

"A little…"

"How much is that?"

"A pack…"

"Mmmhh. And this pain—how long did it last?"

"A good two hours. It hit me in the middle of the night. I was sleeping, dreaming, but I can't quite remember what. And then I woke up because I was hurting… I didn't say anything to my wife, I got up, I took some aspirin, some painkiller, whatever I had on hand, but they didn't help. It hurt very badly here (I put my clenched fist on my chest), as if I were caught in a vise. It was terrifying… but not really enough to call a doctor out at night. And then it went away… But I was short of breath all day yesterday, so my wife absolutely insisted that I come in to see you. I finally gave in because it's been thirty-six hours now, and I'm having a hard time dragging myself around…"

"Mmmhh… I'm going to do an EKG. Stay there."

You get up, go to the stand against the other wall with the baby-scale on it. From the lower shelf you take a small grey case and bring it over here. You open it. You take out an oblong machine the size of a loaf of bread, and a ball of multicolor electric wires. You swab the flat electrodes with a translucent gel and lash them to my wrists, my ankles, using leather thongs.

"Not too tight?"

Then you stick several rubber bulbs to my chest—that is, you try to stick them on. You do your best to squeeze out the air inside and press them hard on my skin, still I hear a little hiss, they fill up again, they slide down my side and land on the sheet.

"With all that hair, it doesn't hold…"

"Mmmhh…"

Eventually you hook each of the electrodes to a colored wire, feeling your way, switching them at the last moment when you've got it wrong. Then, after plugging it into the socket for the electric radiator, you turn the machine on.

The device produces an even hum, the paper roll begins to feed through and display an unintelligible tracing. You press on the top of the machine, you watch the paper band roll out, you wait, you press again, you look at the band, you wait, you press, you look. From time to time, with the tip of your ballpoint, you mark the tape as it feeds out. This goes on for only a few minutes but it feels very long to me. You don't speak. Finally, you unplug the machine, you free me from the electrodes. You wipe the viscous paste from my wrists, my ankles, and my torso with a paper towel.

You roll up the long paper band and set it on your desk. You pile the wires and the machine messily back into the case, you lay the electrodes on the bottom of the sink.

"What do you think?"

You don't answer, you don't look at me. You give a vague wave to tell me I can get dressed.

You lay out the long paper ribbon on the painted-wood surface you use as a desk. You sigh. I sit down beside you. You cut the ribbon into sections of about equal length. You pile them together, you clip them to a cardboard, which you fold and set down before you.

You get up, you go over to the shelves standing in the middle of the room. You look for something. You finally pick up a big soft-bound book with a yellow cover. You come back and sit down. You open the book and pull out a bookmark that you lay on the white surface, between us. On the bookmark I read "Dr. Abraham Sachs."

You leaf through the book, you reach over to a pencil-mug and take out a tiny ruler graded on both sides. You measure the waves traced on the tape, you hold your breath, I see sweat beading at your temples.

You swallow, and you say, "I think you'll have to go to the hospital…"

I heave a big sigh. You raise your head, you look at me, and there's fear—terror —in your eyes. I smile at you, and your fear turns into perplexity.

376

I say, "I knew it. It had to happen eventually."

You take off your glasses, you pull a tissue out of your pocket, you wipe your forehead. You're greying slightly, I'd never noticed before, probably because your hair was often long and greasy, rather unkempt, all these years, and recently it's short, and always clean.

"What... what do you mean?"

"I just knew it, that's all. At my age, it's a thing that can happen, right?"

"Uhh... yes. But..."

"But this is bad."

You nod your head and drop your eyes. I've never seen you like this.

"I'd like you to go to the hospital immediately. I'm going to call an ambulance and alert the cardiac emergency service."

"Don't do that, Doctor. I'm not going."

I see you start. "What are you saying? Of course you are! They'll—"

"They're not going to save me. It's a bad heart attack, is that it?"

Speechless, you nod your head. Then you say, "You've had a massive infarction. The whole heart is suffocating. If we don't give you..."

"Yes, I've read a little bit about it. To unblock the heart arteries, you have to give certain drugs within a few hours after the clot forms. My pain started the night before last. It's too late. And it's just as well that way."

You open your mouth but I lay my hand on your arm. "I'm going home."

"What?"

"I'm going back to my house, and you're not going to say anything, or do anything. I want to go home and die in peace. I don't want to go die in the hospital."

"But your wife—"

"I'll tell her the situation. I warned her a long time ago. She's a believer, she'll be able to pray. It would have been much harder to see her go first."

"I don't understand."

"I know, Doctor, and I'm very sorry for that. How much do I owe you?"

You didn't want to let me pay for the visit. I said that if you made me leave without settling up, it would deprive me of my peace of mind. You stayed silent for a long time, and then your shoulders slumped, you nodded your head, and you filled out a Social Security form in my name. I asked for the EKG tape; I asked you to write on it what I had, and to make out a paper saying you had advised me to go into the hospital. I don't want anyone to accuse you of negligence. But I won't tell Thérèse. I don't want her living in anguish waiting for me to die. I feel relieved. Almost happy. Less unhappy, anyhow.

For you, I imagine this has been a shock. For seven years now, I've been coming to see you three times a year—examination, blood-pressure monitoring, weighing, a few words about the rain and the fine weather, and then the prescription slip for the sole medication I take… An uncomplicated patient. An uncomplicated ending.

❀

As I was leaving your office, with your hand already on the doorknob, I looked you straight in the eyes and I said, "My wife and I had a son…"

"I didn't know that."

"Yes, of course—we don't ever mention it."

"What… what happened to him?"

"He was… a very sensitive boy. When I went hunting, he never wanted to join me, it made him suffer to see me kill a rabbit or a partridge. I always thought he'd eventually toughen up… He was in his last year of the science track at the lycée. He was doing very well at it, but his teachers always said he had more of a literary mind. He made excellent grades in philosophy… One day, he came home from the lycée and for once his mother and I weren't there to greet him… We never did understand what happened. He set down his bookbag on the table, he took my shotgun from the wall, he loaded it, he went up to his room and…"

Your hand came to rest on my shoulder. I looked at you, I smiled at you. "I'm… glad to have seen you today, Doctor."

And then I left, without looking back. Without saying what I had to say to you. I wanted you to know it, but I couldn't. It doesn't matter anymore. After I'm dead, eventually someone will tell you that our son's name was Bruno.

CONSULTATION: IMPOSSIBLE
(Sixth Episode)

The man coming out looks tired. I pick up my shopping bag, I stand, I go in. You follow me and point to the two armchairs facing the desk. "Sit down…"

I set my shopping bag on the floor. I stay standing, near one of the chairs. Behind me, you run water, soap your hands.

"Do sit down, please."

I lift off my scarf, I sit on the very edge of the chair. You dry your hands, you come over to me, you pull out your swivel chair, you sit down, you look at me sadly, you say:

"What can I do for you, Madame… ?"

"Ummm… I don't know exactly."

"I don't think we've met before?"

"No, it's my first time here, my cousin—Madame Boulanger—told me about you, you took good care of her son."

"That's nice of her."

"So I decided to come in, you see it's hard for me, I wasn't too sure how to explain what I—you know, I don't much like to go to the doctor, I never needed to even for my pregnancies, well yes for the children I never hesitated, because we— I mean my brothers and sisters—there were eight of us so our father and mother didn't call one in very often and I had a little sister died of rheumatoid arthritis when she was six because there was no Social Security back then and you didn't bother the doctor over nothing because seeing how it was just before the war—it was Doctor Molina at the time—he was the only one for the whole district and he went around to housecalls on his bicycle. So you see, doctors—I don't dare call one in over nothing, but on this—"

"Yes?"

"Well this, it's been going on for too long, my husband's complaining, so I decided to come talk to you, I should tell you it was hard to do because for one thing I didn't know when your hours were and sometimes I'd come too early, sometimes I'd come too late, or else there were way too many people ahead of me, the last time it was Saturday three weeks ago there was some man who looked awfully sick that you kept in with you for a long time and then there was still somebody else ahead of me so I could tell there wouldn't be time to see you before I had to go to the school to pick up the children I tend…"

I stop. You've crossed your hands, you're leaning on your desk, you're listening to me.

"So. So I came because I have to decide some day, you know? it can't go on this way…"

"Yes?"

"Well, for six months already—"

The telephone rings.

"Excuse me." You pick up, sighing. A loud shout causes you to put the receiver away from your ear. "Hello? Hello? Who is this, Madame?"

The yelling keeps up at the other end of the line and you're just stunned, you shake your head hard. Then you take a deep breath and in a very low serious tone you say, "Hello, this is the Provincial Credit Bank, to whom do you wish to speak?"

The yelling stops short. You go on. "This is Doctor Sachs, Madame, what's the trouble? Calm down, or I can't help you… Just now?… Where is he? On his bed or on the floor?… Yes? on his side?… Yes, you did the right thing, he's out of danger now… Fine, where do you live?… No, no danger, it'll be over by the time I get there… Yes, right away, but tell me where!"

I see you quickly scrawl a number and three words. "Fine. I'm on my way."

You hang up. "I'm terribly sorry—an emergency—Can you wait till I get back?"

I'm already up. "No, no, I have to get home, but don't worry about it, I'll call Madame Leblanc, she'll give me an appointment. I know how it is, an emergency can't wait. Look, I've been meaning to come for six months, I can certainly wait another three days."

I stand up, I collect my scarf and my shopping bag, and I head for the door. You open it, let me go ahead of you, you say goodbye while you're unbuttoning your white coat and you go back into the consulting room. I tie my scarf back on my head, I take my bicycle, and I go home. Just as I'm about to turn the corner, you pass me in your car and I see you drive into one of the housing projects. It's no fun having to rush off like that. It sounded serious, some people have it hard. And I think how even if I'd had an appointment it wouldn't have been any different, emergencies can't wait, when you gotta go you gotta go, but really, for once I actually managed to see the doctor—it's just my luck!

IN THE WAITING ROOM

First I hear the inner door, then the connecting door, open rather abruptly. A woman comes out—"Goodbye, Doctor"—hurriedly buttoning her raincoat, and leaves the waiting room. The old gentleman picks up his cap and his little booklet from the low table and gets to his feet because he's next.

You appear on the threshold, you've put on your jacket without your pullover, the old gentleman steps forward but you raise your hand to him.

"Excuse me, I've just had a call, an emergency, I've got to get over there right away. If you'd like to wait, I'll be back in… in a half-hour. Otherwise, I can give you an appointment this evening?"

The elderly gentleman turns to me, we shake our heads no, we'll wait, he takes his seat again, I uncross and recross my legs.

You close the door, you lock it and you hurry to the exit. Your car shoots off at top speed.

I look at my watch. I see that the gentleman is watching me.

"Time goes faster when you're reading," he says.

"Yes…"

"It tires me out quick, reading."

"I see…"

"But I really don't mind waiting, seeing how the Doctor always takes the time to do an examination and listen to my chest proper."

He falls silent. Then, as he sees I'm still looking at him, he goes on, "Is this your first time here?"

"Yes."

"He's a good doctor, Dr. Sachs. He's very gentle with children… with everyone else too, actually. Nowadays he has a very busy practice, but he's always a good doctor, he's patient and he's not stuck-up. I've been coming to him a long time now, and I'm very satisfied. Course, he doesn't suit everyone, but that's always the way. Some folks even say he's going to leave town, but I've been hearing that since the first time I came, so I don't put much stock in it. It's just talk... I don't know a lot of doctors that would apologize like that and run out to an emergency. I know a lot of them would just tell the person to go over to the hospital and leave it at that. I don't think that's right, with all we pay in on the insurance, doctors make a good living, they can at least put themselves out a little for an emergency... In fact, that's how he got to be my doctor. If he hadn't taken the trouble that day, I wouldn't be here having this chat with you..."

He stops talking, he stands up. "Excuse me, could you watch my things for a moment?" I nod; this is the second time he's asked since he got here. He turns and leaves the waiting room.

I take up my reading again, but soon, through the wall, I hear the telephone ring a long time in your office. You must have forgotten to switch on the answering machine.

ON THE LEAFLET

In a notebook dating from twenty years ago, I found this tract:

WE ARE ALL NAZI DOCTORS!

There is the fantasy:

"Doctors know physiology, pathology, semiology, therapeutics.

Doctors diagnose illnesses through the most modern investigative procedures.

Doctors provide sick people with the most recent, effective, sophisticated treatments.

Doctors offer every patient ready access to the care most appropriate to his condition, with respect for his personality, his convictions, his aspirations, and his life choices.

Doctors bring mankind whatever is needed to avoid suffering, decline, and death."

And then there is the reality:

Doctors begin by touching other people's bodies so as to put a finger on what hurts.

Doctors choose among innumerable theories and schools of thought, personal opinions, antiquated prejudices, irrational beliefs.

Doctors arrange that from one day to the next, a "friend" who could easily have waited three weeks gets care ahead of a dozen other people who have been waiting three months for treatment.

Doctors take pride in the number of patients they see in a day.

Doctors conceal from everyone—especially from themselves—that they have no idea what nine-tenths of their patients are saying, and that they're wrong about what the rest are saying.

Doctors claim to have become confidants. They declare that they treat souls just as much as, if not more than, they do bodies, and they're are proud of it, those bastards.

Doctors preach a lie.

A doctor's words are words of death, promises of pain, incantations of black magic, doorways to torture. Doctors have become the clergy of the only universal religion: The Church of Fortunate and Well-Deserved Health. They determine its dogmas, its obligations, its unavoidable tithe. They prescribe its prayers, its barbaric rituals; they rank the worshippers into quite distinct categories according to the favors done them. Among them are high priests, inquisitors, worker-monks, and a whole barnyard of minions/executors who carry out the menial tasks whereby the flocks are tagged, examined, measured, weighed, photographed, classified, by their most intimate and mysterious characteristics. Nothing will escape them, from the gene that codes for hair color to the makeup of the smallest squamous cell on the sole of the foot. The cataloguing of the human race is on the march, and the doctors are in the front ranks. They no longer diagnose; they sentence. They no longer comfort, they test. They no longer heal, they tally.

Everyone else mourns the dead. Doctors cut them up.

Doctors are simultaneously whores and pimps, dealers and cops. Doctors opposed to abortion have always aborted their own wives or daughters when they deemed it "necessary." Doctors are torturers trained in camps called hospitals.

Hospitals are made for parking those abnormals, those deviants called "the sick," and for leading them back to the paths of righteousness—that is, back to the job. No matter if they weep or howl, if they cannot sleep or if they spend their days vomiting. What counts isn't what people are saying through their sickness; what counts is the doctors' opinion of the condition they should be in after the treatment. Doctors bleed, twist, slice, rape, screw, rip, disjoint, enslave, normalize.

AND YOU AND I WILL BE PART OF THAT WORLD!

Choosing to be a doctor is choosing not between two specialties or two styles of practice, but more important, between two roles: "Doctor" or *caregiver.*

Physicians are more often doctors than caregivers: it's more comfortable, more gratifying, it looks better for parties and dinners, it looks better in the picture.

The Doctor "knows," and his knowledge prevails over everything else. The caregiver seeks primarily to ease sufferings. The Doctor expects patients and symptoms to fit the analytic format his school inculcated in him; the caregiver does his best (questioning his meager certainties) to understand even slightly the things that happen to people. The Doctor prescribes, the caregiver bandages. The Doctor cultivates talk and power. The caregiver suffers.

As for the patient: no matter which he's dealing with, either way he's going to croak. But in what key?

B.S., February 8, 1977

Twenty years later, I haven't changed my opinion.

Doctors are evil:

A young medical student is listening to a discussion between his father and his uncle, both doctors. The uncle is a retired specialist—respected, famous, decorated—and a former deputy-chairman of the Ordre Régional.* The student questions him about this curious organization, established under the wartime Vichy government: Does it truly ensure the integrity of the profession? Why, it certainly does! declares the older man. And it also averts some catastrophes! Take this story for example: a couple consults a very highly regarded gynecologist. This is the nineteen-fifties, so the husband stays out in the waiting room. The wife is gorgeous, but—how shall I say it—a shade simpleminded. The doctor finds her appealing. He has her lie down on the table, he spreads a drape modestly over her face, and he carries out "a tiny procedure." The woman is naive, but she's not a fool. She can tell the difference between a speculum and a man's prick. And besides, the stuff running down her thighs afterwards is no antiseptic liquid. She doesn't speak up then and there, but she does tell her husband. The husband (can you imagine?) takes his wife's word, simpleton though she is. He files a complaint, in his wife's name, with the Order's board.

"And? And?" asks the student.

"And? They settled amicably!"

"What do you mean, 'amicably'?"

"Well yes! If they'd sued him, his career would've been wrecked! Do you realize?"

And the old fellow doesn't understand why his student-nephew cries, "But that's just what he deserved!"

---

*A conservative county medical society, affiliated with a national organization.

Doctors are puffed up with self-importance and incompetence:

A woman comes to the doctor saying she hurts. Where? In an embarrassing place. Where's that? There. Where there? There, in the anus, but a little higher up. Inside. Her general practitioner examines her, but can't figure it out: her rectum is perfect, nothing wrong there, it shouldn't be hurting her, what's she talking about? He sends the patient to a specialist. The specialist examines her in a teaching seminar—where the big chiefs show their students how to examine an asshole in thoroughly humiliating fashion. First, you have three patients undress at a time, in three booths. Then you have them come out one after the other, climb onto the table, kneel with their butts in the air in front of the six students and the two nurses. First you insert the metal thingamajig, fast and hard—just to see if that hurts—then you put the finger in, after slipping a rubber glove on so's you don't get filthy, and you push it in up to the hilt. Obviously, the longer the finger the better. "What about here, madame—does that hurt? There? There? Tell me." Well, yes, it does indeed hurt. And yet, objectively, medically, there's no reason why this lady should be hurting—her rectum's perfect, that's all there is to it, what's she talking about? Get dressed that'll be five hundred francs. For treatment, see your G.P. "But between you and me, gentlemen, it's all in her head."

She comes out, she swallows this pill and that to deal with the pain. And so it goes for a year or two. Finally, the pain disappears. Or else she and the pain get used to each other. One day, she notices that she's bleeding. She goes back to see her G.P. You're bleeding from where? From an embarrassing place. Which one? That one. The anus again? Well, it's some disease! The G.P. can't figure it out. He sends her to another specialist. This one sees her in private, he can tell she's frightened, she tells him that the last time it didn't go awfully well, so to avoid hurting her he doesn't stick the metal thingy all the way up into her rectum. And because he sees nothing, he says it must be hemorrhoids. There now—a little elastic band here, a little vein-toning there, all set, soon be gone no trace. No such luck—it keeps on bleeding. The woman tells herself it's all in her head, like last time. One day, though, she decides that enough is enough. She goes back to see the specialist, it doesn't seem right to him either and he scolds her, saying, "Oh, you should have come in sooner," never considering that maybe he could have suggested that… This time he does use the longest thingamajig, and he sticks it up her, and bingo! Not an inch past where he'd stopped looking the last time, just around a bend, he runs into a cauliflower-size—even bigger—tumor. From the look on his face it's certainly cancer. And from then on it stops being the slightest bit funny. Because the patient exits the tranquil world of the boulevard specialists to enter the world of the hospital wards. A surgeon tells her, "I'm gonna just take that right out of you, no problem, don't worry, afterwards you'll be good as new." No such luck: when he opens her up, things are less rosy than he thought. Not only has the cauliflower gone and spread outside the gardenpatch; it's started eating at her liver besides. Three, four, five metastases. Ohh my. Bad. "This exceeds my competence as a provincial surgeon, I'm sending you to a liver man in the capital, you'll see, he's a great guy."

The capital specialist is polite, courteous, paternal, reassuring. "Yes, it's serious, but it's not hopeless. There's always something more we can do. First, we'll give you some targeted chemotherapy, to 'reduce' these nasty metastases. The only thing is, for the best chance of success (says the plump stately Professor), not all drugs work equally well. In fact, to be frank, most of them are ineffective, and very, very toxic. We don't advise them for you. Now it just so happens that I've been using a revolutionary new substance, one that's absolutely going to change the outlook for this sort of disease. Of course, it's still experimental in man, but in animal tests it's been shown to be very very *very* promising. If you agree to let us use it on you, you would of course be one of the very first to benefit from it… Then, if the metastases and you—both—follow the protocol very diligently, we'll be able to operate, and we'll graft on a brand new liver. The conditions? They're not so terribly draconian, we just implant a tiny pump under your skin, and then feed the drug in at a steady dose, no bother for you…"

The patient agrees. What else can she do? They keep promising her she'll come out of this fine. "You're a fighter, and so are we! We'll fight this thing together, and you'll see—with the help of our cutting-edge medication, we'll beat these nasty metastases! Just think ahead to your liver transplant!" A few months later, wasted, emaciated, skeletal, the patient dies of a long and painful illness. In the last days, though, the doctors decide it would be useful to throw her a dose of their famous "lytic cocktail" through the IV drip, to minimize the suffering of the people around her. Eventually she's sleeping so much that she doesn't realize she's dying.

An edifying tale, you'll say. And where's the kicker? Back in that little paragraph that's standard in every good medical text. I quote:

"Given the high risk of recurrence, the impossibility of excluding the presence of other secondary sites of the initial cancer, and the small number of available graft organs, *liver transplantation is never indicated for treating hepatic metastases.*"

❂

Doctors lie not because they're afraid to tell the truth but because-patients-would-rather-not-know-the-truth. We're certainly not going to force them!

Doctors put patients through torment not to make them suffer but because-they-want-to-try-everything-to-save-their-patients. We're certainly not going to reproach them!

Doctors experiment not because they're sadistic but because-we-must-advance-science. We're certainly not going to stand in their way!

TREATMENT (FRIDAY, APRIL 4)

One day, in a survey of doctors (their turn does come up), some idiot discovered a less-than-glorious set of facts. He found that doctors drink, take drugs, get depressed, smoke, fuck badly, gamble at racetracks and casinos, beat their nearest and dearest, neglect their children, and when they can't stand their stupid lives any longer (and who knows better what horrors life holds in store), they kill themselves. And all of that statistically more often than the ordinary unenlightened citizen of the "general population."

What better way to say that doctors are poor schmucks, who don't even manage to derive some personal benefit, some private fulfillment, from their goddamn job? What better way to say that doctors croak despite all their knowledge?

But before doing themselves in, all doctors are torturers. And while G.P.s may mostly be little kapos, the hospital chiefs—with a few exceptions—are real big Mengeles.

I was doing my rotation in pediatrics. One afternoon, I was told to keep watch over a premature infant. I had no choice. It was obligatory. They were short of personnel, and every student was required to "dedicate" a certain number of his nights to the neonatal life-support unit. I had to spend a whole night in a room where a seven-and-a-half-month shrimp was hanging on, for better or worse—a little human lobster who was in hot water from being ripped untimely from his mother's womb. He was laid out on his back in a plastic box. One tube was threaded into his nostril to aspirate secretions from his lungs, another was poked through the skin on his belly to deliver a nutrient solution directly into his stomach. One tube was attached to a foot, another to the top of his naked skull. He must have weighed three-and-a-half pounds, maybe four. Beneath the plastic hood, his gasps were barely audible, amid the noise of the machines and the crying of the newborns hospitalized in the next room.

He was called Sylvain. I thought to myself, "It's not even a nice name."

It hurt me to see him, that little bit of a human being. His limbs were fastened by bands to the four corners of the box. Now and then he would bring his minuscule fist to his mouth, he'd lean his head toward it, his tongue would suck the space that separated them, and then at the cost of superhuman effort, for a few seconds, he managed to nurse at his fingers.

His eyes were wide open. The room lights were filtered and the walls were painted (if I remember rightly) a deep red. A spotlight bathed the wall above his head.

I untied his hand.

I'd been forbidden to do that, supposedly because he might tear out his tubes, but he never came near them. He only wanted to nurse at his fist.

I watched him cry, suck, breathe, suck, nurse, sigh, sleep, suck.

He was born on September 9, and this was the 13th of October.

I was sitting on a hard plastic chair, in that room that was more like a broom closet than a treatment chamber.

I was sleepy. I would doze off, but every so often he would begin to cry as he slept, and I would sit up with a start, wondering if he was in pain or if he was dreaming, or if he was crying because babies "cry for no reason but their immature nervous systems," as the doctors say.

At regular intervals, I was supposed to hook a syringe of sugar solution onto an electric pump and attach it to the feeding catheter.

Every hour, I was supposed to take his pulse at the fold of the groin, and count his respirations.

Every four hours, I was supposed to check his blood pressure and his temperature.

This preemie, this infant, this human being, they asked me to touch as little as possible, except for those required actions, but I would put on gloves, I'd insert my hands through the openings in his box, I would stroke him with the tips of my rubber-clad fingers. I would put my mouth against the Plexiglass and talk to him, I'd tell him stories, I'd hum him songs.

Every half hour, I was supposed to draw off the secretions from his lungs. This meant starting the aspirator machinery, attaching a clean catheter, feeding it into his nostrils, and aspirating.

He would start to turn blue and suffocate each time I did this, but they'd told me it was necessary to go on aspirating, relentlessly, until "nothing more came into the bottle."

Every four hours, I was supposed to give him an intramuscular antibiotic shot in the buttock. The first time I did it, he began howling, then he stopped breathing, he writhed with pain for several long minutes, and I thought I'd killed him. I stared at him, paralyzed, unable to do a thing, not daring to go call for help, guilty of having handled the thing like a clumsy idiot and having caused his death.

Certainly they'd told me where and how to insert my needle, and I'd done it as prescribed. *But they hadn't told me it would hurt him so much.*

I didn't give him the other shots, I emptied the vials into the washbasin. I did not aspirate him every half-hour. I watched him, I laid my ear against the incubator, and I only aspirated him when his breathing began to gurgle, and then I did it just enough to rid him of what was bothering him.

Toward dawn I took off my gloves, I soaped my hands for ten minutes, and I slipped them, naked, onto him, to stroke him. His fingers closed around my little finger, his fist pulled it to his mouth, and he suckled on it. I stood there against the box, I watched him, and I cried and couldn't stop.

TREATMENT (FRIDAY, APRIL 4)

In the morning, when I left, I hated the people who had stuck the two of us there without considering what it meant.

I hated the nurses for never thinking to look in—for even a second—through the doorway.

I hated the doctors who delegate their torturer role and go off to dine and smoke a cigar in the tranquillity of their bourgeois interiors.

I hated the resident who, at breakfast, gave me a cynical talk on how it was just one more premature newborn with a malformation, among so many. That you don't bring your feelings into it. That the kid had been put in an incubator on principle, but that it wasn't at all certain he would reach the weight required to be operated on for his malformation, and that, even if he did, they'd think twice about doing it, because his brain was probably grilled to a crisp—like *this*, he finished, biting into his toast.

And above all I hated the parents of this little bit of a thing, because if he had been my child, I would have spent my every day and night at his side.

I don't know what ever happened to him. I don't know if he died from not getting the treatment I was told to give him. I don't know if he was operated on. When I left the unit, I swore to myself I'd come back everyday, but I didn't have the strength. When I finally got up the courage to come back, the room was empty, and I didn't dare ask after him.

During ten years of studies, I learned to palpate, manipulate, cut, suture, bandage, set casts, take out foreign bodies with tweezers, put my finger up or thread tubes into every possible orifice, inject, perfuse, percuss, shake, do a "good diagnosis," give nurses orders, write out an observation as per the rules of the art, and make a few prescriptions, *but during all those years, no one ever taught me how to relieve pain, or how to keep it from occurring. No one ever told me that I could sit by the bedside of a dying person and hold his hand and talk with him.*

Morphine has been in use since 1805, but here, in this millennial land, in this land of Lights, this land of Culture, it took until the end of the twentieth century for doctors—those paragons of virtue and humanity who make us the envy of the entire planet—to understand that in infants, silence is the sign of terrible suffering, and to decide to give them morphine to relieve them.

Never mind that I'm only a little kapo, I'm still one of those torturers. I was trained by torturers and I do the same job they do. I won't have children. I don't want to see them die, I don't want to see them suffer, I don't want to make them suffer.

I love you, Pauline, but I will not be the torturer of your children. Of our children.

THE CASE OF DR. SACHS

102

PAULINE KASSER

Shivering, I put down the pages. You were huddled in the big sagging armchair. Without a word, I took you by the hand, I drew you into the bedroom, I lay down beside you, I set a finger on your mouth and I said:

"Not so long ago, women were shouting, 'A child *if* I want it, *when* I want it.' Well, freedom is indivisible. If a man doesn't want a child, no one has the right to make him have one. Not even 'his' wife. And above all not 'in the name of their love.' Love is not a relationship of power. I know, many women think otherwise. They want to be mothers at all costs because that gives them a terrible power. And they hold men in contempt because it's very easy for them to make children and leave men out of the picture, whereas men cannot do the same to women. But those women are incapable of loving or of being loved, because they put mother-hood ahead of their companion. When you raise children, you must give them a positive image of the other sex. And for that, I'll always have greater trust in a man who respects women than in any woman who detests men.

"You suffer from living, my love, but you are alive. If you had wanted to die, you would already have crashed into the pylon, there by the bridge. And you don't spend your time suffering. I know your body, I know what brings it to climax, I know what thrills it. You're dying of desire to have children, you're dying of desire to be a father. There are too many children in what you write and in what you say for anything else to be true. But you're so furious with all the 'bad parents,' real or fantasy, that you worry about being yet one more bad parent...

"Yes, I want to be filled by you, and to see you holding a tiny human in your arms. Like you, I fear to see them suffer, and I fear dying myself before they're on their own, because I know life is risky! But since I met you, I know where my place is, where my desire is. I don't want children by anyone but you, but I will never have children against your will."

I sat up on the bed.

TREATMENT (FRIDAY, APRIL 4)

TREATMENT (FRIDAY, APRIL 4)

"... After my abortion, when you came to my room, you were talking about contraception... the woman lying in the next bed asked you if an IUD was a hundred-percent reliable. You answered slyly that the only totally reliable method was abstinence. Since you have no more intention than I do—stop me if I'm wrong—of utilizing that method, we assume the risks together. If my IUD fails, I will have an abortion. That wouldn't be a sacrifice, it would be a choice."

You cried, "Absolutely not! I don't want you to have an abortion!"

"Why?"

"I love you, I will not make you abort a child we'd have together! That would be abominable!"

"Then... if the device fails, we'd keep it?"

"Uhhh... yes!"

"But I don't get it! That child, those children who are "accidental"—there could easily be several such!—you agree to welcome them and have them run the risks of living, but you forbid yourself *desired* children?"

103

THE FIRE CHIEF

Your telephone rang once, twice, and a half-awake voice answered me. "Yes? What—"

I heard a loud noise, a curse, laughter, and your voice again. "Yes—I'm sorry, I dropped the phone."

"Yes, good evening, Doctor, it's Captain Gentile. Excuse me for bothering you at home at this hour, I know you're not on call tonight, but... there's been an accident. Near the bridge, again. A car hit the pylon..."

"Shit! Kids again?"

"No. There's only one victim—a man... It's—I don't know how to tell you this... He's very, very critical. The rescue squad got up here, they've managed to stabilize him somewhat, but before they take him in to the hospital we'd like you to come over, if it's not too much trouble. It's somebody you know..."

"Who?"

When I told you, there was a long silence, and finally you said, "I'll be right there."

I put down the portable phone and signaled to my colleague, who sighed and shook his head. I went back toward the accident site. The car was completely wrapped around the steel pylon, and the pylon had buckled. For the thirtieth time I wondered how fast he'd been going—had to be at least seventy-five, for that impact. Apparently he was heading home. How did he manage to miss that turn? He must have made it ten thousand times, he knew that road like the inside of his pocket, did he fall asleep? At this hour, that could be it, but it's so stupid!

I felt an icy sweat slide down my back. The guys from the ambulance squad took it all in stride, it didn't touch them more than that, but all my own people were in the same state as me, that's why I called you. We were all his patients. None of us had the courage, at three in the morning, to go and tell his family that Doctor Boulle had just had an accident.

SOLO DIALOGUES

VI

THE PAGE PROOFS

The first sheet bears a title:

PRIVY/CHAMBER
by X.X.

and a biographical notice: "X.X. was born in 1954. He lives and works in Xxxxxxx. *PRIVY/CHAMBER* is the first fiction he has published," and a handwritten note:
   "Dear Bruno,

   Here at last are the proofs of your story. Please look them over and let us know under what name you'd like to publish it. Claude and I are very pleased to welcome this piece to our pages.
In hopes of reading many more!
   Best regards,

Danièle"

The text begins on the following page:

Where there's the stink of shit,
there's the stink of life.
Antonin Artaud

...It's hard to talk about this.

It's not the kind of thing you talk about to friends, at a café or at the house, you know. It's not even the kind of thing you can talk about to your wife. Although, of course, I'm not married, so I can't really say... But I don't see myself talking about it to my wife. Or my wife talking about it to me. What do you think?

...Still, it really is an everyday fact, you see, it's not like a person only does it once or twice a year, no, this thing—this is really all the time. Well I know there are people who only do it once a week, sometimes less, and who are pretty unhappy about the fact, especially women, because apparently it's mainly them who've got problems in that area. Anyhow—it's a part of life. For everybody. Like eating, drinking, or sleeping. Or dying. It's one of the few things that everybody really has in common, no getting around it, like, sooner or later you gotta do it. Whereas the rest—wife and kids, house and car—you can live without, lots of folks live without, but *that*, never mind if people never talk about it, you can't. I think the hardest thing for me, actually, is not being able to talk about it to anybody. But that doesn't tell you why I'm here...

Actually, I don't know myself, see, it's more like I wonder—I wonder if everything's completely normal. Nothing's bothering me, but I worry about it, you know what I'm saying? I wonder if...

See, I've read a lot about the subject—how sicknesses would spread when people used to do it any old place, and actually I know in some parts of the world, the very first hygiene thing—the thing they set up before they do anything else—is telling people it should be done in very particular places, off out of the way, at a distance from water sources, to avoid contamination... I remember thinking when I read that, It's funny, because actually, here's this important function that's completely indispensable for the individual person, and yet at the same time, for the group it's dangerous. I thought what a contradiction, the idea that these microbes do us good, you and me, by turning beef bourguignon or beaujolais into... into energy—actually, just the way they turn ferns into oil three hundred kilometers underground—and then at the same time, if people do it any old place, it can be fatal... Funny, isn't it? And even so, they've still found a smart use for that whole process, because the polio vaccine, the one you drank on a sugar cube, you know? I read—stop me if I'm wrong—that the reason they gave it by mouth wasn't to keep from giving shots, but because it works a different way from the vaccine they inject, right? The injectable vaccine is a killed virus, and the drinkable vaccine is a live one—a weakened form, it doesn't give you polio, it just immunizes against it—and when they give it to a kid, it colonizes the intestine and then the kid just naturally passes it on to a playmate, because children, even when they're toilet-trained, I mean, even when a kid can do it by himself, it's still not all that clean, they play, they run, they hit a ball around, they don't give it much thought, they just go in a hurry when they suddenly feel they have to go, they wipe themselves with paper, they think the paper keeps their hands clean but you know, I read—a while ago already—that that's completely an illusion: actually the paper is porous, the stuff comes through, even if you don't realize, even if you use it real thick, I know I—that's what I used to do when I was ten or twelve, I must have already read that thing by then, and it obsessed me so much I'd put twelve layers, I'd use up a package in two days, my mother would bawl me out because they were constantly having to buy more and she'd wonder why, and my father would yell at me all the time because in our building the plumbing was old and it would clog up over any little thing. My mother always bought regular paper, you know, the kind you got in trains, those little squares folded in half, slightly stiff, slightly waxed, for a long time I used to think of it as cheap quality compared to the soft kind, but actually that shiny kind is more waterproof, but whatever, I would pile eight or ten sheets together, and when I finished wiping once, I'd throw them away and take ten more sheets, and so on, by the end that made a big load, especially if it didn't come away clean the first time. In fact, yeah, now that I mention it, that's a problem I've never resolved: how do you know if it gets clean the first time? It's rare that you don't pick up anything the first swipe. It's sort of a surprise when it does happen, but it's rare, mostly you pick up something, so you gotta do it again, to get what's left, and when there's still a little left—I mean, when you see on the paper that there's still something, a trace— you're tempted to keep wiping until it comes up *perfectly* clean...

So that can go on a while, and you can see why the pipes would clog. I had a nightmare once—everything overflowed, I had to plunge my hands in to pull everything out and put it into pails, and when the pails were full I didn't know what to do with the rest, of course, and I felt like there I was in the process of pulling everything out of the bowl that I'd put into there for years, ever since we'd been living there, and of course that was ridiculous because after all my father and my mother lived there too, but when I think about it, I always imagined that my father and my mother never went to the bathroom, or at least, if they did go, my father only went in to piss, in fact you could hear him do it, the walls were made of cardboard, as for my mother, very simple, I don't think I ever saw her go in there except to stand on the seat to stack the shelves with the packets of paper that she'd bring back from the supermarket... When I think about it now, I say that's ridiculous, of course she went, but it must've been early in the morning, when I was still sleeping, or during the day while I was at school... You see, when you're a kid you don't imagine that your parents screw, but that I always knew—it made such a lot of noise, with the bedsprings and my father's groans—sure, it didn't give me much desire to do like him, but that's another story... What *I* had, though, is I could never imagine my mother going in there, and closing the door, and... Even now I have trouble saying it because I can't imagine her lifting up her dress, yet I have no problem picturing my father opening his fly and pissing, he would do it anywhere, when we'd go on vacation in the car we'd drive a long time and sometimes he'd pull over along the road, he'd get out, plant himself at the edge of the shoulder, and I only understood later what he was doing when I got big enough for him to invite me to get out with him. Me, naturally, I didn't want to... I thought I'd never be able to piss as far as him, so I was always careful to go just before we left or as soon as we got there, never during the trip, and besides, outdoors you have to hurry, I always liked to take my time, even back then, at age ten or twelve, I would spend hours...

When I was a kid, that was the only place I could be peaceful to read. I read a lot, everything, especially novels, and I figured out early that books—that was really a separate place, special, like a house you go into and from one room to the next you plunge into different worlds, you meet different people, killers and whores, pretty innocent girls, tormented doctors—yes, I know that's a ridiculous idea!—mad geniuses and victims... Everything came up for discussion in there, from sex to torture—in a disguised way, of course, at least in the books I could get hold of—but never that particular place, and here it's one of the few things everybody *has to* do, everybody knows that, it's like in movies: some guy gets thrown into a dungeon or he falls down into a wild-animal trap, and he's there for days; when he comes out, he's dead of hunger, he's bearded, shaggy-haired, emaciated, but there's not a hint that he must have had to relieve himself, at least in the first few days, even if later on he had nothing to eat or drink... Whenever I saw that in a movie, I'd think right away of the smell, I could smell the stink of the hole they were pulling him out of, I would imagine what was under the pile of straw at the end of the cell, under the branches and leaves at the bottom of the bottomless pit. You know... I would think of that immediately. And in novels, I was always trying to figure out the moment when one character or another could have snuck out to go to the bathroom.

Very early, I worked it out so my mother wouldn't ask me to do things, and after a while, I did it without even thinking about it—the way I'd set the needle back on a record over and over again on the old Teppaz phonograph with one hand and never take my eyes off my book—say I was in the midst of reading a *Tarzan* or a *Harry Dickson*, and vaguely, in the distance, I'd hear my mother start talking to herself, some little thing like "Oh shit! We're outta bread!" or "What crappy tomatoes," and right away I'd know she was going to come looking for me to send me downstairs. As long as I was going, she'd make a list of other things she needed, and that's what annoyed me: if I only had to go down for a baguette or a pound of tomatoes, it would take me five minutes, but she'd charge into my room yelling, "Go get me a half a bread," and then like "and a jar of cream and two peppers and three lemons and four Petits-Suisses and five eggs and six bananas." Except, since she'd say it all real fast fiveggzensixbananasenfour and since naturally I kept on reading, I only heard some kind of vague words and I didn't always remember everything too well. I would never dare ask her to repeat it, because she would have smacked me: "I'm sick and tired of this, you never listen to me!" and she'd hit so hard that I'd walk around with a mark on my cheek the whole day, and when my father came home at night and saw it he'd start hollering, and she'd be crying even before he raised a hand to her, naturally I didn't want to hear that. So I'd go down scared, instead of taking the elevator I'd rush down the stairs—we lived on the ninth floor—and then try to remember what she'd said, and sometimes I did, but sometimes not, and I'd come on back with the half-loaf, six peppers, five lemons, four jars of cream, three bananas, two eggs, and even at that I would've been crying in front of the grocery lady to get her to give me just one Petit-Suisse out of the six-pack, Oh yes yes ma'am that's what my mother said, I was sure, I couldn't be wrong, and I'd climb back up thinking I must have screwed up, and I'd go in all shaking and put everything on the table, and I'd leave the kitchen and I'd hear my mother yelling, "What the hell did you do to me here? Whadju do?" and that was it—not only would I get a licking, fine, that I was used to, but the worst thing was that she'd roar into my room and take my book and she'd rip it into a million pieces, if it was one I bought at the bookstall, or if it came from the library she'd confiscate it and she'd go return it the next Saturday and bawl out the librarians: "I'm sick of your damn books, when he reads he just gets lost, don't you lend him any more books, if I see them in my house again I'll throw them in the fire!" I knew very well that wasn't true, she was too scared my father would knock her down if they had to replace them… So anyhow, whenever I heard her open the fridge, "Oh what shit there's never anything in this damn house!" I would just automatically, without even thinking, without dropping the book, I'd get up, I'd go out to the hallway and into the toilet just as she was leaving the kitchen to look for me and no way anyone could get me out of there if I didn't want to come.

I'd stay in there sometimes three-quarters of an hour, an hour, it would drive her crazy, but when she'd come knock on the door, I'd say, "I think I'm sick," that would stop her short. I should mention that when I was little—I don't remember it, of course, but I heard the story a hundred times—I had this really bad thing, an "acute intestinal intussusception." Yeah, I guess you'd know what that is, but I had to go look it up in a medical book. What really got me most was finding out it's this totally dumb thing: the intestine doubles back on itself like a sock, it cramps, starts swelling up, it hurts like hell, and if you don't do something the kid can get a blockage and die of it. And the way they examine for it—the barium enema is it?—is also a way of treating it: they put this material in through the anus, the radiologist watches the opaque liquid fill the intestine, the sock area unfolds under the pressure of the liquid, and the child feels better. It only happens to children under four or five years old, right? and most of the time it doesn't happen again. But that—well, my mother didn't know that. I suppose the doctor must have told her at the time, but she never really listened to what doctors said to her, she didn't care an awful lot about my health, I was always late getting my vaccinations, but that thing, for years she thought it could come back. The first time, obviously, I was two or three years old, I'd started crying and rolling on the floor, I turned white for a quarter of an hour, that must have scared the hell out of her, and then it went away, and it happened again a half-hour later and I got over it, and then it hit me again twenty minutes later, and after four or five times she gave me a smack because she thought I was faking, but when I started vomiting and then bleeding from the bottom, she ran me to the hospital and the doctor diagnosed it right away, adding it was a good thing she came in because I would've been a goner, and she goes: "I thought he was putting it on! He'd writhe around for five minutes and then he'd go back to playing," and he says, "Exactly, that's it, that's typical for this…" So she got so scared thinking I could have died and it would've been her fault that the first time she knocked at the door to get me to come out and I said I didn't feel good, that I hurt, she went out to do her marketing herself, maybe she was afraid I'd start rolling on the floor with pain in front of everybody in the grocery store… That's how I got peace and quiet.

…The funniest thing is, when I think about it, that outside of that I've never had any other problem, oh I must have caught some stomach bug now and then, but maybe three times at most, and constipation I don't even know what it is, and that's probably why I started to wonder about things, to get interested in the matter at a, let's call it—you'll laugh—a more intellectual level, but after all, why not? I wouldn't want to be a doctor, there are some things that make me puke, but this doesn't. When I started working, the thing that disgusted the other nursing aides, I could tell, was coming in mornings to find the bedridden patients soaking in their sheets, and when they heard me say "Can I give you a hand?" they would let me, for them it was a blessing from heaven, a co-worker who was strong enough to move these hundred-and-fifty, two-hundred-pound paralytics and who wasn't afraid to put his hands into their shit… And then, little by little, I started doing it all by myself—lift the patient up with one hand, wash him with the other, dry him, change his sheet, all in a second… If ever I had kids, I'm sure that—I'm sure their mother would be delighted to let me take care of them…

…I've never really had a girlfriend—that is, a woman friend. In fact, friends in general I've never really had, either. I don't see who I could've talked to about my—about my interests. And besides, I don't know how anyone could live with a person who spends his time locked up in—

…It's gone on a long time. I started thinking about this, I must have been six-teen or seventeen. I'd already started spending time in the bathroom. I'd go in when I got up in the morning, I'd take along my book, or a class text, even some-times some homework I had to finish. My father'd already died of his cirrhosis by then, my mother never went, nobody bothered me. I'd set up a portable bookcase, and a pulldown desk-ledge on the facing wall. Once I was sitting, I would lower it in front of me and I could read and write, both. My mother never said a thing to me anymore, she wouldn't dare; when my father got sick I was already fifteen, I was two heads taller than she was. That last year I was carrying my father from the bed to the chair and from the chair to the bed practically every day; he weighed eighty pounds when he died. The doctor had asked us to keep track of how his stools looked, to collect his urine, because he had fluid in his belly and the doctor was giving him medicine to make him piss, but that also gave him diar-rhea. He had a bed-flask and a basin next to him, and I was the one who took care of emptying them. My mother didn't want to go near him. It didn't bother me, but it upset her. I told her that since she was doing the cooking, it was better, healthier, if I took care of him.

…Well then, when my mother died of her uterine cancer, I kept the apart-ment, I'd been paying the rent on it anyhow since I started working, so all my lit-tle arrangements are still there, between the toilet and the kitchen there was a broom closet, I knocked down the wall to make it bigger, so I could put in my books, all the articles I clipped, so I could have everything at my fingertips—except when I'm at work, of course, I spend most of my time there. I've had a radio for a long time, I put in a little TV once, but I never turned it on, it made me feel like there was someone watching me. I do everything in there, my taxes… lots of times I fall asleep reading… and then I wake up at the sound of water flushing through the pipes from the people upstairs, they're like everybody else, they've got their little ways, and I can always tell just about what time it is when I hear all that water running down behind me, on the other side of the wall…

…When you think about it, your guts aren't just passive plumbing, they're not simply the equivalent of the pipes that run to the sewers, they're much more com-plicated, more sophisticated, they break down foodstuffs into different nutrients, they let enough water through to make the stool liquid for the first two-thirds of the way, and they take it up again at the end, to recycle it into the general circula-tion… And the rectum, when you consider it, what a marvel of sensitivity *that* is! You know—this is the first time I've ever been able to talk to somebody about this, so I'm making the most of it!—when you look very carefully at people eating, you see them every now and then in the course of the meal, or a little afterwards in the café, they lean from left to right, or from right to left, they lift up one buttock to let out some gas, making it look as though they're just talking to their neighbor, and their tense face relaxes right after... Well, didn't you ever think about how terrifically sensitive the rectum must be, for a person to know without the slightest doubt that what he's going to let loose is a fart and not something else? So, see, I started reading, thinking, studying the subject, and God knows there's plenty to read on it, and I asked myself more and more complex questions... How much a person eliminates in a life, in ratio to his weight, or in volume—see what I mean—and when you think how we're six billion people by now and how each individual produces anywhere from a half-liter to two liters of urine a day, and between three and twenty-five stools a week—it depends on their age, of course, but also on the sanitary conditions and the alimentary customs of the population—I wondered if the number of liters of urine and kilos of shit produced by each country might not be an indicator of the standard of living, and if it could be calculated...

...But I'm getting carried away, talking, talking... You, it's good, you listen to me, you understand, it's not the kind of thing a person talks about at the job, and yet at my job we're right in the middle of it all the time... And you understand, I can't make any friends—I'd have to invite them to come to my house now and then, at least for a drink. But what if they needed to go to the bathroom, I couldn't tell them no. And it would make them laugh—a guy who spends his time in there, with his books, his journals, his radio. I can just hear the lousy jokes pouring out, like, "Well, I'll say one thing, you don't take any crap!" and that—well, look, I just wouldn't stand for it.

PROGNOSIS

(Thursday, June 26)

And when it's all over, I'll live.

Raphael Marcoeur

104

MADAME LEBLANC

I walk into the waiting room. It's empty, but the connecting door to the consulting room is closed and I hear a murmur through the wall. He must be with a patient.

I take off my raincoat. I hang it in the metal cupboard and put on my office coat. The wall clock shows ten forty-five, I lay the newspapers out on the low table.

There were a lot of people, I don't believe I've ever seen such a burial in the district. What a terrible thing, really, to die at that age, and with such suffering, almost three months in a coma. That really makes me sad. I didn't know Doctor Boulle, I'd never been his patient, but some of our friends, and several people who work with my husband who live at Deuxmonts or at Marquay—they went to him; it was an awful shock to them. And I put myself in their shoes, if *you* were to die so horribly—for me it would be even worse... Well, it couldn't be worse than for Madame Kasser, when I think how she's expecting twins! Last month, when you told me that, you were in heaven, you were floating a yard off the ground. I was a little uneasy, myself. I've seen those programs about multiple births. All the parents say it's hard, and the doctors say the pregnancy can often get complicated. So I asked you if it worried you a little, really. You thought about it, and you said, "Sure, but life is full of risks..."

I put away the toys in the children's corner.

Today, you both came to the funeral, you looked very sad. But what broke my heart was seeing Doctor Boulle's daughter. Losing your father like that at seventeen—that must be terrible. There were so many people there. It looked as if the whole district came. There were all your colleagues, of course, and the whole municipal council of Deuxmonts, but the mayors of the other nearby towns too—

Monsieur Burgelin, but also M. Host and M. Noguez, the mayors of Marquay and Lavallée... The Deuxmonts church isn't very big, so there were some people couldn't get in. It's a little surprising that he wanted to be buried in Deuxmonts. He came from the Southwest, I understand. I thought he'd be buried down there. But apparently he wanted to stay here... Naturally, people were moved that he would be buried right in the area... He *had* been here for fifteen years, after all... There was a whole group of youngsters around his daughter—classmates from the lycée, I imagine, but young people from town too. And lots of families with their children... His patients even went to visit him at the hospital, while he was on life support: when he didn't come out of the coma, you got the administration there to put him in a room with a viewing window on one side of the rotunda. I didn't visit him, myself, I didn't know him well enough, but twice last month I went with my sister to the premature nursery; her grandchild was born at eight months, and they kept him in an incubator for two weeks. The two units are next door to each other, they share a corridor, and Doctor Boulle's room was in the middle. The last time, when we got there, there was a lady and a little boy eight or nine years old, looking at him through the glass. When I left a half-hour later, they were still there. I was talking with my niece, and I saw Madame Boulle and her daughter coming in at the other end of the corridor and heading for the room. At the sight of them, the lady took her little boy by the hand and went past us on her way out. She was crying very hard...

I pick up all the little books scattered around, and line them up on the shelves.

I saw them again today, her and her little boy, they were waiting at the cemetery. When the coffin came in, they stayed a little to the side... Doctor Boulle was very much loved, he had a lot of patients. But lately several people were saying that just before his accident he was edgy, short-tempered, he looked tired, that's probably why he fell asleep at the wheel. If only he'd buckled his seatbelt... For the people in Deuxmonts, it's a catastrophe, because his substitute—they don't like her at all. Apparently she talks down to everybody, and she's not very understanding. At the cemetery, today, Christiane—the wife of a man who works with my husband—told me she'd asked her for a renewal slip on the Pill, and the doctor—I forget her name—told her that the Pill gives you cancer and that anyhow two children wasn't enough, she should have more. Obviously, Christiane didn't like that one bit, and I think she's going to come to you. In fact, since the accident, I'm getting a lot more requests for appointments and housecalls from Deuxmonts people... They know you were the one they called in, the night it happened. So all the time Dr. Boulle was still in the coma, his patients would stop in here sometimes just to ask for word on him... Some of them couldn't accept it. They really believed he'd come out of it, with all the progress in treatment... Last week, I asked you if a person could come out of such a long coma without some effects.

You thought about it, you sighed, and you said, "Sometimes... Sometimes, the will to live is so strong that certain people do come out of it."

I run the dustrag over the furniture.

Now that he's dead, there's some talk about his substitute taking over permanently... I'd think twice about that. Doctor Boulle certainly wouldn't have wanted to leave his practice to a doctor his patients don't like. She'd already been covering for him several months. As long as it was only a day here, a week there, it was tolerable, but now... Sometimes, you don't really know what people are like until you've seen them on a daily basis. So when you mentioned opening this office Thursdays, taking on a substitute doctor, and possibly a woman, I was afraid you might be thinking of her, but you told me *Absolutely not,* and since I knew she'd been to see Monsieur Guilloux one day when you were off, I figured she hadn't done exactly what she should have... That's another thing, that breaks my heart too. It's several months now since Monsieur Guilloux was operated on, and he's not doing too well—he doesn't get out of bed any more, but he is still alive... What a calvary, for him and for his wife both...

I sweep the waiting room. Through the wall I hear the telephone ringing and then Doctor Bouadjio's voice. For almost three months now he's been coming in to replace you every Thursday, and during your vacations. The first time he came to visit the office, I was surprised: he's taller than you are! But he's nice, very nice. He'd brought along his little girl, a tiny bug three years old running all around, she laughed and laughed and he did too. He talks and laughs so loud, sometimes, that you can hear him from the street. Obviously, at first people asked me who he was. A black doctor in Play—it seemed odd to them. But I explained that he was no beginner, that he's almost as old as you, that he's been practicing already for a long time at the hospital, in pediatrics, but that one day he got tired of staying closed up within four walls and decided to work out in the country. So while he's building up a practice he fills in for other doctors. When people heard that—that he was a pediatrician—lots of patients brought their kids to him, and Thursday evenings are always booked solid, sometimes two weeks ahead. Not only that, he works hard daytimes as well. I have to say, he's very pleasant, very funny, very comforting with elderly people. And besides, everyone sees that you and he get along well, that you discuss the patients, that you're a team, in a way. Of course, he doesn't suit everyone, but that's always the way. Madame Renard is a little scared of him, I hear; but Monsieur Renard likes him a lot and when he asks him to stop by the house, she always finds some excuse for getting out to do her errands, so they're alone there to talk... Doctor Bouadjio told me that one morning they talked for an hour about the time back when Monsieur Renard used to do healing, and he was really interested in that, because where he comes from, there were

PROGNOSIS (THURSDAY, JUNE 26)

also old people who used to have that kind of gift… I'm sure that when he sets up his practice, he'll get himself a clientèle very quickly. But I hope we'll keep him with us for a while. We couldn't have done better.

I vacuum. The waiting-room door opens, the postman appears, he sees me, hands me the mail, leaves. I drop the packet on my desk and I finish vacuuming. I put the vacuum cleaner away in the cupboard, I pick up the mail, I undo the elastic, I set aside the magazines, the ads, I put aside a personal letter for you, another for Doctor Bouadjio, and the envelopes from the lab. And that makes me think of the insurance document that you were supposed to return to Doctor Boulle the night before his accident, and that we've kept here since. Several times I reminded you that you hadn't left the envelope off for him, and I even offered to take it over, I was a little worried we'd forget, or misplace it—that happens sometimes with letters from specialists, you put them in the wrong folder by mistake and three weeks later, when you can't locate them, I have to go through all the files to find them—but you said again that you would take it over yourself, so I finally just slipped it into the appointment book, because there at least it can't get lost, and seeing it reminds us. Naturally, lately, since we heard Dr. Boulle died, I haven't paid it much mind, but now, you really will have to go and take it to his—

The door opens, Doctor Bouadjio comes out, carrying before him a basket with a babbling baby in it and followed by a young woman I never saw before.

"Hello, Madame Leblanc," he says as he sees me.

"Hello, Doctor! Hello, Madame!"

She opens the waiting-room door for him, he goes out, she follows, through the window I see her open the car door, he sets the basket on the back seat.

Meanwhile, automatically, I go into the study, I look around for the appointment book, it's lying next the the telephone. I open it up; the envelope is gone. Just then, Doctor Bouadjio comes in and, as he always does, with his big smile and his deep voice, he asks me, "How are you today?" He takes my hand, shakes it warmly with his other hand on top, and and suddenly I see you again—this morning, at the cemetery, a little apart, while everyone was filing up to toss a handful of earth on Dr. Boulle's coffin—I see you standing beside the lady with a little eight-year-old boy clinging to her, you're holding her hand that same way for a long while without speaking, then you take the envelope out of your pocket, you give it to her, she reads the document inside, she nods her head, she looks at you, and then she moves off, haggard, clutching her little boy, the sheet crumpled in her hand, like that woman in I can't remember what movie, at the end of some love story.

105

EDMOND BOUADJIO

"Hello, Madame Leblanc, so how are you today?"

"Fine, doctor," she answers, looking vague.

"You're still feeling the shock a bit…"

Her eyes fill. I hand her the appointment book. "I've already done one consult and two housecalls, and I've got another one… and a bunch of appointments this afternoon!"

"Lot of work, this week…"

✳

She leaves my office. I like her very much, she's a charming and intelligent woman. Very sensitive.

I set the rattle on the baby-scale, I toss the vaccine packaging and leaflet into the wastebasket, and I sit down.

Bruno's little black notebook is lying on the wooden surface, next to the cardboard file he gave me as he left.

On the day's page I log in this morning's activities. Monsieur Guilloux, housecall. Madame Radiguet, housecall. Baby Aube Laurens, office visit.

I leaf back through the book, to my first day here.

Monsieur Guilloux, already back then…

Monsieur V.: A small man, not old but unkempt. A mouth full of broken tooth stumps. Traveling peddler, if I recall. He made a funny face when he saw me; he had trouble explaining what he wanted. He'd come in to have his penis examined. He was worried it was too short: "What… what do you think?" I hesitated, then I told him, in all seriousness, "My father always said, 'The javelin always counts for less than the warrior.'"

Robert G.: Pain in left elbow.

PROGNOSIS (THURSDAY, JUNE 26)

Albertine E.: (*She drinks, but she's always denied it*, you said later.) She called me in to see her mother, but she had "a little thing that was bothering her." She hemmed and hawed over taking off her shirt, but it must have been hurting her too much to wait any longer. A huge infected herpes lesion covered her left breast.

Denise R.: She came in to show me her husband's lab test results… (*And spent an hour talking to you about her office boss? Yes, she does that to me too, now and then…*)

Mahmoud, Mardouk, Yasmina and Tassadit R., with their parents… As he was leaving the father told me, "It's good that the Doctor's not alone anymore. He's been looking tired lately."

Savina de T.: Gorgeous girl. Aristocratic. Tall and slim, waist like a fashion model. Certificate of non-contagion. She was going off to teach a children's class on the environment.

Jean-Paul M.: He brought in his uncle, his father's brother, a retarded man with bronchitis. (Your story on them: *All three live together in the one mansion. Actually, the "father" is sterile, and Jean-Paul is the son of his retarded uncle. His mother died when he was ten or twelve. Once, after an accident, he needed a transfusion, and it was his uncle who gave the blood. They both have a very rare blood type. That's when he realized… .He's studying genetics at the Tourmens medical school. He's always the one who takes care of his uncle. Of his father.*)

Monsieur R.: "Call me Marcel!"

Madame Elizabeth N.: Checkup on her aortic prosthesis. (*When she was operated on, her husband couldn't sleep for three months; all night long he kept hearing the valve clicking…*)

Monsieur Michel L.: Followup on his neuroleptic treatment. (*He had a hallucinational delirium a few weeks ago: he saw the hole in the ozone layer in his living-room, and in his terror he beat up his wife…*)

Madame D.: Suicide by barbiturates.

Madame Marie-Thérèse F.: (*Her husband just died, they hated each other, but she's completely lost.*)

Monsieur Jacques S.: train conductor. Nocturnal epileptic fit. (You warned me: *If that happens, the main thing is, don't put him in the hospital; he only has these attacks during his sleep. If the company finds out, he'll lose his job…*)

Monsieur Jules H.: a centenarian. Convalescing from appendectomy! (*The surgeons were afraid to go in. He wasn't ready to die, though, and he told them, "Go ahead, operate! At a hundred years old, I'm not letting myself get knocked off by an appendix!"* He reminded me of old Toumani, who had those same long arms, those same eyes…)

Madame Germaine L.: She was surprised to see me here instead of Bruno. She asked me very curtly where she could possibly have caught her venereal disease. "I never sit on toilet seats without wiping them, and I've never had intercourse with anyone but my husband, so I don't see how—" Suddenly she went white, and she got up and left.

The telephone rings once, and Madame Leblanc picks up.

I hear her answer, "Doctor's office—Oh, hello, Doctor! Yes, he's here, I'll put you through," then call out, "Doctor! It's Dr. Sachs."

I pick up. "Hi, Bruno."

"Hi, Edmond. How's it going?"

"Not bad, not bad at all. Missing the office?"

"No, not really, but… I wanted to be sure things were going…"

"With a pearl like Madame Leblanc, nothing can go wrong," I say, raising my voice.

"I think she's pleased with you, too. Umm—Are you… giving some thought to what I proposed the other day?"

"Yes I am. And I've started reading the material you gave me. We'll talk about it Sunday, at the transfer of powers."

I hear him laugh. "Okay… Uhh—nobody died?"

"Why do you ask that?"

"Because… It's a little stupid… I don't know if this is just my imagination, but I have the feeling it's always when I'm away that my patients die, especially on Thursdays… Well, that's how it seems. Whenever I go to register a death it's always some other doctor's patient. But that's stupid, of course. People don't pick the day they'll die…"

"Well, Monsieur Guilloux did die this morning. Very peacefully, with all the morphine he needed…"

"Oh. Last week he was still puttering, he was building a boat in a bottle."

"Since Monday he hadn't gotten up. He just stayed huddled in his bed, with his ear glued to his radio. His wife would make him take his morphine in little sips…. She was amazed he wasn't suffering. She was convinced a cancer patient has to suffer—that nothing can help them."

"I see. So even she thought that…"

I come out of my office. I tell Madame Leblanc about Monsieur Guilloux's death this morning at around six. She nods sadly. I look at the appointment book. To show me how to get to Monsieur Lejeune's house, in a place called Calicot, Madame Leblanc traces the route on the big military map tacked above her desk.

I look at the clock on the wall. Eleven-fifteen. I've got time to go there and come back to read a little.

PROGNOSIS (THURSDAY, JUNE 26)

106

CONSULTATION: IMPOSSIBLE
(Seventh and Last Episode)

Riding past the doctor's office on my bike, I look at my watch, twelve-ten, there's a car in the courtyard, but it isn't his. He's not there. Through the waiting-room window I see Madame Leblanc come out of the consulting room. She's got her raincoat on and she's about to leave. I go on my way, and then I think it's too stupid—I should have gone back weeks ago, I really should tell him, last time we did leave things up in the air, when I think how I didn't even have time to—And suddenly I just make up my mind, I put a foot down to the ground to let a car go by in the oncoming lane, I cross the road in front of the project, and I turn back toward the office pushing my bike, there's no—, I have to—last time it took me by surprise, getting interrupted like that, and then weeks went by and I had other things on my mind, but after a while I felt ashamed, I mean, when you start something you've got to finish it, I don't know what he must think of me but now it bothers me, and at the same time I was shy to go in again, but now it keeps me up at night. I ought go in now, since Madame Leblanc is still there. That way it'll be over with.

I go into the courtyard, stand my bike against the wall, I take my wallet out of the basket on the luggage carrier, and I go in.

I push open the waiting-room door. Madame Leblanc isn't there. The two doors to the inside office are open. I hear papers rustling. I take three steps and I stop, in the middle of the room. A big black man comes out of the office and smiles at me with all his white teeth.

"Madame? Can I help you?"

"Uhh… Doctor Sachs isn't in?"

"No, I'm sorry, he's off for the week, I'm standing in for him. Can I do something for you?"

"Umm… well, I wanted to tell him—are you a doctor too?"

I'm mad at myself for asking that, I sound stupid. Of course he's a doctor, if he's standing in for him. He smiles at me. "I am indeed. Can I help you?"

"Well, it's that the other day when I came in to see Dr. Sachs, I was having a problem—you know—I couldn't decide because it was going on for six months and every time I thought about coming in either I didn't know the office hours, or I'd come too early or I'd come too late, or else there were way too many people ahead of me—like one Saturday there was a man who looked very sick and the doctor kept him in there with him a long time—anyhow, when I finally managed to see him, we got cut off kind of short because he got an emergency call, a youngster who was having convulsions—it wasn't the doctor who told me that, it was somebody from the project on the Lavinié road, and you know how it is, in little towns people talk, so naturally even though convulsions don't kill a person— I know, because my brother had one when he was little and he never got another one after that—you still have to go, so we broke off kind of quick... But anyhow, I'm really glad I found you here, I thought Madame Leblanc was still here but I wouldn't really have known what to say to her, it's a little too personal, but with you it's not the same, you're a doctor, I can really tell *you*, and you can tell the doctor, is that all right with you? Could you tell him that Madame Guérin came by, that since I saw him things are going much better, that really did me a lot of good, and I didn't realize when I left—and the doctor was in such a hurry that I didn't think of it... And then the other day, suddenly, I said to myself, Oh no, I can't believe it! I'd be embarrassed to tell Madame Leblanc that, but you—I know you'll keep this between us, you can tell him when he comes back, okay? Especially tell him that it's going really very much better since I saw him, I really did the right thing coming in, but at the same time I'm ashamed when I think of the good it did me, in all the confusion it went right out of my head, for once I actually got to see the doctor and, just my luck, I completely forgot to pay for the visit."

107

KADDISH

Yisgadal v'yiskadash sh'may rabo
This cadaver, this ash—show me, rabbi
(Look, Ray—I'm writing your damned prayer) *B'olmo deev'ro* Be evermore my brother—but you'll die, you'll see *khirusay* I hear you say *v'yamleekh* disgusted, disarmed, disembodied, undone, *malkhusay* vomiting away your years, a heart dying broken (I'm writing it, I'll say it, since you asked me to; I scream it, I spit it) *B'khayyaykhon uvyomaykhon,* (for you and all the others) *uvkhayay d'khol* (who believed in life) *bays yisroayl Ba agolo* (—that gag, that figment, that trick—) *uviz-man* (all us wise men, chumps) *koreev,* (locked in by life) *V'imru Amen.*

Y'hay sh'may rabo m'vorakh l'olam ulolmay olmayo Yisborakh v'yishtabakh, Yes yes *v'yispoar v'yisromam* yes poor man *v'yisnasay v'yis-hadar* you're finished with saying, you've had it with talking *V'yis-allay, v'yis-hallal* on and on and on—you're done for, your soul faded, cut down, exhausted, crushed, shunned, wrecked, flayed (Do you hear this, Ray? You hear?) *sh'may d'kudsho b'rich-hu* That preying bitch death will never let go your hide...

L'ay-lo Lay low but *min kol birkhoso v'sheeroso* she's surrounding us, beating, gnawing, wearing us down. She's breaking us, freezing us, mining us, won't leave us be, won't quit, won't forget, won't drop us. *Tush-b'choso v'nay-khaymoso, da-a-meeron b'ol moh* She divines all, destroys all *V'imru Amen.*

Y'hay sh'lomo rabo min sh'ma-yo I don't, don't want you to die, to leave, to fall, to founder, don't want Death spearing you, wooing, commanding your spirit "Come to me, Give me all that you are..."

V'khayeem olaynu v'al kol yisroayl, V'imru Amen. O-say shalom You say, "Peace" *bimromov* But move—Dare, poor souls, to revolt, shake off your chains *hu ya-asay shol-lom* enough! weeping on our knees, enough waiting for death to take us too... *Olaynu v'al kol yisroayl...*
Cursed be thou, o Lord Doctor, king of this inferno.

THE CASE OF DR. SACHS

And buddy be thou, Ray—Glory be thine! "Prognosis six months, remissions don't last..." Well, you're up to nine, and you're trumping Death, and you're fucking it over, and you're giving it the finger and the runaround, what you don't give is a good goddamn—you'll live to see our children, they'll jump, they'll live, them too, they'll holler with you: "Fuck you, Death, fuck you—I'm alive! today and tomorrow and forever!"

V'imru Amen.

108

STILL MONSIEUR GUENOT

The telephone rings. I pick up.

"Hello, Edmond? Is that you, Edmond?"

Startled, I respond mechanically. "Yes, it's me! Who's—?"

"Edmond! I've got to talk to you. I haven't been feeling well for the last few days. My neighbor tells me, 'Madame Serling, you should call the doctor in Nilliers,' but I don't want to, I don't care if I die, it's just that I can't go on like this not talking to you, I've got things to tell you, so I want you to come see me, will you? Tell me—will you, Edmond?"

"Madame, I—Hello? hello?"

She's hung up.

I hang up too, and I go out. In the waiting room flooded with sunlight, the wall clock says three p.m. No one wants to go to the doctor on a day like this.

I go stand in front of the military map tacked to the wall behind Madame Leblanc's desk. Nilliers—the name isn't familiar. It's not in this district, I don't even think it's in this county.

I go back into the consulting room, and I phone Madame Leblanc. She's as puzzled as I am.

"Nilliers? No, I don't know it. It's not around here. And what was the name you said?"

"Serling."

"No, I really don't recall... .Did it sound urgent?"

"I don't know. To judge by her voice, yes... Anyhow, I'm not going to pester you any longer, someone's just coming in."

＊

He's standing in the waiting room, his cap in hand. He picks up his briefcase, the prothrombin booklet, the Social Security form and the prescription slip he'd just set down on the low table. I put out my hand.

"Hello, Monsieur—?

"Guenot, René. Hello... uh, Doctor."

I usher him in. The connecting door pulls to slowly by the closer mechanism as I push hard to shut the inner door. "What can I do for you?"

"Wal, I'm here about my prothrombin, like every month... Doctor Sachs isn't in town, I hear?"

"Yes, I'm replacing him for the whole week."

"Everything okay, with his lady?"

"Uhh... I believe so."

"Because they're expecting twins, right? Naturally, in a small town, everybody knows everything... But twins, that's not nothing..."

"Right!"

I point him to a seat, I sit down in the swivel chair and pull out his file.

He opens an envelope and takes out the report of his latest blood test, he lays it on the table and his cap on the chair. "It went down since last time..."

"Really? Let's see... Thirty-three percent... Last time you had thirty-seven— yes, it's a bit lower."

Out of the corner of my eye, I see him take off his jacket, his knit vest, and undo his belt. "Okay, well maybe you could have a look at me. Should I get undressed?"

"Please."

He takes off his trousers, lays them on the chair, and pulls off his undershirt. "Socks off too?"

"If you want."

"I lie down?"

"Yes please."

He lies down. I bring a chair over to the cot.

I examine him from head to foot, starting by taking his blood pressure; then I take it again at the end.

"You already did that!"

"I know... But sometimes it's lower at the end of a visit. Especially when a person isn't used to the doctor..."

"Uhh... that's true, I haven't—people like... your kind... I mean..."

I smile. "I understand very well."

"But if Dr. Sachs puts us in your hands, that means you must be a good doctor, just like him..."

"I try... Hm—one-thirty over eighty."

"Ah—like last time! That's good!"

I push the chair back toward the window; I offer a hand to help him up. "You can get dressed now."

I go back toward the desk, but I sense that he's still standing behind me. "Shouldn't I get weighed?"

"Uh… Yes, if you like."

He climbs onto the scale. "Did I lose any?"

"No, no change since last time."

"Should I get dressed?"

"Please."

While I fill out his form, he puts on his shirt, his socks, his trousers, his shoes, then he picks up his cap and sits down.

I write out his prescription.

"On the blood test, you don't forget to put 'at home' or else they don't pay it back."

"Here you are."

He takes a bill folded in four from his wallet, and stuffs the change into his pocket.

Just as I'm putting my hand on the doorknob, he looks me straight in the eye. "He's a good doctor, Dr. Sachs… Are you going to take over for him?"

I start laughing. "No! Absolutely not! I'll be standing in for him on Thursdays, and during his vacations. And… I might arrange to work with him a little more in the future…"

"Ah! That's good. He really does have a lot of work, now. When my wife called him, the day I got sick, he had less, but still these days he takes the time to do a real examination, like you. When I come out of here, it bothers me a little seeing a lot of people waiting to go in; so if you come work with him—that's the idea, right?—I think it would be good for him, and for the patients too. I'm sure you'll get used to things… Old Man Renard told me you had an uncle who was a bone-setter, that so?"

I laugh again—darn that Monsieur Marcel! "Kind of…"

"So then it runs in the family! It's like Dr. Sachs, his father delivered babies, I think… Well, that makes me feel better that you're not taking his place, because—I got nothing against you, just the opposite, but you understand, Dr. Sachs—it's a good thing my wife called him when I got sick because they told me at the hospital, if he didn't put me in, I'da been finished, but this way I came through it okay and heck! If he—if the two of you keep on taking care of me good, I can last a long time more. It gives me comfort to know Dr. Sachs isn't gonna be alone anymore because well, people talk, you know, in the beginning they were saying, "I guess he hasn't got too many patients, you never have to wait for long at his office, when you call him he always comes the same day, he never refuses anybody, so it wouldn't be a big surprise if he just up and left some day," and even now, I still hear the same thing, especially now he's got his ladyfriend, but of course all that's just talk, right? Would he a bothered to set up a practice here if he was just gonna leave all of a sudden?"

109

THE READING

Doctor Bruno Sachs
SUFFERING, TREATING, WRITING
A Colloquium on Literature and Medicine
Tourmens

"For my father"

When I was a child, or just barely adolescent, I never went to sleep at night without thinking, *Some day I'll have to die.*

Wrapped in my sheets, I would pray. In that period, it was all I had for combatting terror. Later, I went through a great many paper tissues.

Much later, I saw thirty-five-year-old men nailed to their beds by brain tumors—or by the surgery that had lifted it out of them, old women eviscerated; little girls with abdomens distended from lymphosarcoma whose mothers hadn't managed to disguise it by dressing them in clothes two sizes too big; men and women no longer able to sleep and moaning, "My liver's fucked," fucking liver, that Jew of the body—it gets all the blame even if it has nothing to do with the problem, but when it's big and hard and riven and lumpy with tumor, when your fingers can make out metastases under the skin, you feel your eyes avoiding the patient's, you hear your voice turning nasal... Nazi-al... you feel very stupid and very young at the same time, young enough to bawl.

Like everyone else, I suppose, for a long time I wondered how I would die.

I began—it was easier—by making a list of the diseases I wouldn't get. Obviously, at the age when I could ask the question, I was no longer going to die by some obstetrical accident or by sudden infant death. I'd be spared cancer of the uterus or the ovaries. And then very quickly the thing got less clear. Breast cancer does occur in men. Highway accidents happen to anyone. And then there are bursting aneurysms, those small malformations of the arteries that dilate over time and then explode one day without warning as you're shoving a desk or lifting a couch. As you can imagine, I soon abandoned my count. There was—after all—more to life than that.

And then, one day, I saw dead people. And they showed me that death defies our imagination.

Dead people, people like you and me—I've seen all shapes and colors.

People dead of cardiac insufficiency, blue from suffocation.

People white with bloodloss from a perforated stomach.

Women yellow as a quince from getting aborted by a shithead with a medical license.

Men of sixty, red with apoplexy, sprawled across their beds.

Wasted cancer patients, shattered children, crumpled cripples contorted for the rest of time.

I've seen drowned women who'd just lain themselves down with their arms crossed in a creek; hanged men calmly sticking their tongues out at their shitty life in a deserted shack, or bobbing gently against a treetrunk in a garden. I've seen widowers who put their papers in order, did the dishes and cleaned the house, fed the cat and turned out all the lights, then went and stretched out in the dark in the basement, on old potato sacks so as not to splash blood all around, and put a bullet through their heads.

All these dead taught me something paradoxical, something unbearable and yet incontrovertible: that it is less painful to consider one's death than to love. For our bodies live through, and thanks to, the body of the Other, of the beloved.

Loving means being powerless against time, and knowing it.

Loving means knowing love will last just so long—maybe a whole lifetime, but only that long.

Loving means knowing that unless you die first, you'll see your beloved die. That you will see life and love die in the beloved's body, even before he or she dies. And seeing the beloved die, you will yourself die a living death.

What will become of my body when my beloved is gone? What will become of my life? What will become of your body when I am dead?

I don't know; my patients have not taught me that.

They have only shown me that there is every reason to fear life, none to fear death.

The dead are not frightened. They do not move, they say nothing. Their mouths are often open, for they are tired of having kept them shut for so long. Their eyelids are slack, their skin is yellow, and their hands no longer speak. A corpse is cold. Cold and limp. Not cold like death, but cold. Except when it is in its bed, beneath the sheets, when it has just died.

You, the doctor—they call you and they say, brokenhearted:

I found him in the morning when I went to get him up for breakfast, he never comes in so late for it usually, even on Sunday, he's a person who can't stay in bed, but this time…

Or else it's panic the howls the screams the tears the hair torn out, the ashes on the head the imploring on the knees, Why why why, It's not true it's not true it's not true, Not him not him not him, Do something doctor it can't be he couldn't do this to me.

So then you start dumbly applying your stethoscope to a gurgling stomach, vaguely palpating a chest no longer rising to a breath, peering into eyes as blank as a red mullet's in a frypan. To act as if. To be able to say that there was nothing to be done, that you couldn't do a thing. So nobody can say that you did nothing.

Or else it's some old man or woman falling dead suddenly in the courtyard, on the carpet, or at the bottom of the staircase, and having to be carried to the bed, turned over—ohmygod he's so thin I didn't realize, ohmygod she's so heavy you'd never know—and you peel off your jacket you roll up your sleeves, *Here, I'll help*— Thanks doctor, that's right, she/he needs to be made ready…

Undressing the body in order to clothe him/her (all clean, all pretty) in the dress or the suit that he, that she had picked out that time coming back from the cemetery when we bought the plot together, on the stone there's our names but not the dates of course, the stonecutter did it for us that way so nobody has to worry about it you know in the confusion when the time comes, and besides I'm still here now, but when I go, the children are too far away, they won't do things the way we would, so we decided to just take care of it so there's nothing more to worry about, Here, could you just help me pull off this soiled nightgown (or the checked nightshirt that buttons partway and has to come off over the head—even when they're not stiff yet it's hard, the arms are pale and icy and heavy as marble, but slippery too, loose at the joints). When I think how he always had pain in his shoulder I would never have believed I could just pick it up like that to undress him, and then that heavy undershirt she always wore (and the necklace, the chain, the Cross, the Saint-Frusquin medal), Let's leave that on her, wait a minute I'm going to dab a little cologne that'll freshen him up (and lemmerubyou and lemmepatyou) before we slip on his freshly ironed white shirt, the pink blouse she wore to the grand-daughter's wedding, she even told her she wanted to see her again looking pretty like that, poor thing, she never thought that would be the last one (a finger to the collar, smoothed out, touched up as well, and then gotta see about down below, pull off the sheets left covering the lower belly, business of not seeing not yet casting a glance at that area, with the hairs grizzled gray tarnished around genitals so pale shriveled collapsed gone, useless a long time now—lest he or she has already started to empty out, belly-rumbling noises heard while we were grooming the upstairs, and lest the vague smells ignored till now should turn to mephitic fumes with the lifting of the sheet, buttocks and genitals bathed in shit), Never mind we'll boil it and there's some bleach, but we're not leaving him like that he was always so clean she was always so well-groomed remember (and lemmerubyou and lemmewipeyou and once the problem's taken care of, the sheet balled up in the bathtub, he comes back she brings back some old rags and a couple of diaper pads that date from) our great-aunt we had with us in the house seven years ago she was getting senile and she was letting herself go, so we had to put those on her and when she left for the hospital I don't know why she hung onto them just in case, but she didn't suspect they'd be for (protecting her, putting them in her underpants or his shorts pulled on with such trouble because the legs are heavier yet, slacker, as if the whole body was still hanging on and the skirt that's a little better but), The trousers, oh is that rough! For a man who wouldn't even let me help him put on his socks (as you tuck in the shirttails) gotta tighten the belt three more holes so it holds. (And a pair of shoes, very polished very shiny.) And the tie around the neck this one was his favorite (or else) The cameo her niece gave her for our anniv—Oh, no, her watch! I almost forgot it (and when it's all done, you slip a clean sheet under the now presentable body, that's not too complicated, just roll the sheet, line it up along the body, turn the person onto it toward you he doesn't resist, he lets it happen, you pull the sheet under from the other side smooth it out and that's it), Now just needs a touch of the comb and it'll be perfect (except he's still got his mouth and one eye open but you fix that with a wet cotton pad on the eyelid, a scarf to hold the jaw in place with the knot on top of the skull like an Easter egg for a few hours) when the children get here, that'll hold it, they'll see him looking fine (now there's the tears she wipes with a corner of her handkerchief, the nose he rubs with the cuff of his sleeve) pretty as the day of the little guy's communion, Ah, our little guy, how we loved him! She never got over that seeing him pass away like that, imagine, Doctor—leukemia… But excuse me, I'm taking your time, if you want to come wash your hands (and herelemmerubyou with the a worn chunk of soap in a chipped basin and herelemmewipeyou with a worn washrag and still not be too sure the smell'll go away and you button up your sleeves, you go back into the room, you collect your things, stethoscope no use now, dummy bloodpressure cuff, you could pump at his arm for a hundred years and the pressure will never be lower than it is today…

Way before I became a doctor, I was writing. But when you're a doctor, what use is writing?

I would have liked, I already had the idea—I have it now, in any case—of putting down on paper the name of every patient I've seen die. Of every baby I've seen born.

And, while I'm at it, the names of all the people who've come in to see me, who've ever called me out to the house. But which ones? The ones I actually did treat? The ones who called me in for somebody else (because *you always treat the person who asks for something,* even if he says it's not for himself)? The ones who only stopped me in the street with some trivial question? The ones who didn't sit down in the waiting room and left when they saw me? The ones who only asked me for some routine certificate? The ones who make an appointment and forget to come? The ones whose reason for coming you never understand?

Maybe I could have or should have done it, but I didn't do it. You don't think of doing that sort of thing when you start treating people. These days, doctors are encouraged to shovel everything into a computer, for the sake of epidemiology, statistics, accountants. But no one seems interested in etching the names and faces of people into memory, or recalling the first encounter, the early feelings, the surprises, the comic details, the tragic stories, the failures of understanding, the silences. I've seen thousands of people go by, but at this exact moment I couldn't readily call up more than a dozen of them—twenty with some time, maybe fifty if I strained a little, but not many more…

So, I think that writing, for a doctor like for anyone else, is a way to take the measure of what we don't remember, what we don't retain. You write to try to knit up the holes in evanescent reality with bits of string, tie knots in transparent veils, knowing that they're going to tear open somewhere else. One writes against memory, not with it.

One writes to measure loss.

110

MADAME SERLING

The electronic directory informs me that a Monsieur Serling, Edmond lives at the other end of the county. His number is nearly identical to ours at the Play medical office, except that the last two digits are reversed: 43 instead of 34.

It rings. Once, twice. Someone picks up. "Hello?"

The voice is an elderly man's.

"Hello, Monsieur Edmond Serling?

"This is he."

"Excuse me for troubling you… This is Doctor Bouadjio, I'm a doctor in Play, the other side of Tourmens. I received a call from a woman who had the wrong number…"

❁

When I finish talking to him, he remains silent for a long while. "I don't understand… I think it's a bad prank… My mother lived near Nilliers, three hundred kilometers from here. But she couldn't have telephoned you. She died twenty years ago."

"I'm very sorry. I don't know who could have—"

"Can you tell me again what… this woman said to you?"

I repeat it, I remember it exactly, for the old woman's voice—her weariness and her anxiety—are still vivid in my memory.

❁

Again, he is silent; then:

"It's strange, you see… I don't want to burden you with these old stories, but… my mother died suddenly. A heart attack. She wasn't feeling well and her neighbor had been urging her to call the doctor, since she had a telephone. At the time, a good many older people didn't. I had one installed for her, but she would never use it... We had a falling out, over some stupid thing..."

His voice tightens.

"When they found her, she was sitting in her armchair with the telephone in her hand... I had always believed that when she died, she was trying to call the doctor."

111

HOW IT ENDS

The medical doctor hereunder signed certifies that the death of the person designated on facing page, which occurred on (Date) at (Time) is real *and* permanent.

TOWNSHIP

LAST NAME (Any medical or legal obstacle to burial? YES/NO); FIRST NAME (Organ or body donor? YES/NO); AGE (Commitment to immediate enclosure in airtight coffin? YES/NO); SEX (Commitment to immediate enclosure in plain coffin? YES/NO); DOMICILE.

PHYSICIAN'S AGREEMENT TO CARRY OUT THE FOLLOWING PROCEDURES

Cremation YES/NO, Embalming or other conservation YES/NO, Transport of body to gravesite YES/NO

TO BE COMPLETED AND SEALED BY PHYSICIAN

TOWNSHIP: DATE OF DEATH:

Confidential and anonymous information re: cause of death

I-CAUSE OF DEATH: a) Immediate cause (Nature of terminal developments, of any complications; or nature of the fatal *lesion* in cases of accident of other violent death) (Here mention, if appropriate, postoperative death), resulting from: b) Underlying cause (Nature of causative disorder or of accident, suicide, or homicide)

II-SUPPLEMENTARY INFORMATION: Any morbid (or physiologic) condition that may have contributed to fatality (but not submissible under I as Cause of Death properly speaking) (Here mention, if appropriate, the pathologic mental condition that may have underlain suicide) (See examples below)

Has autopsy been done? YES/NO

_____

Signature and seal of Physician

THE CASE OF DR. SACHS

Death by illness: I. a) Bronchial pneumonia, b) Measles, II. Rickets

Death by accident: I. a) Skull fracture, b) Fall in stairwell, II. Chronic alcoholism

Death by suicide: I. a) Heart wound by bullet, b) Suicide by firearm, II. Melancholia

Death by homicide: I. a) Severing of femoral artery, b) Homicide by stabbing, II. Family conflict

112

IN THE WAITING ROOM

I close the cardboard folder, I stretch, I stand up, I realize that the doorbell at the entrance hasn't rung for a very long time.

I step out into the waiting room and I let the connecting door close behind me. The window is open, the sunlight is playing through the cherry tree.

I sit down beneath the wall-clock. I cross my arms, I stretch out my legs, I close my eyes.

Through the wall, I seem to hear a child laughing. The little girl, probably. The little boy was very close-mouthed before he went in, he clung to his mother. But he eventually starts laughing, too, and I hear you laugh in turn.

I consider your proposal. I see myself fastening my shingle up beside yours, and I recall one of the texts I just read, where you wrote something like this:

"Medicine is a sickness that strikes all doctors, in varying ways. Some derive lasting benefits. Others decide one day to turn in their white coats, because that is the only chance of cure—at the cost of a few scars.

"Like it or not, once a doctor always a doctor. But we don't have to make other people pay for it; and we don't have to die of it."

EPILOGUE

I hear the doorknob turn. The door opens, you come out. You step aside for the pregnant woman and her two children. As I stand, you stop me with a gesture.

"Can you give me another moment—I have a call to make."

I can't help smiling. I sit back down. The wall-clock says five after twelve. I wait. I hear your voice through the wall, but it drowns in the background music from a loudspeaker on the wall.

A few minutes later, the door opens again.

You cast a direct glance at the clock, a circular glance at the room, as if to check that I'm the only one left. Lastly you look at me, and you greet me.

"Come in, please."

You pull back to let me go by. You stretch a hand toward the two small armchairs in front of the desk.

I enter hugging the book against my chest.

"Sit down."

You close the door, pushing hard. You sit down in the swivel chair. You look up at me. You discover that I'm still standing. "Do sit down, please."

As I do so, you ask, your tone detached, "What can I do for you?"

I consider what to say. I gaze at you, smiling.

The walls are white, the ceiling is perfectly smooth, without the slightest trace of mildew. At my left is a cot. You sit before me, at a little desk with drawers, on which stands a single telephone. You are wearing a white coat with short sleeves.

You're older than I imagined, forty at least. Your face is marked with small scars. Your hair is greying; it's a little thin, but it's short and clean. You must have cut yourself shaving this morning, because your neck bears a few traces of dried blood. You have an aquiline nose, stooped shoulders, a slight paunch.

You smile back. One of your upper incisors is chipped.

"What can I do for you?"

You gaze at me, visibly intrigued. You await my answer, but I say nothing. I've laid the book on my knees.

You cross your hands, you lean toward me. "Yes—I'm listening... ?"

"I phoned you yesterday afternoon, to make an appointment. But I'm not here about an illness."

You frown, and you smile in spite of yourself. "I don't understand…"

"I know there's a different name on the shingle, but you are Martin Winckler, aren't you? You *are* the person who wrote *The Case of Dr. Sachs?*"

I set the book on the desk.

"I just finished reading it this minute, in the waiting room."